WISH YOU WERE HERE

A BLUEBIRD BASIN ROMANCE

JESS K HARDY

Copyright © 2025 by Jess K Hardy

All rights reserved.

This is a work of fiction. Names, characters, places, and incidents either are the product of the author's imagination or are used fictitiously. Any resemblance to actual persons, living or dead, events, or locales is entirely coincidental.

No part of this book may be reproduced in any form or by any electronic or mechanical means, including by AI or machine learning algorithms, including information storage and retrieval systems, without the express written permission of the copyright holder. Unauthorized use, including the use of any AI or automated systems to analyze, replicate, or generate content based on this work, is strictly prohibited.

Edited by: Emerald Edits and VB Edits

Published by Pinkity Publishing LLC

A NOTE TO MY READERS

This book includes discussions of and experiences with drug and alcohol abuse, addiction, relapse, trauma, child abuse, parental death, heartbreak, yearning, pining, groveling, forgiving, healing, and... knotting 😈

*To everyone who refused to give up without a fight,
this one's for you.*

THEN

He reminded her of the ocean. It was his hair, she thought, running her fingers through his soft, golden waves. It was his smile, so bright, like sunlight sparkling over the water. It was his body, the liquid way he moved, the warmth of him surrounding her. It was his eyes, so blue she could swim through them, lie on her back and float around them, dive headfirst and sink to the bottom of them. She loved his eyes. Loved the way he looked at her, like she was Christmas morning. Like she was the present he'd wished for all year.

"Davis," he whispered, his breath a gentle caress, a summer breeze against her neck even though it was a strange, frozen spring night. It was too cold to roll the windows down. So they steamed them up instead with their breaths, with the heat kindled between their bodies, making the air around them glow. It protected them, the steam. Hiding them in the back seat of her car. Close, secret, tangled.

His hands branded her thighs, his need stoking a fire inside her as she rocked against him. Finally. *Finally.*

"Kev." His name slipped between her lips, a prayer, a wish offered up to the stars.

Kev. Touching me. Holding me. Kissing me. Finally.

His palms slid to her hips, and flames raced along her spine, licked at her throat, seared a circular path around her heart. A lasso cinching. *He can have it.* "You can have it."

"Have what?" he asked.

"Nothing." *Everything.* Her arms wrapping around his shoulders. Her chest rising and falling, pressed against his. Her months of wanting, needing, loving. He could have it all. Always. Forever. *Finally.*

"Davis, baby."

I love it when you call me baby.

His lips were soft on her jaw, his fingers harder, digging in, gripping. "Davis."

Yes. Say it again. Say my name like it's a secret. Our secret.

She reached for him, her fingers gliding under his shirt, down the firm plane of his abs, grasping the button of his jeans.

"Davis." He caught her wrists, stilling her, holding her in place.

Anything you want. I'll do it. I'll do anything for you. I love you. I love you. God, I am so in love with—

"Davis, we can't."

"W-what?" she stuttered, forcing her heavy eyelids open.

"We have to stop."

"We do?" *No. Please. Not again.* "Why?"

"Because you shouldn't." His head turned toward the window. "I mean, we shouldn't."

She sensed more than felt him pulling away. The way he always did. Any time they got close like this. Any time she let go of the last lingering thought in her head and sank so deeply into him she couldn't see the surface. And she always let him. Always.

But not this time.

"I don't want to stop," she said, trying to hold him close even though he was rigid in her arms—stiff, gone. "Please, Kev. I need you."

"I'm sorry." He still wouldn't look at her, still stared at the window he couldn't see through. *Why won't you look at me?* "I shouldn't have let it get this far."

Rushed, frantic, clutching at him like he was sand already spilling through her fingers, she kissed his shoulder, his neck, his throat, jaw. "Please."

"I'm sorry." So much finality in the words. So much distance. "The rules."

Control spilled through her fingers too. Humiliation for putting up even this small fight churned in her stomach. Shame for wanting him so badly, wanting the one thing he couldn't give her, made the cold night air finally reach her, seep into her bones, harden everything inside her.

She wanted to cry. She wanted to shut down. She wanted to be more understanding, more patient, less selfish. But she wanted him too much.

"Okay," she said.

Only that wasn't what you said, was it?

With an understanding smile, she slid off his lap and sat beside him, told him it was fine. Everything was fine.

Only that wasn't what you did.

Her hurt, angry voice still echoed through the trees. The car door slamming still cracked between her ears like thunder. Like the thunder that had rumbled under heavy, bruised clouds. Even though the sky didn't surrender a single drop of rain that day. It held it all in while she'd held her breath, held all the soft parts of herself together with her arms wrapped tightly around her middle.

The stairs along the side of the house stretched out like rotten teeth. Loose railings, chipped paint, wood so weathered it frayed at the edges. She took each step slowly, silently. The seventh stair creaked, bowing beneath her foot.

Would it break? Would she fall? Plummet through the air until she met the hard, bare ground that looked like it may have been lush and green years ago? Would she land near the rusted swing set that had been shiny and new once upon a time before this place started to die? Before it took everything she loved with it?

They'd left the door at the top of the stairs cracked, like they knew she'd followed them. Even though she knew they hadn't. They never would have let her come. She wasn't supposed to be here. It was wrong of her to be here. But it was wrong of him to be here too.

Everything is wrong.

The room was dark, silent, cold. No heat. No steam. Nothing glowed. Naked walls, cigarette smoke thick in the air, something else. Vinegar. Burning her eyes, her nose. A mattress on the floor.

Kev.

Adrenaline blurred her vision, making his pale skin flicker. Here and then gone, here and then gone. His hand resting limply on his bare chest sparked like a severed power line with every racing beat of her heart.

Kev. Sprawled across the mattress. In another woman's arms. Turned away. Eyes closed. Sleeping. Just sleeping. *He's only sleeping.*

"You're okay," she tried to tell him through vocal cords that wouldn't work. Only a useless rasp, a fist closing around her throat. "Don't go. Stay with me. Please stay with me." No sound. No movement. *This can't be happening. This can't be real.*

That broken-down house with its bare walls and creaking steps. The acrid smell she'd never get out of her hair or her clothes. Madigan on his knees beside the mattress, his blood-shot eyes flashing from panic-stricken to outright terrified when he noticed her. When he held out his hand, shouting at her to stay back while Cole wrapped her in his arms, spinning her, making her look away.

She didn't struggle then. She didn't struggle now as the room faded to ash, every sight and sound and smell floating to the ground like curled leaves from a burning tree.

Except for Kev. Kev stayed.

He sat up. Turned his head. Finally looked at her through hollow, empty eyes. And told her what she already knew. He told her the truth.

"This," he said, "is all your fault."

Her world heaved, a scream clawing its way up her throat before her hands covered her mouth and shoved it back down. Her stomach roiled as she climbed out of bed, stumbled to the toilet, fell to her knees.

That dream. Every night for the last two weeks the nightmare had haunted her. Jolting her awake to scream silently into the darkness. Making her race to her bathroom, making her sick until she couldn't breathe, until her ribs ached, until there was nothing left. Every night.

This is all your fault.

Cool porcelain against her cheek had become her only real comfort. And she knew this wasn't healthy. The way she couldn't eat wasn't healthy. The way her clothes hung from her shoulders and her hips wasn't healthy. Fighting to stay awake every night, terrified of the moment sleep would win, wasn't healthy. Staggering through her days numb, scared, only half alive, wasn't healthy. She was not healthy. She was sinking, falling, vanishing. Nothing. Nothing but dreams and memories and questions with no answers.

"I can't," she told her cold, empty bathroom, her voice a broken rasp. But at least it was her voice. At least she could hear it. So many nights since he'd left, since he'd started fading away, she couldn't. Couldn't find her voice. Tonight was different. Tonight she was too tired, too sick, too empty. Or maybe the pain was finally too loud. "I can't."

Pushing herself up to her feet, she staggered into her room, tore a piece of paper from the pad on her desk and uncapped a pen.

I love you, she wrote, her hand trembling, the letters barely legible. *But I can't do this anymore. I can't be this nothing anymore. Not for you. Not for anyone.*

As soon as she saw the words on the page, she knew. The fight was over. She'd tried. She'd lost.

So she did what she couldn't do that frozen night in her car. What she couldn't do all those weeks she'd stayed by Kev's side, watching him pull away, absorbing his silence, becoming someone she didn't recognize. Convincing herself it wasn't her fault, even though she knew it was. She did what she couldn't even do when she found him in that house, on that mattress with that woman clinging to him. What she hadn't been able to do any night since. Every night he didn't write her or send a message for her or maybe even think about her. Every night he slept while she couldn't.

She crumpled the piece of paper in her fist, closed her eyes on the hot sting of fresh tears. And while her heart shattered into so many unrecognizable pieces she knew they'd never fit back together again, leaving her with sharp, jagged scars for the rest of her life, she whispered the one thing she knew was true into the darkness. The one wound that would never heal. "You never loved me anyway."

And then she let him go.

CHAPTER ONE

DAVIS

Dirt scrabbled beneath her tires as she whipped her bike around a banked turn. Rising from her seat, she thrust her elbows out and pedaled hard to launch off the boulder she and her mom had designed this part of the track around. With each pedal stroke, her lungs burned, her quads screamed.

Let them scream, she thought. *Let them burn. This pain is better. This pain is healthy. This pain is important.*

Even though she and the men from Little Timber—the sober living home that had moved operations onto the mountain last year; the home run by Matthew Madigan, her mom's soulmate and her new stepdad—had been working their fingers to the bone every day, the mountain biking course was still nowhere near finished. Probably wouldn't be until next fall. But this track was almost done. Only this one stretch about halfway down that still needed refining.

"Shit," she barked, locking her arms straight, throwing her weight back to clear the enormous tree root jutting across her path. "Shit!" again when her pedal scraped along the jagged rock she still couldn't figure out how to avoid.

She shouldn't be going so fast. Shouldn't be this all-out on an unfinished track. Then again, she shouldn't have done a lot of things.

Her back tire skidded out on a patch of dry pine needles, velocity vanishing, handlebars looming as momentum yanked her forward. Pushing herself upright with a grunt while a bead of sweat dripped down her nose, she pedaled harder. Saving herself.

This was where life felt real again, where *she* felt real again, bombing down a single-track, pushing herself to the limits, hunting pain, hunting fear. Hunting the moment where nothing mattered but the next jump, the next pedal stroke, the next breath. This was how she survived. This was how she lived without him.

THE MID-JULY SUN WAS MERCILESS. An unrelenting dry heat baked Davis's shoulders as she dismounted her bike at the lodge and pulled off her helmet. Yanking her water bottle out of its holder, she squeezed a stream of no longer cold water into her mouth, over her face and neck, down the back of her tank top. Then she stared at the mountain she'd just destroyed herself climbing up and riding back down.

Thanks to a change in the wind, Bluebird Basin had earned a brief reprieve from the forest fire smoke looming over the western horizon. Today, she was vibrant, green and clear and beautiful. Bought and run by her grandfather, then passed to her mother and grandmother after he died four years ago, this ski hill was her home. It was the place where she'd always felt like she belonged. Where she'd always felt safe. Where she was fighting like hell to feel safe again.

"Good ride?" a deep voice asked from the lodge deck above her.

"Heck yeah," she answered, looking up to meet Madigan's crystal blue eyes, taking in his silvery-black hair, his broad shoulders, his ruggedly handsome face half hidden by a thick, dark beard. Despite the shit show that was her own life, she was still unbelievably stoked her mom had found a second chance at love with the sexy pirate rock-star. A man who loved her mom so much, Davis constantly caught him staring at her, all heart-eyed and dreamy. A man who'd overcome his own addictions and now dedicated his life to helping other men overcome theirs. A man who was just a genuinely good human being. Unlike her father, who she'd always thought was good, until he showed her and everyone else how wrong they'd been.

When Murphy barked at her from Madigan's side, snapping her out of her thoughts, she couldn't help but smile. The giant man. The giant Saint Bernard. Best friends from the moment they met.

"That's great," Madigan replied with a firm nod. Then his chest expanded through a deep breath, his lips pressing into a grim, apprehensive line. And she knew. She knew it in the tightness spreading across her shoulders, pulling at the skin along the nape of her neck. She knew it in the bruise aching beneath her sternum, the pressure clamping around her ribcage. She just knew.

"When you have a chance." He gripped the railing with his tattooed fingers, his knuckles turning white around the words HOPE on one hand, FEAR on the other. "Can we talk?"

Forcing lightness into her tone, she said, "You bet." Because nothing was more important than making sure the people around her didn't worry anymore. Making sure nobody had a reason to ask her if she was okay, even though they all knew she wasn't. The same way she knew what—or who—Madigan wanted to talk to her about. And with his next nod, solemn as a priest, it was clear he knew it too. "Just let me shower first."

"Take your time," he said.

She would have laughed at the irony if laughing was a thing she did anymore. Since time was the one thing she was about to run out of.

THE SHOWER WAS so cold her skin pebbled and her teeth chattered. Cutting down trees all day, digging out trails, riding until her muscles ached, until her blisters had blisters, taking ice-cold showers afterward. Everything hurt. All the time. That was the point.

She'd never realized how healing physical pain could be, how vital. She couldn't sleep without it now, without her body being sore and worked and so exhausted her mind had no other choice but to submit. All the work had made her hungry again too. She'd even gained back a few pounds in the last two weeks.

Staring at herself in the mirror—damp blond curls curtaining her face, blue eyes still a little hollow, still not the same, but brighter—she almost recognized the woman staring back. One day and then another, another step, another breath. She was better. She was healing. She wasn't ready, because she'd never be ready. But she was better. It would have to be enough.

When she stepped out onto the deck ten minutes later, she paused for a moment, letting herself breathe. *You can do this*, she told herself. *This is easy.*

"Hey, Madigan," she said, taking a seat in the big brown Adirondack chair next to him, noticing that his rocked and hers didn't. It felt so much like her life, like she was fixed, stuck, motionless while the rest of the world moved on.

"Hey, Davis," he replied while Murphy whined then walked over to place his big head in her lap.

"What's up?" she asked, running her fingers over Murphy's soft nose, wanting to get this over with. Wanting to fast-forward to the next part. The part where they'd all moved on. Where it wasn't the Great Big Fucking Deal in her life anymore, the thing always looming over her, holding her back, keeping her stuck.

"I'm not going to beat around the bush," Madigan said, staring out at the mountain. This must have been some skill he'd honed while working with the Little Timber men: when to make eye contact and when not to. Because he never missed. "Kev is getting out of rehab tomorrow."

He'd been gone for a month. Thirty days. Thirty days to get clean again. Thirty days Madigan had fought for. Thirty days to avoid jail time for breaking his parole. Thirty days that had felt more like thirty years. That felt like less than thirty seconds now.

"Okay" was all she said. It was all she could say. It wasn't like she'd circled the date in red ink on her calendar—or had needed to since it was already circled on her skin, her heart, her every thought. She knew it was tomorrow.

This moment apparently called for eye contact, because Madigan turned to face her. "I know we talked about it before. I know you said you'd be okay with him coming back here. But if you've changed your mind, I need to know. You need to tell me."

"It's fine." It wouldn't be enough for him, her clipped, brittle reply. So she added, "I mean, seeing him again will be hard." Using that word, *hard*, felt like using the word *tall* to describe Mount Everest. Technically true, but such a blatant minimization it might as well have been a lie. "But he needs you. He needs to be here." *And I need to be okay with it.*

By the exhale sailing slowly through Madigan's nose, the muscles clenching tightly in his jaw, she knew she hadn't convinced him.

"I'll keep him busy," he said anyway, running his knuckles roughly through his beard. "He'll need to be busy. You might not even see him very much. Not if you don't want to." His throat bobbed through a swallow. "Davis, I know this situation is not good for you. It's not what any of us would have chosen. I mean, you've just finally started to—" He cut himself off with a shake of his head. "You know what I mean."

And she did. She'd just finally started to sleep, to eat, to train. To smile.

"But I believe Kev can get well again. I believe he can stay that way this time." Looking down at his hands, he said, "I have to believe it. I have to try."

She looked down at his hands too, HOPE and FEAR seeming almost too on the nose for the moment.

"I feel responsible," he admitted softly.

That, at least, she understood. And there was some consolation, knowing she wasn't the only one. The only difference being that Madigan might be absolved of his guilt someday. She never would.

"But I feel responsible for you too," he said, the words rushed, his expression pained in a way she needed to convince him wasn't necessary. Because if she was going to survive this conversation, if she was going to survive Kev coming back tomorrow, every day after, people couldn't look at her with pained expressions. They couldn't treat her like she might break at any moment.

"If you want me to find somewhere else for him to go," Madigan said. "I will. I have friends with other homes who would probably take him. Bluebird Basin is your home first."

This conversation had gone on long enough. "I appreciate that you're worried about me," she said. "But it's fine." And here came the lie she'd been practicing in the mirror, repeating it enough times that she could finally say the words out loud without feeling sick. Not enough times to believe it, though. Because that number, enough to erase the last eight months of loving him more than she'd thought it was possible to love someone, didn't exist. "We were never that serious anyway," she said, clenching her jaw against the bile rising up her throat, hoping he didn't notice. "More like really good friends."

Madigan's eye twitched. And if that was the only hint he'd give her that he knew she was full of shit, she'd take it and be grateful.

"His rehab facility is a couple of hours away," he said, even though she already knew that too.

Thanks to some snooping, she knew his facility was tucked into the Bitterroot Mountains near Hamilton. She knew it was called Willow Creek Recovery Center. Thanks to their website, she knew what his room probably looked like. That he'd gone to individual therapy once a day, group therapy twice a day, participated in activities like basketball and tennis and tai chi, even karaoke. That he might have spent time in the meditation room, the art room, the exercise gym, the pool, swimming laps or floating on his back in the quiet water.

"I should be back with him around four." Madigan scratched his head. "If you wanted to be here...or not."

Maybe she should be here. Maybe a strong, mature woman would stand firm in her home when the man who broke her heart came back. But she wasn't that woman. And, luckily, her friend and Madigan's old bandmate, Cole Sanderson, had offered to get her "outrageously caffeinated" at Glazed and Confused so she didn't have to pretend that she was.

"I'm good," she said. "I'm hanging with Cole and Mira tomorrow afternoon." She felt bad about it, knowing how many promises Madigan had already heard in his lifetime that had been broken, knowing this one didn't stand a chance. But she swiped her finger across her chest anyway, just like her grandpa used to do, and said, "I'll be fine. Cross my heart."

She wouldn't be fine. They both knew it. But Madigan nodded anyway. Because promises made on broken hearts didn't count.

CHAPTER TWO

KEV

"Do you feel ready?"

Kev's right knee bounced. It always bounced when he was nervous. Or excited. Or just...breathing. But he didn't want to look nervous, so he leaned forward, pressing his elbows into his knees, and said, "I think so. Yeah."

When Rick's bushy brows floated up, Kev flashed him a grin. "I mean, totally. I'm totally ready."

"Kev," Rick said. "You don't need to set me at ease right now."

"I'm not—"

"That's your *I'm setting everyone else at ease so they don't see how not at ease I am* smile." Rick, his calm, soft-spoken, sixty-something counselor, peered at him over his wire-rimmed glasses. "I know it pretty well by now."

Kev liked Rick. He had round cheeks, a bushy gray beard, and a demeanor Kev could only describe as jolly. He was basically the Black Santa Claus of rehab—if Santa wore corduroy pants and sweater vests.

"It's okay to be nervous," Rick continued. "It's okay to worry more about yourself than anyone else right now. It's okay to not be okay."

Worry? Worry didn't even cover it. But Kev let his smile flatten into something less enthusiastic, wondering if even that was just another way he tried to please everyone around him. *Smile. Don't smile. Laugh. Don't laugh. Be happy. Be quiet. Be invisible.*

He'd learned a lot here at Willow Creek over the last month. About his abandonment issues, his newly diagnosed depression and anxiety—*thank fuck for Lexapro*—even that he actually liked yoga, and not just in the snow. But he still hadn't been able to figure out this one thing. This emotions thing. This letting himself feel however he needed to feel thing. This idea that he was allowed to take up space. That he was safe. Because he'd never felt safe a day in his life. And he certainly didn't now.

How does someone feel safe? he thought just as Rick asked, "What are you thinking about right now?"

He wouldn't tell him, wouldn't ask the question. It was too big, so much bigger than those five words. Bigger than the hour they had left together.

"Um." Kev twisted his lips. *What would a person leaving rehab say to their counselor?* "I just... I don't want to mess up again."

Rick nodded sagely. But Kev sagged in his chair, recognizing all the things he'd kept hidden behind the weak, flimsy admission. All the things he'd kept hidden from everyone here. From the kind people trying so hard to help him get back on his feet. Even though he still wasn't sure he'd ever been on his feet to begin with. His counselors, the other patients here, his psychiatrist, his nurse practitioner, even the weird guy in housekeeping. They all knew about his addiction, his relapse. Hell, they even knew a little about his parents, his grandparents, his years in foster care, his time in juvie, in jail. They knew as much about him as anyone else did. But they still didn't *know* him. And they sure as hell didn't know about her.

They didn't know about her soft hair or her infectious laughter. They didn't know the way she smelled after she'd taken a shower:

sweet, herbal, minty. They didn't know how he'd never in his entire life been as happy as he'd been when he was with her. They didn't know how badly he'd let her down. How badly he'd ruined everything. How he'd never be able to trust himself again. Because he loved her. *God*, he loved her. And he'd chosen the drugs anyway.

He couldn't even bring himself to say her name anymore, not out loud. Fear and guilt kept her locked up tight inside his chest, kept his mouth clamped shut. So they didn't know her.

But Madigan did.

He knew what Kev had done. He knew everything. And he'd be here soon to pick him up. When that happened, all of Kev's hard work to keep her hidden over the last thirty days wouldn't matter for shit.

His knee bounced harder. He should have found another sober living home to go to. He should have made better choices. He should have let her go. He should let her go now.

"I can feel you spiraling," Rick said, sliding his glasses up his nose. "It's okay, Kev. It's normal to spiral when you discharge from rehab. It won't be easy. Nothing about recovery is easy. But you will get through this. If you're open, honest, and patient, and you trust yourself and the good people around you. You will get through this, one—"

"—day at a time," Kev finished.

"I was going to say minute. Maybe even second."

Despite himself, despite the way the phrase grated with how many times he'd heard it in the last four weeks, Kev laughed. "Fair."

Rick pointed at him. "You are a different man today than you were yesterday. You'll be a different man tomorrow. We've all done things we've regretted, but that doesn't mean we're not allowed to continue to grow. Regret doesn't mean that you're stuck. Guilt doesn't mean that what you've done is unforgivable." Rick leaned forward, spreading his corduroy-clad legs wide, interlacing his fingers between them. "Even if nobody else ever forgives you, you're still allowed to forgive yourself. You're still allowed to give yourself grace."

Kev nodded, but only because it was what he was supposed to do. Not because he believed it. Why would he believe something that would never happen? Even if everyone he'd ever hurt forgave him, he'd never forgive himself.

"You don't agree," Rick said, eyes narrowed, seeing straight through him. "But you will. One day, you will."

Watching Madigan and Rick talk about him—both occasionally glancing over to where he sat, eventually shaking hands like they were passing the baton in the world's most tragic relay race—was a special kind of fucked up. But even though Kev was definitely the elephant in this room, the relief of having them both here, of seeing Madigan again, was bone deep. He knew in some philosophical way that it made sense, his tendency to cling. Clay. Madigan. Rick. They were father figures, the kind he'd always wanted. And he collected them like baseball cards.

"Ready?" Madigan asked, his hands stuffed into the pockets of his jeans, his brow deeply furrowed. He looked worried, tired, sad. Which made Kev feel even worse.

"Yep." The word barely made any sound. So he cleared his throat and tried again. "I'm ready."

"Keep in touch, Kev," Rick said with an outstretched hand. "You have my email and my number."

Clasping Rick's hand, Kev shook it while giving him a careful smile. Not so bright that Rick would call him out for faking again, but not dim enough to be honest either. Rick was a busy man who treated hundreds of Kevs every year. They wouldn't keep in touch. He knew it better than anyone. Even so, he said, "You bet."

Hoisting his bag over his shoulder, Kev trailed behind Madigan through the automatic doors. A shiver ghosted over his skin when they *whoosh*ed closed behind him. Under the sky stretching out above the parking lot, the world seemed suddenly too big, too open. His palms started to itch, his chest drawing tight, ice trickling through his veins.

"Kev?" Madigan asked, staring back at him because he'd stopped walking. Because he stood still on hot concrete with his eyes wide and his hand pressed over his thundering heart. "You good?"

It's just panic, he told himself, searching for his coping strategies. *Focus on the ground under your feet, the scent of smoke in the air, the muted sunlight reflecting off Lydia's rear windshield.*

This last one calmed him more than anything. Lydia, Madigan's Suburban. Familiarity, comfort, consistency. He knew how soft her velvety upholstered seats would feel beneath him. How her air conditioner would blow just enough barely cool air to keep them from breaking into a sweat. How good Madigan's cassette tapes would sound even through Lydia's ancient speakers.

Taking a breath, then blowing it out slowly, Kev said, "Getting there."

"It's...a lot." Madigan glanced down at his boots. When he raised his head again, meeting Kev's stare, Kev thought he might say something else, toss out some empty encouragement, some poignant words of wisdom he really wasn't ready to hear. But Madigan only turned around and started walking toward Lydia again.

Forest fires raged through Idaho, and a hazy blanket of smoke had settled over the trees along the highway, turning the sky gray and the sun red. Even though the smoke was smothering, it didn't hold a candle to the heavy silence inside Madigan's truck. Kev should probably say something. *Thanks for saving my life. Thanks for putting me in there. Thanks for letting me come back. How is she? Is she okay? Did she miss me? Does she hate me?*

Unable to make himself say any of those things, Kev settled on "Lydia looks good."

Madigan turned his head slightly while a gruff and scraggly voice singing about a girl with the sun in her eyes filled the ensuing quiet.

And then he said, "Actually, now that you mention it, she does look good. Better than she has in a while."

Kev's attention funneled, narrowing in on the change in Madigan's tone, the tight pull in the corner of his mouth.

Tapping his fingers on the steering wheel, Madigan said, "It was pretty bad there for a while. She went through a rough patch where she just wouldn't start. We tried everything, but none of it seemed to help. And then something changed. Like maybe she just needed some time off the road. I think she's turned a corner now. Almost back to her old self."

With his knee bouncing and his throat burning, Kev said, so quietly he barely heard it himself, "That's good."

"She's still got a light out somewhere, though," Madigan added. "She's still...dim."

Even though his voice was soft, Madigan's words roared between Kev's ears. Because they weren't talking about Lydia. They were talking about Davis. *He* was the rough patch. *He* was the corner she had to turn away from. *He* was the reason her light had dimmed. And it was a knife twisting in his heart.

He still had no idea why he'd done it. He still couldn't find a reason. *Why did I give her up so easily? Why did I run? How will I ever stay clean if I couldn't stay clean for her?*

"You'll never have all the answers," Madigan said to the road in front of them, making Kev wonder why everyone always seemed to know his mind better than he did. "Doesn't mean you won't come out the other side."

Turning his face to the window, Kev watched the trees slip by, thinking that if the next words out of Madigan's mouth had anything to do with taking things one day at a time, he might open the door and jump.

Instead of reciting platitudes, Madigan asked, "Have you spoken to Thom or Trisha?"

"No," Kev said. And he didn't think he ever would. Thom, his old drug buddy and Little Timber roommate. And Thom's sister Trisha, his one-time girlfriend, a relationship that had defined the word toxic. He thought they'd become his past, another life. Until Thom had followed him, found him. And then, they'd only had to ask, to offer, and he'd willingly followed them off the mountain, back to their house, the house where he used to live with them, use with them. The house where he'd descended into addiction. Where he'd turned his back on everything good and sweet and perfect in his life. "I haven't heard from either of them. Not since..."

Sensing his struggle to finish the sentence, Madigan asked, "Do you want to know how they're doing? It seemed like you and Trisha might have been...close."

Kev's head whipped around at the implication in Madigan's tone. "No," he insisted. "We aren't close. We were once, years ago. But no. Not now."

With a slow nod that Kev hated, because it seemed so unconvinced, Madigan flexed his fingers around the steering wheel and said, "Okay."

Kev wanted to say more, to make sure Madigan knew that while he might have fucked up with drugs, he hadn't fucked around on Davis. But it would require so many words, spark so many other conversations he wasn't up to having. So he only said, "But sure. Are they okay?"

"I offered to find rehab placements for both of them," Madigan said. "Thom declined. But Trisha is in a facility in eastern Montana. Last I heard, she's doing well."

Kev wasn't surprised about Thom. But Trisha, who'd never once expressed a desire to stop using, shocked him. "That's good." He turned to look out the window again. "Thank you for doing that."

"We all deserve second chances," Madigan said. "All of us."

It was obvious, the way he'd meant that Kev deserved them too. Luckily, instead of talking about how Madigan was wrong, they spent the rest of the drive in the same silent, smothering haze that choked the mountains around them. The haze that only lifted once they reached Bluebird.

"You'll be alone in here for now," Madigan said while Kev set his bag down on the couch. "We have an opening since Sam went home, but I'm sure we'll fill it soon."

Sitting on his old bed, Kev glanced around at the log walls, the vaulted ceiling, the dressers and bookshelves and old-timey skiing posters on the walls, feeling the familiarity of the place like a ghost of someone he used to know hovering over his shoulder.

This was his cabin. The one he'd shared with Clay, and then with Thom. The one where his life had finally started to feel whole and then had unraveled so quickly he couldn't even find where the thread had snagged.

When his roving attention landed on the Little Timber House Rules listed on the far wall, the code of conduct all the men agreed to live by, the rules he'd need to agree to live by again, he bit his cheek.

With a grim resignation, he read rule number one: We Don't Use.

Broke that one.

Rule number two: We Don't Swear.

Broke that one too.

When he scanned down to rule number five—We Don't Have Guests or Overnight Visitors Without Approval—his jaw clenched in a painful, involuntary spasm. He'd nearly broken that rule with Davis once. That time in his life when he'd been lucky enough to have her in his arms, surrounded by her, so close they shared breaths, felt like a dream now. Something that happened to someone else. Someone who had no idea how good he'd had it. Someone he wished he could go back in time and scream at, grab by the shoulders and shake until he figured it out. Until he decided not to blow up his entire life.

"Sounds good," Kev replied flatly, turning away from the rules until his gaze landed on the romance book he'd been reading before he'd left, still splayed out on his nightstand, frozen in time. He remembered it was about a cowboy with a secret, tragic past who'd moved onto a rich woman's ranch for the summer and turned her quiet world upside down. He huffed a dark laugh at the irony.

"I know the other guys are excited to see you again," Madigan said. "But I've asked them to hold off until you come to visit them or until work starts tomorrow." He ruffled his salt-and-pepper curls. Curls that seemed a lot saltier since Kev had last seen him. "I figured you might want some time to yourself to process being back. I wanted to leave it up to you."

In that moment, Kev sensed the weight pressing down on Madigan's shoulders, noticed the permanent furrow between his brows, the way he kept his hands buried in his pockets.

"It wasn't your fault," Kev said, wondering with a sharp, painful twinge if Madigan felt responsible for what he'd done. "I'm sure you didn't think it was. But just in case you did—it wasn't."

Since Kev couldn't look up, didn't dare, the bed sinking under his hips was his only warning that Madigan had sat down next to him.

"We don't have to talk about it now," Madigan said. "I'm sure you talked about it enough in rehab."

He hadn't, actually. He'd talked at Willow Creek. He'd had to. But he'd only revealed enough to convince everyone that he was diving deep. Even though the things he'd admitted to—that the cravings had gotten the better of him; that his roommate had convinced him to leave and he hadn't had the strength to say no; that he'd just had a really bad day—had barely scratched the surface of the truth. The truth, the *reason*, was still there, hiding inside him. Lurking in a place so dark even he couldn't see it.

"But I'm not going to lie to you and tell you that I don't feel guilty," Madigan said. "Your relapse wasn't my fault. I know better than that. But I wish I would have been here for you. I wish I hadn't left." He shrugged. "That's all."

Kev's heart sank. Madigan and Ashley had been out of the country on their honeymoon when he'd decided to take off in the middle of the night. They'd had to cut their trip short. Kev had known that much. But hearing Madigan's regret, the guilt in his voice because of him, his choices, his actions? He could barely breathe through the pressure in his chest, the acid burn in his throat.

"I didn't know you and Thom knew each other," Madigan went on. "I didn't know you had a history with him and his sister."

"Because I didn't tell you," Kev admitted, still not sure why he'd kept his past with Thom, his relationship with Trish, to himself. Maybe because they were a door some small part of him had wanted to keep open, some escape hatch he'd convinced himself was harmless to have. "I didn't tell anyone. I'm so stupid," he whispered harshly, balling his hands into tight fists.

Madigan's palm was a heavy weight on his knee, his fingers squeezing gently until the bouncing stopped. "Not gonna argue with you on that one."

Kev laughed miserably.

"We're all stupid, Kev. We all make bad choices. Some worse than others. But rarely do we choose to do something that doesn't make some sort of sense to us at the time." He squeezed his knee again, and Kev's mind reeled.

What sense did it make to leave you? he wanted to shout. *To leave this place? To throw nine months of sobriety down the drain? To leave her?*

"But we can work through all of that later," Madigan said, and when he stood from the bed, all Kev wanted to do was curl up on his side, pull a pillow over his head, and sleep until the sun came up.

Unfortunately, Madigan had other plans. "Come on," he said. "We've got some paperwork to deal with in the lodge."

Fear gripped him, its claws long and sharp. "The lodge? Really?" *Ashley, Maude Alice, Davis.* The lodge was their space. He couldn't go there, not yet. "You can't bring it here? The paperwork?" He swallowed down a fraction of his nerves, leveling his voice out as much as he could. "I, um, I'm pretty tired."

"She's not here," Madigan told him, and Kev's shoulders curled inward. Whether in relief or disappointment, he wasn't sure. "And

Ashley and Maude Alice are in town shopping. In case you're worried about seeing them too."

"Oh." Kev clasped his hands in his lap, stared down at them, scowled at the evidence of the fingernail biting habit he'd developed around the same time everything had gone to shit. "I didn't mean... I mean, I wasn't worried they'd be there. Or, I wouldn't have minded if they were. They live here. They'll be around." *She'll be around.* "I know that. It's fine. I'm fine."

"Clearly," Madigan said, his lips twisting to the side in an amused grin when Kev looked back up at him. "Get up. Let's get this over with, and then you can sleep."

CHAPTER THREE

DAVIS

Cole and Mira tried their hardest to distract her with raspberry tarts and almost impossible to believe stories about the Makers—Cole and Madigan's '90s grunge band—and far too many cups of espresso. It had almost worked too. But when Davis pulled into the Bluebird parking lot while afternoon started its lazy orange shift into evening, when she saw Madigan's truck back in its usual spot, an earthquake big enough to reduce the mountain to rubble wouldn't have distracted her from the sharp ache in her chest, the pain making it hard to breathe.

He was here. Kev was here. Probably in his cabin. Probably unpacking. So close she could feel him. Tiny vibrations under her skin, a hand cupping her cheek, fingers curling around her neck.

"Fuck," she whispered, dropping her forehead to rest against her steering wheel. Her mouth was dry, her hands trembling, her pulse pounding in her throat. She should just go to his cabin. Get it over with. She should go knock on his door and say *Hi. Welcome back. I'm glad you're safe. I'm glad you're doing well.* And then leave. And it would be done.

She wouldn't call it closure, because they'd have to actually talk about what happened for it to be closure. And that would never happen. But at least it would be done. At least she could take the final step away from him and move on to whatever came next.

Her keys shook in her fingers when she slid them out of the ignition. Her knees buckled when she stepped out of her car. Her vision swam when she tried to stand, static threatening the edges, the worst head rush she'd ever had in her life nearly knocking her over. It was all too much.

Not today, she told herself, cowardly relief rushing through her with every slowed beat of her heart. *Not today*.

It was late, anyway. He'd be tired. And she'd had enough caffeine in the last few hours to incapacitate a horse. Tomorrow would be better. Tomorrow she'd find him, let him see her. Let him see that she wasn't broken. She wasn't damaged because he'd left. Because he'd chosen drugs instead of her. Because he'd chosen someone else. She wasn't hurt that he hadn't sent her a single letter from rehab. It wasn't like she'd sent him anything either, not one of the hundreds of notes she'd written him, crammed inside the shoebox in her closet. She'd acknowledge that he was here to recover. She'd let him know that she was here to work and train and live her life. And it would be done.

Taking the steps to the lodge one at a time, she grasped the railing, not trusting her legs, weak and wobbly like she'd just ridden every one of the fifty miles she'd been training for. *Adrenaline, cortisol, vasodilation. Normal biochemical reactions to stress. You are fine. You will be fine.*

Once she reached the top step, she listened for voices, footsteps, anything. The only sounds were the muted whir of the ice maker in the kitchen, the ticking of her grandfather's clock. The dining hall was empty. She was safe. *Thank god.*

She rolled her shoulders and started walking. It was going to be okay. It was all going to be fine. She could hide in her room for a while before dinner, pull herself together, get her head on—

"Davis?"

CHAPTER THREE

Her heart stopped mid-beat, her lungs seizing. But she didn't turn around. She couldn't.

"Davis," he said again, and despite the softness of it, his voice was a tidal wave crashing over her head, sweeping her feet out from under her. Or maybe it was quicksand, gripping, pulling, depthless. Because she couldn't move. She couldn't breathe.

He was here. He was *here*. Right behind her. Back in the dining hall, back in her world. Back, like he'd never left. She'd wondered how it would feel, hearing his voice again, feeling his presence. Her hands fisted at the familiarity of it, because even now, even after everything, they ached to touch him, to feel him.

"Davis, please."

Please?

The temperature shifted, climbing as anger, hot and sudden and welcome, lit her up, melting her from her frozen spot in the middle of the room.

Did he just say please? *Did that just happen? How had he treated every please she'd ever said to him? What had she gotten back when she'd said* please talk to me? Please look at me? *When she'd begged him, pleaded with him? Desperate to stay by his side when he'd so obviously already left hers?*

Do not look at his eyes, she warned herself as she turned around. *They'll be too beautiful, deep blue, deep as the ocean. Do not look at his lips, so soft, so pink against his clean shave. Do not look at his shoulders or his chest, fuller now, bigger. Do not look at his shirt, because you know that one. You've felt it under your fingertips, your palms, grasped it in your fists. Do not look.*

"Hello, Kev," she heard herself say, her gaze glued to some safe spot on the floor. "Welcome back."

Slowly, he rose from his chair, the dull rasp of metal legs sliding against carpet as foreboding as a snake in the grass.

She closed her eyes.

"Can you look at me?" he asked, barely more than a whisper.

Do not look. Do not look. Please don't look. But it was futile.

Because when it came to him, when it came to Kevin Lowes, she was so weak.

Raising her eyes, she struggled not to stumble back a step, braced herself to keep the wounded gasp from flying out of her lungs. It had been so long since she'd seen him, since she'd seen this version of him, she'd almost forgotten it had existed.

She'd expected to see the Kev who'd gone silent, the one who'd pulled away so hard she still felt the ripples of his absence spreading out around her. She'd expected to see the Kev who'd vanished right in front of her eyes. The Kev who was pale and skinny and so distant he might as well have been a cardboard cutout. But there was color in this Kev's cheeks, clarity in his eyes, steadiness in his gaze. This Kev had rewound time.

She'd met this Kev eight months ago. When she'd looked down at him through the window in her mom's office. When he'd smiled up at her, standing in the snow with Madigan. Even though she'd just returned to Red Falls as a flailing and mildly depressed grad school dropout, she'd smiled at him, a smile that had spread like wildfire from her lips to her chest to her fingers and toes. Because in that moment, she'd known, *known* it deep in her belly, that she was exactly where she was supposed to be.

Looking at him now, she had no idea where that place was anymore.

"I've missed you," he said.

Her mouth dropped open. Because he didn't get to miss her. He definitely didn't get to tell her that he missed her. Who the hell did he think he was?

His brows slid together. "I mean," he said, reading the barely contained anger in her expression, backpedaling away from it. "You look good."

She didn't, she knew. Not like he did. Standing in front of her, tall and golden, with sun-kissed skin and new muscles filling out his shirt, *he* looked good. Aside from the fingernails he'd started biting before he'd left—a habit rehab apparently hadn't broken him of—he looked healthy. He looked vibrant.

Why did he get to look vibrant? Why did he get to be healthy and golden while every day she fought tooth and nail to keep one step ahead of the shadows lurking constantly behind her? The shadows of him, of what they were, of what she'd thought they were, always nipping at her heels, grasping at her ankles.

"Davis," he said. "I'm so—"

"I'm glad you're doing well," she cut across him, backing away when he tried to take a step toward her. He couldn't apologize. Not here. Not now, with the glowing orange sunlight slanting in through the windows. Not with her grandpa's clock over the door ticking and the ice maker humming and all the other normal and mundane things that insisted on continuing to exist like nothing had changed. He couldn't. It would break her, and he'd already broken her once. "I'm glad you're safe."

His mouth opened, then it slowly closed, whatever he was about to say remaining caught between his lips. Caught in the resigned expression that threatened to core her out, in his round eyes and sinking shoulders. In the realization that she was not okay. That *they* were not okay.

"Oh, um. Thank you," he said. And when he raised his hand an inch from his side, an inch toward her, before lowering it again, a tear slipped down her cheek.

"Shit," she said to no one, maybe to everyone, to the entire universe, as she swiped furiously at her cheek, wiping it dry.

The sound he made might have been a groan. It might have been a whimper. It might have been something she'd replay in her mind on an endless loop for the rest of her life.

"Oh. Davis." Madigan's voice from across the room jolted her, like hands appearing out of thin air to clap in front of her face. "You're home."

She swore again, turning away, hating that Madigan would see her like this.

"Hey, Boss," Kev said with a wooden brightness as he stepped around her, blocking her from Madigan's view while she dried her eyes one last time. "Took you long enough."

"Are you two—"

"We're fine," Davis said, clearing the tremor from her voice, noticing the paperwork in one of Madigan's hands, the pen in the other, the concern etched deeply between his eyes. "I was just welcoming Kev back. I'll get out of your way."

She took a step, but not quickly enough to miss the way Kev's fingers twitched, flexing at his side like he might reach for her again. So she walked faster, nodding at Madigan on her way out of the dining hall, bumping numbly into the walls, stumbling down the stairs. It wasn't until she was safely behind her closed bedroom door that the brunt force of seeing him again hit her in the chest, taking her to her knees.

The real tears came then, so fast and demanding she could only let them flow. But this would be the last time she'd cry over him. The hard part was over, and she'd survived it. She was still breathing. Still here.

When Murphy scratched on her door, she opened it, accepting the comfort of her dog, curling up next to his big, furry body on her bed and letting her tears fall into his scruff.

CHAPTER FOUR

KEV

"Yo, space cadet!"

Kev's head snapped up, and he met Tex's stare. The thin, middle-aged white man's hands were on his hips, one eyebrow cocked under the tattered brim of his one-hundred-year-old cowboy hat. He looked like he'd been standing there for a while, waiting, watching Kev toil away on his section of the mountain biking trail in the shade of a cluster of pines whose dry brown needles blanketed the ground he'd been mindlessly driving his shovel into.

He'd requested the shovel today. Needed that particular job. Needed to thrust the sharp, pointed edge into the ground over and over until he couldn't feel anything but the vibrations rattling his bones. Couldn't hear anything but the rasping scrape of metal on dirt. Couldn't hear her flat, cold words echoing between his ears. *I'm glad you're doing well. We're fine. I'll get out of your way.*

"Sorry," Kev said, pulling out the T-shirt he'd stripped off earlier in the day and stuffed into his back pocket. The T-shirt he'd grabbed from the Little Timber community-clothes pile, because aside from one pair of jeans and a flannel, he didn't have any clothes of his own. In jail, he'd worn a blue jumpsuit. In rehab, he'd borrowed tagless shirts and drawstring-free hoodies and sweats. The clothes Madigan got for the men who needed them here were nicer, but they were still shared. Still not his.

Using the borrowed shirt to wipe the sweat beading on his brow, he asked, "Did you say something?"

"Just to pack it in." Tex tilted his head down the trail where all the other men were packing up, clapping each other on their backs, smiling in the late afternoon sun. "It's quittin' time."

"Sure, man," Kev said, realizing how heavy faked lightness could feel. Like a balloon filled with concrete. "Sounds good."

It had been a week since he'd left Willow Creek. A week of trying to slip back into the groove of Little Timber days. A week he'd spent hoping Madigan and the guys didn't see all the ways he was failing. He couldn't be present. He couldn't be here. He couldn't get her out of his head.

From the moment he'd seen Davis in the dining hall, the rigid set of her shoulders, the determination in her tightly clenched jaw, that single fucking tear she hadn't been able to hold back—the tear he'd made her cry just by existing in her world again—he'd remembered what pain was. Pain wasn't physical. It wasn't craving or depression or even the body-shaking spasms of withdrawal. It was making Davis Thompson cry. It was the gulf between them that he'd dug out himself. It was knowing how badly he'd fucked everything up. That no matter how badly he wanted to, no matter how hard he might try, he'd never be able to fix what he'd broken.

And now that he was back, he suffered that pain every day, because he saw her every day. Walking through the dining hall, when she helped them work on the course, when she raced her bike down the finished trails so fast it terrified him. When she made small talk with the other guys, her bright smile fading to a dull glow whenever her eyes met his.

Each time he saw her, each time she didn't speak to him, each time he couldn't summon the courage to speak to her, something inside his chest twisted, cranked, *tick-tick-tick*ing louder and louder.

Threatening to explode. Threatening to wrench the earth-shattering *roar* out from the place beneath his ribs where he'd been keeping it caged. Where it needed to stay. Because he'd brought this all on himself. Because if anyone deserved to roar, it was her. And she was silence personified.

After packing up his tools, he headed down the mountain a few paces behind the other guys. Behind Tex and Ace and Stanley and several new guys Kev didn't really know yet. Everything had changed so quickly. No Clay. No Brian. No Sam. People he'd cared about, people he'd thought had cared about him too, all of them gone now, moving on while he'd stumbled backward.

"I think we need a group tonight," Ace, a tall, friendly man from the Crow Nation who'd come to Little Timber only a couple weeks before Kev had decided to leave, called out over his sun-bronzed shoulder.

"Absolutely, brother," Tex agreed, fanning his narrow face with his hat. "Haven't had one in over a week."

When Stanley said, "I know I need it," Kev couldn't help but notice how loud all the guys were being. So loud he'd hear them even though he'd fallen far behind. "I've got lots of things to get off my chest. It's been a rough week."

"And it does no good keeping it all in," Ace said. "Right?"

All the men agreed in low, conspicuous murmurs, and Kev shook his head while sunlight pierced the trees, shadow and light dancing down the trail back to their cabins.

He'd done this before too, back when he was doing well. Banded together with the guys to subtly—or not so subtly—call one of the other men out. Someone who was withdrawing or hiding or not fully embracing the process. All the things he was currently doing. All the things the guys were apparently not content with letting him get away with anymore.

He should be grateful they were looking out for him. This was why he'd come back to Little Timber, after all. To get better. To get well. Hopefully to stay that way this time. But he just didn't have it in him to pretend. As hard as he'd tried, he couldn't find the energy to convince them that he was okay. To set them at ease and make them stop worrying about him. It used to be so easy, flashing smiles, laughing at jokes, being whatever he needed to be to skate by, go unnoticed, be safe.

It was fucking next to impossible now.

"What do you think, Kev?" Tex asked, waiting on the trail until Kev caught up with him. "A group sound good?"

"Sounds real good," he said, forcing a stale grin onto his face while he snatched Tex's hat from his hands and put it on. "How do I look?" He tugged on the brim, working harder to seem okay, making the impossible possible, smiling wide enough to pop his dimple. "You know, I used to be a cowboy too." So many years ago. Back when his childhood was happy for half a second.

"Damn." Tex clicked his tongue. "You look like one of the studs on your romance book covers, you handsome bastard. Why don't I look like that?"

Kev repositioned the hat, shading his eyes. "Back on my grandparents' ranch," he said around the dull ache in his chest, "I used to spend more time on a horse than off." Sunlight dimmed, shadows enveloping him at the memory of how it all ended. "Never had a hat like this, though."

"Well"—before Kev could react, Tex snatched the hat, flipping it back onto his head—"if you want to be a *real* cowboy, you'll have to get one of your own."

Feeling his smile slip, like holding it there on his face was as draining as holding a boulder above his head, Kev said, "I might just do that."

"Come on, pup." Tex threw an arm around Kev's shoulders. "But do me a favor, don't tell Boss I called you a bastard. My old back can't handle bathroom duty anymore."

"Oh. Hi, guys."

Kev wheeled around, her sweet voice grabbing his shoulders and spinning.

"I didn't see you there."

As a chorus of *Hi* and *Hello* and *Hey, Davis* erupted around him, his gaze followed her every move, tracking her while she hopped off her bike and removed her helmet. While she shook out her hair, her golden waves falling around her shoulders, glowing in the afternoon sunlight.

"How's training going?" Ace asked her.

Kev hadn't heard it from her, because they didn't talk. But Tex had told him that she was training for a mountain biking race. Something about "fifty miles of pure hell." Kev had actually laughed, relating to that more than he'd wanted to.

"Good," she said. "Better now that the smoke's cleared out again. How's the trail?" When she pointed her chin up the path they'd been clearing all day, Kev narrowly avoided clutching at his chest, remembering the feel of her chin under his fingertips, his lips against her throat. That one night in the back seat of her car, the softness of her skin, the delicate line of her jaw when he'd kissed her there. It was imprinted on his memory in permanent ink.

"Getting better, but still sketchy," a new kid named Brayden told her. "Be careful if you're gonna ride it."

Brayden was barely twenty-one years old and classically good looking, with dark brown hair, a jawline chiseled from marble, and one of those irresistibly charismatic personalities that drew everyone in.

Kev squinted at him, overtaken by a sudden bone-deep jealousy. Especially when Davis tossed a grin Brayden's way and said, "Thanks for the heads up, B. I think I'll give it a try."

B? She calls him B? Grinding his teeth together, Kev wanted to tell her that Brayden—because there was no way in hell he'd ever call him *B*—was wrong. The trail was not better. He wanted to warn her that it was still too dangerous. It was uneven and narrow and riddled with rocks and roots. But he wasn't the guy who could tell her these things anymore. He wasn't the guy who could put her helmet back on for her, clicking the chin strap into place, letting his fingers graze the curve of her cheek, brush that soft curl back off her shoulder. He was the guy who could only press his lips together into a neutral, well-meaning grin when their gazes caught, letting even that go when her smile flattened out in response.

She was so quiet around him now, so reserved. He despised it more than if she'd shoved him, slapped him, screamed in his face, told him she resented him and that he was a terrible person and she'd never, ever forgive him. It would hurt like a sword through his gut, but he'd take it over the silence draining him slowly through a thousand tiny cuts.

But silence was all he got while she hopped back onto her bike. Polite, reserved, awful silence. Maybe it was what he deserved, seeing as silence was all he'd given her in the weeks before he left. Was she healing from the thousands of tiny cuts he'd given her then without meaning to? Without even knowing it? Was the way she always seemed to ride off in the other direction, all her silence, all her polite smiles and chilled, guarded expressions his payback? Was this his karma?

Watching her go, he wondered for the first time if she wasn't just mad at him for what he'd done. He wondered if she actually hated him.

"Have I mentioned how much I love this firepit?" Madigan asked, sitting on a stump with his jeans-clad legs spread wide, directly across from Kev while the rest of the Little Timber men sat on their own logs or stumps around the crackling flames in the clearing between their cabins. "I don't know why it never occurred to me to put one out here."

"Maybe Cole is just smarter than you," Tex suggested.

While most of the guys laughed, and Kev pretended to as he stared up at the scattered stars twinkling above them, Madigan scoffed. "Please. I outscored that little punk on every test in school." He scratched his head. "Until I dropped out."

"Don't be mad, Boss," Brayden said. "It's okay when our friends are smarter than we are. What?" he cried, flinching when Stanley smacked his arm.

"You don't know Boss well enough to give him hell yet," Stanley grumbled, only half joking.

Kev felt a little smug at the way Brayden's shoulders caved in. But then he regretted it. He'd been Brayden more than once, the new guy just trying to fit in. Trying to make friends, to find his place in a world he wasn't even sure he belonged in yet. He'd give him a pass, even if Davis did call him *B*.

"So," Madigan said, and Kev stiffened. He knew that *so*. He felt the weight of that *so* like hands pressing down on his shoulders. Shit was about to get real. "I've been thinking about something lately."

"Here we go." A smile slanted across Ace's handsome face. "Boss has been *thinking*."

A few of the guys snorted. Kev's stomach roiled.

With a charitable laugh, Madigan said, "I've been thinking about how we show up for each other here. I think it can be hard for men, in particular, to support each other." His deep voice echoed around the suddenly quiet firepit. "The distant and surface-level way we interact with other men isn't necessarily our fault. It's something that's deeply ingrained in our society. It's something we learned on the playground as kids, especially in my generation. Be tough, don't cry, don't hold hands or hug each other, don't support each other in a way that anyone else might see or judge. But as adults, as men trying to break the chain of unhealthy habits, I think it's important to challenge our deeply ingrained beliefs. With that said, I'm wondering, before you came here, how did you support the men in your lives? How did they support you? Did you have healthy male relationships?"

"I'm not even sure I know what a healthy male relationship is," Stanley said, and Kev took that one like a gut punch. The other guys must have too, judging by the nods and affirmative grunts around the firepit.

"Okay. Let's start there." While he tossed another log onto the fire, Madigan asked, "What is a healthy male relationship? What does it look like? Feel like?"

"I don't know," Brayden said, his shoulders jerking into a shrug. "You're, like, friends. Like my boy Mikey. He's got my back."

Madigan nodded evenly. "So a healthy male relationship has something to do with being able to count on each other."

Everyone agreed. And Kev thought of the few real friends in his life. Of Thom. He might have played a big role in convincing him to leave Little Timber, but he always had his back too. Even now, if Kev needed him, he knew Thom would be there. Probably high. Most likely broke. But he'd be there. That had to count for something.

"A lot of us have issues with abandonment," Madigan said, interrupting Kev's thoughts with a piercing blue-eyed stare in his direction. "So it would make sense that being accountable is important in a relationship. It might feel like the most important thing to us."

Kev blew out a relieved exhale, thinking, *yes, exactly that*. Until Tex spoke up.

"I'm not so sure," he said, pulling off his hat and cradling it in his lap. "There are lots of people from my past, guys who I thought were my friends, who were always there while I was using, always ready to hook me up or share my scores or get into trouble with me. But I'm not sure any of them were there when I really needed them. I mean, I haven't heard from a single one of them since I've been living here. That can't be healthy, right? Just being there for each other during the good times?"

Despite the fire's heat, Kev shivered. Thom and Trish, they were good-times-only people in his life. On their side of the relationship for sure, but also on his. He didn't know if either of them were struggling. He didn't even think about checking in on Trish at her rehab. And part of that, he knew, was for self-protection, severing himself from that world since he was obviously too weak to keep one foot inside it, even one toe. But still, maybe he didn't have friends. Maybe, he thought while his stomach sank like he'd been eating bricks instead of the meager diet of cheese sandwiches and peanut butter crackers he'd been managing to force down lately, he didn't know what a friend was. Let alone how to be one.

"That's a good point," Madigan said, his attention settling on the fire. "An important part of any healthy relationship is being there for each other through the good times *and* the bad times. Standing by each other's sides when we're happy, but also when we're emotional or quiet or angry. I think men can have a difficult time with this. With the emotional side of relationships. I know I used to."

"I don't speak for the entire transmasc community," one of the new guys named Noah said. He was a stocky white trans man around Kev's age with jet black hair, a trimmed black beard, and demeanor so quiet he'd quickly become Kev's favorite person to work the trails with. "And I'm not sure I've ever been a highly emotional person. But I feel it. Since I transitioned, I feel a pressure to be more...stoic, I guess. More locked down. I don't know if I put that pressure on myself or if it comes from society." He huffed a laugh. "Probably both. But it's definitely there. I definitely see it in my relationships with other men."

To a chorus of thoughtful hums, Madigan said, "Thank you for that perspective, Noah." Then he asked, "So why, as men, do we feel like we need to be stoic? How is it helping us? Why do we feel like we need to hold our emotions back, especially with each other?"

"Because emotions are scary," Stanley said, his hands resting on his round belly. "I mean, that's why I drank. I'd get overwhelmed at work or at home, and all I wanted to do was get to that place where I felt nothing."

"This is true," Madigan agreed. "Emotions can be scary, and a lot of us drank or used to avoid having to feel them. But maybe we wouldn't have tried so hard to blank out if we hadn't been led to believe that feeling something, that being emotional, was somehow wrong or bad, or"—he nodded at Noah—"not how men were supposed to behave."

Noah nodded back.

"Maybe," Madigan continued, bringing the point home, "emotions would be less scary if we didn't believe that being emotional would lead to being laughed at or called out or even punished. If we didn't believe that being emotional would lead to being alone."

Ace whistled. "That's heavy, Boss."

Kev would have agreed if he wasn't so busy trying to stop his heart from pounding. He knew, even though it felt like it, that Madigan wasn't talking about him, using his life, his childhood, as fodder for group. He knew it because Madigan would never do something like that. But he also knew it because he wasn't the only man around the firepit who looked rocked. Most of them did. Eyes wide. Mouths open. Hands rubbing over faces. Even so, it still hit so close to home, to Kev's home, that panic twisted inside him.

After a moment, Madigan asked, "How would it feel if you had friends who would come to your side and sit with you without judgment no matter how emotional you were? And how would you feel about sitting with your friends when they were going through hard times? Not judging, not trying to fix everything, just being there. Even if they were emotional. Even if they were angry or sad. Even if they were crying."

While all the men stared at Madigan, joined in silence, a deep black hole spiraled out from Kev's belly, threatening to swallow him whole. Because he'd had that once. He'd had her.

Davis had been there for him. She'd sat with him. Even when he'd pulled away from her, from everyone. She'd stayed. And he'd let her. He knew he was hurting her. He knew he wasn't good enough for her. But he couldn't let her go.

Maybe it was good she wasn't talking to him anymore, as awful as it felt. Because he didn't want to hurt her again, and he clearly didn't know how to be a friend.

"I used to feel scared," Tex said, cutting through the quiet tension in the air. "I used to be afraid of my feelings. Afraid of what it might mean if I felt genuine love and affection for another man. Settling for the bare minimum of what a friendship should be because anything was better than being alone."

"You don't feel that way anymore?" Madigan asked.

Tex shook his head, then settled his hat back into place on top of it. "Nah. It's just like you said, deeply ingrained beliefs holding us back. I'll prove it too." He glanced around, his gaze landing on each of the men, one at a time. "Guys," he said with complete sincerity, "I care about you. I care about all of you—even you, Brayden." This earned him some much-needed laughs. "And I will always be here for you, through the good times and the bad times. And I hope like hell you'll be there for me too."

"Always," Ace said, giving Tex's outstretched fist a bump.

Kev wanted to do the same, nod and smile and bump Tex's fist. But his arm wouldn't move. The truth was, he didn't actually know if he could be there for Tex or the other men. He didn't know if he could be there for anyone, not in the ways that mattered. How could he expect other people to trust him or rely on him when he couldn't even trust himself?

When Stanley gave Tex's fist a bump from his other side and said, "You can count on me," Madigan grinned at the men like a proud parent. Which made Kev feel even worse. He'd done nothing to earn anyone's pride.

"Lots of love around this fire tonight," Madigan said, "Let's keep that love going, keep questioning our preconceived notions of what male friendships should look like, dig deep when emotions make us uncomfortable, and make our own rules about how we want to be there for each other."

After a minute of thoughtful silence, the fire popped, and Madigan asked, "Does anyone else have anything they want to talk about before we wrap up?"

It was subtle, hips shifting on logs, heads turning, eyes flickering in the firelight. But Kev knew they were all looking at him now. He was supposed to say something, talk about what it was like coming back, how he was settling in. That was the deal. That was what was expected of him here. He was supposed to be honest, open up, lay all his worries out there so these men could carry some of their weight for him. Because holding it all in, carrying it all by himself, was bad and led to bad things.

There was just one problem: he'd never been able to open up. Even when he was here before, he hadn't opened up. He'd just lied. Lied that he was happy. Lied that he was fine. Lied because he couldn't find the words to say how he really felt. Lied because he'd spent most of his life believing that being seen but not heard meant being safe. That being quiet and fine and happy and not emotional was how to not wake up with bruises on his skin.

He'd been lying since he'd gotten back too, brushing off concerns, pretending he was making the transition easily. Pretending another bit of his heart didn't break every time Davis walked or rode by without talking to him, without even looking at him. Pretending he wasn't sinking deeper and deeper into the bleak emptiness of not having the first fucking clue how to make things better.

What he was doing, how he was living, was obviously not working. So what if he just stopped? What if he stopped pretending everything was fine for five fucking minutes? Because he was so exhausted by all of it.

What was he really risking here in this place with these men by telling them the truth? He knew what he was risking by continuing to lie. He was risking everything staying exactly as it was, exactly the same.

Well, fuck that.

"I'm...struggling." His voice was shaky, his hands cold and trembling. He kept going anyway. "I'm struggling, being back. But I'm not ready to talk about it."

Of all the things he'd already disclosed, the things he'd done and the things that had been done to him that he'd admitted to in groups like this, these simple words might have been the hardest he'd ever pushed out of his mouth. He was expecting blowback. One of the guys would call him out for hiding. Another would put pressure on him to say something real. Maybe they'd tell him to stop being afraid of his emotions. But that didn't happen.

It surprised him, but nowhere near as much as the smile breaking out beneath Madigan's beard, the understanding expression on his face when he said, "That's fair, Kev. And when you are ready, we'll all be here to listen."

While he helped the men stamp out the fire, Kev wondered what the hell had just happened. He'd never seen Madigan so accepting of someone after they chose *not* to participate in the discussion. But maybe, just by being honest, just by telling the truth even though all he'd wanted to do was gloss everything over with more easygoing lies, he'd actually done something right for once.

CHAPTER FIVE

DAVIS

She heard the men before she saw them, their boisterous laughter ricocheting off the dining hall walls, echoing down into the stairwell where she stood. It was strange, the different voices as the men staying with Madigan changed. She didn't recognize all the new guys yet, and sometimes she missed Sam's tinny chuckle. She really missed Clay's booming guffaws. When he was gone, she'd missed Kev's warm laughter too, the way his eyes would water when he really got going. She'd missed it so much she used to wake up in the middle of the night convinced she could hear it. Like he was back, standing outside her window. Like he'd never left her at all.

It was a confusing kind of pain, knowing she'd miss it again. Knowing that the next time he left, which he eventually would—whether he got better and moved on or got worse and ran again—he'd leave for good. All she'd have of him, of his laughter, of the time when it felt like the sun had chosen to shine directly on her, were the few videos and pictures of him on her phone she hadn't been able to make herself delete.

Since the guys, and therefore Kev, were in the dining hall, she considered turning around, heading back down the stairs and waiting in her room until they returned to their cabins. But she'd already turned around so many times since Kev had gotten back. Making sure she always worked on a different part of the course than he did. Doubling back on the trails when she saw him about to cross her path. Turning away from the sound of his voice. Sometimes turning toward it when the trees between them were thick enough to hide behind.

Over the last week, she'd developed her own addiction. She'd watch him when he couldn't see her, relief settling into her when he yanked saplings out of the ground with his bare hands or hurled branches taller than he was into the slash pile. Obsessed with his sun-kissed skin, his rippling muscles, how healthy and alive he looked.

But it was moments like this one that were the hardest. Running into the men in a situation where she couldn't just wave and ride past. Where she'd need to say hello at the very least. Where her gaze would snag on his, and she'd see it all right there in his eyes. The eagerness. The unspoken words trapped behind his lips.

Because while she wanted to watch him when he wasn't looking, he wanted to talk to her when she was.

How? How could she make small talk with him? How could she ask him how he liked her grandma's lasagna or talk to him about the fucking weather when the weight of all the words they hadn't said to each other, the words he so clearly wanted to say to her but she refused to listen to, pushed her into the ground?

She couldn't.

So she turned around, heading back down the stairs, until her mom said, "Hey, sweetie."

Shit. "Hey, Mom," she said, spinning back.

"Were you coming up?"

Trying to soothe the concerned frown her mom had worn for the last month with the fake smile Davis had perfected over the same amount of time, she said, "Uh, yeah. Just wanted to grab a bite before I head out."

"You're going out?"

There was true surprise in her mom's voice, probably because even Davis couldn't remember the last time she'd gone out.

"Yep," she said with more fake smiling. "I'm meeting Callie and Olivia at Jimmy's."

Without another word, her mom grabbed her by her shoulders and pulled her into a big, full-on parent hug. The kind that was a little too tight, lasted a little too long, and meant a little too much. When she finally released her from the hug, still holding on to her arms, she said, "That's wonderful, sweetie." Then, quietly, "He's in there. Kev. They're just finishing with dinner. I didn't know if you'd want a heads-up."

"It's fine," Davis said, her arms hanging limply at her sides, her heart beating limply in her chest. "I mean, it's been a little awkward. But it's fine."

Her mom stared at her for a moment, long enough to make it clear she didn't believe her. And when she opened her mouth, the words *are you sure you're okay?* broadcasting from her apprehensive expression, Davis had never been so happy to feel her phone buzz in her pocket. Until she pulled it out and saw the caller ID.

"Who is it?" her mom asked.

Davis's exhale could have powered an entire wind farm. "It's Dad."

"Chuck? He's calling you?"

Since he'd tried to sabotage Madigan and Little Timber, secretly drugging the men—including Kev—in an unforgivable bid to win her mom back. Since both she and her mom had told him to stay out of their lives, her dad had only tried to text her. Each text, each attempt to reach her, to apologize, filled her with an all-consuming rage. Not only because she was furious with him for lying, for hurting the men —for hurting Kev—but also because, despite her best efforts, she missed him. She missed their weekends. She missed skiing with him, playing cards, going hiking and fishing in the summer.

She couldn't help it. It was embedded in her genetic makeup, rooted in her brain's hard-wired insistence on maintaining parental attachment. And he was taking advantage of it by not honoring her request to be left alone, by continuing to text, by progressing to calling.

"He's apparently unwilling to respect the eighty different ways I've asked him to stop contacting me," she said.

When her phone buzzed again, her mom asked, "Are you going to answer?"

"No." Clicking the side button, Davis sent the call to voicemail. "I'm not." *Not now. Not ever.*

Pressing her lips together, her mom sighed. "Okay," she said, looping an arm around Davis's shoulder, squeezing her into her side. "Come get some dinner before you go."

Once they were in the dining hall and her mom split off for the kitchen, Davis wanted nothing more than to follow her. To disappear behind the counter, hide next to the walk-in freezer, eat her dinner in peace. But how long could she keep that up?

Kev was here. It was a fact. He wasn't going away anytime soon. She needed to figure out how to be in the same room as him. She needed to feel comfortable in her own home again. It was time to reclaim her space, plant her flag in the ground and say *you may have broken my heart, but you haven't broken me.*

With a fortifying breath, she approached Madigan and the men like she was approaching the gallows. Her footsteps were slow, her hands cold and clammy, her heart a riot in her chest. But she held her head high and, with a surprisingly steady voice, said, "Hey, guys."

"Hey, Davis," Madigan replied, sitting at the head of the three tables they'd pushed together. "How's it going?"

"Good." She made herself smile. Then she made herself meet Kev's waiting stare, refusing to look away. Refusing to back down even when the ache in her chest made her eyes water. Refusing to do anything but stand her ground and ask, "How's the lasagna?"

"Fuck. That's gotta be so stressful," Olivia said, her hazel eyes going wide under her blunt black bangs while she poured beer into Davis's glass until the pitcher of Cold Smoke ran dry.

Sitting opposite her best friends since kindergarten in a dimly lit back corner booth at Jimmy's and with a smile so flat it barely existed, Davis nodded at her friends. She ran her fingers over the cracked vinyl seats, waiting for the house band to get going so the jukebox could stop playing an endless loop of depressing country songs.

Yeah, Willie Nelson, I'm well aware that only memories remain...

Flagging the waitress down for a refill, Callie said, "Seriously. So intense. Like, you just don't talk to him? At all?"

"Not really," Davis admitted. "We say *hi* sometimes. At dinner tonight I asked him how the lasagna was. I mean, I asked all the men, but..."

"Good god." Olivia's brows crashed into each other. "What did he say?"

Davis tucked a curl behind her ear, then squeezed the shiver trying to race up her neck at the memory of Kev locking eyes with her, waiting until all the other men had quieted down to tilt his lips into the barest hint of a grin and give her his answer.

"Um, he said it was good." *And my entire body melted into the center of the earth when I remembered the way he used to whisper that word into my ear.*

"Good? That's it?" Callie looked...angry—worried? Affronted? All of the above?—while she toyed with the long blond braid hanging down from her chin-length bob. "After all he's put you through? The best he could do was *good*?"

"Like I said." Davis shrugged. "We don't really talk."

She wanted to say more. Explain that it wasn't only that she and Kev didn't talk to each other. It was how much he so obviously *wanted* to talk to her. How much he maybe wanted to apologize, to explain what happened, to try and make her understand. It was how hard she hid from that apology. Feeling more and more like a coward with every passing day. She wanted to tell them about yesterday afternoon when she'd ridden past his cabin even though she could have taken a much shorter route back to the lodge. When he'd been sitting on his porch, reading a book in his pair of faded jeans and nothing else. Not even shoes.

She wanted to monopolize the conversation, taking the rest of the night to describe the way Kev had looked at her in deliberate, excruciating detail. The way he'd slowly lowered his book and risen from his chair. She wanted to confess the way her gaze had drifted across his bare chest, voyaged down his abs. How she'd nearly fallen off her bike when she reached the muscles cutting like a V toward his jeans. How he'd finally broken his silence when she'd wobbled, shouting, "Are you okay?" Like he couldn't help himself. Like it was reflexive. She wanted to tell them how she'd cried behind her sunglasses because she hadn't been able to say a single word back to him. She'd just put her head down, stood from her seat, and pedaled harder.

She wanted to say all these things, but she wondered if her best friends would even understand something she barely understood herself.

"Well, it's probably easier that way." Olivia tugged her high pony tight. "I mean, it's not like you really want to talk to him anyway. Right?"

With matching expectant expressions, her friends stared at her, watching, waiting, wondering. Her third beer was likely to blame, but staying in the Strong Woman Keeping It All Together character she'd been playing all night seemed impossible. She just couldn't do it anymore. "I don't really know what I want."

"Hey." Sensing her resignation, her bone-deep weariness, Callie reached out to take her hand. "It's okay. I wouldn't really know what I'd want if I was in your shoes either. There's no right or wrong way to get through this."

Olivia took her other hand. "Seriously, Davis. You can feel however you need to feel for as long as you need to feel it. We're always here for you. No matter what."

Davis smiled. She believed them. One hundred percent. But it didn't make the pressure orbiting her ribs any less intense. "Thanks, guys."

"You know, there's only one thing that will fix this situation." Squeezing her hand, Olivia said, "Let's go dance until we don't even know what planet we're on, let alone if there's a guy named Kev living on it too."

Two hours later, hot and sweaty, her silk shirt clinging to her chest, her voice hoarse from screaming the lyrics to the band's classic rock covers everyone in the entire bar knew all the words to, Davis could almost convince herself that things were normal. That if there was a guy named Kev living on this planet, she didn't even know him.

"My, my. What have we here?" came a familiar voice behind her.

Spinning around, she shouted, "Cole!" and threw her arms around the timelessly cool older man's neck, succumbing to the bizarre alcohol-induced belief that anyone you ever saw randomly at a bar was a person you hadn't seen in years.

"Hey, Cole," Callie and Olivia said at the same time, still dancing, still laughing.

Easing out of the hug, Cole gave Davis a wry, knowing grin. "Having fun?"

She rolled her eyes at his *you'll regret this in the morning* tone. "Yes. As a matter of fact, I am."

"I guess you needed to let off some steam," he said, considering her in the worried parent way he sometimes did when he remembered the thirty years that stretched out between them. "Makes sense."

"Yeah, well..." Davis sighed, then waved at her friends to let them know she was taking a break. "What are you doing here?" she asked, following Cole to the bar.

Hopping onto a barstool while she climbed onto the one next to him, he said, "Mira and Linda are having a mother-daughter spa weekend in Bozeman. Ian's on a date with Brendan. I got lonely. And hungry. So I came in to pick up some food." Parental all over again, he asked, "Are you staying in town tonight?"

"Hadn't planned on it," she said. "I was going to Uber back up."

Cole laughed out loud. "There's Uber service in Red Falls? You're kidding, right?"

"There is," she said smugly, then conceded, "Well, it's really only Bud with his side-by-side. He lives for any excuse to drive that thing around."

"I think we're gonna head," Callie said, rosy-cheeked, a sweaty strand of hair clinging to her cheek as she joined them at the bar. "Are you sure you don't want to stay over at my place?"

"Thanks," Davis said. "But I'm okay. I'll just Uber—"

"I'll give her a ride up," Cole said.

Davis spun toward him on her stool. "You will?"

"I rode in Bud's side-by-side once." He shuddered. "Fucking terrifying. Besides, I haven't seen Mad in a while." Pulling out his phone, he moved his thumbs across the screen, then gave whatever message came back to him a smile—the kind that only tilted one corner of his lips. "How about that?" he said. "He's still awake."

"Madigan is awake after ten?" Davis gasped, making a show of her shock. "Impossible."

While Cole paid for his food, Davis gave Callie and Olivia hugs goodbye, then they walked out to his Volvo.

"Hottest. Car. Ever," she mocked, sliding into the passenger seat.

Clicking his seat belt, Cole scoffed. "This Volvo aggression will not stand, man."

Davis squinted at him. "What's that one from? *Anchorman* or something?"

He made a sharp, throaty noise of indignation. "Sometimes I worry about you young people. It's from *The Big Lebowski*. Buckle up, please. Then hand me my burger."

Aside from PJ Harvey singing about a rooftop in Brooklyn through the speakers and the wind whipping through Davis's hair, the drive back up to Bluebird was quiet. Not awkward, just quiet, still. Or maybe she was too buzzed to notice the difference.

She had her window rolled down, and her head was tilted out the side so she could see the stars. It took forever to get dark in the summer in Montana, so they'd just come out, bright, twinkling freckles spreading across the darkening sky.

"Are you okay?" Cole asked her at some point.

Another star revealed itself, and she said, "Not really."

Through her peripheral vision, she saw his head bob. She liked a lot of things about Cole. He was funny, his chaotic energy mirrored hers, and he was a perfect match for Mira. She remembered taking a few pictures of them at Madigan and her mom's wedding and thinking, *Wow, those two are totally going to bang. And then they're going to get married.* But the thing she liked most about him was that he never pried. He never gave her advice unless she asked for it. She trusted him to listen, to just be there. Maybe that's why she felt safe enough to say, "I miss him, Cole. So much it hurts."

She'd said it quietly, sending the words up to the night sky above her, to the stars that were always there whether she could see them or not. But Cole had heard them too, his hand wrapping around hers for a silent moment, his fingers squeezing.

"I'm sorry, Davis."

She breathed in, inhaling the rapidly cooling air—cedar and pine and the mustiness of a dirt road she'd traveled over too many times to count. A lifetime's worth of memories tangled in the scent. "It'll get better," she said, wanting to believe it. Wanting it more than anything. "It has to."

They pulled into the parking lot, and it was only when she got out of the car that she finally realized how much she'd had to drink. She swayed on her feet, the rudely bright floodlights making her eyes burn and her head ache.

"Oof," she said, while Cole slipped his keys into his pants pocket. "I think I'm gonna walk around for a little bit. Get some air before I try to sleep. Otherwise, you know." She twirled a finger through the air. "Spinny head."

"Probably not a bad idea." Unzipping his hoodie, he wrapped it around her shoulders. "This one's my second favorite," he said while she slid her arms into his soft, warm sleeves. "So you can't keep it, but you can have it tonight."

Pulling the zipper up, she said, "Thanks, Cole. You're a good friend."

He pointed his chin toward the trees. "Don't get lost out there, yeah?"

Fairly certain he meant something more than the obvious by the statement, she promised, "I won't." Then she gave him a hug. It was tight but brief, interrupted by Madigan shouting, "Yo, Cole!" from the lodge deck.

"Yo, Mad!" Cole shouted back, a smile shooting across his face.

After Cole gave her shoulder a quick squeeze and walked toward the stairs, Davis pulled up her hood, buried her hands in her pockets, and walked the other way into the trees. Hoping not to get lost.

CHAPTER SIX

DAVIS

THE NIGHT WAS BEAUTIFUL. Cool but not cold, and the wind had changed direction, blowing the lingering forest fire smoke south, leaving the sky crisp and clear. It was quiet out here too, so quiet she could hear the pine needles snapping under her feet.

She used to take walks like this all the time with her grandpa. They were both night owls, and sometimes, when everyone else had gone to sleep, they'd find each other in the dining hall and sneak out to walk the cross-country trails. She'd hold on to the middle finger of his left hand, the one he'd lost the tip of in a lawn mowing accident, the one he'd called his *nubbin*. When she was young, he'd tell her stories about pirates and giants and mermaids. She'd tell him about whatever video game she'd been playing or book she'd been reading for school. He'd pretend to care about the games and care almost too much about the books.

When she got older, their conversations shifted, deeper questions requiring longer walks: Why was there so much pain in the world? Was life designed or a string of cosmic good luck? Did aliens exist, and if so, what would they think of humanity?

No matter what they talked about, no matter if she'd been eight or eighteen, they'd always ended their walks the same way. They'd stare up at the speckled darkness, make a wish on a certain star, then hurl pinecones high enough to try and knock it out of the sky. Which, of course, they never did. But that wasn't the point. The point was to not let the walk end, to delay it as long as possible, so they could keep talking and laughing until there were no pinecones left.

She missed her grandpa, so much sometimes it made her want to believe in ghosts. Made her wish he was one just so she could talk to him again. Just so she could have one more story. Ask one more question. Throw one more pinecone.

"Davis?"

It was a phantom whisper through the trees. "Who's there?" she shouted, spinning around, fumbling with her phone to turn on the flashlight, half expecting to see her grandpa standing right in front of her. *Shit*, maybe she *was* losing her mind.

When her flashlight finally flared to life, her heart gave a brutal kick, rebounding so violently from fear to relief to pain she wondered if it would ever beat normally again.

Standing a few feet away, his hands in the air, his fingers splayed wide, Kev squinted at her, one eye closed against the light blazing from her phone. His hair was mussed, wet, like he'd just showered. He was wearing a white long-sleeve T-shirt that hugged his chest and navy sweatpants that hung low on his hips, and his bare toes stuck out from a pair of flip-flops.

"Don't scream," he said. "Don't bust me. I'm out past curfew."

"I see that," she snapped for some reason, clearly a symptom of complete neurological collapse. "Why are you out past curfew?"

When he quirked an amused brow at her tone, she bit down, shooting him a *don't look at me like that. You actually did run away in the middle of the night, or have you already forgotten* kind of expression.

Lowering his hands to his sides, his amusement vanishing, he said, "I couldn't sleep." While he cleared a soft scratchiness from his throat, she turned off her flashlight, thrusting them into darkness until her eyes adjusted to the moonlight again.

"I didn't mean to scare you," he said. "I mean, I didn't even know you'd be out here. Why...are you out here?"

"What? I can't go for a walk on my own property now?" She didn't mean to give the words such sharp edges. But there they were, jagged and cutting.

"Of course you can. That's not what I meant." His chin drop was subtle, easily missed. But she'd studied his subtleties the way explorers studied their maps. Charting the tightness in the corners of his mouth. The furrow that sank between his brows. The way he pinched the bridge of his nose between his thumb and first two fingers. The way he rolled his right shoulder, only once and always the right. The way he'd told her in hundreds of tiny gestures that he was struggling. The way she'd been unable to do a single fucking thing about any of them.

"I just wanted to make sure you were okay," he said. Then he glanced through the trees, frowning at the cabin lights in the distance, that furrow sinking between his brows again, his expression trying to tell her even now that he was struggling, that those cabins were somewhere he didn't want to be. "But I'll head back. Get out of your way."

"No, wait." She stepped toward him, then halted, pulling the hand trying to reach for him back to her side. Because she didn't step toward him anymore. She didn't reach for him. She didn't tell him things like *no, wait*. Only she did, because that was her voice. Those were her words. "I mean, you don't have to go back just because I'm out here." Planting her feet into the ground, she pinned her hands at her sides. No longer trusting a single booze-soaked cell in her body. "This is a big resort. Lots of trails. Plenty of room for the both of us."

Slowly, pointedly, he raised a brow. "You sure about that, Davis?"

There was a lot left unsaid in his question. A lot he didn't need to say. She knew how large his presence loomed in her world. He was everywhere. Always. And she was doing everything she could to avoid him.

"Yes," she insisted. "Mostly."

A thick, sticky silence wedged itself between them. She didn't know how long they stood inside it, watching each other. But it felt like an eternity.

"Davis," he eventually said. "Can we please talk?"

He took a step toward her, and she flinched, panicked, stumbling back and tripping over a tree root. And then he was there, his hands big and warm and impossibly *on* her. One curled around her arm, the other behind her back, pulling her close, keeping her from falling. Keeping her from breathing.

He was so strong, his grip on her so firm, his clean, soapy scent almost unbearable in its familiarity. All she could see were his eyes shining in the moonlight. All she could hear was her heart beating, her blood rushing wild in her ears. All she could feel was the heat from his body warming hers, the ragged bursts of his breath against her lips.

"I've got you," he said. It was only a whisper. It was the loudest thing she'd ever heard.

With every breath, his body pressed more tightly against hers, intensity rippling off his shoulders. Shoulders she'd grabbed at some point. Shoulders she was clinging to like a lifeline. Shoulders she needed to let go of. *Let go, Davis. Let him go.*

"Sorry," she said, still clinging. "I-I tripped. I'm so"—she gasped when his hand fisted in her sweatshirt, tightening against her back—"clumsy."

His eyes narrowed, a bit of the haze over them clearing while his nostrils flared. "Davis?" he asked, a corner of his mouth hitching. "Are you drunk?"

"No," she replied, the lie catching in her throat. "Maybe. Sort of. I don't know."

It could have been a trick of the moonlight, the smile that seemed to spread across his face. Even if it was only a trick, she had to look away from this person she hadn't seen in so long. This man with

Kev's dimple, his smell. This man who held her like Kev used to hold her, before he'd stopped touching her.

She'd thought his silence had been cruel. His slow disappearance had nearly cracked her in half. But these were nothing compared to the sharp torment of Kev's old smile shining down on her now.

"I'm okay," she lied, easing out of his grip while he released her arm and unclenched his fist at her back.

Still so close, not stepping away, he wrapped his fingers around her hoodie's drawstrings. "This is Cole's?" he asked, voice low. "Isn't it?"

She glanced down at the Seattle Mariners logo on her chest. "Yeah. He drove me home. Let me borrow it because I was cold."

"That's good." He tugged on one of the drawstrings. And even though it was gentle, she felt that tug in every single one of her erogenous zones. Maybe even a few new ones. *Inner ankles, anyone?* "You shouldn't drink and drive."

A fragile laugh slipped out of her. "You're really giving me a lecture on responsibility?"

Huffing through his nose, he tugged on the other drawstring, pulling her closer. And she went to him. It was just that easy. He pulled, she followed, the tug drawing her toward him as irresistible as gravity. But where had following that tug gotten them? Where had it gotten her? Ignored? Abandoned? Betrayed?

She couldn't go to him. She shouldn't even be talking to him. She definitely shouldn't be alone with him. They were over, and this would only make everything hurt so much worse.

"Kev, you can't do this," she whispered, trying to pull away, to step back, to leave. Not moving a single muscle.

"Can't do what?" He didn't pull her closer, but he didn't let her go either. He only stood there, staring at her, focusing all his attention on her. Subsuming her in a way nothing in her life ever had before she met him. In a way he hadn't done for so long the feeling of it now was like sticking her frozen hands into a bonfire.

"You can't just touch me or look at me the way you're looking at me," she said, staying cold, staying frozen, because at least she wouldn't get burned. At least this moment wouldn't leave more scars. "You've been gone for so long. Even before you left, you were gone. Just...gone. And I know some of it was my fault."

He reeled back. "You what? No—"

"But you can't just suddenly be *here* now. You can't just suddenly be *you* again. Too much has happened. It's all too much." *It hurts too much*, she thought. *I can't hurt like this anymore.*

Releasing her strings, stepping back, he said, "I know." He scrubbed a hand over his face. "I know I can't. I know I shouldn't. I know I should stay away from you. I know if you hadn't been drinking tonight, you wouldn't even be standing here with me. You wouldn't be speaking to me. I know I should turn around right now." His exhale was a self-deprecating *puh*. "But I'm weak, Davis. I'm so fucking weak. And I know I can't touch you. I know I can't look at you. But, *god*, I wish I could. I wish we could talk, because the silence..." He closed his eyes, a second too long to be a blink. "It's destroying me. I wish you'd just let me talk to you. I wish you'd let me tell you—"

"*You* wish?" she asked harshly. "*You?*" Her anger was unexpected. A meteoric flash, a fire roaring to life behind her sternum, stinging her eyes. Maybe there was no way out of this conversation without some burns, some scars. "You don't think *I've* wished?" Visions assaulted her, limbs tangled together, his arm hanging off the side of the mattress, another woman's arm draped over his waist. Images she would sell her soul to have wiped from her memory. "You don't think I've wished every single night since you—" She couldn't even finish the sentence. "No, Kev. You can't do this. You can't... wish."

"Whoa. Okay." His hands flew back into the air, his eyes wide, rounded with fear. "Okay, you're right. I know."

"But you don't know," she said, her voice breaking as the alcohol and the night air and the nearness of him pressed in on her. Grinding her palm into her chest, she pushed against a pain so intense it made her eyes water. "Kev, you do not know." Because he didn't. And not just about Thom's sister—whose name she'd never learned. He didn't know the other things she'd seen either. How terrified she'd been. He didn't know what she'd had to watch Madigan do to him to wake him up. He didn't even know she'd been there at all.

A part of her was dimly aware she should just tell him what happened while he'd been unconscious, so high on heroin his eyes never once opened, not even when Madigan and Cole carried him down the stairs, loaded him into Madigan's truck, and took him to the hospital. She should tell him what she'd seen, let him deal with it so she didn't have to anymore. But that would mean finding out for sure. Because even though it sure as shit looked like it, she still didn't know if he'd been unfaithful to her. And maybe it made her a coward, maybe it made her weak too, but she was fine going to her grave never finding out.

"You're right," he said, running his trembling hands through his damp hair, interlacing his fingers behind his head. He looked up at the sky, his expression raw and pleading, before he released a jagged breath, lowered his hands back to his sides, and met her stare. "You're right," he repeated, his voice edging back toward calm. "I don't know. But I want to. What can I do? Please tell me what I can do to fix this. I'll do anything. I'll work harder. I'll participate in every group. I'll read every book. I'll journal until my fingers bleed. I'll do everything Madigan says. I'll crawl on my hands and knees. Please let me fix this. You have to know how sorry I—"

"Stop." Hot tears filled her eyes, spilling down her cheeks. "Kev, you can't."

"I can't what?" There was so much desperation in his voice, the moonlight turning his haunted face pale.

Say it, Davis. Just fucking say it. "You can't fix this. You can't fix *us*."

His eyes shone, refusing to leave hers. "Davis, please."

"I thought I could handle you coming back here," she said, wrapping her arms around her middle, trying to physically hold herself together, to keep herself from shattering. Because she would not shatter. Not again. "I thought I could be strong and handle it, because this is where you need to be. Here with Madigan and the men, it's where you need to be. I know that. But it's so hard. It's so much harder than I thought it was going to be." Even now, with anger and hurt churning inside her, all she wanted was to crawl into his arms so he could hold her, kiss her, tell her everything would be all right. She wasn't strong enough for this. She wasn't strong enough to keep her distance while he was so close.

"Do you want me to leave?" He blinked a single tear free. A tear that found every crack in her resolve, exploiting every weakness in the wall she was trying to build between them. A tear she wanted to brush dry with her thumb, kiss away until she tasted the salt of it on her lips. "I'll leave," he said. "I can find another home. I can leave the entire state if you need me to. I'll do anything for a chance. Let me prove it to you that I can get better. That I can *be* better. I know I don't deserve one. I know I don't deserve—*Fuck*." He swiped at his cheek when the tear tried to roll. "I know I don't deserve you. I never did. But I'll do anything, Davis. Anything. Just tell me what to do."

"I don't want you to go," she said, fighting to keep her voice steady, fighting to keep her heart steady when the thought of him leaving her again shook the ground beneath her feet. She didn't want him to leave. But she'd *never* wanted him to leave. She'd never wanted to lose him. And even though she wished more than anything that she hadn't, she had lost him. Then she'd almost lost herself.

She'd spent the last eight months loving him, then worrying about him, being terrified for him, then being devastated by him. She wasn't even sure who she was anymore, if not in relation to him. Now that he was here, now that he was safe, she needed to find out. She needed to focus on herself. And he needed to focus on himself too.

"I need time," she told him while another tear rolled down his cheek. "I need space to get used to having you here again. Because I can feel you wanting to talk to me. Every time I see you, I can feel it." She brought her hand up to cover the penetrating pang in her chest.

"Right here. And it's like I'm going to have a heart attack. Like it's all going to cave in."

He nodded fiercely. Like he knew. Like he felt it too.

"I need to not feel this way anymore," she said. "I need to be able to walk by you without worrying that this"—she motioned between them, her hand passing through the sea of tension, an ocean of want and need and regret that stretched to the horizon—"is going to happen. I need to be able to breathe again."

"Okay," he said. "I can do that. I'll give you all the space I can. All the time you need. I promise." His throat bobbed, his chin dropping toward his chest. "Just don't give up on me."

Giving in to that tug between them one last time, and because she couldn't stop herself even if she wanted to, she stepped to him, reached out, and took his face between her hands. The warmth of his skin sent a lightning bolt of need surging down her spine. She wanted so much more already. So much more than this little touch. She wanted to smooth her thumb over the furrow between his brows. To brush his bangs back off his forehead. To beg the sun to rise so she could see him more clearly, lose herself in the blue of his eyes, study the golden glint of his stubble, memorize the curve of his lips, knowing this might be the last time she'd ever see him so close.

Grasping her hand, he interlaced his fingers through hers. "I would never ask you to promise me back, because you don't owe me anything. But please, Davis." He turned his head, pressing his lips into her palm, making her close her eyes to hold back the tears burning behind her lids. Tears that pushed through to wet her lashes when he said, "Please don't need forever."

And with one final kiss to her palm, he let go of her hand, turned around, and walked away.

CHAPTER SEVEN

KEV

Mounting his steps, Kev threw his door open, slammed it so hard behind him a picture fell off the wall, and ground out a miserable and frustrated and probably way too loud "fuck!"

He didn't know what would happen when he came back to Bluebird, and he obviously hadn't thought it through. Because hurting Davis all over again had not been part of the plan. Yet here he was, causing her more pain, making her cry. Making her feel uncomfortable in her own home. When would he ever figure this life shit out? Twenty-eight years, and he still didn't have a single fucking clue.

Footsteps thundered up his stairs. The *fuck* had definitely been too loud.

Kev sat on his bed, pinching the bridge of his nose while Tex and Ace and Stanley burst into his cabin like the Kool-Aid Man and his two skinny cousins.

"What's going on?" Tex asked, ripping off his hat so fast his wispy reddish-blond hair fell into his eyes.

"We heard banging and"—Stanley lowered his voice, looking around like Madigan might magically sprout up from the area rug—"*swearing.*"

"You good?" Ace asked, sitting beside Kev on the bed.

No, he was definitely not good. "I'm fine," he said. And while Tex scoffed, Kev's jaw clenched, his obvious not-fineness exploding out of him. "I'm just so fucking tired of fucking up all the time!"

"Shh." Stanley winced. "You don't want to get bathroom—"

"Why not?" Kev asked, staring plaintively at him. "Maybe I need bathroom duty. Maybe I need bathroom duty until my back breaks and my hands fall off."

"Oh boy." Holding his hat in his lap, Tex took a seat on Kev's couch. "What happened?"

"Nothing."

"There's a whole lot of something in that nothing," Ace said, a brow arched.

"If you need to get it out"—Stanley groaned as he bent his knobby, arthritic knees and sat down beside Tex—"now's the time. This is a circle of trust. You're safe with us."

Safe? What a joke. He wasn't safe anywhere, not from the idiot who'd always be there with him, fucking everything up.

Burying his hands in his hair and pulling hard, he backed himself away from the edge. As impossible as it was, as destroyed as he felt, he couldn't fall into this well. The same fucking well he'd fallen into over and over again when anything went wrong. It was too easy. Blaming himself for everything was too easy. Hating himself was too easy. He wasn't here for things to be easy. He was here to get better. Learn. Grow. Be healthier. And healthy people talked about their problems. Healthy people asked their friends for help. Healthy people stayed out of the well. "I just ran into Davis."

Only silence surrounded him. Until Tex said, "Go on."

"She"—he tried to clear the thorns lodged in his throat—"it's hurting her. Me being here. She said I couldn't fix it. That I couldn't fix us."

Ace blew out a long, careful breath. "She told you that?"

"Yeah."

"Well," Tex said plainly. "That's good."

Kev whipped his head up, bringing a scowl along for the ride. "What do you mean, that's good? How is that good? How is me hurting the"—*woman I love*—"hurting Davis good?"

"It's good because she's being honest," Tex said, his tone making it clear that this was something Kev should already know. "She's telling you how she feels. You two will never get past this point, whatever that looks like, without being honest with each other."

"And at least she's talking to you," Stanley added with an apologetic smile stretching out under his bulb of a nose. "That's gotta be a step in the right direction, don't you think?"

They were right. Didn't make it any easier to hear.

Kev flopped back onto his bed. "Why did I do it?" He closed his eyes, refusing to cry in front of these guys because, no matter what Madigan had said, emotions were fucking scary. "I had everything. I had her. Why?"

"Have you talked about this stuff with Boss?" Tex asked. "Because you should."

Kev shook his head. "No. This is literally the most I've talked about her with anyone."

"Hmm," Stanley murmured. "Why don't you want to talk about her?"

"I don't know," Kev said. "It's hard. I'm embarrassed or something." He swiped angrily at the tears that wouldn't stop falling, showing the men his fingers. "And whenever I think about her, this keeps happening."

"What?" Tex was unimpressed. "Your fingers keep getting wet?"

Reaching back, Kev grabbed a pillow and threw it at Tex's face.

"Nothing wrong with crying," Ace said, plucking Kev's romance book from his nightstand and squinting at the back cover. "I cried yesterday while I was on the phone with my mom."

Resting his hands on his belly, looking a little like a bear about to settle in for a long nap, Stanley said, "I cried at a commercial about laundry detergent just this morning."

"And I cried after stubbing my toe on my dresser last night

because it hurt and I was tired," Tex said. And while Kev wondered if he'd ever find his way back to where these men were, how healthy they all seemed, Tex leaned in. "But since you're talking about Davis now," he said, "you might as well keep going."

Kev rolled his right shoulder. *Be like these men*, he thought. *Be willing to cry over commercials and stubbed toes and broken hearts.* "She wants more time," he admitted. "She wants space. She said she can feel me wanting to talk to her, and it's too hard."

"That's reasonable," Ace said. "You do kind of look like a kettle about to blow whenever she's around."

"No, you look more like an eager little puppy." Stanley twirled his finger in the air. "Spinning in circles and wagging your tail just trying to get her to look at you."

"I do not," Kev insisted, even though he knew they were right.

"What is it you young people say?" Tex asked, his solemn tone shifting the mood in the cabin, demanding Kev's attention. "I'm gonna hold your hand when I tell you this. But I think giving Davis some space will be good for both of you. I know you care about her. But you're here to focus on you, Kev. To get well and healthy and stay that way. And I think she knows that. If I were to put myself in Davis's shoes, after everything she's been through, the last thing I'd want to be right now is a distraction for you."

Kev was a kid being yanked back by the shirt collar before accidentally running into traffic. That's how abrupt and disorienting the sensation was, the realization that Davis might be wanting to keep so much distance between them not only to protect herself, but to protect him too.

While Kev continued to spin out, Stanley asked, "So what are you going to do?"

He opened his mouth, tried to form a thought, but nothing came to him.

"I've got an idea," Ace said. "You read romance books, right? They've gotta have some helpful pointers." Raising Kev's current read in his hand, pointing at the bare-chested cowboy on the cover, Ace asked, "What would this dude do in this situation?"

Kev gave the book a dubious once-over. What would handsome loner and rebel Smithson Kane do if the determined and exacting Daphne Beckham told him she wanted space?

"Well," Kev said, "he wouldn't want her to kick him off the ranch. But he wouldn't just let her get away either. So he'd probably honor her wishes. He'd give her space. But." He made a half-hearted smirk. "He'd also do every extra chore he could find. Save random children from runaway horse accidents. Find a reason to lift heavy things whenever she was around. And he'd probably stop wearing shirts."

Tex snorted. "Well, there you go."

"You barely wear shirts now," Stanley said.

"This is true." Ace got to his feet. "You're tits-out as soon as the sun comes up."

"What?" Kev said, feigning innocence. "It's hot. And I don't want to get my shirts all sweaty. I hate doing laundry."

"So if I did all your laundry," Stanley suggested, already looking incredulous, "you'd keep them on?"

With a sheepish grin, Kev admitted, "Probably not."

Stanley rolled his eyes. "That's what I thought."

Everything still hurt, but at least Kev was laughing.

"You settled, then?" Ace asked, bringing the mood back down to the ground as he set Kev's book back on his nightstand. "No more slamming doors?"

Kev shook his head. He wasn't settled, not by a mile. But he did feel better. And now that they'd fished him out of the pool of self-loathing he'd been wallowing in, he could see that something good had come out of his chance meeting with Davis. He'd been so worried, so convinced. But even though she wanted space, he didn't think she hated him. Davis wasn't like him. She hadn't grown up having to hide her emotions. She wore hers like jewelry, gave them out like gifts. Especially when she was keyed up.

He'd noticed the way her breath had caught, her pupils

expanding in the moonlight when he'd pulled her close, keeping her from falling. He'd felt the shudder running through her, the electric spark tensing her muscles, her coiled fingers gripping his shoulders. She'd even touched him. He wasn't sure she'd ever touch him again, and now the shape of her hand was imprinted on his cheek, his lips still tingling from the softness of her palm.

"I'm good," he said, because he could hold out. He could make that one touch last him weeks. Maybe months. And in those months, he'd give her all the space she wanted. While also finding every reason to lift heavy things whenever she was around and never wearing a shirt. "Thanks, guys."

"No problem." Standing up with another, and even longer, grunt, Stanley said, "Just do the same for us when it's our turn."

After Stanley and Ace headed out through the door, Tex set Kev's pillow back on his bed, widened his stance, and said, "I'm sorry things are so hard with Davis right now. But I'm glad you talked to us about it tonight." Then he pursed his lips, and Kev finally understood why they called it a sinking sensation. "I think," Tex said while the floor beneath Kev's feet dropped out, "that you're still holding yourself back here. I think you're still hiding."

He considered pushing back on this, but he was suddenly, profoundly exhausted. Besides, Tex was right.

"I wonder if it's the guilt," Tex said, making Kev's skin pull tight. "I wonder if it's because, deep down, you still don't believe that you deserve to get better. I get that feeling all the time. Like I'm a bad person who's done bad things, so I don't deserve anything good anymore." Sliding his hat back onto his head, he said, "But you do deserve it, Kev. We all do. And I do think you need to talk to Boss. Not about her, but about what's going on in here." Tex pointed at Kev's chest, right over his heart. "And here." He tapped once on Kev's forehead. "He's better at that sort of thing than any of us are. And I'm pretty sure he's been waiting for you."

CHAPTER SEVEN

AFTER A SURPRISINGLY DEEP sleep and an even more surprisingly decent day working the trails, Kev stared at the door to the office Ashley and Madigan shared, wondering if his decent day was about to course correct. Blowing a stream of air through his lips, he raised his fist and knocked.

"Come in," Ashley called out.

Turning the knob with a hand he was determined to keep steady, Kev popped his head inside and said, "Hey."

"Kev?" Madigan shot up from his desk like Kev had just run in screaming that the cabins were infested with termites. "Is everything okay?"

"Oh, yeah." He ruffled his hair, already failing in his attempts to not fidget. "I just wanted to talk to you. Do you have a minute?"

Madigan and Ashley shared a look, then Ashley closed her laptop and walked to the door, letting Kev in.

"I'll just go check on dinner," she said with a smile and a small pat on his arm he wouldn't have called unmotherly. Then she stared at him for a moment, and he couldn't shake the feeling that she wanted to give him a hug. Thankfully, because he wasn't sure if he'd be able to handle a hug from Ashley without getting his fingers all wet again, she only said, "It's good to see you. Looking so healthy." She squeezed his arm gently, kindly. "You're in the right place, Kev. You belong here."

Yeah, he wasn't going to survive this. Not if she said another word to him. She should be mad at him after what he did, after the way he'd hurt her daughter. But she wasn't. It didn't make sense. Emotion wedged itself sharply between his ribs, the kind of emotion that might overwhelm him if he said *thank you* or *that's kind of you* or *I'm sorry* or any of the things he wanted to say to her. And since he stood no chance of surviving a meeting with Madigan after having a complete and total breakdown in his office, all he could do was give Ashley a thin smile.

But then, in a low whisper, she asked, "Did you see the new books I left for you?"

His smile spread. He had noticed the books: a shelf of new historical and western and paranormal romances. "I did," he whispered back while Madigan narrowed his eyes at them. "Thank you."

Squeezing his arm again, she said, "Read the wolf series first. It's so good." Then she straightened, gathered her hair over a shoulder, and glanced back at Madigan. "See you later?"

Brimming with suspicion, Madigan gave her a smile that didn't make it past his lips and said, "You bet."

Once she left, closing the door behind her, Madigan asked, "What's up?"

Kev's feet stapled themselves to the floor, his courage vanishing in a silent but resounding *poof*.

"You know..." He gave a nervy laugh, hooking his thumb over his shoulder toward the door. "It's actually nothing. Never mind. Maybe I'll just come back later."

"Kev. Sit down." The way Madigan said it, it wasn't an order, but it was close enough that Kev knew a smart man would obey. So he did, taking the chair across from Madigan's desk.

"I'm actually glad you came by," Madigan said, then muttered, "Even if I'm not sure that I want to know what you and Ashley were just talking about. But I've been meaning to come see you, check in. I just wasn't sure if you were ready." His head tilted, gaze steady and assessing. "Are you ready?"

Staring down at his hands in his lap, Kev auditioned at least ten different responses. Most were thin attempts at humor to ease the concerned look on Madigan's face. Some were complete deflection. None were honest. Because that was him. That was his life. That was how he got by. He wasn't a liar, but he wasn't honest either. Not with himself, and not with anyone else.

He might not have graduated from high school or made a single good choice in his life, but he could recognize that he was getting a second chance here. A second chance from Madigan. From Ashley.

From the guys. Maybe not from Davis. But if there was even a remote possibility of that, he couldn't keep doing the same things over and over and expect anything to change. He couldn't keep pretending he was fine because he was scared of upsetting everyone around him if he told them the truth. He couldn't keep believing that if he showed when he was feeling angry or sad or worried or just...human, that the people he loved would leave him. Or hurt him. The guys hadn't left him last night. They hadn't hurt him. They'd helped him.

He wasn't a kid anymore. He wasn't *that* kid anymore. He had to try. What was it Rick had told him in rehab? *It's okay to worry more about yourself than everyone else right now. It's okay to not be okay.*

The truth weighing him down wasn't a joke. It wasn't a deflection. It wasn't nice or easy-going or happy. But it was honest. *Tell the truth, Kev. Just tell the truth.*

With his gaze pinned to his hands, he said, "I think I need some help."

It was probably only a moment of hesitation, but it stretched out like a shadow until Madigan asked, "Okay. What kind of help? What can I do?"

Looking up from his hands, not stopping until he met Madigan's stare, Kev said, "Tell me why. Tell me why I relapsed."

"So, you don't know." It was a statement. Not a question. Either way, Kev shook his head.

"I can't stop thinking about it," he said. "Why did I decide that drugs were more important than"—he barely kept himself from saying her name—"than everything." That wasn't a lie. Because she was everything. "I remember my life being good. I was feeling good. Then I remember feeling dull, off. Then I remember feeling...nothing. Just, nothing." He opened his hands up to the ceiling, like the answer might fall right into them. "What's wrong with me? Why don't I know?"

Taking a deep breath, Madigan sat back in his chair. "First of all, you had undiagnosed depression and anxiety. When I picked you up from rehab, that was one of the first things Rick told me. *Kev has clin-*

ical depression and generalized anxiety. I don't think we can blame your relapse entirely on your untreated mental illness, but I think it contributed in ways we weren't keeping an eye out for. You feel better after talking with Rick and your other counselors, right? You feel better now that you're on meds?"

Kev nodded emphatically. "Night and day. I'm still nervous a lot of the time, but it's manageable. And the depression cloud is..." He closed his eyes, feeling for that heavy gray mist, that smothering dullness, that nothingness. Not finding it. "It's lifted."

"If it starts to settle back down," Madigan said in a tone that managed to be severe yet caring at the same time, "you need to let me know. Can you do that?"

"Yeah," Kev said, hoping he was telling the truth now too. "I'll tell you."

Ducking his chin, Madigan said, "Good." Then he added, "But if we take the depression and anxiety out of the picture, why did you relapse? Believe me when I tell you, Kev. I wish I knew. I wish I could tell you why relapses happen. All I can say is that they do."

Kev's hope sank, pulling his shoulders down with it.

"But I can also tell you that having one doesn't mean you'll have another. It doesn't mean anything except for in that moment—for reasons you may figure out or you may not—the addiction was stronger than you were. I should know." The rasp was so familiar that Kev wasn't surprised when he looked up to see Madigan running his knuckles through his beard. "I've had four relapses in my life," Madigan said. "And I only saw two of those coming. The other two... I eventually figured out where I'd fallen down, but it took a while. It took reflection and focus and work. And through that reflection and work, each relapse taught me something about my addiction. Each one made me understand myself better. Each one was a part of my recovery. Just like this one will be a part of yours."

Four relapses... He couldn't imagine going through this three more times. In that moment, he felt for Madigan, for everyone who loved him. His parents and brothers, Cole, anyone who stayed by his side, constantly worried he'd use again each time he kicked.

Would Kev have another relapse? Was he just running on a hamster wheel, stuck in a loop of doing well, building a life, and then losing everything? If, somehow, he ever did win Davis back, would he just be forcing her to get stuck in that loop with him?

No. No fucking way.

He needed to stop running, figure his shit out, break the cycle. He needed to ask more questions, get more answers. Whatever it took.

"But how do you explain that to the people around you?" he asked. "How do you tell the people you've hurt"—*tell her*—"that you didn't mean to do it? That you didn't even want to do it? I mean, I know it was my choice. Nobody forced me to get in that car. Nobody forced me to go back into that house. I take full responsibility for my actions. But how do you explain that you don't know *why* you did it?"

Madigan's shoulders rose and fell. "Sometimes you can't. Sometimes all you can do is show them that you're trying to learn from your mistakes and get back on the right path." Clasping his hands on his desk, he raised a brow in a stern, knowing expression. "And I don't mean show them by pretending to be perfect."

Kev had to work not to glower, every instinct inside him wanting to shoot back with *I don't pretend to be perfect*. But that would have been a lie. And he was trying to be honest. So he only asked, "What do you mean?"

"I mean," Madigan said, "we don't show them by insisting we're fine all the time. Which is a thing addicts do, you know. The *I'm fine* thing. I think I missed it with you because you're really good at it. I should have caught it, dug deeper. But"—he sighed—"I guess I'm not perfect either. This was a good reminder."

While Kev tried not to let the guilt swallow him whole, Madigan hit his stride. "So instead of going through our lives pretending nothing's wrong, pretending we're fine—which only distances us from everyone else anyway—we show the people we love and trust that we're trying by letting them in. We show them our struggle. We let them know when we're feeling the pull. We ask them to help us. We *let* them help us. Just like you're doing right now. Because if I've learned anything after four relapses, it's that we can't do this alone."

Despite how much he wanted to believe him, questions and doubts ping-ponged wildly through Kev's mind. *Won't that just make them leave? Won't that annoy them? Won't showing her my struggle make her realize I'm too messed up to be with? Won't she think I'm broken beyond fixing?*

Since he couldn't bring himself to ask any of these, he only said, "That's, like, really hard."

"Don't I fucking know it."

"Boss?" Kev's eyes bulged. "Did you just say a swear word?"

"Yes, I did. I'll take bathroom duty for it too."

When Kev's lips twitched, Madigan smiled and said, "Look, you did a thing you regret. But you are not a bad person, Kev. *Nobody* here thinks that." The emphasis on the word, the way Madigan stared directly into his eyes when he said it, the meaning behind those three simple syllables, knocked the wind out of Kev like a kick to the ribs. "You did everything we need to do after we relapse. You went to rehab. You cleaned yourself up. And now you're here, searching for answers, learning more about yourself, trying to make amends, recommitting to your recovery." His gaze shifted to the side, settling somewhere in the middle distance. And with a slow, deliberate nod, he said, "This is the way."

"Is that..." Kev blinked. "Did you just quote *The Mandalorian?*"

His attention snapping back to the here and now, Madigan scoffed, waving a hand through the air. "Don't overthink it."

"No, you did," Kev insisted while a laugh tried to bubble up in his chest. "You even sounded like him."

"Fine. Whatever," Madigan said, giving in. "It's a great show with a good message about the importance of having a moral code. And Baby Yoda is cute."

Kev snorted. "The cutest."

Silence found them again, then Madigan asked, "I've wanted to let you settle in a little first. But I've been meaning to ask you, do you want to go to therapy? I know someone. A therapist."

"Your old girlfriend?"

Coughing on his next inhale, Madigan blurted out, "How the hell did you know that?"

Kev shrugged. "Everyone knows that. It's, like, Little Timber lore."

Tugging on the collar of the snug black t-shirt he filled out in a way Kev only wished he could, Madigan said, "Well, she wasn't my girlfriend. We were just... We had—we were friends. That's all. And she's good at her job, if you want to see her."

Kev considered it. He said he'd do whatever it took, and if Madigan insisted on it, he'd do this too. But after a full month of nearly daily talk therapy, both individually and in groups at rehab, he was a little psychoanalyzed out. "Maybe later?" he suggested. "After rehab, I could use a break."

"That's fair." Madigan nodded. "The offer isn't going anywhere." Then he asked out of the absolute blue, "You used to live on a ranch, though, right? With horses?"

"Yeah," Kev said warily, expecting the question about as much as if Madigan had asked him if he'd ever wanted to be a circus clown. "With my grandparents when I was a kid."

"Did you like it?"

Embarrassed to go overboard, Kev said an almost criminally low-key "sure" about some of the best years of his life, some of the *only* good years of his childhood.

Glancing down at his desk, Madigan said, "There's something here. Something I've been thinking you might..." The rest of the sentence got lost in the fray while he shuffled through some papers. "Ah. Here it is." He held up a pamphlet. On the cover, a silhouette of a horse stood proudly beneath the words *Equine Therapy at Strawberry Farms*.

"What's this?" Kev asked while Madigan passed him the pamphlet.

"There's a woman in town, Jen Shaw. She's Mira's friend. Mira from Glazed and Confused. Cole's Mira. Do you know her?"

"I know Mira," Kev said, the words weaving around a sharp lump in his throat. A lump reminding him of all the ways he'd hurt Cole—and Mira too, he was sure—by running off while Cole had been watching Little Timber. "But I've never met Jen."

"She's a speech therapist at the nursing home in town, but she also does this horse therapy stuff at her barn. She reached out to me a while ago about partnering with Little Timber." He winced. "I'd kind of forgotten about it, if I'm being honest. But when she sent me this the other day, I immediately thought of you."

Kev opened the pamphlet, scanned the pictures of horses grazing in a field at sunset, someone grooming a chestnut coat, a red-haired woman touching her forehead to a big bay's muzzle. That thing ratcheting tight in his chest unwound a click at the sense memory of the velvety warmth of that part of a horse. "How does she use horses for therapy?"

"I'm not entirely sure," Madigan admitted. "Look, I don't know the first thing about horses. So I've been reluctant to move forward with this because it's so out of my wheelhouse. But it's not out of yours. Jen is passionate about this treatment, and the bit of research I looked at seemed pretty solid. I think it could be a helpful option for the men who come to stay here. If you're interested. If you're willing. I'd like you to try it out for me, like a pilot program."

The immediate record scratch was deafening. Must have been because there was no way in hell Madigan had actually just said that to him. "You want *me* to try it out?"

"Yes."

"Me?" Kev asked again, pointing a thumb at his chest. "This guy?" He needed to be extra sure because nobody ever asked him to do anything like this. Nobody ever asked Kevin Lowes to do important things. They asked Kevin Lowes to stay out of the way so he didn't mess up all the important things other people did.

"Yes, Kev." Madigan didn't bother hiding his amusement. "That guy."

"Are you sure?"

With a half smile, he said, "Aside from marrying Ashley, I don't think I've ever been so sure about anything."

There was a sudden, solid weight in the room. And even though he didn't know what it was, even though it pressed down on his shoulders, it wasn't heavy. It wasn't a burden. It was…nice, centering.

"Okay," he said, despite having no firm concept of what he was agreeing to, only knowing that his blood felt charged, sparking through his veins. "When can I start?"

CHAPTER EIGHT

KEV

THE SCENT HIT him as soon as he hopped out of Madigan's truck and his feet touched the ground. Earthy, musty, nostalgic. *Horse.* The sound found him next, distant whinnying, closer snorts, hooves crunching over grass.

Strawberry Farms was lush and green, white fencing marking off several rectangular pastures housing horses of all different shapes and sizes. Grassy hills rose to the west, climbing to meet the steep, rocky face of the mountain range towering above them. Everywhere Kev looked, he saw land and sky and horse. Everywhere he looked, he saw reminders of the only place that had ever truly felt like home.

"Jen said to meet her at the main barn." Madigan scanned the grounds, squinting into the early morning sun. "There are four barns out here. Which one is the main one?"

All four barns were painted red with white trim, weathered but well cared for. Some were smaller than others, but Kev pointed at the only one with an actual door. The one with country music playing through an open window. "That's it."

They hadn't taken three steps toward the main barn when the

actual door flew wide open, and Jen rushed out, followed by an enormous matted orange tabby cat that looked like it had seen some shit.

Jen wore a faded blue ball cap with her red ponytail threaded through the hole in the back, a plaid button-down shirt with the sleeves rolled up, a pair of dusty jeans, even dustier work boots, and an electric smile. Kev thought she might be in her late forties or early fifties, and the lines extending from her eyes seemed so comfortable there. Like she was a person who smiled a lot. As a person who used to smile a lot too, it set him at ease in a way he couldn't really describe.

"Hi, guys," she said, reaching out to shake Kev's hand, and then Madigan's while the cat wove in and out of Kev's legs. "Don't mind Eleanor," she said, and Kev thought *Eleanor? That cat is* not *an Eleanor.* "Barn cats are such hussies." She laughed. "I am *so* excited you're here. Seriously. I've wanted to do this for so long."

In the pasture beside them, a white Appaloosa pony speckled with black spots let loose an ear-piercing whinny, sending the cat running.

"They're hungry," Jen explained with a breezy laugh. "I figured I'd wait until you got here so we could feed them breakfast together."

Kev felt that thing wash over him. That profound tingling sensation of being in the right place at the right time with the right people. He'd felt it the first day he'd walked into Little Timber. He'd felt it the first time he saw Davis. He'd even felt it when he was twelve and had to move onto his grandparents' farm. When his grandmother had taken one look at him, pulled him into her arms, and said, "It's all going to be okay. You're safe now." Since he'd forgotten how to trust adults at the time, he'd fought against the sensation then. He embraced it wholeheartedly now.

"That sounds amazing," he said. Because it did.

"What time should I pick him up?" Madigan asked. "I've got some errands to run in town, but I'll head back up to Bluebird if you'll be keeping him for a while."

"Can I stay all day?" Kev asked with an eagerness he immediately smothered. "I mean, it's Saturday, so we don't have any trail work. And only if it's okay with you, Jen. If not, that's totally cool."

Her electric smile turned one click shy of blinding. "Are you kidding? You can absolutely stay all day."

"This is really great," Madigan said. Only he didn't say it. He croaked it, his voice thick with emotion.

Kev refused to look at him. Because when Madigan got emotional, everyone got emotional. He was like a one-man superspreader event for feelings. Even though Kev wasn't sure if it was something his grandmother had said or something he'd just made up, the phrase *there's no crying in horse stuff* popped into his head.

Clearing his throat, Madigan said, "Just call or text me when you're done, okay?"

"Thanks, Boss." Kev made a valiant attempt at a steady nod, but it was too late, the contagion was out, the emotions had spread.

Squeezing Kev's shoulder, Madigan sniffed once. Then he cleared his throat a second time and made his way back to Lydia, knuckling his eyes dry on the way.

"Come on, Kev," Jen said, blessedly all business as she turned around and led him toward the main barn. "We've got some paperwork to fill out." The pony blew out another extremely pissed-off whinny. "And some very impatient horses to feed."

"This is Clyde," Jen said, pouring a scoop of sweet feed into an enormous buckskin draft horse's bucket. "He's huge, but he's as sweet as they come."

Lowering the wheelbarrow holding three kinds of feed back to the ground, Kev introduced himself. "Hey, big guy," he said, scratching Clyde between his ears after the horse thrust his nose into his bucket.

"And this little ball of sass is Maggie."

The Appy pony had abandoned whinnying in favor of whipping

her head up and down like a maniac, occasionally adding a double-barrel donkey kick high enough to take a person's head off.

"Jeez," Kev said. "She's intense."

"Ponies, am I right?" Jen poured a small scoop of pellets into Maggie's bucket. "She was my daughter's first mare. Dumped her more times than I can count. She's retired now, except for running all the horses in whatever pasture she's living in, of course."

"Big Alpha Mare Energy."

Jen laughed. "Enormous." After feeding the rest of the horses in the pasture, she turned to face him. "So, Madigan told me a little about you."

Kev's eyes went wide. "Oh, um—"

"Nothing too specific," she added quickly, dropping the scoop back into the wheelbarrow. "Just that you used to work on your grandparents' ranch. You seem really comfortable around horses."

"Oh, yeah," he said, relief washing over him that she only knew that much. That she wasn't imagining him alone in an empty house or rolled onto his side on a jail cot or passed out on a mattress on the floor. "They had quarter horses mostly. We used them for moving cattle, some roping, trail riding, that sort of stuff. A rodeo every once in a while just for fun."

"That's great," she said, adjusting her ball cap. "But, fair warning, what we do here might feel a little different."

"Okay?" He picked up the wheelbarrow, walking beside her back toward the main barn. "How is it different?"

"I am so glad you asked," she said with a smile he felt like a pat on the back. A little gold star. Like he'd asked the right question. Done the right thing. It shouldn't have affected him so much, the validation. But it did. It always had. Maybe that was why he was so messed up. Maybe it was why he tried so hard to please. A person probably shouldn't be as starved for simple praise as he was.

"A lot of the time, our relationships with horses are transactional," Jen explained. "We tend to use them for some purpose that benefits us. Just like you said—sometimes we train them so we can show them or take them to rodeos. Sometimes we put them to work on ranches. Sometimes they're destined for the track. The horses in this program"—she looked around her farm, at the three front pastures, some horses still eating quietly, others ambling toward their water troughs or out to the middle of the pastures to graze—"they're all pretty mellow, calm, bombproof. Most of them have survived years of kids' lessons and summer camps and tourist trail rides. Because of that, they tend to be good babysitters. But they're also highly skilled at reading people."

Kev nodded, suddenly worried about what some worldly old horse might think of him.

"If we're willing, we can learn a lot about ourselves through the way they see us. This program is about relationship building, accountability, focus, trust, and honesty." She met his gaze head-on with an unwavering blue-eyed stare. "Because I promise you, these horses will know when you're full of shit."

"I don't want to be full of shit." He winced at the words that should have popped up in a thought bubble above his head rather than straight out of his mouth. "I mean," he hedged, "that all sounds really good to me. When Madigan told me about this place, I don't know." He ruffled his hair, fighting the heat trying to rush up his throat. "It felt...right. Like it was exactly what I needed."

"You know what, Kev?" She gave him one of those smiles that was also kind of a frown. Knowing and proud. Like that one meme of Robert Redford nodding on a log. "I think you're going to do just fine."

He kicked at the dirt, the heat evading his defenses, shooting up to flood his cheeks.

"Let's go feed the horses in the back pastures," she said. "And then, would you like to go for a ride?"

"Really?" He thought he'd get to hang out with the horses today, maybe do a little barn work. But he hadn't let himself hope for a ride.

"Really," she said. "It's going to be hot as hell this afternoon, so let's get them out early."

CHAPTER EIGHT

AFTER SPENDING twenty minutes doing a meditative practice Jen called mindful grooming, Kev not only had a very clean horse but also an unexpectedly calm mind. He'd never paid much attention to grooming a horse before. He'd always just brushed off the biggest dirt clumps, thrown on a saddle, and gotten to work.

Now, sitting on top of Clyde, walking down a wide treelined gravel road next to Jen, who rode a fine-boned black thoroughbred named Tom Collins, Kev said, "That was really different for me. The grooming thing."

"How so?" she asked.

"I guess it was the first time I ever thought about what it was like for the horse." He adjusted his helmet. He'd never worn a helmet before either and definitely would've preferred a cowboy hat. Not that he was about to tell Jen that after she'd thrust the helmet toward him with a steely *this is nonnegotiable* look in her eyes. "Like, here I am," he said, trying to explain. "This person they've never even met before in their space, brushing their coat, picking up their hooves, moving them around. And I always expected them to just let me. I always expected them to trust me."

"Pretty wild, huh?" she said. "But the wildest part is that they usually do just trust us. Horses will follow us through thunderstorms, across rivers, down mountains so steep or over jumps so high it literally puts their lives at risk. They'll do all of that and more for us, trusting us the entire time. Whether we deserve it or not."

Golden sunlight filtered through the trees, warming his face, his hands, chasing out the morning chill. Sunlight. Warmth. Golden. All the things Davis had been to him. "It kind of makes you realize how important it is."

"How important what is?" Jen asked, studying him closely, listening intently.

He'd never had to do anything to earn Davis's trust. She'd just given it to him. From the instant they'd met, she'd trusted him. She'd been his warmth, his sunlight. Until he'd turned his back on her. *Who the hell turns their back on sunlight?*

"To make sure you deserve it," he eventually said.

Birds trilled to each other in the trees. The horse's hooves crunched softly over gravel. And Jen said, "Thank you for sharing that with me, Kev. You're a very thoughtful person."

Before he could find the words to respond, to tell her she was wrong and that he was selfish and thoughtless, she asked, "Do you want to go faster?"

His first instinct was to say *yes, absolutely, let's go*. Itching to escape this conversation, escape the guilt gnawing at his belly. But that was what he always did. The restless energy churning relentlessly inside him was always ready to jump, to move, to run. Even if he had nothing to run away from anymore. Nothing but himself. Nothing but his own fear of sitting still. *Christ*, he was tired of running. He was so indescribably tired.

"Can we stay slow today?" He felt self-conscious asking for it, too exposed somehow. But how exposed must his horse feel right now? At the mercy of this stranger on his back? And yet Clyde kept walking, kept putting one hoof in front of the other with his head low, his ears forward, his back swaying calmly from side to side under Kev's saddle. *Trust.* "If you don't mind."

"Slow is good," Jen said with a gentle smile. "Slow is important. Sometimes I forget that too."

They walked in silence, the temperature rising rapidly as the two lanes of what Kev thought was probably an old logging road narrowed into a single overgrown trail.

"This is a good spot to turn around," Jen said. "The trail gets pretty primitive from here on out."

"Sounds good." Sliding his reins to the left to turn Clyde around, urging him on with a squeeze of his heels, Kev saw a horse standing alone in a pasture at the back of Jen's property, staring at him.

"Who's that?" They hadn't fed that horse, he would have remembered if they had. Because she was spectacular.

"Oh, yeah," Jen said. "I forgot that I fed her before you got here. That's River. She's beautiful, isn't she?"

River was a bay so dark she looked dipped in chocolate, with a thick black mane, a white blaze flowing like milk from her forehead down to her nose, white socks on her front legs, and a long white tail that billowed behind her in the breeze.

"She's amazing," he said. "Why is she all the way back here?" *Why is she all alone?* he wondered inwardly.

"She's all the way back here," Jen said, urging Tom Collins closer to River's fence, "because once we put her in this pasture to deworm her and test her for Coggins, she refused to let anyone come near her again." Jen pointed her chin down the fence, where Eleanor sat licking her paws, her fuzzy belly folding over the sides of the rail. "Anyone but the barn cat, anyway."

"No kidding?" Kev couldn't stop staring at the mare. Mainly because she wouldn't stop staring at him.

"No kidding." Jen's laugh was a little sad. "She's an American Mustang. My ex—" She cut herself off. "My *estranged* husband adopted her from a BLM corral years ago. It was part of some Mustang Makeover challenge. He competes—competed," she corrected again, "in cutting competitions, and he thought she would be his next winner. Turns out, she didn't want to be made over."

Kev pressed his lips together while River swished her tail viciously at a fly trying to land on her flank. "I guess not."

"I can't really blame her," Jen said. "The roundups of our wild horses can be horrific. Who knows what she's been through, what scars she has that we can't see."

Kev's left eye twitched, some old bruise deep inside him starting to ache. "She doesn't trust us anymore."

"No. She does not." Jen leaned forward, resting her arms on her saddle's pommel. "It's too bad. She really is a gorgeous mare."

"What will you do with her?" The thought that something else might happen to this horse, that some other place she thought was her home might be ripped away from her, made his fingers turn icy around his reins.

"Do with her?" Jen repeated, a question in her inflection as well as her creased brow. "I won't do anything with her. She's safe here, Kev. I'll keep feeding her, giving her water, making sure she's healthy. Buying her the occasional toy." Pointing at a red ball with a tug handle in the corner of River's pasture, Jen whispered, "She plays with that one when she thinks nobody's watching."

The tension hiking Kev's shoulders toward his ears slowly eased. She was okay. She was safe.

"And maybe someday," Jen continued, scratching Tom Collins's withers until they started twitching, "she'll let somebody try to earn her trust again. But it won't be me." She sat up and, with a self-deprecating laugh, said, "That mare hates my guts."

Kev couldn't imagine anyone or anything hating Jen. She seemed way too nice. And smart too. But horses could be weird. Like the way River seemed to stare straight into his soul. That was weird.

"Let's head back," Jen said as an excited grin flashed across her face. "It's time for you to learn all about mindful chores."

CHAPTER NINE

DAVIS

She sat on the edge of her bed, staring blankly at her wall, and realized that there was something wrong with her. While she'd spent the entire week showing up every single Little Timber man by cutting the most trail, digging up the most trees, working a solid extra hour every night after they'd called it quits, Kev had spent the entire week giving her all the space in the world, all the time in the universe. He'd barely even looked at her aside from the quick, tight grins he flashed when they happened to cross paths. She knew she was supposed to be feeling better about everything. She should, in fact, feel great.

Because this was what she wanted, wasn't it? Wasn't the fact that she never felt that pull between them anymore, that electric current arcing from her chest to his, keeping them connected, keeping them entangled, exactly why she'd asked him to give her space in the first place?

It was. It absolutely was.

So why was it fucking her up? Why was she losing sleep while her mind replayed in vivid detail the way he laughed with the other men now? Why did she stand under the spray of her shower every night wondering why the smiles he gave to everyone but her were brighter, warmer, more genuine, more...Kev? Why did she sit at her desk pretending to scroll through social media when, really, she scrolled through mental images of him looking lighter and looser every day? Especially now that he was working with Jen and her horses. She'd never seen him so content. Not even when things between them had been good. She'd never seen him glow the way he did lately.

It shouldn't matter anymore, because they were over, and she needed to move on with her life. Whatever that ended up looking like. Whoever she ended up becoming without him, without school, without a fucking clue what she should do next. But she couldn't help but wonder, was it her? Was having her out of his life the reason for his glow? Was he better off without her?

And to make matters worse. Like, so much worse. He'd completely stopped wearing shirts. And with all the work on the trails and whatever Jen had him doing, he was getting ridiculously ripped. In her face, glowing, shirtless, ripped. Every. Single. Day.

She couldn't sit there anymore, staring at walls, wondering, questioning. She needed to get up. She needed to make a plan. There was a life out there for her without him. She just needed to go find it. She needed to get off her ass and find her own fucking glow.

Grabbing her hoodie from her closet, because even though it was warm out, she was always a little cold these days, she glanced at the shoebox on her top shelf. The one filled with all the things she never got to say to Kev—the angry notes, the random thoughts. The goodbye that was still balled up in there somewhere. The goodbye she'd written out after scraping herself off her bathroom floor a month ago. The goodbye she needed to recommit to.

Kev didn't want her to give up on him. But she couldn't give up on herself either. She couldn't forget what he'd done, even if he seemed like he was back—the Kev she'd fallen in love with, the Kev she would have moved mountains to stay with. The Kev she'd thought was the one for her forever.

Closing the closet door, she pulled her hoodie over her head and finally left her bedroom. Maybe she didn't have a life plan, but she could at least help Maude Alice with meal prep. She could at least be useful. But halfway to the stairs, she doubled back when she heard "Seriously? Fine. Whatever. Just, frickin' frick you, dude" from the rental office Madigan had repurposed as a computer lab for the guys during the offseason.

"B?" she said after peeking through the door.

Brayden's head was on the counter, buried in his arms, his dark hair sticking up a little in the back. Even though he was only a few years younger than she was, Davis felt a little protective of him. He seemed like he wasn't sure what he was doing at Little Timber yet. Like he was still trying to figure it all out. Some of the men were like that. It took them time to settle, to find their way. And right now, she sympathized with that plight on a profoundly deep level.

"B?" she tried again. "You okay?"

Looking up, finally noticing her, he winced. "Crap," he said, quickly drying his eyes with two swipes of his fingers, his nails painted black. "Hi, D. Um…" He sniffed, blinking hard up at the ceiling. "I didn't know you were out there."

"I'm sorry," she said, stepping back toward the door, realizing he probably didn't want anyone seeing him like this. "I didn't mean to interrupt."

"You're not interrupting anything. Except me wondering why I'm so fricking bad at this stuff."

"At computers?" she asked.

"No." His laughter was self-deprecating in a charming kind of way. "At, like, life." He pointed a finger at the monitor. "Like this. This should be easy, and I can't figure it out."

"Can I help?"

He straightened, his eyes lighting up. "For real?"

"Of course," she said, coming around the counter when he waved her over. He turned the monitor, and she read, "How to get your GED." A smile burst across her face. "You're getting your GED?"

"Highly doubtful," he grumbled, picking up his pencil, tapping it on the counter. The pencil itself was riddled with teeth marks, like he'd been gnawing on it. "I mean, I want to. But I can't even figure out which test I'm supposed to study for. There's a GED, but also this." He pointed at the screen again. "What the heck is a HiSET?"

"Good question," Davis said, pulling up a stool to sit beside him. "May I?"

Sliding her the mouse, he said, "Absolutely."

After a few minutes of searching and clicking, they learned that HiSET stood for the High School Equivalency Test. And that in Montana, either it or the GED were valid ways of earning a high school equivalency diploma.

Still tapping his eraser, Brayden asked, "So how do I choose? Which one's better?"

"I don't know. But the internet will," she said, typing *what are the differences between the GED and the HiSET* into the search bar. "Okay. First of all, the GED has four tests instead of five."

"Less is more," Brayden said, spinning from side to side on his stool. "GED it is."

"But," she added, "the HiSET is multiple choice, whereas the GED has some fill in the blanks and stuff. The HiSET is a little cheaper too."

Chewing on his pencil again, he pulled it free, asked, "What would you do?" then clamped it back between his teeth.

"Oh, I am a multiple choice girlie. One hundred percent. If I don't know the answer to a question, with multiple choice, at least I might get lucky."

"You make a good point."

Scrolling farther down, she said, "But there are free practice tests available for the GED and the HiSET. So you can just take one of each and see which one you do better on."

He folded his arms on the counter again, letting his forehead drop dramatically on top of them, and groaned. "But what if I suck at both?"

"Well, do you have a study plan?"

"A whaty what?" He raised his head, then dropped it again. "This is probably a stupid idea. I was never any good at school. Never mind."

"I understand how you feel. Making decisions like this, taking chances like this, can seem pretty daunting," she said, refusing to let him talk himself out of this so easily. "But were you motivated in school? Were you into it? Did you care?"

Sitting upright again, he scoffed. "Heck no. For the two years I bothered going to high school, all I cared about was girls and drugs. I was high all the time. I mean *all* the time."

"Well, there you go. You're clearheaded now. You're motivated now." She raised her brows. "Who knows what you'll be good at. And look." Clicking on an external link, she said, "There are free prep classes at the Adult Learning Center in Red Falls twice a week. Oh, and they allow you to attend virtually. We could do them here. I can come and help if you want. If you decide this is what you want to do. Which, by the way, I definitely think you should."

"You do?"

She nodded. "Yes. Knowledge is power, B."

"You know, you're kind of good at this," Brayden said, pointing his pencil at her. "Like, you've been really helpful."

Considering she'd been no help to herself at all lately, it was nice to know she could at least still be helpful to someone else. "So what do you think? You gonna go for it?"

Flipping his pencil into the air, catching it between his fingers like it was a cigarette, he said, "Maybe. Gets pretty boring around here. If anything, it's something to do, right?"

"Sure is," she said. "I'm excited for you. Putting yourself out there is hard."

"It really is." Tilting his head, he chewed on his lip. "Speaking of... Can I say something I have absolutely no business saying?"

"That depends," she said, her eyes narrowing, "on what it is."

"Like I said. It gets boring around here. So we talk a lot, the guys,

I mean. There isn't much that happens around here that we don't all know about eventually."

"Okay," she said slowly, her narrowed eyes tightening into a full-on squint. "What are you getting at?"

"The thing is, putting yourself out there *is* hard. Whether it's for something like trying to get a high school diploma or for trying to apologize for some really shit—crappy," he corrected himself, "thing you've done."

"You can swear around me, B. I'm not going to rat you out."

"Shh. Boss is always right around the corner," he whispered, looking around high and low. "Seriously. It's like a horror movie."

She laughed, half expecting Madigan to walk through the door holding a list of the Little Timber rules, pointing at the no swearing rule just for show.

"Anyway," Brayden said. "I know this is none of my business. But I just gotta say, I have never seen a dude more stuck on a girl than Kev is on you. Or any dude who put himself out there harder to try and make up for his mistakes. I wasn't here when everything went down, but... I don't know." He raised a shoulder. "I guess I've always been the kind of guy who just gave up whenever I've let people down. Like, I'd do something messed up, then I'd just go get high and hope everyone eventually forgot about it. I know," he said, rolling his eyes when she gave him a thin smile. "Shocker I ended up here, right? But Kev? He's, like, totally the opposite. I don't think he'll ever give up trying to make things right with you. Even when he's eighty years old, he'll still be trying. Sitting in his recliner, writing you love poems or something. Don't tell him I told you any of this, okay? I feel like he's finally starting to like me. But I just thought you should know. Kev is legit. He's all-in."

He's all-in, she thought. *And all I can seem to do is shove him out.* "Thanks for telling me that. But me and Kev...it's a really complicated situation."

"Oh, for sure," he said, nodding. "I get that. But, like, what if..." He pointed his chin at the monitor. "What if it's like these tests?

What if it's complicated because you're trying to fill in the blanks or write an essay or something, when really, it's just multiple choice? Or even simpler. What if"—he drew a heart on the already heavily graffitied counter with his pencil—"it's just true or false?"

One of these days, she'd stop being shocked by the hidden depths the Little Timber men possessed. And even though he was sweet and insightful and, yeah, maybe talking about something he shouldn't be talking about, it still didn't keep her from saying "I appreciate that B. But there is no test. No blanks to fill in." She pressed her lips together, just for a second, just to brace herself. "Because there is no Davis and Kev anymore."

"Okay, D." He patted her hand, brushing away her insistence like dandelion fluff, like something that appeared sure and stable on the outside when everyone knew a single breath would scatter it to the wind. "Whatever you say."

It was a *whatever you say* that followed her all throughout helping Maude Alice with dinner. All throughout pretending to eat while Kev and the men sat at the table next to her. While Kev talked and laughed with everyone but her. All throughout last night and today as she milled around her room, avoiding the trails because she just couldn't do it. She couldn't see him, couldn't hear that *whatever you say* when faced with his shirtless torso, his bulging biceps, his straining abs when he tossed huge, heavy logs into the chipper pile like they were twigs.

It was a *whatever you say* that followed her into the dining hall, where she now sat, staring in an almost exhausted indifference at the newest text from her dad. Hating the way he was wearing her down. Wishing he would just leave her alone.

> Chuckle Puppet: Are you ever going to talk to me again? Should I just give up? I don't know what else to do here. I just want to apologize. I just want a chance. Dad.

"I've seen that look before," her grandma said, emerging from the kitchen like she was emerging from the salon. She was such a beautiful woman, so put together, her silver hair always perfectly styled, makeup always perfectly applied. She was nothing short of regal, and Davis wondered, not for the first time, if her mom had secretly been adopted. Or maybe she and her mom just had more of her grandpa in them.

Pointing a finger at her, joining her at the table, her grandma said, "When your mother makes that face, it's almost always because of your dad."

Davis passed her the phone. "Nailed it."

Her grandma's eyebrow flickered while she read Chuck's text, her expression otherwise remaining carefully neutral. "Chuckle Puppet?"

Taking her phone back, Davis said, "Seeing *Dad* on my screen just pissed me off. At least Chuckle Puppet is funny."

"You still aren't speaking to him?"

Davis shook her head.

"I see." Maude Alice Cooke was the kind of person who could fit an entire thesis inside those two words. Davis waited for more discussion on the matter, but her grandma only asked, "How's the training going? I still don't understand why any sane person would ever want to ride a bike that far when perfectly good cars exist."

Because I'm clearly not sane, Davis thought. Saying instead, "Because cars can't go where my bike can go. And training is going great. I can get all the way up the mountain in under two hours now. Hopefully I won't completely embarrass myself at the race in September."

"That's wonderful, dear. Although I can't imagine you'd ever embarrass yourself doing anything."

An invisible fist rammed into Davis's chest. A memory roaring through her mind. That frozen night with Kev in her car. Steamed-up windows. His hands on her thighs, his lips against her throat. That night when she'd put herself so far out there she couldn't find a path back.

That was the night when her world had crashed down. The night he'd pushed her away, and she'd slammed her car door, shouting "Fuck the rules!" at the sky while storming away from him, leaving him alone in the cold. In the dark. That was the night she'd learned how deeply shame could root itself inside a person.

Because that was the night she'd lost him.

Slowly, her grandma's eyes narrowed. They were such a unique color, a pale, rainy gray. Not like Davis's—bright blue, just like her dad's. Which was a thing she used to love sharing with him.

"Davis," her grandma said, "how are you?"

"Oh, you know." She didn't even bother trying to sound convincing. "Fine."

"Let's try that again." Her grandma's warm fingers wrapped around Davis's cold hands as she saw straight through her fake smiles and half-truths the way only a grandparent could. "How are you?"

"Seriously, Grandma," she said, clinging to those half-truths by her fingernails while she attempted her own version of Kev's glowing smile, producing a faint glimmer at best. "I'm good. Each day gets a little better."

"Well, isn't that just wonderful." Davis sensed her grandma's cynicism, the way the word *wonderful* might as well have been *bullshit*. Thankfully, she let Davis's wonderful bullshit slide, rising from the table to kiss the top of her head. "I'm heading over to Glazed and Confused to play cribbage with Linda."

Linda was Mira's mother and Maude Alice's best friend. She was living with cognitive decline now, and Davis knew their weekly cribbage games had just as much to do with their friendship as it did with Maude Alice trying to give Mira a break to run errands or go on dates with Cole.

"Tell her I said hi," Davis said. "Cole and Mira too, if you see them."

"Of course." She placed a hand on Davis's shoulder. "I know I'm not Max. I know you and your grandpa had something so special, a once-in-a-lifetime connection. But if for whatever reason things stop being fine or good or any of those pleasant words, I'm here. I'm always here for you, Davis."

"I know," Davis said. She'd just reached up to squeeze her grandma's fingers when her phone buzzed, snapping her already tenuous mood improvement in half. "Shit."

Smoothing a hand over her hair, her grandma said, "That Chuckle sure is a persistent puppet."

Davis left her phone, and the text from her dad, untouched on the table.

"You know, dear," her grandma said, "nobody would fault you if you talked to him again. He's your father, after all."

"He's a lying, duplicitous prick," Davis grumbled while some annoyingly persistent part of her wondered if her grandma was right.

"True," her grandma said evenly. "But, you know," she sighed, kissed Davis on the head again, and said, "family." Like the word explained everything. And maybe it did.

Maybe families hurt each other sometimes. Maybe families at least tried to work through those hurts. Maybe a good daughter would at least let their father try to apologize. But Davis was still too hurt and angry and lost to sort it all out.

While her grandma walked away, Davis's phone buzzed again. This time, for whatever reason, she picked it up.

> Prof Novak: Hey Davis. How are you? Do you have a second to talk?

Bolting up from her chair, she stared at her phone, her heart rate kicking up a few beats per minute as she typed out:

> Davis: Hi Professor Novak. Sure!

Five seconds later, her phone buzzed with an incoming call.
"Hello?"

"Hi, Davis," he said in his wired, perpetually enthusiastic voice. "How are you?"

"I'm great," she lied again, pacing in front of her table. "How are you?"

"I am fantastic."

The last time she'd spoken to Dr. Ben Novak, it was so he could tell her he'd lost his funding a year and a half into her postgrad and she'd have to find a new mentor, fit herself into a new microbiology lab, and start on a new project. Which, at the time, had been a blow about the same magnitude as a freight train colliding with her at full speed. Even so, that hadn't been the only reason she'd left Missoula. There'd been the stress, the endless lab hours, missing her family, the fact that her relationship with her ex, Patrick, had deteriorated to the point of two bored ships passing in the night. The nagging feeling that she just wasn't interested in research anymore, in school. In any of it. Like she was just going through the motions of someone else's life. Doing what she thought she was supposed to do.

"That's great," she said, adding a hesitant "Um, what's up?"

"Only the best news ever. My new grant went through." Ben was a young professor, early thirties. His chaotic energy had been infectious to her once upon a time. It kind of fizzled in her now. Which, all things considered, might have meant she was excited. The bar was exceptionally low. "We're funded again for the next five years."

She pulled at her lower lip, possibilities turning over in her mind, answers to questions she'd been asking herself for weeks. "Really?"

"Really. Davis, I want you back in the lab."

"You do?" Switching her phone to her other ear, she wiped her suddenly clammy hand off on her shorts. Was this a sign? Was this what she needed? A chance to make a clean break? To get away from the memories, from seeing his face every day? To get away from his smiles and laughter that used to be for her but now seemed to be for everyone *except* her? Was this her chance to get back on her own path?

"Heck yes," Ben said. "Would you want to come back? I spoke to the dean, and you can resume your studies right where you left off. I've felt so bad about letting you and your cohort down. Most of them are coming back. Michael and Anika and Bobbi. And I'm really excited about this new project. You're going to love it. I'll send you all the details. What do you think?"

Her skin buzzed, but she couldn't tell if the electric tingle was from excitement or nerves or just some weird neurological tick heralding a total mental breakdown. "When do you need an answer by?"

"Classes start August twenty-sixth."

"So soon," she thought out loud. *Less than a month.* "Okay. Send me all the information. And I'll get back to you as soon as I can."

"This is so great," he cheered, and she imagined his fist pumping into the air. "I'll email you tonight."

Lowering her phone from her ear, she held it against her chest, countless conflicting emotions floating around her, winking in and out like embers. What was she doing? What was she doing with her life? Did she want to stay here? Did she want to run Bluebird with her mom and grandma? Did she want to go back to school? What did she want?

What the absolute hell do I even want?

Plopping back onto her chair, she groaned. Because aside from the one thing she couldn't have—to go back in time and keep Kev from ever leaving—she didn't know. Then her phone buzzed again.

"Dr. Novak?" she said. He was the type of charmingly absent-minded professor who always forgot something.

"Uh, no." At the familiar voice, her breath froze in her lungs. "Hi, Davis."

"Dad?" The word croaked out of her.

"I'm guessing you didn't see the caller ID."

Pulling herself together after the initial shock of this breach of her defenses, she said, "No. I didn't—"

"Don't hang up." The pleading tone in his voice kept the phone at her ear. "Just let me say one thing."

"Haven't you already said enough?" she asked, hot anger swirling in her chest, bubbling up into her throat. "Haven't you already *done* enough?" It took everything she had to keep her voice down. The last thing she needed was for her mom and Madigan to come running out of their office to see what was wrong.

"Davis, honey. Please."

"I'm sorry, Dad. I have to go. Please don't call me again. Don't text me either. I'm not ready to talk to you." The persistent tug-of-war between guilt and anger and love and hate pulled a bit harder to one side, making her say, "Yet. Just...not yet."

"Okay," he said. "Okay, I understand. I'll be here when you're ready. But I miss you, Davis. And I'm so—"

She mashed the *end call* button, slid her phone across the table so hard it skipped off the other side and thumped onto the floor, and collapsed back into her chair. Her head throbbed, a drum pounding between her temples.

Was this all she did now? Demand space? Avoid hard conversations because she was too sad or angry or hurt? Run away from everything?

She'd promised herself she wouldn't cry anymore, but she would have had better luck keeping the sun from setting in a few hours than keeping the tears from welling in her eyes, clouding her vision. She wanted a break. She wanted a single day of peace. She wanted a hug. The only problem was, the person she really wanted a hug from had been gone for over four years. If he were still here, her grandpa would know what to say. He'd be able to tell her what she should do, make her path clear. And if he couldn't, he'd hug her until all her problems seemed so much smaller.

A cold, wet nose nudged her elbow, a big, furry head wiggling into her lap.

"Hey, Murphy," she said, wiping her cheeks dry. She glanced down, meeting the dog's deep brown eyes. "Where have you been?"

His tail swung from side to side, his fuzzy eyebrows tenting. And then he whined.

"Do you need to go out?"

A sharp increase in tail-wagging velocity was his answer. Maybe he was on to something. Maybe she needed to get some air, go for a ride and clear her head. Maybe then she'd be able to figure out what the hell to do with her life.

Pushing herself up to her feet, she blew out a determined breath and said, "Come on, pal. Let's get out of here."

CHAPTER TEN

DAVIS

Sweat slid between her shoulder blades, dripping from her nose. It felt good, pedaling up the switchbacks, pushing herself to the limit, demolishing her personal best time. Murphy panted like an old man with asthma behind her, but he kept up. Usually he made it about halfway to the top with her, then chilled in the shade until she came back down. But he was all-in right now.

"I'm not slowing down, Murph," she called back to him. "Head down if you need to."

He only barked. Then galloped ahead of her while she rounded another turn.

Smiling into the late afternoon sun, she said, "Fair enough."

With each pedal stroke, thoughts and plans drifted through her mind. Each option shouldering its way through, only to be elbowed out by some other possibility. *I love it here. I should stay. It hurts to be here. I should go. I'm not sure if I want to do research anymore. What the hell else am I going to do? If I left, I could start over. If I left, I could always come back. If I left, I wouldn't have to see him every day. But if I left, I might never see him again. Why do I want to see him again? It's over. But what if it's not over? What if there's a chance?*

Because what if I still love him? Fuck. Fuck. "Fuck!" This last one she shouted so loud that if Bluebird had been covered in snow, the echo might have brought down an avalanche.

When she finally reached the top of the mountain, she was out of breath, out of steam, and not a single step closer to knowing what she should do. Leaning her bike against the upper Moonlight lift shed, she took off her helmet, slung the strap over her handlebars, and pulled her water bottle out of its holder. While she squirted water into her mouth, and then into Murphy's, voices carried up from a trail below her. She couldn't see them, but she could hear them, running chainsaws and weed eaters, shouting at each other over the racket, laughing.

Without so much as a thank-you for the water, Murphy whipped his head up, turned tail, and took off toward the men.

Davis didn't necessarily need to follow him. She could have picked another trail to ride down. She could have ridden back down the way she'd come up. She could have done a lot of things. Which was exactly what her mind kept telling her as she climbed back onto her bike, clipped back into her pedals, and pointed her front tire in the direction of the crew.

She rode slowly, quietly, hoping to skirt by the men. Hoping to catch a glance, just a tiny glimpse of him. Because this was what she did now. This was how she survived. She snuck glances, stole time with him. Time he didn't know he was sharing with her. She knew it was wrong, but she needed it. Craved it. She craved his glowing smiles, his shoulders catching the sunlight, his abs flexing, skin glistening. Her need for him was an itch she could never quite scratch. Between her shoulder blades. Inside her bones. Deep within her beating heart. Impossible to reach.

She skidded to a stop, because there he was. Trimming trees with Brayden and Noah. Lit up by the sun, radiant. He sank to his knees to give Murphy a hug, taking a slobbery lick to the face that, even in her distressed state, managed to tug at a corner of her mouth. After pouring half of his water bottle out for Murphy to lap up, he stood again and took a long sip.

A stream of water slipped over his chin, trickling between his pecs, down the rigid valley of his abs. And then he was smiling, then snorting, then laughing so hard at something Noah said he doubled over, his hands on his knees, his face turning red.

At the sight of it, the sound of it, her smile fell, plummeting boulder-like to the valley floor. Why? Why did he get to laugh like that again? She couldn't laugh like that anymore. Why did this all seem suddenly so easy for him while she was constantly pedaling uphill? Why was he happy and comfortable when her emotions had her in such an unyielding chokehold she was literally shaking, trembling, a volcano about to blow?

Breathing hard, and not from exertion, she was suddenly fueled by a frustration she couldn't reason with, driven by an anger she couldn't control. Animated by months of pain and fear and rage and confusion that refused to be bottled for one more second. Pressure building, steaming out of her ears, every rational thought in her head running for safer ground, she dropped her bike in the dirt and marched out of the trees.

"Hey, D," Brayden called out once he spotted her.

Kev raised his head, his eyes wide. But in less than a blink, his interest in her vanished, his surprise replaced by the same bland grin and tight nod that had become his default greeting for her these days.

"Hey, B!" she shouted back, faking a too-wide smile.

Nothing. Nothing from Kev at all.

When Brayden asked, "How's the ride?" and Kev returned to his trimming, clipping away like she wasn't even there, not even tempted to look at her when she'd been going so far as to hide in the trees like a creepy-ass stalker just so she could steal a single look at him, she fucking lost it. Game over. The end.

Now she understood why they called it seeing red, because there was nothing around her that wasn't cast in a blaring warning light:

the trees, the sky, the alarmed faces of men who recognized the impending devastation of a woman about to completely lose her shit.

Glaring daggers at him, barely capable of controlling her fingers, she fumbled through unclipping her helmet strap.

"Davis?" he asked, backing slowly away from the pyroclastic cloud she'd morphed into.

Finally yanking her helmet off her head, she reeled back, grunted, and hurled it at the trees. Only in her current, deranged state, her aim was shit, and she nearly hit him.

"What the heck?" he cried, jumping back, her helmet landing just shy of his feet. "Jesus, Davis." He picked up the helmet. "Did you just *throw* this at me?"

While she stared at him, not up to explaining that, no, she hadn't thrown it *at* him, she just had no control of her motor functions at the moment, Noah grabbed Brayden by his shirt collar and said, "Uh, we're just gonna head back down. Let you two sort this out."

"Don't kill each other," Brayden called out, laughing while Noah pulled him down the trail.

After looking at Davis, then at Kev, Murphy whined, then barked. It was apparently an *I'm not hanging around for this mess* kind of bark, because he followed behind Noah and Brayden, trotting off until he disappeared behind a cluster of pines.

And then it was only them. Just Kev and her and the trees and the sun and her bike helmet between his hands, hovering in front of his flawless, heaving chest.

"Did you throw this at me?" he asked again, not breaking eye contact.

"No," Davis stated with fire in her veins. "It was an accident."

"An accident," he repeated, his voice calm, almost amused. It was maddening.

"Yes," she repeated back, shoving one hand on her hip while flicking out a finger with the other, pointing it just off to his left. "I meant to throw it at the tree."

"Why did you try to throw your helmet at a tree?"

"I tried to throw it at a tree"—she clenched her jaw so tightly she thought she might end up needing dental work—"because you were *laughing*."

"Hmm. I see." When he started walking toward her, it was like the sun had moved too close to the earth, solar flares looping out in wide arcs, heat lashing her cheeks, her chest. Somewhere, glaciers were melting at alarming rates. His head tilted, studying her, seeing everything. "Is this finally your roar?"

"My what?" she tried to snap but it came out too soft, or maybe it was just muted by the blood rushing in her ears.

"Nothing," he said, following it up with "So, I'm not allowed to laugh anymore?"

"No."

He almost laughed again right there and then. She wanted to scream.

"Okay." He cleared his throat, still moving closer to her. "I'll stop. I'll stop laughing."

Once he was close enough that she could see the tiny beads of sweat glistening on his forehead, his shoulders, his stomach, he offered her helmet back to her.

She took it with a quick swipe.

His brows slid together, all levity slipping from his expression. "Davis, seriously. What's going on?"

Chucking her helmet to the ground at her own feet this time, she said, "Are you allergic to clothes or something? Why don't you ever fucking wear a shirt?" She knew how it sounded. She knew how every word coming out of her mouth sounded. Childish, unreasonable, absurd. She'd lost control. She needed to get it back, tear it out from the claws of indignation that had ripped it away from her.

"No, I'm not allergic to clothes." He looked down at his body. Having no other possible choice, so did she. "See, I'm wearing shorts."

She did, in fact, see.

"I'm not wearing a shirt because it's hot."

"The other men wear shirts," she said, hauling her gaze back up to some spot a solid inch above his head. "Do you mean to tell me the other men aren't"—she fought through a dry swallow—"hot?"

She wondered if anyone in the history of the world had ever worked as hard to hide a smile as he was working now. It looked painful. "No, they're pretty hot too."

Her nostrils flared.

"Sorry," he said, reaching for the shirt sticking out of his back pocket. "I'll put it on."

There, her brain tried to say. *That's better.* But her body disagreed. Because as soon as he snapped the shirt out straight and started to put it on, she yanked it out of his hands and threw it into the trees. Hitting her mark this time.

With his empty hands splayed wide, he stared up at the branch his shirt now dangled from. His expression was so ridiculous, so utterly baffled, that when he said, "You just threw my shirt onto a tree," she couldn't hold herself together anymore.

The worry, the pain, the hurt, the endless longing, the bottomless well of missing him. It all came out in a single broken laugh, followed by another, and then another. And then she was gone. Laughing hard. And he was laughing too.

There they were, laughing together just like they used to, when the most ridiculous things were so funny they could barely catch their breaths. While the familiarity of it swirled warmly around her, he moved into her space, reaching out to brush a stray curl out of her eyes. So close. So strong. So perfect. So Kev.

"Why have you been ignoring me?" she asked, breathing it into the small space he'd kept between them.

His brows crowded together. "What do you mean?"

"You never talk to me anymore." The words poured out of her, cascading in a rush like water from spring snowmelt. "You barely even look at me."

"Isn't that what you wanted?" he asked. "You asked for space. I've been trying to give it to you."

"I don't want you to ignore me." She hated how irrational she sounded. Give me space, but not too much. Leave me alone, but still want me. Don't talk to me, but keep wishing you could. It was unfair. It was pathetic. It was embarrassing.

He took a deep breath. "What do you want me to do?"

Hold me. Kiss me. Never have changed. Never have pulled away. Never have left.

"I don't know," she answered honestly. "I wish I did. But I don't."

He brushed his knuckles over her cheek. A velvety softness, gentling her. His velvety soft voice gentling her too. "I'm glad you didn't say you wanted me to put my shirt on again. Because that one in the tree is the only one I have up here."

The tension in her shoulders broke as another laugh huffed out of her, as she leaned into his touch. It felt so good. So right. Even though she knew it was wrong. How was it possible to be both at the same time? The worst idea? The most perfect sensation?

Meeting his stare, she asked, "Why are you so happy?"

The furrow sank more deeply between his brows while he searched her face. "What do you mean?"

It took her a moment to form her thoughts into something coherent. Something he might understand. Because even through her anger and frustration, she wanted him to understand. She wanted to be clear.

"You seem so happy," she eventually said. "I see you on the trails, in the dining hall, sitting on your porch, hanging out with Madigan and the men. I see you everywhere. And you seem like you're doing so well. Like you're a little happier each day. While I'm..." She couldn't say it. She couldn't say *while I'm more and more miserable, more heartbroken, more alone.* "Was it me?" she asked through a body-wide tremble. "Was being with me what made you sad? Am I what made you leave?"

Her throat tightened, burning hotter with each word. But she had to know. He'd been so unhappy with her at the end. Since the night in her car, he'd only grown more and more despondent, withdrawn, dim. No matter how hard she tried to make him smile or laugh, there was no joy left in him. No light. And now he was alive again, vibrant, glowing, happy. Truly happy. If she was the reason, if he was happier without her, it would make the decision for her. She would leave. Because she wasn't happier without him. She still missed him, still felt the space he used to fill beside her burning like a phantom limb.

Closing her eyes, she asked, "Is your life better without me in it? Because if it is—"

"Are you fucking kidding me right now?" He cupped her face with a ferocity that tore a gasp from her lungs, wrenching her eyes open.

Even with all the work he'd been doing this summer, even with the determination in the way he held her, his hands were still so impossibly soft.

"Davis Thompson, you were and still are the best thing that has ever happened to me in my entire fucking life. If I'm happy right now, it's because I get to see you every day when I thought for a long time I might never see you again. If I'm happy, it's because I'm doing everything I can to be a better man. Because I'm starting to understand myself a little better. Because I'm refusing to just go through the motions this time or force myself to be perfect. If I'm happy, it's because I think I'm on a path. One I'm actually excited to follow. One I hope and pray every single night will lead me back to you." He brushed his thumb over her lower lip, a ghost of a touch that haunted every cell in her body. "I'm also happy because I've been on Lexapro for six weeks."

Her gaze jumped to his. "You have?"

He nodded, moving farther into her space, backing her into the woods until they were hidden in the shade. Her eyes wanted to close again. Her head wanted to tilt. Her lips wanted to part. Her heart wanted to leap out of her chest and into his hands.

"I told you all about it," he said.

She scoffed weakly. "No, you definitely did not."

"I did," he insisted. His fingers curled around the nape of her neck, squeezing gently, melting her muscles. "In my letters."

"You didn't write me any letters." He was so close now, his lips hovering over hers, just out of reach, a breath away. She could almost feel them, so full, so warm. "I wanted you to. I went to the mailbox every morning. Checked my email ten times a day. I figured you wouldn't, but I wanted you to."

"I wrote you a letter every day in rehab," he told her. "Sometimes two. I just wasn't sure if you'd want to hear from me, so I didn't send them. I didn't want to upset you, Davis. I didn't want to hurt you." He rolled his right shoulder, only once. "Any more than I already had."

Pressure mounted behind her eyes, doubling with every one of his words, his confessions. "I thought you'd forgotten about me."

His grip tightened around her neck. Not painful, just real. "Forget?" He shook his head. "I could live a thousand lifetimes, and I would remember you in every single one of them. I'd make it my mission to search for you. I'd never give up until I found you again. And I won't give up now. Unless you tell me to. But you'll have to tell me, Davis. Otherwise, I'll keep coming for you. I won't stop."

His breath smelled like mint and his skin smelled like sunshine. She wanted to taste both. "No," she said, doing everything in her power not to reach for him, to slide her hands over his chest. She shouldn't say more. She had to say more. "I don't want you to give up. I don't want you to stop."

Intensity flared in his eyes, and in the space of one breath, he dropped his forehead to hers. In the space of another, he tilted her chin, angling her up to him. A third breath, and his lips brushed over hers, barely touching one corner of her mouth, then the other.

Desperate for him, needing him like something essential, something vital like air or water or heat, she parted her lips, searched for his. But then his hand dropped to her low back, and something cold and dark slinked down her spine.

That same hand had dropped from the mattress in that house. While another hand had slithered over his waist, a palm pressing possessively over his stomach, long, slender fingers, chipped red nail polish. A nose nestled into his hair. A body wrapped tightly around his.

What was she thinking? What was she doing? How had she let this happen?

Breaking away, she pushed him back. "Stop."

He blinked, his eyes unfocused, chest heaving. "Stop?"

A leg hooked over his thigh. Bare breasts pressing into his bare back. "I can't."

"Davis? What happened? What—"

"This was a mistake." She stumbled back. "I can't do this. I'm sorry."

Before he could stop her, she ran to her bike, yanked it up from the dirt, and took off down the trail as fast as she could, barely able to see through the tears streaming down her cheeks.

"Davis, wait!" she heard him call out behind her. Then she heard his footsteps thundering down the trail. "Wait!"

She couldn't wait. She couldn't be near him. As desperately as she wanted to, she couldn't pretend that they could get through this when he hadn't just chosen the drugs over her. He'd chosen another woman too. She couldn't stop seeing it. Couldn't stop seeing *them*.

She'd only let go of her handlebars long enough to brush her tears away. But in that split second, her front tire hit a tree root, tucked in, and her bike bucked, launching her over the handlebars.

She screamed, landing hard on her shoulder before rolling to her hands and knees.

"Jesus Christ!" Kev shouted, taking massive bounding steps, leaping over the root to slide onto his knees at her side. "Are you okay?"

Her world spun, her shoulder aching, knees burning. "I'm fine."

"You aren't wearing your helmet."

She'd left it behind. He held it in his hands now.

Setting the helmet on the ground, he looked her over, pushing her hair out of her eyes. "Did you hit your head?"

"I don't think so." She looked down at her hands, at the streaks of dirt on her gloves that would have been cuts on her palms if she hadn't been wearing them. "I'm okay."

When she tried to stand up, her right knee buckled, pain lancing through her thigh.

"You're not fine," Kev said, holding her elbow to steady her. "You're bleeding."

Only then did she notice the red stream trickling down her leg. It was a small cut. It would heal.

When he said, "You hurt yourself," something inside her snapped like a bone breaking in half.

"No," she cried. And even though her knee burned and her shoulder ached, she yanked her elbow out of his grip and wheeled on him. "No, Kev. *I* did not hurt myself."

"Okay," he said, visibly confused. "But—"

"*You* hurt me," she said, the tears that hadn't stopped falling swelling in a fresh wave. "This"—she raised her hands, showing him the dirt on her palms, slashing a hand down across her knee—"is nothing. What you did... You hurt me so much worse."

He recoiled, like she'd slapped him. "I know I did. I know. And I'll do whatever it takes—"

"You don't know!" She'd said it to him before. She practically screamed it now, wishing she could shove him, slap him, something. Anything. "I loved you, Kev," she pushed out through a broken sob, knowing this would bruise him more than any shove, hurt him more than any slap. "I was so in love with you. I knew I'd never love anyone as much as I loved you." Her throat burned, her voice so hoarse it scraped out of her. "And you didn't care. You broke my fucking heart!"

Despite his utterly stunned silence, she pressed on. Because she couldn't stop. "You don't know what I had to see," she said. "You don't know what it was like to be in that house. In that room. To see you in that bed with"—her stomach cramped, nausea gripping her as the truth she never wanted him to know poured out of her like blood from a wound—"that woman."

"Davis." His face went white. Not pale, but *white*. "What are you talking about?"

She couldn't keep the tears from falling. Just like she couldn't keep this secret for him anymore. She couldn't keep hurting herself just to protect him.

"That day," she said, her voice shuddering. "The day you left. We f-found you." She shivered, like the temperature had dropped fifty degrees in the space of a few heartbeats. "There were needles on the floor, on the bed. And you were in her arms. Thom's sister. You were together. You were *with* her."

It was like watching a solar eclipse, just as staggering, the way his expression fell, the light dying in his eyes.

"There was a moment, this horrible moment when I thought we'd gotten there too late," she told him, wanting him to understand how scared she'd been. Needing him to know all the ways that day had changed her. "I thought you were already gone. And then I had to watch Madigan spray that shit into your nose. We waited and waited. And I prayed. I'm not religious, but that day I was. That day I prayed for you to wake up. To be okay. To open your eyes and just be okay."

He stared at her. Unblinking. Unmoving. She'd never seen him look so terrified, so broken. She would have felt awful about it if she hadn't been shattering too. No, that wasn't true. She'd already shattered. She'd been in pieces since it had happened. Now she was just peeling off the tape that had been holding her together, finally letting him see all the cracks he'd left behind.

"You never opened your eyes," she said. "But you started moving after Madigan gave you a second dose. I was so relieved. I was so happy you were still with me. But when Madigan tried to pick you up and carry you out of that place, she...clung to you." Bile rose in her throat, forcing her to swallow it back down. "She didn't want to let you go. And I wondered, does she love him too?"

"You were there?" The words rasped out of him, stone scraping against stone. "Why?"

Why? "What do you mean?" she said, pushing back, shaking her head at him. "Why wouldn't I be there?"

"I mean," he ground out with barely controlled anger, a muscle in his jaw flickering, "why the hell did Madigan bring you to that house?"

"Seriously?" She pulled up to her full height, refusing to let him distract her. "*That's* what you're upset about? After what I just told you, you're mad because I was there?"

She wasn't even sure he'd heard her, but his anger seemed to fade, confusion flooding in to fill the void it left behind. "Why did he think that was okay? It doesn't make sense." He swiped a palm across his forehead, like he couldn't understand it, like it rocked the foundation of everything he'd believed was true. "You should never have seen that."

Pointing a finger into his chest, she said, "No. I shouldn't have. Nobody should ever have to see the man they love in another woman's bed. Nobody should ever have to see the person they love so pale and sick and wonder whether they're still breathing. Nobody."

Like someone had snapped their fingers in front of his face, he woke up, emerging from the haze of shock to grasp her hand and flatten it firmly over his heart. "You're right. Nobody should have to see that. I should never have done that to you. I should never have done any of it. But I promise you, Trisha and I—"

"Trisha?" Davis asked. She'd wondered for so long. And now those two syllables clicked into place in all the stories she'd told herself since that night. The final missing piece to the worst puzzle she'd ever had to put together. "That's her name?"

Closing his eyes, he curled his fingers around hers until she could see his fingertips digging into his chest. "Trisha was *not* in bed with me when I...when I fell asleep. I was alone. She must have crawled in after."

"After you left," she said. "After you left me."

His chin sank toward his chest, his head turning back and forth. "I don't know how to do this," he said, muttering it to himself. "I don't know how to make you understand." When he looked up again, determination blazed in his eyes. "I did leave you. But I left for the drugs. I left because something is wrong with me. Not for someone else. *Never* for someone else."

"But I saw you with her when she was here visiting Thom. You were standing so close. She had her hand around your neck. It was intimate, Kev. When you hadn't been intimate like that with me in so —" Her throat spasmed, cutting her off.

"*Fuck*, Davis." While he scrubbed his hand over his face, she watched the realization of everything she'd seen, everything she knew, crash over him.

It was too much. Too heavy. What if the weight of it all derailed him? What if her honesty made him leave again? What if it made him use again? Despite his insistence that there was something wrong with him, what if she was actually the unhealthy thing in his life? What if she was holding him back? What if all she'd ever do with him was constantly walk on eggshells, wondering if any truth or real emotion she showed him would only send him back to that mattress with a needle in his arm?

That was why she hadn't been able to make him come back to her when he'd started distancing himself. That was why she hadn't been able to take care of herself and let him go. She'd been too scared then. Too scared of saying the wrong thing, doing the wrong thing, being the reason he relapsed.

She was still too scared.

"We weren't intimate," he explained, his bloodshot eyes pleading with her to listen, to believe him. "I can see how it might have looked that way, but there was nothing close or warm or romantic about that moment. She was offering me drugs. And I was fucking dying inside because I knew I wasn't going to be able to say no. I knew it was over. It was one of the lowest points of my life."

"You really weren't with her?" She wanted to believe him. She wanted it so badly. "You really didn't...sleep with her?"

"Trisha and I were together years ago. But I swear on my

goddamned life, there is nothing between us now. I swear I was alone when I used. I fucked up. I know I did. And I hate that you saw me like that. I hate that I scared you. I'll never get over it. But I was *not* with another woman. Please believe me. Please, Davis. You are the only woman I want. You're the only woman I will *ever* want."

She waited for it, for the relief, for the cracks in her heart to stitch themselves back together, for the scars to start healing. But there was nothing. Nothing but a sweeping, bone-deep sorrow.

"I believe you," she said, because she knew he was telling the truth. But in that moment, she also knew it didn't matter. Maybe he hadn't left because he'd wanted another woman. But he had left because of her, because she hadn't known how to help him stay.

"Please tell me we can try again," he said, raising her hand to his lips, brushing her knuckles over his cheek. "I'll do anything. Can we try? Can you give me a chance? I'm really working—"

"I can't." The words sliced through her.

He pressed his thumb into her palm, the pressure its own kind of plea. "Why?"

Because I'm not good for you. Because I didn't support you when you needed it the most. Because I couldn't leave you when you'd started leaving me. Because I'm selfish and greedy and so ashamed I can barely look at myself in the mirror. Because I can't be around you without wanting you. Because I love you so much I can't breathe. "Because I'm leaving."

"What? You're—"

"I'm probably leaving," she amended while his hand dropped to his side, taking hers with it. But not letting go.

"Where? Where are you going?"

"Back to Missoula. My professor got new funding. I think... I'm pretty sure I'm going to finish my master's." Her resolve, what little she had of it in the face of his crushed expression, faltered. "I'm almost positive."

Time slowed, each second stretching out like the shadows surrounding them in the fading sunlight. Silently, they breathed the same air, filling their lungs with earth and pine. And she could see the instant it all caught up with him, his jaw unclenching, his shoulders sinking. Acceptance settling into him. Because deep down, he must have known it was for the best too.

He deserved a clear, uncomplicated chance at recovery. He deserved time to focus on himself. He deserved a partner who knew how to support him. Who knew what to do and say and didn't shout things like *fuck the rules!* when he'd known he needed them, and she'd needed him too much to care.

He loosened his grip on her, and she pulled her hand free.

"How long?" he asked. "How long do I have?" He shook his head. "I mean, how long until you leave?"

"A month."

Grinding the heel of his palm into his chest, he said, "Okay." Then he backed away. One step. Two. "That's... It's great." He tried to smile, but there was too much pain behind it. "You deserve great things, Davis. You deserve everything."

She couldn't hold herself together much longer. She had to go. She had to get away.

"Thanks," she choked out, fighting back the river of tears trying to leave its banks. "I should probably finish my ride."

"Wait. What about your knee?" It was a straw grasp. They both knew it.

"Don't worry," she told him, picking up her helmet. "It doesn't hurt."

Silently, even while all the things left unsaid between them howled between her ears, he watched her walk back to her bike.

Not letting herself wince at the sharp sting in her knee when she stepped over the frame, she turned to him one last time, and with a steadiness she didn't possess, she said, "Goodbye, Kev."

And then she rode away from him, letting gravity pull her down the mountain, faster and faster until the wind turned the tears streaming down her cheeks to salt.

CHAPTER ELEVEN

KEV

SHE'D BEEN THERE. She'd seen him. In one of the worst, weakest, most reprehensible moments of his life, Davis had seen him. And Madigan had let it happen.

Kev didn't think it was possible to feel worse about his relapse. About what he'd done. He didn't think the self-hatred could cut any deeper. But just like he'd been about everything else in his life, he'd been so indescribably wrong.

Blazing down the trail with a fury that threatened to engulf him until he was nothing but walking flames, he reached the clearing at the base of the mountain and turned toward the cabins. The men were all there, hanging out around the firepit, talking about nothing the way they always did at the end of the workday. And there was the man himself, Matthew Madigan, standing with his legs wide, his hands on his hips, like some instinctual part of him knew what was coming for him and was already braced for it.

"Hey, Kev," Brayden called out, oblivious to the rage radiating from Kev's core, the impending meltdown about to level the entire state. "How'd it go up there?"

Slowly, Madigan turned Kev's way, his smile falling by degrees with every inch that vanished between them. "Kev?" he said cautiously, squaring off. "You cool?"

Gathering all the air left in his lungs, harnessing the nuclear rage bubbling through his veins, he whipped his finger out in Madigan's direction and roared, "Fuck you, *Boss!*"

And then everything slowed while his words echoed through eternity, the loudness of his own voice feeling wrong in his ears, the full understanding of what he'd just done falling to the ground like radioactive ash. His brain screamed at him to run, to hide, that fists and belts were coming for him. And even though he knew they weren't, he charged past the sea of wide eyes and open mouths and raced up the steps to the safety of his cabin.

The last thing he heard before he slammed his door was Brayden muttering, "He's gonna have bathroom duty until the end of time." And Madigan ordering the men to "Get back to your cabins. Now."

It only took twenty seconds before Madigan's boots hit his stairs, climbing slowly, deliberately, each step like a thunderclap, like a hole punched into a wall, plaster exploding into the air.

"Kev," Madigan said, not bothering to knock. "I'm coming in."

"No. Leave me alone." Kev felt exactly like he sounded. Like a terrified kid who just wanted to scream into his pillow, kick his feet on his bed, throw his toys at the wall. A kid who'd never been able to do any of those things.

"Not happening," Madigan said. The door swung open, and he appeared, somehow even more massive than usual, filling the entire frame. "Mind telling me what that was all about?"

Meeting Madigan's stare, Kev fought not to cower, not to let his fear overwhelm him. "You let her come," he ground out. "What the hell is wrong with you?"

"Kev," Madigan warned, his brows snapping together. "You need to calm down right now. And let who come?"

"Davis." Interlacing his fingers in his lap, Kev squeezed so hard something cracked. "You brought Davis with you that day. Why the fuck would you do that? Why the fuck would you put her through that?" *Put* me *through that.* "Why would you let her see me like that?"

"Ah." He didn't just see Madigan's chest move through a deep, understanding sigh, he felt it, the energy in the room shifting, cooling from red to blue. Somehow, Madigan could do that, cool off an entire room with a single deep breath, staving off a nuclear explosion by his refusal to react. "I understand that you're angry with me right now." He motioned to the couch. "But can I sit?"

Reluctantly, but not knowing what else to do in the face of Madigan's levelheaded composure, Kev nodded.

Lowering himself slowly to the couch, Madigan said, "To answer your question, I didn't bring Davis."

Kev scoffed.

"I'm telling the truth, Kev. Never in a million years would I betray your or any of the men's trust like that. Never in a million years would I have put Davis in a situation that could have been potentially dangerous for her. Believe me, I never wanted her to see you like that. *I* never wanted to see you like that."

Ignoring the second part, Kev asked, "If you didn't bring her, how'd she get there?"

"She snuck out. Followed us down the mountain with her headlights off. I didn't even know she was in the house until it was too late. I tried to get her to leave. Cole and I begged her. But"—Madigan's shoulders hinted at a shrug—"you know Davis."

"She's stubborn," Kev said, not adding *it's one of the things I love about her* even though it was right there on the tip of his tongue.

"She wouldn't budge. I would have carried her out over my shoulder if I hadn't had more important things to deal with at the time."

Like saving my life.

"Why didn't you tell me?" Kev hated the tremble in his voice, the desperation, the outright surrender, because he knew he'd lost. He knew she'd been right. He couldn't fix what he'd broken. He couldn't fix them. "I've been trying to make things right with her. But after that, after what she saw, things will never be right between us again." He slumped, curling in on himself. "I just wish I'd known. I wish I'd known that I never stood a chance."

Leaning forward, resting his elbows on his knees, Madigan said, "I wanted to. I've struggled with it until this moment. In fact, I almost did tell you after I picked you up from rehab."

"Oh my god," Kev said, realization dawning, stabbing him in his chest. "I finally get it." He would have laughed at his own stupidity if he wasn't so mortified. "That's why you asked me about Trisha that day. That's why you said you thought we were close. Because you'd found us in bed together. You and Davis and Cole had found us in bed together." His head fell into his hands. How could things keep getting worse? "Jesus, Madigan. You thought I was being unfaithful to Davis too."

"I didn't think that," Madigan said severely. "I didn't make that leap. I've passed out with people after using too."

"I would never have done that to her," Kev insisted into his palms. Then he raised his head. "Never. I love her."

"I know you do, Kev. But I love Davis too. And I didn't feel like it was my place to tell you that she'd followed us. I figured if she wanted you to know, she'd tell you herself. But maybe I was wrong." He ran his FEAR hand roughly through his hair. "Maybe I should have told you. Maybe I messed up too."

Kev could never keep anger up for very long. It always faded as quickly as it arrived, pouring out of him like water from a hose, leaving him empty and cold. "No, you're right," he said, acknowledging the impossible position he'd put Madigan in. "It was up to her to tell me." And now that she had, it really was over.

"I'm sorry, Kev. Either way, I'm sorry."

He only nodded, a weak little tuck of his chin, adrenaline siphoning out of him until his muscles felt like rubber and his bones like twigs.

"Were you two able to talk about it?" Madigan asked. "Or was it a dropped bomb kind of situation?"

While his knee started bouncing, Kev said, "There's probably still a crater up there where it exploded."

Air rushed out of Madigan's nose. "Shit."

"Yeah."

"What do you need? How can I help?"

What had been a tolerable, dull pressure behind his eyes transformed into an unholy sting. "There's nothing anyone can do. It's too late. It's done."

"Are you sure? Maybe you both just need more time. It's amazing what time can do."

Kev looked at him, incredulous, wondering how he could be so cruel. "But we don't have time. That's the point."

Madigan frowned. "Why not?"

"Because she's leaving."

"What do you mean?" he asked, his scowl deepening into something more like confusion.

"Well, she's *probably* leaving," Kev said, keeping the tiniest vestige of hope alive, even though he knew it was worthless. Why wouldn't she go? He'd made it impossible for her to be here. "Next month. You know, going back to school."

Madigan rose to his feet like a six-foot-tall tsunami. "Seriously?"

Wondering how many secrets existed on this mountain, Kev realized—"You didn't know."

Sitting down again, crashing hard, Madigan rested his head on the back of Kev's couch, looking up helplessly at the vaulted ceiling. "No, I did not. And I'm pretty sure Ashley doesn't know either."

Kev sighed. "I figured everyone knew but me." *Just like everything else.*

"Not this time."

"Sorry, Boss."

Leaning forward again, the worried lines in his forehead smoothing out, Madigan said, "Don't worry about us, Kev. Don't even worry about Davis. How are you? How are *you* doing?"

Without warning—and scaring him a little—laughter burst out of him.

"Kev?"

Shoving the bizarre emotional outburst down, Kev said, "I'm not about to run off and start using again, if that's what you mean."

Madigan's patient, waiting expression didn't falter.

"But I'm not good. I'm pretty fucking far from good."

"I'll ask it again, then. What do you need? How can I help?"

Pushing on his thigh, trying and failing to still his jumping knee, Kev considered the question. "I think I need some space," he said, fully aware of the irony of the words coming out of his mouth. "I need to be alone. At least for tonight."

Madigan studied him for a moment. Then, as if coming to some agreement with himself, he said, "Okay. I'll tell everyone to wait until tomorrow to come talk to you." He arched a brow. "Because after that scene out there, you know they're going to want to."

"Yeah." Kev nodded. "I know."

Before he left, Madigan leaned over, squeezed Kev's knee—which immediately stopped bouncing—and said, "You're still getting bathroom duty. For a week."

Even though Kev had known it was coming, he groaned.

"Don't be too hard on yourself tonight, though. Today was heavy." Giving him a strange, unreadable look, Madigan said, "But tomorrow? Who knows. Things might feel lighter."

After Madigan left his cabin, Kev opened his nightstand drawer and pulled out the stack of letters he'd written to Davis while he'd been in rehab. Letters he'd never sent. Letters she'd never read. His thoughts. His fears. His regret. His love. All of it so completely worthless now.

Putting the letters back, he slid the drawer closed, rolled onto his side, and stared at his wall while the light grew dim, watching it fade until it was so dark he couldn't see anything anymore.

CHAPTER ELEVEN

B<small>ANG</small>, *bang, bang.*

Kev's eyes sprung open, his heart rocketing into his throat. At first he thought it was thunder rattling his walls. But his cabin was bright, sunlight pouring in through his windows.

Bang, bang, bang.

It was the door. Someone was here. He checked his clock. Ten thirty a.m. Madigan must have let him sleep in.

"Kev!" The voice shouting at him was deep and booming and so wonderfully familiar Kev's puffy, swollen eyes misted. "You in there? I didn't drive all the way out here from Billings just to wait on your porch for you to decide to wake up."

Sitting up in his bed, Kev said, "Clay?"

"The one and only."

"W-what are you doing here?" he asked, pinching his nose, squeezing his eyes shut until his emotions settled.

"Open the door, and I'll tell you."

Kev wanted to open the door. He wanted to see Clay's gap-toothed smile, his shiny bald head, get wrapped up in his big bear arms. As far as adopted father figures went, they didn't get much better than his old cabinmate. But he was a raw nerve, a man walking around without his skin on, the hottest mess west of the Mississippi.

"Kev!"

"Okay," he said. "I'm coming."

Climbing off the bed, Kev glanced down at himself. He'd fallen asleep in yesterday's clothes and his shorts were wrinkled, his T-shirt creased. Reaching up, he tried to smooth out his bedhead, his curls sticking out at wild angles that refused to be tamed.

Walking to the door, because he knew Clay wouldn't care what he looked like, he grasped the knob, held his breath, and turned.

"Jeez." Clay winced, sucking air in through his teeth. "You look like shit."

Okay, maybe he would care.

"That's actually better than I feel," Kev said, trying to smile, trying to set Clay at ease even now, even after one of the worst days of his life. And then he grunted. Because Clay had him wrapped up tight in those big bear arms, squeezing so hard he lifted him clear off the ground. So hard that if he had broken down in tears, it would only have been because he was in actual physical pain. Which was...kind of nice.

"Boss called me last night. Told me what happened," Clay said, letting Kev go. "I came as soon as I could."

"You drove all the way over here? Just for me?" Kev's mind went blank, short-circuiting in a puff of white smoke.

Stepping past him into his cabin, straightening his shirt over a belly Kev thought looked a bit less round than the last time he'd seen him, Clay said, "Of course. You're my friend. That's what friends do."

It didn't hit him until that very moment just how much he'd missed Clay. It was a physical presence in the room, solid and substantial. Just like the man himself.

"I would have come to see you in rehab too. If you hadn't told me not to."

"Oh, yeah." Kev ruffled his hair. "Sorry." He hadn't wanted to see anyone during his first couple of weeks in rehab. Too embarrassed. Too depressed. After that, he'd just wanted to get out. Get back here. Get back to her. So she could leave.

Clay sat on Kev's couch. Then he patted the cushion next to him and said, "Sit down, son."

Son. The word had a direct line to Kev's tear ducts. But he wouldn't cry. Not this early in the morning. Not every time anyone said anything even slightly emotional.

When he joined Clay on the couch, they sat in silence for a moment, listening to the birds chatter outside the windows, the wind whisper through the pines. Turning to look at him, Clay said quietly, but with a punishing gravity, "I'm sorry about Davis."

Davis. Another tear duct-hotline word.

"I'm sorry about your relapse," he continued. Kev couldn't meet Clay's gaze, but it bored into him anyway, seeing everything he should probably stop wasting so much energy trying to hide. "I'm sorry I wasn't here for you. I'm sorry you went through rehab, and now you're going through this, feeling like you're better off going through it alone. I'm sorry about all of it."

Letting the words sink in, letting the apology mean everything Clay wanted it to mean, Kev listened, absorbed, and then he nodded. If he couldn't let himself be open and accepting with Clay, a man who'd just driven four hours to sit with him, he knew he'd never feel safe opening up to anyone. He also knew where that had gotten him, being scared and closed off. He'd known where that path led for most of his twenty-eight years. Nowhere good.

"I thought I could get her back," he admitted. "I thought if I just worked hard enough and gave it my all and did whatever she needed me to do, I might get another chance. And now, after what she saw, it's just...over."

Clay sighed deeply, then said, "I am going to tell you something that might be hard for you to hear."

Kev raised his head, meeting Clay's deep, brown-eyed stare, wondering what could possibly be worse than what Davis had already told him. Nothing. Nothing would ever be worse than that. "Okay."

"I care about you," Clay said. "And I care about Davis. But I think you might have forgotten something important."

Kev waited, sensing it coming, a heaping, bitter spoonful of brutal perspective.

"Kev," Clay said. "You are not here for Davis. You"—he pointed a finger at Kev's chest, echoing the sentiment Kev had heard enough times now that he knew it must be true—"are here for you. You are here for *your* health. For *your* life. You can't just skip over that part because you think someone else is more important. I don't know why you decided to use again." His expression fell, determined lines creasing his eyes, bracketing his mouth. "But I can't help but think it had something to do with her."

"No," Kev insisted, his blood heating, because if he knew one thing, it was this. "It was *not* her fault."

Leaning back, giving Kev space, Clay said, "I know. I never said it was. I don't think Davis would hurt a fly if it was buzzing on her nose."

"She wouldn't." Kev could tolerate a lot of things, but anyone believing his fuck-up was somehow Davis's fault was not one of them.

"But sometimes when we're thinking about someone else, worrying about someone else, wishing we could be different for someone else." Clay's brows rose a suggestive inch. "We can lose track of ourselves. We can lose focus. We can fall down."

Tears pricked at Kev's eyes again, and he fought like hell to hold them back. "I love her, Clay. I love her so much. She's all I want."

"And that's the problem," Clay said kindly. "You need to want other things. She can't be everything for you right now. You have to decide that *you* are the most important person in your world. I know that's something you're not good at. It's probably something you've never done a single day in your life. But that's why you're here. *That* is the work. If a future exists for you and Davis, it can't exist without this commitment from you. At least for now, you have to choose you. You have to focus on you. You owe this to yourself, Kev. Maybe you owe it to Davis too."

Clay's words stung, salt in each of his thousands of wounds. But the sting was necessary. It was real. Because Clay was right. And deep down, Kev had known it for a while. "But what if by choosing me," he said, giving voice to his deepest insecurities, his oldest fears, the feeling always churning inside him that he wasn't worth anything, "I end up losing her?"

Clay only stared at him meaningfully, that meaning being: *then she wasn't the right person for you in the first place.* And Kev was glad he didn't say it. Because even if it was true, he couldn't hear it.

Kev blew out a shaky breath. "I don't think I know how to choose myself."

"I know," Clay said. "But just like everything else, we commit to the process. We dedicate ourselves to learning. We figure it out, one day at a—"

"No," Kev blurted out, half tempted to cover Clay's mouth with his hand. "Don't say it."

"Okay, okay." Clay chuckled, his belly jiggling. "But it's true. Trust the process. Trust the men. Trust Madigan. Hell, you might even learn to trust yourself."

Kev turned Clay's words over in his mind as the cabin grew quiet, as Clay's expression sobered. As he said, "I'm proud of you, Kev. I'm proud of you for going to rehab, for coming back here. I'm proud of you for loving Davis as much as you do. I'm proud of you for just being you. Because you are a good, kind, caring young man. And I will be so unbelievably proud of you the day you decide to believe it too."

Kev's vision blurred, his chin wobbling, his nose stinging. *Fuck*, he was going to cry again. And this time it was going to be bad, torrential, an emotional flood he couldn't possibly hold back.

"Oh, come here," Clay said, pulling him into a side hug so snug and warm Kev had no choice but to fold himself into it. "At some point, you have to let go and let yourself feel it all. You're safe here. You're safe now."

And there on his couch, while Clay repeated his grandmother's words to him, rocking him just like she used to when he was a kid, Kev let go, let himself feel it all, and wept until his throat was raw and his eyes were swollen.

"You don't need to be happy all the time," Clay said, still rocking him. "It's not a fatal flaw if people see you fall apart. Nobody will yell at you anymore if you need to have a moment."

Clay knew a bit about his past, about his dad, about how dangerous it had been for Kev to be in the way or be noticeable at all when he was young. And while Kev appreciated the sentiment, believing it was much harder. Because Clay didn't know how bad it had really been for him. He didn't know about the fear, the hunger, the loneliness. The canned peaches sitting on otherwise empty pantry shelves. The story of a kid left to fend for himself.

"I'm serious, Kev," Clay said. "Nobody will punish you for this."

Kev sniffed, then mumbled, "Madigan gave me bathroom duty for a week."

With a deep chuckle, Clay said, "Okay, fine. But to be fair, I think you deserved that one." Then he gave him one more squeeze and said, "Feels good to cry sometimes, doesn't it?"

Even though his eyes burned and his sinuses ached, Kev nodded.

Pulling back, Clay said, "I probably can't drive out here every time you need to have a good old-fashioned breakdown. But I'm just a phone call away. Always."

Kev remembered the group they'd had around the firepit weeks ago. The conversation they'd had about the ways men showed up for each other. About what a healthy male friendship looked like. He hadn't really known before. He thought he might know now. "Thank you, Clay. It means a lot to me that you came here. I really miss you."

Without hesitation, Clay said, "I miss you too, son. But now"—his right eyebrow jumped—"I've gotta go. I have a brunch date with Maude Alice."

While some of the weight pressing on his shoulders lifted like fog burning off the mountains in the morning, Kev asked, "Did you just say 'date'?"

His brown cheeks went cherry-red. "Yes, sir."

Kev wiped his eyes dry, smiled, and said, "Well, shit."

"Careful, there." Clay laughed. "You want bathroom duty for two weeks?"

Pushing up from the couch while Clay did the same, Kev considered holding out his hand for a shake, then realized it wasn't what he wanted. Pulling Clay into a hug instead, he said, "Thanks for coming."

Hugging him back, Clay asked, "Are you gonna be okay?"

When the answer came to him, he was surprised by the certainty that arrived with it, the path unfolding clearly in front of him when it had been so impossible to see anything clearly only the night before.

Was it the path he wanted? Maybe not. But it was the path he needed to take. And he was going to do whatever it took to stay on it, even if it meant taking things one day at a time, even if it meant letting Davis go for a while, even if it meant that she might never come back.

"Yeah," he said. "I think I will."

CHAPTER TWELVE

DAVIS

As much as she wanted it to, reading the email from Professor Novak for the third time in as many days didn't change the effect the words had on her. The new research proposal—engineering microbes to target specific cancer cells for site-directed chemotherapy—sounded interesting. She'd be studying the same bacterial strain she'd been working with before she left school. The funding was solid for the next five years. Her lab mates were all returning. And she couldn't summon a single ounce of enthusiasm.

She'd never been this person before. She'd always known where she was going, what she was supposed to do. Or at least what everyone expected her to do. She didn't recognize this inertia, this indifference, this apathy. Maybe she was depressed too. Maybe she should get on fucking Lexapro.

The knock on her door was a signature. The same three little taps her mom had used for as long as Davis could remember.

"Hi, honey," her mom said, peeking her head inside. "Can I come in?"

"Sure." Flipping her laptop closed, Davis swiveled around in her desk chair. "What's up?"

Her mom crossed the room to sit on the edge of Davis's bed. When she started wringing her hands in her lap, Davis asked, "Mom? You okay?" Because if she'd come in here to deliver bad news, the new, indecisive, and, quite frankly, flailing version of herself wasn't sure she could handle it.

"Davis, sweetie."

Honey and *sweetie*? This couldn't be good.

"I've given you a few days to tell me, and you haven't. So I'm just going to come right out and say it. Kev told Madigan that you were thinking about going back to school. And then Madigan told me."

Davis groaned, circling her fingertips into her abruptly pounding temples. "Shit."

"Did you not feel like you could tell me?" Hurt rang through her mom's words. "You know I'll support you in whatever you want to do. You know that, right?"

This wasn't necessarily true. Her mom hadn't exactly agreed with her choice to leave school in the first place. And she definitely hadn't wanted Davis to stay at Bluebird, at least not initially. But what Davis was going through now, the paralyzing hesitance... She barely knew how to explain it to herself, let alone to anyone else.

"I didn't tell you yet," she said, staring at the pink nail polish she'd applied last night to feel like she was at least making an attempt at self-care. It was already chipped. "Because I've apparently decided that denial is a good look this summer."

With a soft laugh that faded into an apologetic sigh, her mom tilted her head to the side, her blond curls—a little darker and longer than Davis's—bunching up on her shoulder. "Want to talk about it?"

"I don't know," Davis said while frustration prickled her skin. "I feel like I'm just floating here. Like I'm"—she looked around her room, waving a hand to encompass so many things she couldn't find the words for. *Like I'm stuck. Like what I want is too close to me here, considering I can't have it. Like I don't know how to jump to the next thing anymore. Like I'm completely and totally*—"lost."

"Oh, sweetie."

"So I might leave. I might go back to school." She raised and lowered a shoulder, back to staring at her hands in her lap. "Professor Novak has a spot for me again. Everything sounds really good. I just... I haven't made up my mind yet." She bit down, interlacing her fingers and squeezing, a little pain to keep the pressure brewing behind her eyes at bay. "Because I can't seem to make up my mind anymore. About whether I want to do research anymore. About whether I want to move back to Missoula. About anything. Because every time I think of leaving, I feel sick. But every time I think of staying, I feel even worse."

Rising from the bed, her mom knelt at Davis's feet, taking a hold of her hands. "Every time you think of leaving *him*, you mean."

Biting her cheek, convinced that if she said a single word, she'd fall apart, crumble like dead flowers in a vase, she nodded.

"I haven't ever been through what you're going through," her mom said. "And it's something I never would have wished for you. Or for Kev. It's hard to be on the outside of it. Because it's obvious that both of you are struggling. It's obvious that you both still care about each other. It's obvious that you're both hurting."

Reaching up to wipe away the tear rolling down Davis's cheek, the first brittle flower petal floating to the ground, her mom said, "One of the hardest things to do in life is forgive. But do you think you could? Could you forgive him? Is he worth a second chance? Is he worth trying to trust him again? Because if the answer to any of those questions is yes, even if the answer is maybe, then it's no wonder you're having a hard time deciding what to do. It's no wonder you're feeling a little lost."

"I don't know," Davis said. "I want to forgive him. I do. But what if I forgive him, and he does it again? What if I give him a second chance, and he breaks my heart even worse than the first time? The ghosting, the silence, the nonstop worry. I can't go through that again." She closed her eyes, pushing out the memories of waking up in a cold sweat with a scream frozen in her lungs. "I can't."

"I know." Her mom squeezed her hands, her honey-brown eyes

misting over. "I can't see you like that again either. But it's hard seeing you like this too. I just wish there was something I could do. I wish I could snap my fingers and make it all better."

Blinking another tear free, Davis asked, "How do I get over this feeling that if I even consider staying, forgiving him, that I'm being stupid or naïve or weak? I mean, you never forgave Dad, right? Not after the divorce? Not after he drugged the men? You were strong. You held your ground. Shouldn't I hold my ground too?"

"First of all," her mom said, her tone skewing maternal. "Kev is *nothing* like your dad. And second." The muscles in her jaw flickered, her lips twisting. "I...have forgiven him. Your dad."

"What?" Davis pulled a hand free of her mom's hold to wipe her eyes. "Since when? We haven't even spoken to him since Flannelfest."

"Actually." She cleared her throat. "I spoke to him last week."

Davis must not have heard her correctly. "I'm sorry. You what?"

"Sweetie, I haven't wanted to make a big deal out of this because your relationship with your father is just that—yours. And after what he did to Kev, I wouldn't blame you if you never said another word to him for the rest of your life. But Madigan is big on forgiveness. And a few months ago, your dad reached out to see if we would meet him for coffee. So we did."

Davis's head spun, and not just in a figurative sense. She was dizzy, confused, thrown so hard that the reality she landed in was *not* the one she'd woken up in that morning. How could her mom have forgiven him? How? "You are seriously blowing my mind right now, Mom. And not in a good way."

With a tight half smile, she said, "Believe me, I'm still furious with your father for what he did. I'll never forget it. But I don't feel like I'm a weaker person for listening to him. I don't feel stupid or naïve for letting him apologize and try to make things right. Neither does Madigan." She reached up, brushing a stray curl off Davis's cheek. "And you won't be a weak or stupid or naïve person if you let

Kev apologize either. Not even if you give him a second chance. Not even if you decide he's worth it."

"I won't?"

She shook her head. "No. You'll just be a woman who's following her heart. Which can be a really fucking terrifying thing to be sometimes."

Through an abrupt, frail laugh, Davis said, "True story."

"But I have to believe," she said, her voice going soft, "that everyone on this planet deserves a second chance. Maybe not a third. Definitely not a fourth." Pulling a tissue from the box on Davis's nightstand, she handed it to her. "But second chances give us room to be imperfect. They give us room to be human. Without them, we'd probably all end up on our own."

Maybe her mom was right. Maybe Kev deserved more than she was giving him. Maybe he at least deserved to be heard when all she'd done each time he'd tried to apologize was run away. Maybe he deserved a second chance. Maybe they both did.

Davis blew her nose and threw the tissue into the trash, then she threw her arms around her mom. "Thank you," she said, the scent of her mom's floral shampoo filtering in through her stuffed-up nose. "I know I'm not easy to talk to. But thank you for always trying. And sometimes you even help."

Her mom snorted, and Davis hugged her even more tightly.

"I love you, Mom."

"I love you too," she said. "More than anything in this world. But right now, I have got to get up off my knees. In fact, it might be too late. I'm not sure I'll ever be able to straighten them again."

"Not yet," Davis said, holding on, not letting her go. "Please. Just a few more seconds."

Squeezing her back like she really meant it, like she knew exactly how much Davis needed it, like she needed it too, her mom whispered, "You've got such a big heart, sweetie. Now you just need to follow it."

CHAPTER THIRTEEN

KEV

SHE STOOD DIRECTLY in the path of the late afternoon sun, a black silhouette against a flood of orange light, difficult to see at all without squinting.

Hiding in plain sight? Kev thought with a smirk. *Nice try, but I am a master of that particular trick.*

"How we doing today, River?" he asked, keeping his voice low, petting Eleanor's matted fur from her perch on the fence.

Every day after he was done working with Jen and her other horses, he'd find himself out here, standing at her fence. He'd wait. He'd watch. Sometimes he talked to River while she either turned around and ambled toward the other side of her pasture or stood in one place, locking eyes with him in a staring contest she always won. He wasn't sure why he kept coming out here to be with this mare who seemed to want nothing more than to be left alone. But he did, every day. And maybe it was working. Because today, she'd come closer to the fence, to him, than she ever had before.

"I've got something for you." Slowly, he pulled the brightest and reddest apple he'd found in Jen's stash from his pocket and held it out over the fence.

Her right ear flicked toward him, and then her left.

His lips curved into a smile. "Are you hungry?"

She blinked at him, her long, black lashes feathering her cheeks.

"It's all yours, if you want it." He was tempted to shield his eyes from the piercing sunlight, but he didn't want to startle her with too much movement. He really needed to get himself a hat. He'd managed to save up a few bucks. Maybe he'd ask Madigan for a Goodwill trip. "All you have to do is come and get it."

He could have sworn River narrowed her eyes at him, sizing him up, ultimately deciding he wasn't worth the effort. He almost put the apple back in his pocket, but then Eleanor chirped a little meow, and River turned, swished her tail, and took a single step in his direction.

He barely breathed.

She took another step.

"Atta girl," he whispered. "I'm not so bad. Promise."

After another step that brought her within six feet of him, she looked at the cat, then at the apple, then she looked up at him, then back at the apple again. She was so close, just a few more steps. All she had to do was—

"Kev? You okay?"

Damn.

"Hey, Jen," he said. "I'm good. Just saying hi to River." When he turned back toward the mare, she was already heading to the other side of her pasture with Eleanor trailing behind her, chattering up a storm.

"I saw that," Jen said, joining him at the fence. "Sorry I interrupted. She was really close, though. I think she likes you."

Heat flooded his cheeks, his blush intensifying while he gathered his nerve to ask, "Do you think I could try to work with her? Train her? Like, when I'm done with the therapy stuff."

During his time at Strawberry Farms, he'd mindfully groomed, meditated on horseback while riding the trails, and learned how to do groundwork without any lead lines, running and turning and jumping with the horses because they *wanted* to run and turn and jump with him. Because they trusted him. He'd never experienced anything so exhilarating as sprinting as fast as he could before sliding to a dead stop with a one-thousand-pound horse doing the exact same thing beside him.

When he spent time with the horses, he felt focused, calm, centered. They didn't care if he was happy or sad or quiet. They only cared that he was there, giving them his full attention, listening, learning, trying. Even cleaning stalls gave him a sense of peace, starting with something filthy and foul—because some of Jen's horses absolutely destroyed their stalls—and cleaning it up, smoothing the fresh shavings out, making it nice. He was even gaining an appreciation for the nineties country music station Jen always streamed through the barn speakers, believe it or not.

He still thought about Davis every second of every day. They hadn't talked since the bomb-drop on the trails, and it still hurt whenever he saw her, like he was a fresh bruise and she was the thumb pressing down. But he could see it in her eyes, the way he pressed down on her too.

He wasn't giving up on her, on them. He couldn't. He was only trying to listen to Clay and Tex and focus on himself. Because while he owed Davis so many things, none of them were as important as working his ass off to figure out how he'd fallen apart. It was the only way to make sure that if she ever did consider letting him back into her life, she'd never have to worry about him hurting her like that again.

And somehow, though he wasn't sure how yet, River was part of that work. There was something about her story, something about those scars she had that nobody else could see.

"Do you really want this?" Jen asked, giving him a troubled look. "Because I want you to be here for you, Kev. Not to help me train my horses for free."

Setting the apple on top of the fence for River to eat once they were out of sight, Kev turned to walk with Jen back toward the barn. "I think this *would* be for me," he said, kicking at a rock in his path. "I feel like she and I..." He wasn't sure how to say what he wanted to say without sounding ridiculous. *It doesn't matter if you sound ridiculous.* "I think we might have a lot in common. I want to help her. If I can."

"Then yes. Absolutely." Jen smiled up at him. "That would be amazing."

"Really?"

"Are you kidding?" She scoffed. "I think River is one lucky mare that you're interested in working with her. I certainly don't have the time to do it. She deserves more of a chance than I've been able to give her." Slowing to a stop, she turned to face him. "But I just want you to prepare yourself, because she may not come around. Even with all the time and patience and understanding we can give them, some horses who've been mistreated never learn to trust again. It won't be your fault or your failure if she doesn't, okay?"

Fighting the urge to rub at the ache in his chest, at the bruise in the perfect shape of Davis's thumb, he said, "Yeah, okay." And though they walked the rest of the way in silence, his mind churned. *She may never come around. No matter what I do, she may never trust me again. I have to find a way to be okay with it. I have to find a—*

"Shit," Jen hissed, reaching an arm out, soccer-momming him back a step as a big, red four-seater side-by-side came tearing down the driveway. "Not again."

He was about to ask what was not-againing when she took off, marching toward the side-by-side with purpose.

"Sorry, Jen," Bud from the hardware store said, opening the driver's side door and stepping out. "Jimmy cut him off, and I found him wandering around town. I tried to drive him to his hotel this time. I really did. But he would only let me drive him here."

Jen exhaled sharply through her nose. "It's okay, Bud. Thank you for making sure he's safe."

Bud repositioned his blue trucker hat on his head, looked a little like he wanted to say something else, changed his mind, then nodded. Finally noticing Kev standing there—they'd met a few times when

Kev had used his *I'm too high to drive* Uber services—Bud said, "Oh. Hey, Kev. Wanna help us out?"

"Um, sure," Kev said warily. While Bud walked around to the back seat, Kev followed behind with extreme caution, half expecting snakes to jump out when Jen opened the door. But she only shook her head, stepped to the side, and said, "Kev, meet Scott Shaw. My husband."

Kev peered into the side-by-side at the middle-aged dark-haired man currently passed out cold in the back seat. "Is he okay?"

"He'll have a mother of a hangover." Bud sighed, also shaking his head. "But he'll survive."

"Come on," Jen said in a way that sounded rehearsed, practiced, like this wasn't the first time this had happened. Like it wouldn't be the last. "Let's get him into the barn."

While Kev and Bud rolled Scott out of the side-by-side, the smell of whiskey rolled out with him, practically seeping from his pores. Barely getting him onto his feet, they slung his thick, muscular, and outrageously heavy arms over their shoulders. The dude was taller than Madigan and absolutely yoked.

"Who er you?" Scott grumbled, his head wobbling on his neck while he tried to take Kev in.

Before Kev could answer, Scott's brown eyes lit up, his lips slanting into a sloppy but somehow also disarming smile. "There she is," he slurred, his gaze focusing entirely on Jen. "Hey, darlin'."

"Don't *hey, darlin'* me," Jen snapped, turning away and striding toward the barn to open the door. "You can't keep doing this, Scott."

Bud grunted while he and Kev more or less dragged Scott through the door and down the hall, depositing him onto a couch in the room off Jen's office that seemed set up for estranged husbands who needed to sleep off day-long benders. There was a soft pillow for his head, a warm blanket for the rest of him, a little lamp on a table, a glass that looked like it had been filled with water somewhat recently.

Kev wondered if this had been Scott's office when he'd still lived here. Especially when he noticed the far wall, where there were at least twenty pictures of Scott either standing next to or sitting on top of a well-muscled, broad-chested buckskin, each one with some sort of ribbon or championship buckle around its neck. Each one showing the man currently sprawled face down on the couch smiling, well groomed, handsome as hell, and brimming with confidence, looking like someone in complete control of his world.

And then there was the picture above the couch of that same buckskin, standing in its pasture with the sun glowing behind it and an epitaph engraved on the plaque at the bottom of the frame that read:

Rebel Doc Hollywood "Bucky"
2010-2021
Now you can eat all the pizza you want, big guy

"I'm sorry," Scott said, rolling onto his side and nestling into his pillow while Jen knelt beside the couch and pulled the covers over him. "Don't hate me, darlin'. Just needed to see your face."

"Jen, I'm gonna head back to work," Bud said softly from the door. "If you're all good here, that is."

Looking at Bud over her shoulder, her red braid sliding across her back, she said, "I'm good. Thanks again, Bud. I'll Venmo you for the ride."

He took off his hat, held it in front of his chest. "Come on, Jen. I'll just refund you. He's always on the house. You know that."

Reaching out behind her, she squeezed Bud's hand. Then she turned back to her husband and sighed while Eleanor climbed onto the couch and nestled herself into the nook of Scott's bent knees. "See you next time."

"Probably so," Bud said. Then he nodded at Kev before walking through the door.

The entire scene was so recurrently bleak, and Kev suddenly felt like an intruder. Especially when Scott grabbed Jen's hand. When he said "I'm sorry" again, and she told him, "I know, Scott. You're always sorry." Especially when he closed his eyes, and she brushed his hair back off his forehead, tucking the blanket in around him, never letting go of his hand.

And then it wasn't Scott and Jen in that room anymore. It was Kev passed out on that couch. It was Davis kneeling beside him, taking care of him, making sure he was safe and warm while he slept it off. It was Kev sprawled out on a mattress on the floor. It was Davis watching Madigan pump him full of Narcan. It was Davis telling him, "I'm glad you're doing well. I'm glad you're safe," when he'd returned to Bluebird. It was the meaning behind those words he hadn't truly understood until now. He hadn't understood, because he hadn't ever put himself in her shoes. He hadn't been where he was now, watching the fallout, seeing the worry and the pain and the fucking indefensible selfishness of all of it.

In that moment, with awareness blazing through him like a bolt of lightning that started at his feet and shot for the sky, he knew it would never be him on that mattress again. It would never be him on that couch. It would never be someone he loved having to watch. Having to say "I'm glad you're safe" after he'd decided to throw his entire life away for something that only wanted to destroy him.

He was done. For good.

When Jen dropped her head, resting her forehead on the couch, still holding Scott's hand, Kev didn't think she was crying. He didn't even think she was sad. Just utterly exhausted.

"How often does he—"

"Too often," she said, her voice muffled and far away.

He wanted to tell Jen that he was sorry too, that she shouldn't have to deal with this, that her husband needed to get his shit together. But the hypocrisy of that would have been laughable. And nothing about this situation was funny.

Raising her head, she said, "It's not his fault." Like she knew the way Kev had been judging him, like maybe she thought Kev had been judging her too. "He lost a lot, his horse, people he loved, family, one right after the other. It was like watching dominoes fall." Looking at Scott again, she said, "This was how he coped. But he just couldn't ever pull himself out of it." She tugged his covers up a little higher. "And I couldn't stay in it with him anymore."

Kev understood how they'd ended up this way. More than he ever wanted to. He also knew there wasn't anything he could say to make it better, because that thing didn't exist. But he could help. So he walked to the table, picked up the empty glass, and said, "I'll go get him some fresh water."

Jen's eyes were dry but so dim, the vibrant sparkle he was so used to seeing in them muted when she said, "Thanks, Kev."

Thirty minutes later, after they'd left Scott sleeping in the spare room and Madigan arrived to pick him up, Kev climbed into Lydia, shut the door, and said with unshakable conviction and a clear, solid, resolute voice, "I'm never using drugs again. Never."

Turning slowly in his seat, Madigan stared at him. Then he wrapped his hand around Kev's neck. Pulling him so close their foreheads touched, he said, "Everyone's situation is different. But the day I said that sentence out loud was the day I stopped using for good too." He gave Kev's neck a firm squeeze, let him go, and then drove them home.

While the winding gravel road up to Bluebird churned under Lydia's tires, Kev's thoughts wandered, playing through his life since he'd returned from rehab. Until they latched on to something so tightly it felt like a revelation.

He'd been going about everything all wrong, jumping over steps, racing wildly toward some finish line that seemed to get farther away the faster he ran toward it. So terrified he'd never get there that he couldn't ever just be *here*. He needed to slow down. He needed to back up, retrace his steps, and start again at the beginning.

He knew Madigan and Clay and Tex were right. He knew he was supposed to focus on himself and his journey toward recovery right now. But what they didn't understand was that Davis was part of that journey. He couldn't separate the two. If he was on a path, she was the trees on either side of him, the clear blue sky above his head, the sunlight warming his face and showing him where to go. If he took a step, he took it toward her. Could he continue down his path without those things? He could. And he would. But not without a fight.

She'd probably never love him again—he could see that much. But she'd thought this entire time that he hadn't loved her. She'd thought he wanted someone else. He'd wronged her in so many ways, broken her heart, hurt her, betrayed her trust. But never like that. He'd never wanted anyone else. He'd never wanted anyone but her. And as important as it was for her to know that, he thought it might be even more important for him to tell her, show her, holding nothing back, hiding no single part of himself. Even if it hurt. Even if his old scars were already starting to redden and burn. If she was willing to hear him out, he'd open every single one of those scars back up for her without hesitation.

He'd always known she was worth fighting for. But right then, he decided that he was worth fighting for too. He knew what he had to do. He knew the next step he needed to take. He just hoped it wasn't too late.

CHAPTER FOURTEEN

DAVIS

"You're certainly chipper lately," Davis said while her grandmother flitted around the kitchen, whistling while she worked like Snow White's lesser known eighth dwarf: Unhingedsy. "What gives?"

Chopping carrots with a distant smile, and what Davis might have thought was a blush if her grandma was the type of woman to succumb to such an undignified thing, she said, "I'm no more or less chipper than normal."

"*Sure*," Davis said, drawing the word out while she chopped celery to help prep for dinner. "Whatever you say."

Pointing the tip of her knife Davis's way, her grandma said, "What about you? You're chipper too. At least compared to how sad you've..." She turned back to her carrots, letting the obvious remain unstated. "You just seem happier. Has something changed?"

"Not really," Davis said. Only it wasn't necessarily true. Talking to her mom earlier had helped. A lot. And for the first time in weeks, months, really, she felt a little hopeful. Like maybe she could talk to Kev. Like she wouldn't be losing a part of herself by letting him back into her life. Like maybe they could try. Maybe there was something still there.

"Oh my god," she said, wheeling on her grandma. "You're whistling *again*! What is going on?"

Wandering into the kitchen, Madigan said, "Couldn't have anything to do with Clay's visit, could it?"

"Clay's coming back?" Davis asked, eyes wide. "When?"

"He was already here. You missed him," her grandma said, adding "But *I* didn't" under her breath.

"I missed him?" Davis turned to Madigan.

"He was here a few days ago," Madigan said.

"He was? Why did he…" The stoic, almost tender expression Madigan gave her answered her question before she finished asking it. He'd come for Kev. Probably after she'd told him…everything. "Oh," she said, because what else was there to say?

Glancing down at the small package he held in his hands, Madigan asked, "Can we talk for a minute? In private?" He deferred to her grandma. "Unless you still need her, Maude Alice."

Waving him off, still floating in a cloud of post-Clay visit bliss, her grandma said, "She's all yours."

DAVIS ALWAYS APPRECIATED the way Madigan filled a room. And it wasn't just that he was big. His *presence* was big. Even now, while he sat on the edge of her bed, picking up his package and staring at it, toying nervously with the bit of string that tied it together while she sat at her desk and waited, his presence was imposing. "How are you, Davis?"

"You told Mom I was thinking of leaving." She didn't ask it like a question. Didn't necessarily state it like an accusation either. It was somewhere in between.

He looked up, regret suspended in his bright blue eyes. "I wasn't going to. But she could tell I was sitting on a secret the second I walked into the lodge that night. I didn't want to lie to her."

"And Kev told you."

"He was upset." He huffed a wry laugh. "He was *very* upset."

"Is that why Clay was here?"

"Yes," he said, running his knuckles through his beard. "I felt like I needed to call in the big guns to keep Kev on track, show him some support. He didn't really have a lot of that, of support, when he was..." He let the thought fade out, always careful not to share too much about the Little Timber men. Even though she would have given him just about anything to bend that rule a little right now. To give her a glimpse into Kev's life. Into the past they'd never really talked about. "But I think it helped," he said. "I hope it did, anyway."

"Me too," she said, meaning it. Ever since talking with her mom, some of the bolts in the metal plate she'd welded over her heart had worked themselves free. Not enough to remove it. But it was looser, letting some light in. "I never wanted to upset him. Through all of this, I never wanted to hurt him."

Madigan met her stare, his brow creased. "Of course you didn't, Davis. Nobody would think that."

"It's just, sometimes I get scared," she admitted, because apparently today was the day when all her deepest fears decided to pop up and tumble out of her. "I get scared that something I'll say or do will make him leave again. Make him use again." *And it will be all my fault again.*

"I understand," Madigan said calmly. "It's actually a very common fear, Davis. It's a fear I hear from a lot of family members and loved ones. It's a fear I have too sometimes. But we—addicts—are exceptionally good at finding reasons to use all by ourselves. No assistance required, believe me."

She let herself laugh at that.

"Look," he said, and she thought *here we go.* "I know more than most that there are no guarantees in life. Especially not with addicts. But I really think, I really *believe*, that Kev is committed this time.

He's doing the work. He's digging deep. He's learning about himself. He's opening up."

"That's good," she said, because it was. She was happy for him. Proud of him in ways she'd probably never tell anyone. Mad at him for waiting until now, for only figuring his shit out now. But she'd never tell anyone that either.

Madigan took a deep, long, fortifying breath, then said, "I'm telling you this because if I didn't believe that he was committed, if I didn't believe he was doing the work..." He held up the package. "I wouldn't have agreed to bring you this."

Her mouth suddenly so dry it was difficult to speak, she asked, "What is that?"

"I don't know, exactly. But it's something very important to Kev," he said. "After we got back from the barn this afternoon, he practically sprinted to his cabin, coming out with this and asking me to bring it to you. He said he should have given it to you a long time ago. He said he doesn't want to make you feel uncomfortable, though. And that if you don't want it, that I should just bring it back to him. But he said he 'wants you to know.'"

"To know?" Davis repeated, waging an internal war between jumping up to snatch the package from Madigan's hands right now and asking him to leave it on the bed so she could stare at it for the next ten hours. Neither of which, she realized, included not giving it to her. "To know what?"

"He didn't say." Placing the package back in his lap, his expression wavering, confidence slipping, Madigan said, "Maybe I should let you think about this for a minute. Maybe I should go and—"

"No." She held out her hand. "I'll take it."

After a moment's hesitation, he passed her the package. "Thank you, Davis. Thank you for... Well, just thank you." His mission accomplished, he stood from the bed and made his way to her door. Turning back, he said, "It's going to be different around here without you, a little less bright. But I'm happy for you. Your mom is too."

She would have smiled, said thank you, told him she'd miss him.

But the package in her hands consumed her thoughts, made everything else in the entire world irrelevant. Because now that she could see and feel and touch what Kev wanted her to have, what he wanted her to *know*, emotion swelled so rapidly inside her she wasn't sure she'd be able to speak even if she tried.

Wrapped inside white tissue paper and held together with a length of baling twine tied into a pretty little bow were letters. Lots of letters. He'd written her name across the one on top with instructions she could just make out through the tissue paper:

Please read this first.

When she looked up at Madigan again, the letters held loosely in her hands, tears already standing in her eyes, he said, "Murphy's out here." He angled his head toward the hallway. "Do you want him?"

"Yes," she said, her voice already cracking around the edges. "Kev's not the only one who needs the big guns called in for support. Come on, Murph."

Hearing his name, Murphy trotted in through the open door, leaped onto her bed, turned around twice, and flopped down with a deep, satisfied grumble.

"I'm gonna go check on the guys." Madigan wrapped his hand around the doorknob. "See you at dinner?"

"I'll be there," she said distantly, not sure if it was true. Not sure where she'd be if the letters in her hands were what she thought they were.

Once her door snicked closed, she crawled onto her bed, crossed her legs, rubbed Murphy's belly when his thigh popped up, then turned her attention back to the letters. Carefully pulling the twine bow free, she unfolded the tissue paper and picked up the first letter from the pile. Opening the envelope and sliding the piece of paper free, she smiled at his handwriting. It was so much like him, the before him. Maybe the now him too. A little chaotic, slanting in some places, upright in others. Like someone who'd just sprinted to his cabin and grabbed a pen and a piece of paper. Someone who'd tried to make the words as legible as possible even though he was rushing, hurrying to get them all out.

> Davis,
> I know you're leaving. I'll probably spend the rest of my life hoping I wasn't the reason why, even though I'm pretty sure I am. At least part of it. But today was a strange day. This thing happened. It was eye-opening and it made me finally realize what I'd done to you. Something worse than leaving. Something worse than doing drugs again. Something worse than both. I shut you out. I made you feel alone. I was struggling, fading. I know you felt it. I know you were doing everything you could to keep me from slipping away. But you couldn't get to me because I wouldn't let you. You couldn't get to me because I'd built a wall between us.
> I know I only have a few more weeks left with you. I know that may be all I get. If that's what happens, I'll find a way to be okay with it. But I'm not going to shut you out anymore. The walls are coming down. I should have sent these when I wrote them. I'm sending them now. I know you don't owe me anything, but I hope you'll read them. I understand if you won't. But I hope you will.
> Kev

She stared at the letter in her hands, at the words she'd never dared to hope she'd hear from him. Seeing them now cored her out, somehow filling her up at the same time.

Setting down his first letter, she picked up the next. Her name was scrawled across the front. Nothing else. Just her name. She opened the envelope.

The letter was short and devastating.

> *How did this happen? How did I end up here? I don't know. I don't fucking know.*

She picked up the next letter, watching it tremble between her fingers. The envelope was the same, only her name.

> *Davis,*
> *It's weird writing a letter to someone when you know they'll never read it, but I don't have anyone else to talk to. Everyone here is really nice, but they keep asking questions I can't answer. I've never felt so lost. I've never been so scared. I couldn't sleep last night. I have a little window in my room that looks out over the trees. I spent the night staring at the moon, wishing I had a picture of you to stare at instead. I'm so tired. I wish I could fucking sleep.*
> *Kev*

A tear rolled down her nose, dropping onto the next envelope as she opened the third letter.

> *Davis,*
> *I met my counselor today. His name is Rick. I hope he can help me. I didn't sleep again last night. Every time I closed my eyes, I jolted awake again, my heart racing, my stomach so tied up in knots I thought I was going to be sick. I haven't been able to eat much. Rick said that's the first thing we need to work on. Eating and sleeping. Seems simple enough. Also seems impossible. I swear I saw your face in the moon last night. Or maybe I'm just losing my mind.*
> *Kev*

She read his words over and over until the sting of them faded.

Until the images of him waking up with his heart racing, his stomach burning, just like hers had, faded enough to let her move on.

When she read the next few letters, when she saw the way he'd struggled, how alone he'd felt, how *like her* he'd felt, she clutched at each piece of paper like if she just tried hard enough, she could reach through the fibers to find him in that place. She could hold him, rock him in her arms until he finally closed his eyes.

He still wasn't sleeping much. He was eating even less. But by the seventh letter, something changed.

> Davis,
>
> Have you ever sunk to the bottom of a pool and stayed down there so long you started to wonder if you'd make it back to the surface in time? And then when you did, and you took that huge first breath, it was like life coming back to you? Like relief and gratitude filling your lungs? I feel a little like I took that breath today.
>
> I finally slept last night. For sixteen hours. They usually don't let you oversleep here, but I guess they knew I needed it. I'm actually hungry too. Rick started me on an antidepressant a few days ago. He said it's too early for it to be working, but maybe he's wrong, because I feel clearer today. I'm glad I'm here. I still don't know how things fell apart so fast. I don't know why I decided to sink to the bottom. But I'm in the right place. I'm bobbing above the surface again.
>
> I miss you,
> Kev

She ran her fingertip over those last few words.

I miss you. I miss you. I miss you.

How many notes in her box said the same thing? How many times had she written them or thought them while wondering if he missed her too?

She read the next letter. And the next. And the next. Some were rambling. Some only a few sentences long. Each one gave her a glimpse into his world in rehab. His group sessions. His nature walks. His meditation and yoga and journaling. How much he hated journaling, how it reminded him of going to the dentist.

You know it's probably good for you, but you also know it's going to suck.

Which made her laugh.

He told her about his individual counseling with Rick, where they were working on things like honesty and openness and trust. Every day there was some new revelation, some new goal he was trying to reach. She'd never worked half as hard on herself as Kev was working on himself in these letters.

About halfway through the pile, he started writing her full name and address on the envelopes. By the last few, he'd even put a stamp on them. Somehow, she'd been holding herself more or less together. It was the stamp that finally broke her. She wasn't sure why, but that's when the sobs came, the ugly crying that shook her entire body until Murphy put his head in her lap and stared up at her with his big brown eyes, whimpering softly.

Kev had almost sent these letters. So close to it, he'd paid for the postage. And she understood why he didn't. Because at that time, she wasn't sure if she would have opened them, let alone read them. Even though she'd checked her mailbox every day, she'd been so hurt and angry she might have thrown any letters he'd sent her away. She might have even done something unforgiveable like burned them. And then she would have missed so much. She would have missed his thoughtful, funny, brutally real words. She would have missed this.

Dear Davis,
Madigan is coming to get me tomorrow. He's bringing me

home. Knowing him, he's already made sure you're okay with me coming back to Bluebird. If that's true, all I can say is thank you. I wouldn't have blamed you for saying no. But you'll never know what it means to me that you said yes.

I'm nervous about leaving this place and going back to the real world. But I can't wait to see you. Just to see your face again, Davis. You have no idea how much I miss your face. I'm terrified too, though. Because once I see you, then I'll know what you think of me. I'll know the answer to all the questions I've been asking myself since I got here. Questions like how are you feeling? Are you angry? Are you hurting? Are you sad? Happy? Thriving? Do you hate me? Have you missed me? Do you still love me? Do you? Because I still love you. Maybe I shouldn't say that, but it's true. I have never stopped loving you. I'm not sure if I ever will. I know that may be hard to believe after what I did to you. And I understand if you hate me. I understand if you never want to talk to me again. I'll understand if you take one look at me when I get back and turn around. It will crush me, but I'll understand.

I haven't sent any of these letters to you. I probably won't send this one either. But I can't tell you how much you've helped me in here. Just being able to write to you. To feel like I'm talking to you again. Just to remember your smile and your laugh and what it felt like being with you, just hanging out. Just talking. Nobody will ever understand how amazing just talking to Davis Thompson is. God, I miss it.

It's important in recovery to do something called making amends. I need to make amends with you. I wanted to do it in person, and I hope I'll be able to. But I also realize that you might not want to hear what I have to say.

Considering that the definition of making amends is to

correct a mistake a person has made, I know that what I did to you might be too much to ever make amends for. It's definitely not something I can do in one letter. Or even in one day. Making amends for what I did to you will take time. It will take effort. It will take work. So I thought I'd at least try to apologize in this letter.

I've thought about it a lot, how to apologize to you. I could tell you that I've never been sorrier for anything in my life than I am for the way I hurt you. For lying to you. For scaring you. For pulling away. For leaving. For using drugs again. And I am. I am so fucking sorry. I wish I could go back in time. I wish I never would have gotten into that car. I wish I'd never picked up that needle. But I did. And I have to own it. So even though I am sorry, my apology to you is going to be a lot more than that. My apology to you is my commitment to working harder, getting better, being better. My apology to you is not expecting forgiveness until I've earned it. My apology to you is realizing that I may never earn it and being okay with it.

I know it's not enough. Not even close. But right now, it's everything I have.

I love you. Forever.

Kev

Setting the letter down on top of the scattered pile of his words, his love, his heartbreaking honesty, she gave in, letting herself cry, letting herself weep for him, and for her. For them. For what they'd been. For whatever they were now. For whatever they could be.

For the first time in months, she knew exactly what she needed to do.

Climbing off her bed, she opened her closet door. Then, with tears streaming down her cheeks and Murphy galloping hot on her heels, she ran from her room, from the lodge, racing down the pine-covered path toward the cabins. She had to see him. She had to show him. She had to make sure that he knew too.

Charging up his steps while Murphy hung back to sniff and mark all the trees he'd already sniffed and marked hundreds of times, Davis pounded on his door while her heart pounded on her ribs.

The door swung open, and with wide eyes, he said, "Davis?"

"Jesus Christ," she panted, gaping at his bare chest, at the soft trail of golden hair disappearing beneath a towel wrapped so low around his waist it clung to those V-shaped muscles like it had been painted on him. "Are you ever not shirtless?"

"What?" He looked down, his damp curls brushing against his shoulders. "Oh, sorry. I just got back from doing bathroom duty, and I had to take a shower before dinner."

"You got bathroom duty?" she asked. "Why? What did you do?"

"I told Madigan to fuck off, more or less."

Her eyes bulged. "You *what?*"

"Davis." He took a step toward her, scanning her face while the clean, soapy scent of his recently showered body infiltrated her senses. "Have you been crying?"

"Yes, I've been crying," she answered quickly. Because of course she'd been crying. Because only someone without a heart would have gotten through his words with dry eyes. "I got your letters."

"Did you"—he reached up to squeeze the back of his neck—"read them?"

Working extremely hard to not look down at what his upward reach had done to the precise location of his towel, she replied, "Every single one."

Somehow, in an effort to not look at his body, she slipped and fell into his eyes, lost, sinking, remembering the way she used to imagine diving into them, floating around in the deep blue pools.

When Murphy barked at them from the bottom of the stairs, quick and high pitched like a slap in the face, she shook herself out, remembering why she'd come, what she was doing there on his porch.

Looking down at the shoebox she'd taken from her closet, she said, "I wrote to you too. While you were gone. They aren't much." She held the box more tightly. Maybe this was a mistake. His letters were so beautiful and emotional. What she'd written, what she'd felt. It all seemed so small now. So simple. "I don't really know what they are."

"Do you want to come in?" he asked.

"I can't come in. You're not allowed to have unauthorized guests in the cabins." Her chest grew tight when she said, "The rules."

"The rules," he repeated softly, a shadow passing over his face, the same shadow passing over her too. Because those two words touched on something. And she wanted to touch whatever it was back about as much as she wanted to touch a needle dipped in poison.

His gaze drifted over her shoulder, the shadow dissolving, replaced by a quirk of his lips. "I could just ask Madigan?"

She turned around just as Madigan walked by with Stanley and Tex.

"Yo, Boss," Kev called out. "Can Davis come into my cabin?"

Like he'd hit a wall of quicksand, Madigan slowed, then stopped, then froze. Only his mouth moved, swinging open briefly before snapping closed again.

"Boss," Tex said, elbowing Madigan in the ribs. "Kev asked you a question."

"Yeah, Boss," Stanley added with a big shit-eating grin. "Answer the man."

As Madigan's gaze shifted between them, his expression somehow relieved and wary at the same time, he held up a hand, his fingers splayed, and said, "Five minutes."

When Tex said, "Only five? Jeez, Boss. That's barely enough time to say hello," Davis couldn't keep the smile from her face. Kev couldn't hide his either. It was full and bright and unguarded. Seeing it again was like standing in a ray of sunlight after what had been the darkest and grayest day, week, month.

"Gotta give 'em ten," Stanley said. "At least."

Sighing so deeply Davis heard it from the porch, Madigan said, "Fine. Ten minutes. But do not be late for dinner."

"Thanks, Boss," Kev said, still smiling at her. "We won't be late."

When Madigan shouted, "And put some clothes on!" Davis fought back a legitimate sigh at Kev's sheepish grin while he shot Madigan a thumbs-up.

Then he stepped back inside his cabin, and she followed him in, her shoebox clutched in her hands and her heart climbing into her throat.

CHAPTER FIFTEEN

KEV

"Just, um, let me get dressed."

While Davis sat on his couch with the box in her hands, Kev rifled through his drawers, grabbed whatever looked pants and shirt shaped, and disappeared into his bathroom. Once he closed the door, he dropped the clothes onto the floor, grasped his sink with both hands, and stared at his reflection.

She's here, he thought at the man staring back at him. *She's in your cabin. She read your letters. Be cool. Don't fuck this up, Lowes. Do not fuck this up.*

After taking five deep breaths he really hoped she couldn't hear through the door, he got dressed, scrubbed a towel over his hair, and pointed a finger at himself in the mirror, mouthing *be cool* one last time.

Finally leaving the safety of his bathroom, he sat on the edge of his bed, directly across from where she sat on his couch. After a beat, he asked, "Are you okay?"

After another beat, she nodded.

"I didn't mean to make you cry, Davis. With the letters. I never wanted to upset you or make you sad. I just wanted you to know."

Her eyes turned glassy, and he watched one tear slip down her cheek.

"Shit," he said, wanting to go to her, wanting to dry every single tear he'd ever made her cry. "I'm doing it again."

"Can you just be quiet?" she asked, raising a hand. "Like, just for a minute? I need to get this out, and I'm not sure I'll be able to if you keep talking."

Since he'd do anything for her, anything she ever asked, he made a key turning in a lock motion against his lips, then threw the key over his shoulder. Which made her smile at least.

"Okay." She took as deep of a breath as he'd taken in his bathroom. "That night... The night I saw you—" She waved her hand in the air.

"The night I relapsed," he said for her.

"After, when I came home, I didn't know what to do. Mom and Grandma, even Madigan, were all freaking out because I couldn't speak. Like, I couldn't get the words out. I couldn't stop crying. I was so scared." When she met his stare, hers was as intense as a storm. "Kev, I was so fucking scared."

There were so many things he wanted to say to her. *I know. I'm sorry. I was so scared too.* But she wanted him to be quiet, so he balled his hands into fists and kept his mouth shut.

"I couldn't sleep either," she said. "Just like you. I had nightmares. I got sick almost every night. I couldn't eat. I lost weight. I lost strength. I didn't recognize myself."

While her voice went soft, the one in his head roared. *Look at what you've done. What you did to her. Never. Never again.*

"I wanted to talk to you," she told him, her gaze flickering to the box in her hands, her fingers tightening around it. "I wanted to scream at you. I wanted to ask you why. I wanted to know what I'd done wrong. I wanted to hold you and pretend none of it ever happened." Looking up at him again while he blinked, because the tears filling his eyes had made her face blur and he needed to see her clearly, she said, "I understand why you never sent me those letters.

And I'm glad you didn't. I wouldn't have read them. I wouldn't have been ready. I was so sure that you'd chosen her over me, that you'd wanted to be *with* her when you didn't want me that way anymore." Dropping her chin to her chest, she repeated, "I wouldn't have read them. And even if I had, I wouldn't have understood. It was the right choice. But because you didn't send them, I had no idea what you were thinking. I had no idea if you even thought about me. I had no idea if I even crossed your mind."

Every day. Every minute. Every fucking second. He didn't tell her this, even though it killed him not to say it.

"But I missed you. Like there was this hole you'd left behind that I kept throwing myself into. I couldn't stay out of it. I was just...buried. And it was really fucking lonely down there, so I started writing to you. Little things. On napkins. Scraps of paper. On my hands. Anything I could find. It helped, somehow. Getting it out. But then, one night," she said, her voice going so quiet he had to lean forward to hear her, "I was lying on the floor in my bathroom after waking up sick and terrified again, and I thought, I can't do this anymore. I can't miss him like this anymore. I can't *be* like this anymore. I can't keep burying myself inside this Kev-shaped hole."

He bit down, grinding his teeth together.

"So I told myself it was over," she said while his throat closed up and his eyes burned. "I told myself I had to move on. I told myself I had to let you go because if I didn't, I was going to disappear."

When her voice broke, it took everything in him not to fall to her knees and beg for forgiveness. Beg her not to cry. Do whatever he could to keep her from hurting for one more second because of him.

"So I did. I let you go. And slowly, things got better. I started riding my bike more, training harder. I started sleeping again. Eating again. I'd almost convinced myself I was over you. But it was a lie, because I still missed you. I missed my friend. I missed taking walks with you. I missed just talking to you. Because just talking to Kevin Lowes was pretty fucking amazing too."

A laugh tumbled out of him. It was the kind of laugh that never made sense. Laughing through tears. Laughing even though it hurt.

"So I kept writing." She looked down at the box in her hands. "All these little notes. Little messages to you." When she looked back up at him, uncertainty tugged her brows together. "These are my thoughts, my feelings. But some of them aren't very nice. If you don't want to read them, I understand."

Not giving himself time to think about whether this would be good for him, he held out his hands. "I want to read them."

"Are you sure?"

"Yes."

She leaned forward, and despite how badly he wanted to, when he took the box from her hands, he was careful not to brush his fingers over hers.

Working the lid off the box, he looked inside, pinning his lips between his teeth. There were so many of them. Corners torn off menus, folded napkins, light pink journal paper, matchbooks, receipts. Her tidy handwriting scrawled across each one. His heart rate picked up, the idea of reading these notes not three feet away from her making his palms itch. But he didn't care. If he couldn't realize the way every word, every thought, every bit of honesty in this box was a gift, then there truly was no hope for him.

Starting with a cocktail napkin, he unfolded the thin white paper, revealing the words *I wish I didn't miss you so much* hidden inside. He brushed his thumb over the black ink, over the embossed detailing, the letters M and S. He wondered where she'd been when she found this napkin, what she'd been doing while wishing she didn't miss him.

Setting the napkin beside him, he pulled out a piece of journal paper.

What the fuck is wrong with you?

He almost laughed, because he wished he knew.

There were more like that. More angry words written quickly.

> *Why did you do it?*
> *Did you ever care about me?*
> *Did you ever love me?*
> *Nobody has ever hurt me this much.*

That last one made his stomach burn, a sour taste surging into his mouth. But he kept reading.

> *I am so lost.*
> *Maybe this is all a dream. Maybe I'll wake up.*
> *Fuck you!*
> *Why can't I hate you?*

Her anger was hard to take. But it was her sadness that cut into him, making him struggle to keep going.

> *Why wasn't I enough?*
> *When will I get better?*
> *When will this be over?*
> *I want my life back.*

The note she'd written on a matchbook from Randy's shook between his trembling fingers.

> *I still love you. I wish I didn't.*

It was a knife in his chest, claws scraping across his heart. But he kept reading. He kept listening to her, letting her yell at him now when she hadn't been able to then. Eventually finding notes with some promise. Notes that almost made him smile. The beginnings of conversations they didn't get to have. Words that felt more like the start of something rather than the end.

I was never this bored before you left.
Do they have romance books where you are?
I saw someone with a bouncing knee today and cried.
I think Murphy misses you.
I got stung by a fucking bee on my ass.
That one country song you sing all the wrong words to was playing at the grocery store. I can't even get away from you when I'm buying chips.
You would have liked the moon tonight. Maybe you saw it too.

The more he read, the more he noticed one statement recurring. A statement she'd written at least fifteen times. And seeing it, reading it over and over again, made something bubble up inside him. Something sweet and heavy. Something he probably shouldn't let himself feel. Hope.

I wish you were here.
I wish you were here.
I wish you were here.

But there was one note he hadn't read yet. One that was crumpled into a ball in the corner of the shoebox. All the other notes had been folded carefully or tossed in. This note had pain and anger and hurt etched into every crinkled edge.

"You don't have to read that one," she said when he pulled the crumpled note out of the box. She didn't look him in the eye when she said it, so he knew she was wrong. He did have to read it. He wasn't there for her then, when she'd needed him, when she'd written it. He wasn't about to run from her now.

He uncrumpled the note, carefully spreading it flat. And then he read the words she must have written to him that night. When she'd decided to let him go.

I love you. But I can't do this anymore. I can't be this nothing anymore. Not for you. Not for anyone.

He'd done hard things in his life, but not reacting to her words, keeping his expression neutral while he held the exact moment he'd lost her in his hands? It wasn't hard. It was impossible. That note, that was when his choices had almost broken her. He'd broken himself when he'd made them, but he never wanted to break her too. And it killed him, knowing he'd come so close to doing it anyway.

Even though her words were tattooed on his heart now, scars he'd feel with every beat it took for the rest of his life, he realized it was good that she'd written them. Because she should have let him go. She should have forgotten about him. And maybe he should have let her. But that was a future he couldn't even imagine. He wasn't that strong.

Carefully, he placed the final note on top of all her other admissions. Her questions. Her anger and rage and confusion and hurt.

Their ten minutes long since passed, he put the lid back on the box, closed his eyes, and said, "Thank you."

Her voice shuddered. "I'm sorry if those were hard to—"

And that was it. That was the raggedy end of his self-control snapping.

He slid off the bed, landing on his knees, drawing a sharp gasp from her lips. But he couldn't listen to *her* apologize to *him*. There was no fucking way.

Taking her hands in his, he stared deeply into her glassy blue eyes, hoping she could see the honesty in his and know he was telling her the truth.

"Davis," he said, "please don't be sorry. You have *nothing* to be sorry about. This was all me. And I am so, so"—he hung his head, worried he might start crying again and not wanting a single tremor in his voice when he said—"sorry." He forced his gaze back up to meet hers. "I'm sorry I hurt you. I'm sorry you felt lost. I'm sorry you couldn't eat. I'm sorry you couldn't sleep. I'm sorry that knowing you couldn't hate me makes me happy." *I'm sorry that knowing you might still love me makes me even happier*, he thought but didn't say.

"You were always more than enough. You were everything. You *are* everything." Giving her a hint of a smile, he said, "I'm sorry you were bored. I'm sorry you got stung by a fucking bee. I'm sorry that country song made you think of me while you were just trying to buy chips—although I know all the words to it now because Jen listens to nothing but country classics in the barn. I'm kind of sad it isn't actually 'Hoop Shootin' Boogie,' to be honest."

When she choked out a laugh, he said, "And I'm sorry you wished I was here. I wish I'd been here too. I wish I'd never left. I wish I'd talked to you. I wish I'd done everything differently. I'm sorry. I'm sorry. I'm so fucking sorry." His voice trailed off, his shoulders sinking, his chin falling to his chest. He didn't know what else to say.

"Kev." At least she was still holding his hands. At least she hadn't let go. "Look at me."

Shaking his head, he closed his eyes against a surge of welling tears, his emotions finding all the cracks in the dam he'd tried so hard to build around them. He pressed his forehead into her knees, using care not to push on the knee she'd cut after her fall, but he had to touch her, feel her, be near her. In case this was his last chance.

When her hands slid out of his, he knew it was over. He'd done everything he could, but it wasn't enough.

And then he felt it, so soft, so faint at first he thought he'd imagined it. But it was there, it was real, her fingers running through his hair, her nails scraping so gently along his scalp, soothing, comforting. Relief. Bliss. Everything.

Still, he couldn't move. Couldn't raise his forehead from the safety of her knees.

Until she cupped his face. Until she said, soft but demanding, "Look at me."

It was one of the hardest things he'd ever done, but he obeyed, lifting his head, opening his eyes, finding hers wet and red and filled with unshed tears.

"I forgive you."

There was no fight left in him, no resistance to the sob finally wrenching itself free from his chest. He collapsed back onto his heels, and she followed him down, kneeling in front of him, letting him fall into her as they cried together, his arms loose around her waist, hers tight around his shoulders.

"I forgive you," she said again, their bodies shaking, breaths shuddering. "For everything."

He pulled back, taking her face between his hands, brushing her tears away with his thumbs while she did the same. They held on to each other then, both on their knees, and he'd never been more grateful that another human being existed, that somehow, he'd been lucky enough to live at the same time as her, end up in the same state as her, the same town, the same ski hill. With all the mistakes he'd made in his life, the bad choices, how he'd made it here now, gazing into her eyes, touching his forehead to hers, lowering his lips to hers—

"It's been way over ten minutes!" Madigan shouted through the door.

"Shit," Kev hissed as they broke apart. He jumped to his feet, pulling Davis up to hers when Madigan warned, "I'm coming in."

The door swung open, Madigan stepped through, and Kev couldn't imagine what they looked like. Two red-eyed kids, their faces still wet with tears, chests heaving, hands at their sides, fingers almost touching.

Slowly, Madigan's disappointed dad expression melted away, leaving only a deep concern behind. "You two okay?"

Kev turned toward Davis, his fingers itching to reach for her, to hold her hand when she said, "We're good. But we need a few more minutes."

While some series of emotions raced too quickly across his face for Kev to pin any one down, Madigan said, "Yeah. Of course. I'm, um,"—he cleared his throat—"just glad you're okay." Then, with one last glance at them, he sniffed, nodded, and closed the door snugly behind him.

"Kev," Davis said, her voice calm and clear, her eyes drying. "I don't really know what all of this means. But I'm so tired of crying. I'm so tired of being sad. All of this feels really heavy right now. And I think we both could use a break from heavy things."

His heart gave a dull, painful *whump*.

Not a break. Please. We don't have enough time.

"This may sound ridiculous." She laughed at herself, and he'd never heard a more perfect sound. "But do you think we could start over?"

His head tilted. "What do you mean?" Because whatever it was, he'd do it. She could ask him to speak to her only in French while standing on his head and he'd find a way to make it work.

"Can we start at the beginning again? Like we just met? Can we be friends?"

Could he do that? Could he only be her friend? Staring down at her, wanting so badly to brush her soft curls back off her shoulders, cup her jaw, and kiss her until the sun went down and came back up again, he had his answer. It wasn't the answer he wanted. But it was the answer they needed.

"Okay." Stepping back, letting himself take an easy breath, he gave her his friendliest smile, held out his hand, and said, "Hi. I'm Kevin Lowes." When she slid her hand into his, sparks skittering across his palm, he added, "It's really nice to meet you."

CHAPTER SIXTEEN

KEV

"And then she asked if we could be friends. And I was like, hell yes we can be friends. You know, because I thought she was about to tell me she was glad we made up, but she still didn't want me around. Like, thanks, but bye. And then at dinner that night we sat across from each other, and I swear I caught her checking me out, like, twenty times. Probably because I was checking her out, like, forty times."

He spun the bright red apple in his hand. "It's been like that for the last few days. We catch each other staring. It's the best feeling, that kick to the ribs I get when she looks at me and then looks away, blushing, smiling, sometimes glancing back again just for a second. Ugh," he groaned, the force of their new *friendliness* racing through his bloodstream at light speed. "And now she wants to go for a walk tonight. Just us. I'm kind of freaking out. I know, I know," he said, laughing at himself. "I've got it bad. Have ever since the first day I laid eyes on her. But, I mean, she's Davis. She's *Davis*," he said with extra emphasis, like that alone could convey all the ways she blew his mind, burrowed under his skin, lit him up from the inside out until he glowed. "You'll understand if you ever get to meet her."

From where she stared at him a safe thirty feet away, River swished her tail, thoroughly unimpressed.

He shrugged. "What?"

He could have sworn she rolled her big brown eyes before dropping her nose back down to the grass, biting off a mouthful of fat green blades.

Leaning back, stretching out in River's very clean pasture since she seemed to only use the northwest corner to do her business, Kev pillowed his head with his non-apple-holding hand and gazed up at a blue sky dotted by small, puffy clouds.

He knew his time with Davis was limited. Less than three weeks to find his way back to a real friendship with her. He didn't dream of trying to convince her to stay. He supported her in whatever she wanted to do, whatever she needed to feel secure and fulfilled and happy. But that didn't mean he wouldn't do everything in his power to convince her to keep him in her life after she left.

He'd also cross his fingers and toes and use every single romance hero trick he'd ever read to maybe at least get a kiss. Just one more kiss from her, and he would die a happy man. He knew, of course, that this was a lie. One would never be enough. But that had to be part of recovery from addiction, right? Learning how to make a little be all he needed? Figuring out how to appreciate just enough of something?

He was about to ask himself if there was such a thing as *just enough* Davis Thompson, when the sound of hooves crunching over grass tickled his ears, growing louder with each step.

Keeping his body still, his eyes on the clouds, he wondered how good a horse's hearing was. Could River hear his heart pounding? His breath catching? Maybe not, because she kept walking in his direction, one slow hoof in front of the other until her earthy, sun-warmed horse smell filled his nose.

Carefully, he slid his eyes to the side, catching her in his peripheral vision. She was maybe six feet away, her eyes on the apple in his hand, her fuzzy nostrils flaring. As slowly as he could, he opened his fingers, making his palm flat while she took another step toward him.

Her warm breath gusted over his skin as she dropped her head to sniff at the apple, her gaze darting back and forth between the fruit and him like she was waiting for him to pounce, to grab her, take her from her herd, from her home.

I won't hurt you, he told her silently, because he'd always been convinced that horses were, at least to some degree, telepathic. *You're safe with me.*

Her nose nudging his palm zeroed out his thoughts, a hyperfocus on the softness of her whiskers, the solid warmth of her muzzle against his skin taking over. Risking the chance that he might scare her off, he turned his head. From his perspective, she was enormous, her body big enough to block out the sun.

While she pawed at the ground next to him, blowing out a quiet, rattling snort, the vulnerability of the moment set in. He was so small lying there in her shadow, insignificant, completely at her mercy. Memories of the sensation buzzed through him like panic, real fear tensing his muscles, his body preparing to either run or curl in on itself, protecting the parts of him that could be seriously injured by a boot or a fist.

Almost as if she could sense him spinning out—because, like he said, horses were telepathic—she finally sank her teeth into the apple in his hand, biting off a chunk, sending his memories skittering back into the darkness. Because only earning Davis's forgiveness had ever made him feel so victorious.

The sound of her chewing so close to his ears sent a shiver down his spine, and after she swallowed another bite, he waited for her to take the rest of the apple from his hand and walk away. But she didn't. She ate the whole thing right there, letting him hold it for her the entire time.

After finishing the last bite, she sniffed his hand for a few seconds to make sure she hadn't missed anything. Then she rose above him, standing her ground. Staring down at him while he stared up at her for what felt like a motionless eternity. Eventually, she dropped her head again, sniffing his knee, his thigh, his belly, his chest.

He was surprised by how okay he was with it, with lying there, holding still, being vulnerable while this horse checked him out. His heart didn't hammer against his ribs. His skin didn't crawl with the need to stand up, to be tall, to be big enough to defend himself if he needed to. His knee didn't even want to bounce. Even when she nudged his hip, softly at first, then hard enough to make him roll a little. Even when she did it again, rolling him all the way over onto his belly. Even then, he just rested his cheek on his folded arms while she sniffed his shoulder, his back, his butt. While she nuzzled at his back pocket where, *shit*, he'd stashed a couple of mints from Jen's office.

"You want one of those?" he asked, keeping his voice as calm as possible. "They're my favorites too."

She only snorted, and when he felt her teeth close around his pocket and tug, a tiny zing of panic shot through him. She was a very big horse, after all. And these were his only pair of jeans.

"I can get one out for you," he suggested when she nipped at his pocket again. She was way too close to his ass, and he kind of liked his ass. He had, in his humble opinion, a good ass. A good ass he really didn't want River to bite.

Gingerly, he reached back and pushed her nose out of the way, something he had to do twice because she just nudged him right back the first time. Then he fished one of the mints out of his pocket. With one more half roll, he ended up on his back again. Holding the mint in his closed palm, he told her, "I'm gonna sit up now, okay?"

Her tail swished, whipping through the air as she watched him like there was a non-zero chance he was actually a snake wearing a human suit. But she didn't bolt.

Pushing himself up to his elbows, he waited, made sure she was still cool. Then he sat up all the way. "I just have to unwrap it," he said before tearing the clear plastic wrapper with his teeth and dropping the mint back into his hand. "Still want it?"

Even though she seemed smaller now that he was upright, she was still intimidating as hell. And *man*, she was beautiful, so dark and shiny, so well built. He wanted to reach out and run his fingers down her nose, over the white blaze flowing between her eyes, scratch that place just under her forelock where most horses love to be scratched. But this was about trust. And trust had to be earned.

Holding out his open hand, he waited for her to make a move. In half a breath, she went for it, gathering the mint into her mouth and crunching it in utter bliss. He made a mental note to get more mints after she snatched the second one even more enthusiastically than the first.

Once the crunching was done, she licked his palm, then nudged his hand.

"That's all I've got," he told her. "I'll get more next time—Hey." He braced himself with a hand on the ground while she nudged his shoulder, pushing him. When she did it again, he laughed out loud. He'd been pushed around a lot in his life—by circumstance, by loss, by his dad, by the system. After twenty-eight years of weathering those blows, there was something almost cathartic about being pushed around by a horse. He wondered if it was cathartic for her too. It must have been, because she didn't want to stop.

So he only sat in the soft grass, under the warm sunshine, letting her nudge him, push him, sniff him, rustle his hair with her muzzle while he laughed like he hadn't laughed in a very long time.

Eventually, she lost interest in him and walked away to graze in the far corner of her pasture. The one with what looked like a little white shed tucked into the trees behind it.

With a smile still stretched out wide across his face, Kev stood up, stretched out his back, and left the mare to her peace and quiet. Hoping he also left one step closer to earning her trust.

CHAPTER SEVENTEEN

DAVIS

Sitting next to Brayden at the ski rental counter after making sure he had a fresh notebook, a fully stocked mechanical pencil, and a plate of cheese and crackers—because she could never retain information on an empty stomach and she wanted to give him the best possible chance for success today—Davis clicked the *join meeting* button and waited for the adult learning center to accept their request.

"Why am I so nervous?" Brayden asked, chewing on his mechanical pencil until it made a cracking noise.

"You're nervous because this type of stuff can be nerve racking," she said. *Nerve racking like deciding to be friends with a man who still stars in every single one of your fantasies. A man you can't stop looking at or thinking about. A man you're a few short hours away from meeting up with for your first friendly walk...* "And because you care. If you didn't, you wouldn't be trying to bite your pencil in half."

Pulling the pencil out of his mouth, he said, "Oops."

"It'll be super chill," she promised him, trying to promise herself the same thing. "We have the camera turned off, and we'll be muted. So you can just relax and listen."

Tapping the pencil on the counter, he said, "Okay. I can do that—Shoot." The host let them into the meeting, the screen showing an empty podium in a small classroom, and Brayden sucked air in through the cute little gap in his teeth. "Here we go."

As the meeting started, a brown-haired, brown-eyed twenty-something instructor stepped up to the podium, and Brayden immediately said, "Ooh, she's hot."

Davis snorted, nudging Brayden's shoulder with hers.

"What?" he laughed, pointing at the computer monitor. "It's good motivation. I'll learn anything she wants to teach me."

When Davis rolled her eyes, someone knocked, and she and Brayden both whipped their heads up to find Ace standing in the doorway with Noah.

"Sorry," Ace said, looking sheepish. "But Brayden told us he was coming over here to learn how to get his GED, and we both thought." Ace and Noah shared a look, then shrugged. "Why not?"

"Really?" Davis jumped up, waving them over. "I love this for you! Here." Giving Ace her stool, she pulled another one over for Noah. "Sit. The instructor just started. I'll go get more paper and pencils." She held up a finger as a smile shot across her face. "And more snacks."

Stepping around the counter, looking back as all three men settled in, their faces lit up from the computer monitor's glow, their expressions some mixture of guarded but determined, the strangest sensation overcame her. For the first time, she realized how much she liked helping the Little Timber men. It made her feel good, useful, when she worked alongside them every day, supporting them in whatever little way she could. She realized how much she was going to miss this, miss them—all of them—when she left. *If* she left.

She also realized they were going to need another computer. Maybe two.

CHAPTER SEVENTEEN

DESPITE HOW MUCH Davis loved having the men from Little Timber on the mountain, later that night, while Ace and Tex and Stanley waved a little too enthusiastically at her, while Brayden smiled a little too brightly when she walked past the firepit on her way to Kev's cabin to pick him up, she really wouldn't have minded just a tiny bit more privacy.

Waving back, her smile tight, cheeks hot, she climbed the steps up to Kev's door.

"Hey," he said after pulling the door open. He was fully dressed —*thank god*—in his faded jeans, a dark heather-gray T-shirt, and a smile. "Oh," he said, popping his head outside. "It's kind of chilly tonight, isn't it?"

"Not too bad," Davis said, though there was a mild nip in the midsummer air. It was a weird time of year in Montana. Blisteringly hot during the day, but the temperatures could drop into the forties at night.

"Hang on." Keeping his door open, he walked to his closet, grabbing a red and black checkered flannel and tying it around his waist. "Just in case," he said, stepping onto his porch, closing his door behind him. "Let's go this way." He angled his head to the porch steps leading away from the firepit. "The guys have been giving me hell since I got back from the barn. Can't even go for a walk without it making front page news around here."

"Good idea," Davis said. "I was surprised they didn't start applauding when I walked by."

Kev snorted. "The restraint that must have taken."

"We should really give them trophies."

Grinning down at her, sliding his hands into his pockets, he said, "Medals at the very least."

For so long, she'd tried *not* to look at him. Not to notice the way his bottom lip was a little fuller than the top. Not to let her gaze trace over the strong line of his jaw or down the straight slope of his nose. Not to connect the dots of the three tiny freckles on his right cheek. Not to lose herself in the deep blue ocean of his eyes, the dark forest of his lashes. Not to appreciate just how beautiful he was. She let herself indulge in it now.

After a long moment he might have spent indulging in looking at her too, he angled his head toward the steps again and asked, "Ready?"

Probably not, she thought. But she nodded, following him down the stairs anyway.

Side by side, they made their way to the cross-country trails. Past the spot where she'd run into him right after he'd gotten back. Where she'd tripped, lost her balance. Where he'd caught her, his hand fisted at her back, his body pressed against hers, his breath ghosting over her lips—

"Ah," she blurted out as she tripped *again,* over literally nothing this time.

His hand shot out for her elbow, steadying her. There was a jolt of electric heat where his fingers wrapped around her skin, so intense her eyelids tried to flutter closed. So sensual her teeth wanted to sink into her lower lip. And she'd willingly agreed to be alone with him? At sunset? In the woods? She was so fucked.

"Careful," he said, his voice low, his hand pulling away almost immediately so he could slide it back into his pocket.

She didn't think it was on purpose, her insistence on tripping whenever he was close enough to catch her. She wasn't a clumsy person by nature. And yet... Maybe even her subconscious wanted his hands on her body. Maybe every single one of her neurons had decided to band together in a coordinated attack to make her feet heavy and her reactions slow in the off chance she'd fall into his arms.

She was so royally fucked.

They walked in silence for a while, but it wasn't an uncomfortable silence. It was weird, the way it felt almost necessary. Like they both needed some time to get away from Bluebird, from Little Timber, from the rest of the world before he could eventually ask her, "How was your day?"

"It was good," she said as they turned down a path that dove into the woods. "I worked the trails with the men this morning, rode twelve miles this afternoon, then helped set the guys up with their class."

"What's the race you're training for? Tex said it was fifty miles or something. That's intense."

"It's just this fundraiser thing," she said, minimizing what the ride actually was, what she was raising funds for, what it meant to her. What it might mean to him. But she wasn't ready to have that conversation yet. They were keeping things light, and that conversation would not be light. "I needed something to"—*let me still feel close to you*—"focus on this summer. But yeah, I hope I'll be ready. The farthest I've ridden so far is thirty miles, and that made me so sore I could barely walk the next day. But the race isn't until September, so I've got more time."

"I guess you'll have to do some training in Missoula, then? Since you'll be leaving before the race?"

Her steps slowed, the decision she still hadn't made looming like an anvil above her head. "Yeah. I guess so."

When he nodded, his gaze falling to the white Little Timber sneakers most of the guys wore when they couldn't afford their own shoes, she asked, "How was your day?"

Even though the sky had turned a muted, dusky orange after the sun dipped behind the trees, his smile lit up the trail when he said, "It was amazing. There's this horse I'm working with at Jen's. She's a Mustang named River. She's so beautiful, but pretty standoffish. She'd lived most of her life wild until she was caught."

And while he told her all about this horse who didn't trust people, a horse he'd decided to devote his time and energy to, just so she'd have a single friend in the world other than one of the barn cats, something inside Davis's heart shifted, cracking like lake ice in the spring, settling, melting. Because she knew in that moment that she hadn't been wrong about him. Despite what happened between them, despite her doubts and insecurities and the voice in her head that wondered if she could ever trust her own judgment again, she knew that Kev was a good man. Just solidly, wholeheartedly, sincerely good. She'd sensed it the first time she'd seen him from her mom's window. *Known* it deep in her soul.

So maybe her judgment wasn't defective. Maybe he was just a good man who made a bad mistake. A good man who, under previous Kev and Davis circumstances, would be holding her hand on this walk. She kind of wished he'd do it again now, take her hand, interlace his fingers through hers. But his stayed in his pockets. Which was probably for the best.

"That's amazing," she said after he told her how River had shoved him around today. "She sounds like a horse I'd want to be friends with. Prioritizing herself over everyone else. Claiming her space in the world. Not giving a single fuck what anyone thinks."

"Right?" He laughed. "Like, she's all *why should I give you the time of day? What have you got that makes my life any better than it is now? Why should I trust you at all?* It's really making me think about a lot of stuff."

Davis could see it, Kev walking out to River's pasture every day, trying every day, waiting patiently. Not expecting anything, just hoping. She felt a sudden kinship with the mare. "Have you found anything?"

"Hmm?" he murmured, his amused gaze snagging on hers. "Found anything for what?"

Staring up at him as the crickets burst into their nightly serenade, she said, "Anything that makes her life better enough to want you around?"

The wry twist of his lips was so sweet she wanted to taste it. "Mints."

"Mints?"

"She goes off the fucking rails for mints. Those little red and white ones."

"Well, yeah," Davis said with a laugh some might have called a giggle. "Who doesn't love those?"

"I know. They're so good. She nearly tore off my jeans trying to get to them."

A cough exploded out of her so quickly she barely had a chance to catch it in her fist. Pushing the mental image of Kev...*jeansless*, as far back in her mind as it would go, she said, "Cool." Following the eloquence up with, "Um, do you think you'll try to ride her?"

Ride her? Gah. It was getting worse by the second.

"Yeah." He rolled his grinning lips together, his eyes sliding from hers down to her collarbone and not an inch lower. "I hope so, anyway."

"Well then. I, uh"—she stumbled over a pebble, snorted about it, total nervous system failure—"hope she lets you."

Once he was satisfied that she wasn't about to fall again, he looked away, dropped his head back and said, "Beautiful night."

Tearing her gaze from his profile, she joined him in looking up at the sky.

The stars had just begun to reveal themselves, tiny pinpricks of light twinkling in a sea of deep navy, dark purple, wispy pink clouds hovering above the trees. Reaching down for a pinecone, she picked her star, closed her eyes, and wished for something she probably shouldn't wish for.

"What are you doing?" Kev asked while she hurled the pinecone at the sky.

"Making a wish," she replied, finding another pinecone on the side of the trail. "My grandpa and I used to do this. We'd pick a star, make a wish on it, then throw pinecones until we knocked it out of the sky. Which, of course, we never did. But"—she grunted, launching her pinecone at the star as hard as she could—"it feels good."

Stepping off the trail, returning to her side with a handful of pinecones, Kev said, "I want to try." And then he pointed at his star, closed his eyes, took a deep breath, and fired the pinecone into the sky like a high school quarterback.

"What did you wish for?" she asked, her skin drawing tight, her sophomore year football player fantasy apparently still alive and well.

After throwing another pinecone, the motion making his shirt ride up enough to reveal a sliver of smooth skin and toned muscle, he asked, "Is that what you and your grandpa would do? Tell each other your wishes?"

"Yep." She nodded. "Every time." This wasn't even half true. For instance, she didn't tell her grandpa when she'd wished for Trevor Lawlor to kiss her in the fourth grade, or for bigger boobs in the sixth. But desperate times...

Running a hand through his hair, his cheeks stained pink, he said, "Okay. I guess I wished for more."

She cocked her head. And he huffed a laugh at her doglike request for elaboration.

"I, um, wished for more walks like this," he said, toeing at the ground, becoming the human embodiment of the word *bashful*. "More pinecones. More chances to make more wishes with you. Just...more." Before she could respond, not that she had any idea what to say, he asked, "What did you wish for?"

The crickets stopped singing. The breeze died down. And they stood facing each other in the silence. *I wished for your hand in mine.* "Kind of the same thing," she said.

When he smiled down at her, she wondered if friends did this, wished on stars to have more of each other. Probably not. Friends walked on walks. They didn't smile and gaze and wish. They walked. *Walk, Davis.*

It was clear that self-control was not her strong suit when it came to Kev, but gathering the paltry amount of it she did have, she turned away from him and started back down the path. He didn't let her get far, falling into step with her, silent except for the gravel crunching and pine needles snapping beneath his feet. The sound was ingrained in her DNA, in her memories of her grandfather, her childhood, her entire life here at Bluebird. Even the parts of her life she didn't want to think about. Like the fact that her mom was apparently talking to her dad again.

Angling toward Kev, she asked, "You believe in forgiveness, right?"

He spent some time considering the question, his brow furrowed thoughtfully, head tilted, lips pursed. And she realized that thoughtful, considerate Kev was even sexier than quarterback fantasy Kev.

"I didn't used to," he eventually said. "I'd heard too many apologies that weren't genuine growing up. Too many *sorry*s that meant nothing because I knew he'd do the same thing over and over. And then, when I was using, I made too many worthless apologies of my own. Apologies that meant nothing because I knew *I'd* do the same things over and over. But now?" He made a low humming sound. It wasn't quite a laugh, too self-deprecating. But it was close. "It's safe to say that my feelings have changed. I know how hard it is to truly apologize for something. How scary it can be, for everyone involved. So if the apology is genuine, if it's real, then yeah. I'm listening to it. I'm trying to forgive. It would be pretty hypocritical of me not to."

Steeling herself, she asked, "Even if the apology is from my dad?" She waited for the anger to surface in him, the rage over what her father had done to the men, to him, tricking them into ingesting drugs, trying to get him thrown back behind bars. Trying to ruin their lives. So when he only said, "Sure," she jerked to a stop like she'd run into a brick wall.

"Sure? That's it?"

He shrugged. "If he was truly sorry. If he really meant it. If he was trying to make changes, make amends. Then, yeah. I'd absolutely hear him out. We all fuck up, Davis."

"But his fuck-up was *seriously* fucked up," she said, not entirely sure why she was trying to convince Kev to hold on to the grudge, to nurse his anger the way she'd been nursing hers. "It's unforgiveable, isn't it?"

He turned, facing her like bison faced winter storms, head on, determined to make it through. "We have to be able to change," he said. "To grow. We have to be able to at least try to atone for our fuck-ups, even if we believe they're unforgivable. Even if everyone else thinks they're unforgiveable too. Because if we can't..." When he trailed off, there was so much gravity in the pause, like what he was about to say was substantial. Vital. Like it was the linchpin his future might revolve around.

Running a hand roughly through his hair, he said, "If we can't grow or change or try to be better, how can anyone ever trust us again? How can *you* ever trust me again? How can I ever trust myself?"

Blinking the sting from her eyes, she finally saw things through his. Maybe for the first time. Of course Kev was open to forgiveness. Of course Madigan was too. All the men at Little Timber probably were. Because they'd all made mistakes. Big, life-altering mistakes. They all needed forgiveness, from their families, from their friends. From themselves.

"Do you think I should forgive him?" she asked.

"I don't know." Kev slid his hands back into his pockets. "Has he apologized?"

"I think he wants to," Davis said. "He texts me all the time. He even called me once. But I'm still so mad at him." The breeze picked up again, brushing a curl across her face. She tucked it snuggly behind her ear. "I haven't talked to him since it happened. So I guess I haven't really given him a chance to apologize."

"Wow." Kev rocked back on his heels, giving her a wry smile. "I never thought I'd have anything in common with Chuck, but that is highly relatable content."

"Oh my god." Davis plucked at her collar, pulling it above her chin, pretending to hide inside her shirt. "Okay. I get it. I'm bad at accepting apologies."

When she lowered her shirt again, the amusement that had lit up Kev's expression was gone, his dark, heated gaze rising from the bit of her stomach she'd accidentally exposed, sweeping up her chest, her throat, skating along her jaw.

"I'm only kidding," he said, his voice a little gruff while he met her stare. While flames licked at every inch of skin his attention had roved over. "Relationships with parents can be complicated. Believe me." That furrow sank between his brows again. "I know."

Those two words, *I know*, the almost defeated way he'd said them, made her heart ache. Kev had told her a few things about his dad, none of them good. And he never said a word about his mom. She knew there was more there, a deep pain brewing under the surface. How deep, how bad things had been for him, she wasn't entirely sure. When they'd been together, he didn't seem to like talking about his childhood, and she'd never wanted to make him relive bad memories. She'd never wanted to make him sad or darken the mood in the limited time they ever had alone with each other. So she'd never asked, never pushed. But maybe she should have. Maybe a friend would ask. Maybe a friend would push.

"As for whether you should forgive him?" Kev blew out a breath. "That is some serious father/daughter stuff I have no business commenting on. But I'm here to listen. If you want to talk more about it."

Deciding not to push now. Not on their first friends walk. She only said, "Thank you."

With his hands still deep in his pockets, he smiled. "Anytime."

And since she couldn't just stand there and stare at him all night, she turned away, barely making it a step when he whipped a hand out, hooked his finger into the belt loop of her jeans, and pulled.

"Davis," he whispered, tugging her close enough that her back nestled against his chest, her lungs reaching up and snatching her breath right out of her throat.

Her heart battered her ribs, her head tilting ever-so-slightly as his dipped down, his mouth hovering over the shell of her ear, his breath stirring the hairs at the nape of her neck when he said, "Wait."

"What's happening?" she whispered back, gasping when his hand slipped to her hip, squeezing her there once, a warning to keep still.

As if she could move. As if she wasn't rooted to the spot.

"Look." His voice was low, the warmth of his body enveloping her, his soft curls brushing against her cheek while he reached across her to point into the trees.

The woods were dark, and her vision was hazy, her eyelids growing heavier with each expansion of his chest pressing into her back.

"I don't see anything," she whispered.

When he moved even closer. When he placed his fingers under her chin, skillfully turning her head, angling her in the direction of—

"Whoa," she said in a rush of air. "Look at him."

Between the trees, just far enough away that they weren't in any immediate danger, stood an enormous bull moose. As tall as a house, he flicked his ears back and forth, his antlers flaring wide above his head in the fading light, his gaze soft and focused somewhere farther down the trail.

"Amazing," she whispered, not daring to move a muscle. Because of the moose, of course. Not because Kev's body molded so perfectly to hers. "We hardly ever see them here. But they're my favorite. Ever since I was a kid."

"I don't think he sees us," Kev whispered back, his breath ghosting across her neck, a shiver racing down her spine.

"Not yet," she said, barely making a sound.

Kev's angle changed, his voice and breath and lips dropping from her ear to somewhere just below it. Like he was looking down at her, his gaze hot on the junction of her neck and shoulder. "Should we go?"

But I don't want to go. I want to stay here with you. With your lips at my neck and your hand sliding across my waist...

When the moose started to swing his head their way, some

lingering thread of self-preservation made her say, "Yeah, we should go."

Slowly, he pulled his finger free of her belt loop, giving it one final tug she felt deep in her belly before letting her go.

Then they turned around, heading back toward the cabins in a silence so profound she wondered if the last few minutes had actually happened at all.

CHAPTER EIGHTEEN

KEV

I COULD HAVE TAPPED her shoulder. I could have just whispered her name. But no, I had to hook my fucking finger in her fucking belt loop. I had to pull her against me. Why the hell did I tug on her like that? Why did I grab her hip? Why am I hard right now when this is supposed to be an innocent, friendly walk? An innocent, friendly walk where she looks and smells so good that the need to kiss her is actually ruining my life.

While he tried to shift himself in his jeans as covertly as possible, Kev wondered if this walk had been a mistake. She hadn't said a single word since the moose. She'd only stared straight ahead, looking a little like someone who'd just stepped off a roller coaster they didn't even know they were on. He needed to lighten the mood or he was going to blow this whole *friends* thing before he'd even had the chance to convince her he was worth the effort. *You don't mind if I'm hard as a rock around you all the time, do you? I mean, friends do that, don't they?* After a lengthy inward groan, he forced himself to get a grip.

"Can you believe we actually saw a moose?" he asked, because what else do you ask someone you just saw a moose with while fighting an erection? Shoving his hands back into the safety of his pockets—where he'd been trying to keep them through the whole damn walk so they wouldn't do anything monumentally stupid like tug on her fucking belt loop—he said, "Pretty cool."

"So cool," she agreed, her cheeks flushed as she gathered her hair over her shoulder and fanned her neck.

Was she hot? Was it possible that she was as turned on as he was right now? How could he find out? He had to know. Maybe he could sneak a glance at her shirt, so quickly she wouldn't notice. Just to see if her—*Lock it down*, he warned himself when his cock gave another twitch at the thought of Davis all worked up, her chest heaving, her nipples hard, their pointed tips barely hidden under the white cotton of her shirt.

He bit down, flexing his jaw at the need to shift himself in his jeans again. This was worse than high school. *Friends. Friends. Friends,* he chanted, fighting to get a hold of himself.

While he imagined the least boner-inducing things he could come up with—rotten cheese, wet cardboard, toenail splinters—they walked in silence again and he inhaled deeply, letting the distinctly sharp and piney *Bluebird* scent he'd missed so much while he was gone clear his head.

After a few minutes, she went from fanning her neck to rubbing her arms. It was getting cold. And the soft white shirt hugging all the curves he was dying to mold his palms around wasn't possibly warm enough to keep out the chill.

"Here," he said, untying his flannel from around his waist. The one he'd brought along for the express purpose of giving to her if she needed it. Settling the flannel over her shoulders in the friendliest way possible, he explained, "You look cold."

"A little," she said, sliding her arms through his sleeves, buttoning the top few buttons. "Thanks."

She looked so good wearing his shirt that he was half tempted to tell her to keep it, that it was hers now. Just like his heart. But he only said, "No problem." Then added, "It's so great that you're helping the guys get their GEDs. It's all they can talk about. I think Stanley might come to the next training too."

"Really?" Her face lit up in the rising moonlight, then she frowned. "Hmm," she murmured thoughtfully. "We're going to need a bigger space. And more computers," she said, thinking out loud. "I'll have to talk to Madigan about it. You guys deserve a dedicated space for learning."

A shot of warmth swirled through his bloodstream. He never felt like he deserved anything, and he knew a lot of the guys felt the same way. This was huge, what she was doing, the way she was helping and supporting them, believing in them. At least for now. At least until she left.

"That would be amazing." He bit his cheek. "This kind of thing will help them, I mean us," he corrected even though he wasn't the school type, "more than you know. It'll help the men who stay at Little Timber in the future too."

The word *future* landed between them like a piano plummeting from a skyscraper, with a vibration he felt in his chest, the ground shaking beneath his feet. Would there be a future for her here? For them?

He wondered if she felt it too, because her pace slowed, her chin dipping toward her chest.

In a desperate attempt to fix the vibes, he asked out of nowhere, "What's your favorite color?" then groaned internally. *Favorite color? Jesus, Kev.*

"Uh, green," she answered, probably grateful enough for the shift in mood to humor him. "You?"

He set his jaw, because this was going to sound so pathetic. "Believe it or not." He smiled weakly. "It's also green."

She scoffed, giving him a dubious side-eye. "Be serious."

"I almost lied and answered blue just so I didn't sound like I was trying too hard. But"—he raised a shoulder—"it's green."

"Okay, but what shade of green?" she asked. "Like, leaf green? Or lime green? Or baby-shit green?"

He barked a laugh. "What on earth is baby-shit green?"

Grinning up at him, she said, "You don't know?"

He shook his head, looking down at her, wanting to stay there, locked with her in an infinity mirror of matching smiles.

"It's like a yellowish green," she said. "Almost neon. Mustardy."

"How much baby shit have you seen in your life?"

"Tons," she replied. "I used to babysit all the time."

"I've never been around a baby, so I've never seen it. But maybe baby-shit green would be my favorite." He raised a shoulder. "Impossible to say. Maybe I'll come google it in the computer lab."

"Oh my god, no," she said. And now she was laughing. Like, really laughing. He'd missed this, laughing with her, joking around about stupid shit. It was like a shot to the arm. Like that first sip of water after walking for days with a canteen full of sand. It was so much better than any high he'd ever had.

The thought struck him, so fist-like he nearly grunted. And it reminded him of something Rick had said to him in rehab. Something about the way addiction makes people blind to all the good things in their lives. How once they see it, once they see all the good things they'd sacrificed to their addiction, they'd never unsee it. He thought he saw it now. He never wanted to unsee it again.

"Do not google *show me baby shit*." She was still laughing. "You'll end up on a list somewhere."

"Noted." He pressed his lingering smile between his lips, trying like hell to play it cool. "Actually, it's spring-grass green. You know, when it finally gets warm, and the grass just starts to sprout. It's like... new. It's new green. That's my favorite."

"Kev," she said, and he turned back to find her standing still, her eyes wide. "I'm not lying." She raised her hand, like she was taking an oath. "I swear. But that is my favorite green too. Exactly that."

Click. He took a mental snapshot of her like that, glowing in the moonlight, and saved it in the *Davis* photo album in his mind. "What a coincidence."

They weren't far from the cabins now. He could see the porch lights in the distance. Right then, he hated those lights, hated how close they were. Because it was almost over, their friendly walk. Because if this *had* been a date, if he'd never left and they'd still been together, she wouldn't be about to drop him off, say goodnight, and go on her merry way. He would have walked her back to the lodge like a gentleman. Or he would have at least pretended to be one just so he could press her up against her door, thread his fingers through her hair, and kiss her so thoroughly she'd melt against him, making those needy little noises he still couldn't look at her without hearing.

But since this wasn't a date. Since he *had* left. Since they were only friends, his lonely little cabin would be his last stop tonight.

"But speaking of kids," she said, reeling his focus back in while they started walking again. "Isn't it so weird getting older? I have friends who already have kids. I'm still eating Cinnamon Toast Crunch for breakfast, and my friends are raising literal humans."

"It's *so* weird," he agreed. "I have to borrow most of my clothes, and they're literally responsible for another life."

"Right? It doesn't make sense."

"Do you want kids?" he asked for some absurd reason. Why couldn't he ever break his habit of always saying the first random thing that popped into his head? *Would thinking before you speak just once actually kill you?*

"I don't know," she said, her steps slowing in time with his heart rate because at least she didn't seem completely shocked by the question. "Maybe? What about you?"

"Oh yeah. I want tons of kids." His eyes flew wide, because he'd done it again. And not only had he said this without thinking, he'd also imagined it. Imagined a daughter with Davis's clever blue eyes. A son with her infectious laughter.

And when she asked, "Tons?" he faked a laugh.

"Not tons, obviously," he said. "I mean, not, like, a herd of them or anything."

"How many, then?" she asked, amused.

Enough that they never felt alone. "Two could be good," he said.

"As long as they got along. But three might be better. Although an odd number just seems like one would always be singled out. So, four?"

She'd stopped walking again, so he had too. When he turned to face her, he did it slowly, a little worried about what kind of expression he might find on her face. This was a wild conversation to be having on their first friends walk. It was a topic they'd never discussed even before everything had gone sideways. But when he met her stare, she only looked thoughtful.

"I can see it," she said, her eyes sparkling, a smile playing at her lips. "Kids crawling all over you, waiting in line for you to hold them up with your feet and turn them into airplanes, crowding around you for bedtime stories. You'd make a good dad."

He didn't respond. Partly because he had no idea what to say. Because there were no words to describe what it meant for someone like him to hear something like that. But mostly because his throat was closing up so tightly he knew he'd sound weird if he tried.

Luckily, she took mercy on him. "And then you can finally learn all the wondrously subtle shades of baby-shit green."

"The ultimate upside," he said, laughing to cover for all the ways she'd cracked him wide open with five simple words: *You'd make a good dad.*

While he hoped that she was right, hoping even harder that someday he'd have the chance to find out, they started walking. And before he was even close to ready, his cabin appeared between the trees. The guys had abandoned the firepit, leaving the clearing dim and cold. When they reached his cabin and she started to unbutton his flannel, he couldn't stop himself from covering her hands with his, stilling them.

"Keep it," he said. "For the walk back to the lodge. I'll get it from you later." *Or never.*

Staring down at his hands, she said, "Okay." But when he tried to pull away, she trapped his fingers under her thumbs, keeping him close. "Wait."

He'd wait. He'd stand there all night. He'd stand there forever if she wanted him to. "Davis? Are you okay?"

"Yeah. It's just..." She cleared her throat, still looking at his hands. "It's your nails. You've stopped biting them."

Curling his fingers around hers, he said, "Surprisingly hard habit to break. But I think I've kicked it." Actually, it had been pretty easy. He'd stopped the first night he'd run into her on these same trails. When he'd caught her after she'd tripped. When he'd decided that if he ever got lucky enough to hold her hand again, touch her skin, run one of her curls through his fingers, he wasn't going to do it with jagged, bitten nails.

"That's good," she said. "This was nice. This walk. Talking to you. I've"—she glanced down at her feet—"missed it."

"I've missed it too," he said, edging a hair closer. He'd been following her lead, keeping himself in check, trying to stay friendly. But she was holding his hands now. She was gazing into his eyes. *Fuck it.*

Giving her a lopsided grin, *the* lopsided grin, the one he practiced in the mirror when nobody was looking, the one that showcased his dimple, he said, "Best night I've had in a long time."

While she stared at his lips, hers parted slowly, her pupils dilating, eyelids sinking. Her fingers closed around his, and when she asked, "Kev? Do friends do this?" his heart made a mad dash for his throat.

"D-do what?" he stuttered out. *Fuck.* Was she thinking about kissing him? Had he lopsided-grinned too close to the sun? He wanted to kiss her the way River wanted mints, bad enough to tear a hole in his jeans. Which—if she kissed him right now in his current, riled-up state—might actually happen. And that was the problem. It was too soon. He wanted her too badly. He wouldn't be able to stop once they got started. Not if she didn't want him to.

Panic gripped him, freezing him into a wide-eyed statue of *what the fuck do I even do right now?* So when she let go of his hands and leaned in close, when she said, "this," while resting her cheek against his chest and looping her arms around his waist, he was almost too in his head to register the breathless, soul-shaking relief of having her in his arms again. But he snapped out of it, his panic melting away, releasing him, leaving him loose and warm. Because there it was, the sense of rightness when he had her wrapped in his arms, when he buried his nose into her hair and filled his lungs with her sweet, herbal scent.

Happiness. Joy. Love. Relief. So much relief. It was all there, and he let himself feel it. Because this was what he was fighting for. This connection. This rightness. This hug was the reason. This hug that he thought he might never get again. Holding this beautiful, kind, caring person who noticed he'd stopped biting his nails. Who was willing to pull him close again. Willing to let him sway her from side to side while she pressed her palms into his back. Willing to let him close his eyes and just be with her. So, yes. The answer to her question was yes.

"Friends definitely do this," he said. "All the time."

She breathed a laugh that he felt everywhere her body pressed against his.

When she pulled back, not all the way, just enough to meet his eyes, he asked, "Wanna do it again?"

"What?" Her smile was knee-buckling. "Hug?"

Because he couldn't help himself, he tucked the one curl that insisted on springing free to brush against her cheek behind her ear and said, "Sure. Whenever you want. But I meant meet up for another walk."

"Oh, right." Color filtered into her cheeks. "Um, yeah. Yes. I do."

Sliding his hands back into his pockets, locking them up tight as he took a step away from her, he suggested, "Tomorrow?"

"Tomorrow sounds good," she answered with a nervous little wobble in her voice he'd replay in his head a million times once he was alone in his cabin.

Grinning at her, he said, "Good night, Davis."

She stepped back, said, "Good night, Kev." Then she turned around, heading for the lodge.

Watching her go, trying and failing not to stare at her ass—perfect in every way, even if it was mostly covered by his flannel—he finally blew out the breath that had been trapped in his lungs for the last hour, day, month...

That had gone well. Really well. Maybe he'd be better at this friends thing than he thought. Although he doubted that friends needed to jerk off after hanging out with each other as badly as he did.

Oh well, he thought, climbing the stairs back up to his cabin. *Baby steps.*

CHAPTER NINETEEN

DAVIS

All week long the heat had been brutal on the trails, the sun beating down without mercy, the skies refusing to give them so much as a single cloud. While Davis pulled her rake through the dirt, sweat dripped from her nose, rolled between her breasts, trickled down her ass. But the heat wasn't all bad, because when it was hot, Kev took off his shirt.

She'd become a Pavlovian dog, a drooling mess, and his glistening abs were the loudest dinner bell in the history of humankind.

They were almost done with the final details of this track, and she couldn't wait to try it out. They'd cut a huge section of banked turns into the mountainside, and they'd built a wall ride, a series of skinny bridges, and a sweet ladder drop she was dying to fly over. Almost as much as she was dying to trace those V-shaped muscles darting into Kev's shorts with her tongue.

"Ugh," she groaned, shaking herself out, shaking off the thoughts of how hot his skin would feel under her fingertips, how hard and slippery.

"You okay, Davis?" Tex asked, a wry grin barely concealed under the shadow of his cowboy hat. He'd seen where she'd been looking, who she'd been looking at.

"Yep. Just hot," she replied, wiping the back of her hand across her brow. Not realizing the words that had come out of her mouth until Brayden snorted and said, "I'll bet," under his breath.

Luckily, Kev was busy cutting in a drainage gutter far enough away that he hadn't seen or heard the men catching her staring. But, *holy Hannah,* every time he speared the ground with his shovel, his forearms flexing, his shoulder muscles rippling, she lost all sense, all concept of being surrounded by other people, forgetting that standing there staring at him with her mouth hanging open wasn't socially acceptable.

It was the hug. It had to be. It was being so close to him again, feeling his body beneath her hands, hearing his heart beating wildly against her ear. It was wearing his flannel to bed and returning it to him the next morning without washing it. Just so it smelled a little like her. Just in case he might have noticed, might have brought it to his nose, closed his eyes, and breathed her in.

She'd always been physically attracted to Kev in a way that was almost embarrassing. But now, after all they'd been through, after his letters, after they'd cried together in his cabin, after their hug, she couldn't deny it. She wanted him.

You're the one who wanted to be friends, she reminded herself inwardly while watching him arch his back, his abs stretched out long while he sprayed water from his squirt bottle into his open mouth. Also reminding herself that even though those were some very lucky hydrogen and oxygen atoms, she wasn't one of them. So as much as she might have wanted to, she couldn't just slide herself down his body like that one drop currently sliding over his chin, traveling down his throat, slipping between his pecs...

Before she could follow that one lucky drop farther, he wiped his mouth with the back of his hand, dropped his squirt bottle back to the ground, turned his head...and *winked* at her.

Shit.

Sucking in a breath, she jerked her head down, closed her fingers around her rake, and tried to pretend she'd been working instead of staring. But while he ducked into the trees to finish his dig, she wondered about that wink. About the way his gaze had found hers so easily, like he'd known she'd been watching him. Like he'd put on the entire performance just for her. If that was true, if he was teasing her, it was so unfair it was almost rude. Not that she wanted him to stop. But it made her think of an article she'd read once about a man who'd become a monk and used extreme manual labor to combat his lingering sexual urges. Raking even harder, faster, making each section of the trail so clean someone could eat off it, she could suddenly relate.

When she took a break for her own drink of water, having just barely wrangled back a tenuous grip on her frazzled hormones, he called for her.

"Davis!"

Whipping her head up, frazzled all over again, she shouted back, "Yeah?"

When Kev shouted, "You gotta check this out," she glanced downtrail, catching Ace and Tex looking at her, shaking their heads, smiling, knowing everything.

Feeling herself blush, a surge of heat blooming in her chest, tingling in her cheeks, she asked, "What's up?" in the blandest, friendliest tone she could muster while she set down her rake and walked toward the trees.

"Come here, and I'll show you," he said in a way that wasn't so friendly. A way that made her knees weak and her core simmer.

"Say what you want," she heard Stanley mutter as she followed Kev's voice into the woods. "But the boy's got game."

Pushing through pine boughs thick enough to hide them from the rest of the world, Davis found him kneeling in a clearing, dappled in sunlight, surrounded by a small field of wildflowers. Yellow arnica, magenta fireweed, purple bellflower, scarlet paintbrush.

"Wow," she whispered, barely more than a breath.

He turned his head, gazing up at her, looking like some golden god glowing in a sea of color. "Amazing, right?"

You have no idea, she thought as she went to him. Kneeling beside him, she ran her fingertips over the veiny pink petals of a wild geranium blossom and said, "So amazing."

Plucking a daisy from its stem, he brought it to his nose and breathed in deep. It seemed suddenly so private where they were. Only the birds, the flowers, the muted rays of sunlight finding their way through the trees.

Only them.

"Here," he said, turning to face her while she turned to face him. Carefully, he brushed the strands of hair that had come loose from her ponytail back off her shoulder. Then he slid the stem of the daisy behind her ear. "Beautiful."

She trapped a moan in her throat as his fingers brushed over the shell of her ear. Before she met him, she'd never been touched by a man with Kev's level of confident ease, of attention, of skill. When she'd thought she might never feel it again, might compare every man who ever touched her in the future to Kev and find them lacking, she'd mourned. But now, as his fingers trailed across the angle of her jaw, her moan almost breaking free, her chest rising and falling in rapid waves, his touch felt like a resurrection.

His thumb traced the curve of her lower lip, his eyes going dark, his gaze turning hungry while he said, "Davis?"

Loving the way her name sounded when he said it like that, like she was a dessert he might order, something delicious he couldn't wait to eat, she reached up and wrapped her fingers around his wrist. Her eyelids fluttered at the strong, driving pulse beneath her fingertips when she replied, "Yes?"

His gaze was fixed on her mouth. But slowly, it rose to meet hers, gaining clarity. "Friends don't do this, do they?"

She sighed, feeling him putting the brakes on himself, the intensity in him ramping down.

"Should we stop?" He asked it so quietly she felt more than heard the words. So quietly she could easily have convinced herself she hadn't heard them at all, that she hadn't thought *no, we shouldn't*. But that would have been wrong. Rash. Careless.

So she tried to agree, tried to nod, but this only made his thumb part her lips, opening her wide enough to take it into her mouth. She could do it. It would be so easy here in this sweet, secret place to lean forward, run her tongue along his skin, close her mouth around him, and *suck*—

"Quitting time!" someone yelled out, yanking them apart. Shattering whatever spell the flowers had cast on them.

"Jesus," she gasped, collapsing back on her heels, bracing herself on her hands, still panting as the world stubbornly came back into focus.

Kev only stared at his thumb, his pupils blown while he growled a low and tortured "Fuck."

Watching him, the way his abs flexed as his teeth sank into his lower lip, she said, "I don't think we can be alone together. Like, ever. I don't think we can be trusted to...*friend*."

"I think you're right." He met her stare. "We need a fucking chaperone."

She laughed, the honey-thick tension between them gradually thinning out. "I'll ask my mom."

"What about Maude Alice?" he suggested with a grin that made her glad she was already on her knees. "She'd be game."

"Oh my god." Laughter shook her shoulders. "What is *wrong* with us?"

Licking his lips, a thing she somehow felt all over her body—*fucking magical flowers*—he said, "Nothing."

He was right. Nothing was wrong. Everything was just a bit too right. But it was also too fast. Maybe even dangerous. Only, it didn't feel dangerous. It felt amazing. And after months of feeling miserable, she was having a very hard time not letting herself indulge in a little amazing.

"I know it's wrong," she said, reaching out for him in her mind, sliding her fingers over his round shoulders, up the column of his neck, into the soft curls at his nape. "I know I shouldn't. But Kev." She took a breath, let it out. "I want..."

"What?" he asked, spurring her on, just a light kick since she was already raring to go. "What do you want, Davis?"

Her gaze dropped to his pecs. "I want"—she swallowed—"to put my hands on your chest." She let her eyes sink even lower. "I want to trace my fingers down your abs. I want to feel you, your body. Like, you have no idea—"

"Fuck, Davis." He scrubbed a hand over his face. "You can't say those kinds of things to me."

"I know." Pressing her lips together, she said, "I'm sorry. But it's true."

His hands clenched into fists at his sides. "If I told you all the things I want to do to you right now, you'd probably run away faster than I could catch you."

She highly doubted that, but the image, the visual... And now it was all she could think about: Racing through the trees, running from him while he gave chase. Wondering what would happen if she slowed down. Wondering what would happen if he caught her.

"But I can't. We can't." His jaw muscles feathered. "We're only—"

"Friends," she said, coming to her senses, parking the chase fantasy—but keeping it close enough to take it for a test-drive later. "We're only friends."

"Right." His shoulder sagged, probably in relief. But maybe in regret too. "Friends."

"Okay." She inhaled the sweetness of wildflowers. "Friends. We can do this."

"We can," he agreed firmly while he got to his feet. He reached out for her. "I promise not to call you into the woods again."

Taking his hand, letting it go as soon as she was up and not a second later, she said, "And I promise not to—" *Dream about your breaths coming fast behind me, your footsteps even faster. How hard your body would feel crashing into mine, taking me down to the forest floor...* She cleared her throat. "Be so horny."

Laughter burst out of him. "Same."

His bared golden-god torso gleamed in the afternoon sunlight, and she shook her head at it. "But Kev, you have *got* to start wearing a shirt. It's not fair."

"Sorry." He glanced down at his work boots, giving her a clear view of the flush tinting his cheeks. "I'm, um, probably doing it on purpose a little."

"I knew it," she said, and she might have given his chest a little shove if the prospect of touching his warm skin didn't feel so *un*friendly.

"It's just, when I don't wear a shirt"—his wince was so guilty it needed to serve time—"it makes you look at me. And I guess I'm horny too."

He wasn't the only one blushing now. "That's actually kind of sweet."

"But you're right. I shouldn't," he said. "Because we're not ready. Because we need more time." As soon as the words left his lips, his smile fell, his brow creasing. "Even though we don't have very much of it."

"Kev! Davis!" Tex shouted into the trees. "Time to go."

While she followed him out of the woods, away from the flowers, from the cool, silent shade and back into the sweltering heat and blazing sun, she knew he was right. Her time, *their* time, was running out.

She needed to make a decision. She needed to figure out what she was going to do with her life. She needed to figure out if the growing, undeniable desire to stay, to tell Professor Novak that she wasn't coming back, was because her interests were starting to shift. If helping Brayden and the other men in the computer lab had really sparked something inside her that felt like a different path. If her late-night internet searches for educational grants for nonprofits had really filled her with an enthusiasm she hadn't felt in a long time. Or if it was all just smoke and mirrors, tricks distracting her from the truth: that she was holding on to the past with Kev, hoping there might be a future with him too. Hoping their story wasn't over and willing to sacrifice everything else to find out.

Even if she planned on pressing the daisy he'd given her flat between the pages of a book tonight so she could keep it until she was old and gray, she knew she couldn't sacrifice everything for him again. She couldn't stay here just for him. No matter how good it felt to have his skilled fingers brush over her ear and his thumb trace her lip. No matter that the trees were greener, the sky bluer, the breeze softer when he was near, when he smiled at her, when he reminded her how *right* everything had felt when she'd been his and he'd been hers.

Okay, *fine*, maybe those things mattered a little. But he wasn't hers anymore. She wasn't his. And even if they did end up finding their way back to each other, he couldn't be her reason. He couldn't be her everything. She needed something for herself. She just needed to decide whether that something was in Missoula or right here at home.

CHAPTER TWENTY

KEV

SHIELDING his eyes against the morning sun on his way to meet Madigan in the parking lot, Kev checked himself when he didn't see Lydia in her usual spot, but a white Bluebird Basin utility truck parked there instead.

"Morning," Madigan said, swinging a set of keys around his finger after he dismounted the lodge steps. "You look well rested."

"And you look...weird," he told Madigan, suspicious of the bounce in his step, his cagey grin. "What's happening? Where's Lydia? Did Jen cancel or something?" After sitting with Davis in the flowers yesterday and another—very well-behaved—moonlit walk with her last night, Kev had been buzzing all morning. But his amperage dialed way down at the thought that he might not get to work with River today.

"I'm sorry, pal." Madigan sighed. And while Kev thought *did he just call me 'pal'?* Madigan clasped a hand over his shoulder and said, "Lydia needed some work done this morning. Old girl's got some starter issues. Shannon and Tex have her in the garage."

"Oh, man," Kev said. "Sorry about that, Boss." He knew how important the Suburban was to Madigan. But there wasn't much

Bluebird's short, feisty, and damn good maintenance manager couldn't fix. "I'm sure Shannon will get her sorted out."

"I'm sure she will too." There was that grin again. Cagey, calculating...*squirrelly*.

"We taking the pickup then?" Kev asked, tilting his head toward the Bluebird Basin truck in Lydia's spot.

Swinging the keys around his finger one last time before catching them in his fist, Madigan said, "No. *We're* not." He grabbed Kev's hand and slapped the keys into his palm. "But you are."

Kev stared blankly at the small set of keys, at the yellow smiley face charm grinning up at him. "I am?"

Fishing something out of his back pocket, Madigan said, "Yep. I checked, and this is still valid. Kept forgetting to give it to you after I got you back."

Kev took his driver's license from between Madigan's fingers, the words *I got you back* filtering through about ten different possible translations in his head. *I got you back to Red Falls. I got you back to Bluebird. I got you back to safety. I got you back home...*

"I'll be pretty busy today," Madigan said while Kev wondered what it all meant, getting his license back, getting access to a vehicle, being trusted like this. "And I think with how much time you're spending at the barn, it'll be easier on everyone for you to have some independence getting there and back. Ashley said you can use the pickup. It's stick. You cool with that?"

Kev wasn't great at stick by any stretch, but he'd figure it out. "Yeah. Yeah, I'm cool," he said, scratching his head, unable to stop the heat from creeping up his throat, the mist from clouding his vision at this show of faith. "It's really nice of Ashley to do this for me. It's really nice of both of you. I won't let you down. I promise."

"I know you won't," Madigan said, rock steady, no hesitation, no apprehension. Like he really did trust him. While Kev sank into himself, trying to make sense out of the emotions sweeping through him, Madigan asked, "You're still enjoying working with Jen, right?"

The question yanked him back up to the surface. "Oh, yeah," he said. "It's amazing."

Widening his stance, crossing his arms, Madigan said, "That's great, Kev. Do you think it'll help the other guys?"

"Oh, for sure." His voice rose, enthusiasm ringing through each word. Even though he'd been a little...distracted lately, he'd been meaning to talk to Madigan about Jen's program, about how much it had affected him. "Just the grooming and the groundwork alone would be great for the guys," he said. "It's all about trust and relationship building. It's all about getting real. Because you can't lie to a horse. I'm not even sure you can lie to *yourself* around a horse. They see straight through you. It's, like, honesty bootcamp."

"Hmm." Madigan's lips tipped into a grin. "Maybe I should give it a try too."

Kev could see it: big, bearded, tattooed Boss up on a horse. "You should," he said, grinning too. "I think you'd learn a lot about yourself. And Jen is awesome. She's kind and understanding, but she's no pushover. She really gets it."

"And the horse you're working with?" Madigan asked. "Brook or something?"

"River," Kev said.

"River, that's right. How's it going with River?"

"It's slow," Kev admitted, rubbing his thumb over the smiley face charm. "She might have even more trust issues than I do." It felt strange admitting this out loud, but not necessarily in a bad way. Just a little too sensitive, like freshly healed skin after removing a bandage. "But I'm going to try to halter her today for the first time."

Rocking back on his heels, Madigan said, "Well, whatever haltering is, I hope it goes well. And thank you, Kev. Thank you for trying out this program for me. For opening yourself up to it." He held out his hand. "You've given me a lot to think about."

Kev looked down, momentarily paralyzed. A handshake. Madigan was offering him a handshake. It was a simple gesture, common even. But when Kev took Madigan's hand in his, when he squeezed and shook it once, it didn't feel simple. It felt monumental.

After they let each other go, Kev took a shaky step back and said, "I guess I'd better hit the road."

Madigan stood his ground. "Drive safely. Wear your seat belt."

Gripping his keys tightly until the metal bit into his palm, trying to distract himself from the ache boring into his chest, Kev said, "Thanks, Madigan. I will."

As soon as he pulled up to the barn, Jen came striding out of her office to meet him.

"Madigan told me you'd be driving yourself here today," she said, all smiles while he hopped out of the truck. "Freedom, right?"

Shutting the door, jingling his keys—which made Eleanor tear across the parking lot toward him like he'd rung her dinner bell—Kev said, "Heck yes."

"Congratulations."

He bumped Jen's waiting knuckles with his. "Thanks."

Jen was a vibrant kind of person, always overflowing with energy even though Kev knew she was exhausted from the backbreaking work of running the barn by herself, plus her side job at the nursing home. And then there was the occasional babysitting of her alcoholic husband. And even though she looked happy to see Kev today, even though she was as upbeat as always, hints of deep blue still hung beneath her eyes.

They hadn't really had a chance to talk after Scott had showed up the other day. And even though he knew their situation was none of his business, he cared about Jen. She was good people. He wanted to check in.

While Eleanor wove in and out of his legs, scratching her fuzzy head on his calves, he asked, "Are you okay? You know, since Scott was here?"

Her smile faded. Not all the way, just a small cloud passing over the sun. "I'm okay." She slid her hands into her back pockets and shrugged. "Just another day."

It was clear by her tight jaw and clipped reply that she didn't want to talk about it. And maybe he shouldn't have asked. But at least now, if she did want to talk, hopefully she'd know he'd be there to listen.

While her smile slid back into place, she said, "I have been waiting all morning to tell you something."

"Oh yeah?" he asked, reaching down to pick Eleanor up after she stood with her paws on his thigh and squeaked out the most adorable half-silent meow.

"I was walking Tom Collins down the road past River's pasture yesterday, and she actually came to the fence. She even let Tom sniff her nose."

"She did?" He would have smiled too if Eleanor hadn't chosen that moment to headbutt his chin. Because River never showed any interest in other horses.

"I mean," Jen hedged, "she eventually squealed so loud my ears rang and then took off. But yeah. All the work you're doing with her, I think it's helping. I think you're getting through to her. Whoa, Kev. Are you okay?"

He'd set Eleanor down and stayed there, bracing himself with his hands on his knees. "Yeah," he said, trying not to either pass out or throw up or cry. He wasn't sure which. "It's just been a really emotional week. I think it's all catching up to me at once."

Rubbing his back, Jen asked, "Want to come sit down for a while? I can make a fresh pot of coffee."

Coffee did sound good, but he couldn't wait. Pushing himself back up, waiting for the world to stop spinning, he said, "Actually, would you mind if I started with River today and worked with you after?"

"Not at all." Looping her arm through his, like she wasn't quite sure that he was safe on his own yet, she led him toward the barn door and said, "I bought a fresh bag of mints yesterday. Just for you."

How much candy was too much for a horse to eat? The question rolled vaguely around Kev's mind while he fed River another mint, and then another. But she was there, eating them straight from his palm, following him around her pasture while he told her every detail of how things were going with Davis. Including their hug, their near kiss surrounded by wildflowers, his decision to start wearing shirts. She shook her head at that one.

The mint bribery, the talking, the walking around, it all had a purpose. And that purpose was to lead her to the front gate of her pasture—where he'd hung a simple rope halter.

"Do you know what this is?" he asked once they reached the gate, holding the halter in his hands.

She eyed the rope warily but continued to crunch her mint. Which he took as a positive sign.

"I want to take you for a walk," he told her. "Maybe get out of here for a little bit, see the sights, stretch your legs. But you have to wear this first." He held up the halter, then hung it back on the gate. Turning to face her, he said, "It will go here." Slowly, he reached out to run his hand over her nose.

She balked at the touch, her nostrils flaring. But when he said, "Easy, girl," in a gentle tone while giving her another mint, she settled.

He brushed his palm down her nose, putting the slightest pressure through the contact. Just to see how she'd react. When she lowered her head, not fighting him, he slid his hand up her face, over her forehead, running his fingers along the soft hair under her forelock, scratching her there. She seemed to like it, twitching her lips over his jeans pocket. Or maybe she just wanted more mints.

"Can I show you where else the halter will go?" He wouldn't ever have gone as far as to call the expression on her face *enthused*, but at least she didn't look scared.

Unwrapping another mint, holding it under her nose, he lowered his hand and waited for her to drop her head. When she did, he placed his other hand over her pole, where the halter strap would put pressure behind her ears. And then he braced himself, ready to step back and out of her way in case she whipped her head back up. But she didn't startle, didn't shy. She just crunched her mint, watching him intently from the corner of her eye while he massaged her pole, scratched under her mane, moving his hand all the way down her neck, running it over the length of her back.

"Good girl," he praised. "See? It's not so bad."

The loud breath she blew out through her nostrils wasn't quite a snort. More like a deeply annoyed sigh.

"Should we try it?" he asked, taking the halter from the fence again.

Her eyes went wide, showing their whites. And there was the fear. There was the mistrust.

"River," he said, lowering the halter, letting it dangle by his side. "If you don't want this, you can just back away. I won't force you. And I know you've been through a lot. I have too. Probably nowhere near as much or as bad as you, but I have a hard time trusting people just like you do. The thing is," he told her, pushed the words past the fist closing around his throat, "it's really hard to do this life thing all alone. And there are some amazing people out there. Kind people. Forgiving people." Davis's face bloomed into view. "Beautiful people. I know it's scary. I know it can feel safer to keep everyone at arm's length. I know it's hard to accept even good people into your life when you're worried they'll end up hurting you. Or worse, leaving you." That part was a struggle to get out, a sharp pang in his chest. "But you are surrounded by love here. Nobody will hurt you. I promise."

She blinked, the hard lines around her eyes and her mouth softening.

"Besides." He gave her a flat, apologetic smile. "I'm out of mints."

Pawing at the ground, not believing him, she sniffed at his pocket, nudged his hip with her nose.

"But I know where there are more," he said, lightly brushing the halter along her neck. "A lot more. We just have to trust each other to get there. What do you think?"

"Holy shit," Jen whispered through her fingers, her hand covering her mouth. "I can't believe it."

After leading River around her pasture long enough to feel fairly certain she wouldn't just rear back and bolt the second he opened the gate, Kev took the risk, walking with her down the road back to the barn. Eleanor trotting behind them the entire time.

"I'm out of mints," he told Jen, stopping with River in the parking lot, letting her graze in the small patch of grass beside the barn. "I promised her I'd find more once we got here."

"Oh, sure. Of course," Jen said, wide-eyed. "She can have all the mints. Just"—she held out her hand, like if she didn't, they'd vanish—"hang on."

When she returned from her office with the entire bag of mints in her hand, Kev really did wonder if River might get sick today.

"What a good girl," Jen cooed, slowing her forward progress when River pinned her ears flat back against her head. "That's okay, sweetheart. I'll stay right over here." When Jen's blue eyes met Kev's, they shone like glass. "This is amazing, Kev. You've got a gift. I think you're a natural trainer."

"Oh, um..." He cleared his throat, his cheeks suddenly scalding. "Thanks. I was thinking," he said, playing off how touched he was by the compliment, but also how nervous he was to ask this question.

This question that felt too important. So much more than his desire to give River a richer and fuller life. So much more than worrying that her isolation wasn't good for her. Because the question was about him too. It was about his past, his own isolation, his invisible scars. Nobody should have to live their lives alone. "Have you ever tried to give River a pasture buddy?"

Jen rubbed her chin, looking at River the way a hiker might look at a dormant but rumbling volcano before attempting to hike it. "Once," she said. "But she kicked Clyde so hard he got a bone bruise and had to be on stall rest for two weeks."

"Shoot." Kev winced. But he'd lashed out before too, hadn't he? He'd done things to protect himself that might not have made sense to anyone else. He'd known the fear, the feeling that fists were safer than words. That it was better to be hard than vulnerable. That it was better to fight than it was to trust. "It's just, sometimes I wonder if she's lonely out there all by herself."

"I know. I do too," Jen agreed. "I guess I'd be willing to try again. I'm just not sure who to put with her. It's gotta be the right horse. I think Clyde was a little too *interested*, if you know what I mean. It's gotta be a horse who's willing to give her some space at first. Not some big dumb gelding who immediately tries to sniff her butt."

"What about Maggie?" he asked, playing the ace he'd been holding up his sleeve. "She's such a strong mare. I bet even River would sense it and not try to mess with her. And I can't see Maggie wanting to sniff anyone's butt."

"Maggie..." Jen peered past him to where the pony was grazing in her pasture. "I put her in with the geldings a few months ago to keep the peace when they weren't behaving. But they're pretty stable now, so she can probably move. You know." She flashed him a grin. "It's not a bad idea."

Like she finally realized they were talking about her, River raised her head, making Kev laugh at the huge clump of crab grass sticking wildly out of her mouth.

"Let's put them in the round pen together and see what happens," Jen said. "I'll go grab the pony." Taking a wide, respectful path around River—who pinned her ears back again because she really did seem to dislike her—Jen made her way toward Maggie's pasture. But then she stopped, turned back, and placed her hands on her hips. "I hope I'm not out of line by saying this, Kev. But you seem different lately."

"I do?" he asked, surprised by the statement. Not because he didn't feel different, which he did, on a cellular level. But because he didn't think other people had noticed.

"Yeah." Her head tilted thoughtfully. "You're... I don't know. Lighter."

Holding on to River's lead rope more tightly, using the pressure to ground himself, he said, "I, um. I think it's being here. Doing this program, working with you, working with River. I think it's helping."

He wouldn't tell her about the other reason for the change in him. About how beautiful Davis's eyes looked in the moonlight. How when she'd dropped him off at his cabin last night, she'd stared at his lips for a solid five seconds before realizing it, before blurting out an adorably rattled "good night" as she scampered back to the lodge. How jacked he was to help her with the training ride she'd planned for the weekend.

While River tried to tug him toward the grass again, he said, "I told Madigan this morning that I thought it would help the other guys too."

Jen's smile was so warm he felt it where he stood, a little glow in his cheeks. "Thank you, Kev," she said. "I'm thrilled that you're feeling the benefits of this therapy. And I'm so grateful you were willing to give it a try." Then her smile faltered, the clouds crowding above her again, shadowing her expression. "Life can get pretty heavy. We all deserve a little lightness every once in a while."

Just like she'd been doing for him, he wanted to push the clouds away for her too. He'd thought about asking Madigan if he could spend more time at the barn just to give her a break from the constant chores. Partially because he loved a lot of those chores. Mostly because he remembered another woman in his life who'd worked too hard, someone he should have tried harder to help, someone he wished he'd taken more of the burden from when he'd had the chance. But by the time he found the courage to open his mouth, Jen had already started walking away.

CHAPTER TWENTY-ONE

DAVIS

WHILE REREADING the most recent email from Professor Novak, Davis toyed with a strand of her hair. The email from Ben was kind, but she could tell he was getting frustrated with her refusal to give him an answer. She couldn't blame him. She was frustrated with herself too.

But recently, something had shifted inside her, like a bone healing after a fracture, finally getting stronger even though it was changed. Even though *she* was changed. Even though she would never be the same again. Even though everything in her life felt so different she could barely keep up. She still felt stronger, better, new.

And then there was Kev. She knew she needed to focus on her future, figure out what this stronger, newer, better version of herself wanted. But her problem was the same now as it had been from the moment she'd first laid eyes on him, no matter how hard she tried, no matter how good her intentions were, no matter how much stronger she felt, she couldn't resist him. She couldn't stop thinking about him, finding reasons to be near him, wanting more. Wanting everything.

How the hell was she supposed to make decisions about her near future right now? It was impossible. She needed more time.

Her email pinged, and she creaked out a groan. If it was Professor Novak again, she'd have to recognize it as the sign from the universe that it was. She'd have to answer him. She'd have to make a decision.

"What the fuck?" she said to her laptop. Because the email wasn't from Ben. It was from someone she hadn't heard from in months. Someone she didn't think she'd ever hear from again. It was from her ex.

Hey Davis,
Heard you might be moving back to Missoula. That's cool. Any chance you'd want to grab a drink? I miss your face.
Patrick

She and Patrick hadn't necessarily ended on bad terms. Even so, a shudder tore through her while reading his email, her entire nervous system shouting *no* and *wrong*. Was this what happened when a person went backward? Was this nervous system rebellion the result of trying to step into old footprints, trace old paths, live an old life?

She didn't want any of that. She didn't want to get a drink with the man who'd essentially ignored her for six months while she'd been perfectly fine with it. She didn't want to sink back into that lukewarm bath. She didn't want to keep moving in a direction that got her nowhere.

Burying her face in her hands, she gave in to the endless confusion swirling around her. She couldn't keep doing this, living in this limbo world with one foot in Red Falls and the other constantly reaching out, trying to find solid ground, flailing in empty space instead. She needed to stop trying to do what she thought she was supposed to do, what she thought everyone expected of her. She needed to stick her neck out for once in her life. She needed to grow the fuck up. But first, she needed to get some answers.

"Come in," Madigan called out after she knocked three times.

Pushing the door open, she found him sitting at his desk, sliding a pair of black frames up his nose.

"Are those new?" She pointed her chin toward the glasses.

"Hey, Davis." Pulling them off, he tilted the frames back and forth once before setting them on his desk. "Cole convinced me to get readers. He said I was squinting too much and it was making my crow's feet worse. Which is something I never thought I would care about. But here we are."

"Nothing wrong with wanting to preserve those rugged good looks." She took the seat across from his desk. Trying to smile and feeling the fakeness of it—which, of course, Madigan would see straight through—she said, "You do have a piratey reputation to maintain, after all."

While he sat back in his chair, he squinted at her, already calling her out. "Everything okay?"

Toying with the curled corner of some paper on his desk, she said, "Yep."

Leaning forward again, his blue eyes sparkling but intense, one of his brows rising, he said, "Davis."

Sometimes she wished he wasn't so skilled at reading people. Sometimes she wished they could talk about the weather or something for five minutes before diving headfirst into the hard stuff. But he *was* skilled at reading people, and she wasn't here to talk about the weather. She was here to talk about...everything. Time to dive.

"You know how I'm working with some of the men to get their high school equivalencies," she said.

"Yes." His expression brightened. "I've been meaning to tell you how much it means to me and to the guys that you're helping us out like this."

"Oh. Thanks," she said, ignoring the blood rushing up her throat from his gratitude. "But about that... If it's okay with you—and I'll ask

Mom too—I'd like to clear out one half of the storage room downstairs and move the computer lab in there. It's a bigger space, and the men won't get kicked out of it when Mace gets back at the start of ski season. Because I know you're always working with the guys on their emotional growth. And that's amazing," she added quickly. "But they deserve a chance to work on their educational growth too. And not only for the summer."

A corner of his mouth hitched. "I hadn't really thought about what to do with the lab when the rental shop opened back up again. But I think moving it into the storage room is a fantastic idea. Thank you, Davis."

"And we'll need more desks and chairs. And computers. At least two."

His smile slipped. "You're right." Running his knuckles through his beard, he admitted, "But I don't really have that in the budget."

Fighting not to wring her hands in her lap, not entirely sure why she was so nervous but really not appreciating it, she said, "I've been researching some state-funded opportunities for nonprofits, and there are actually quite a few, several of them focusing on education. So I thought, if you're interested, I could try to apply for them."

"You'd do that?" he asked, his eyes going round. "For us?"

"Of course." She waved him off with a little white lie. "No big."

"It's pretty big, Davis," he insisted. And someday she'd learn not to bother lying around him, not even little white ones. "For these guys, it's huge."

Needing to fidget, because her chest had grown so tight she was worried something inside it might crack—and also because that had been the easy part of this conversation—she picked up a glass paperweight from his desk. "This is cool," she said, rolling the clear orb with a black octopus suspended inside it around her palm. "Is it new too?"

"Ashley got it for me after we watched that one octopus documentary on Netflix. I guess I'd said something about wanting my own octopus friend." He took a deep breath, eyeing her with suspicion.

"But something tells me you're here for more than sentimental paperweight appreciation. Is there something else on your mind?"

Putting his octopus friend back, she said, "I guess I was wondering. Randomly. Out of nowhere. For no particular reason. Um, what made you decide to run a sober living home? Like, what made you know it was what you wanted to do?"

He clasped his hands, resting them on his desk. "Well, I knew I wanted to help other addicts. But I didn't really know how at first. I'd thought about becoming a counselor or a social worker. But if I'm being honest, school was never for me. Then I met this guy who ran his own home in Seattle, and I started working for him. It felt good. It felt like important work. After a while, I thought *I can do this*. And that was that. I moved to Montana a year later, opened Little Timber, and never looked back."

"Cool," she said with a slow nod. "Cool, cool."

"Davis." His voice shifted back into the concerned, parental tone he'd absolutely nailed even though he'd never had kids. "Is there a reason you're asking me this?"

Rolling her neck from side to side, unable to sit still for another second, she stood up, started walking. "It's just, I don't really know what I'm doing with my life. I mean, I have this huge decision to make, right? And, like, I want to go back to school. But I also don't."

"Why don't you want to go back?" he asked while she paced restlessly in front of his desk.

"For one thing, I'm not sure I'm interested in research anymore. And, if I'm being totally honest with myself, I'm not sure I ever was. It just seemed like the thing to do. Like, oh, I'm eighteen. I have no idea what I want from life. I barely even know who I am. But I'm kind of good at math and didn't blow anything up in chemistry. So, yeah, let's go to college and pick a major and then go to grad school and spend all kinds of money because I'm supposed to have all this shit figured out from the jump." Stopping right in front of him, she planted her hands on his desk, her fingers splayed wide, finally letting herself fall into the deep hole of indecision and uncertainty she'd been tiptoeing around for months. "But I don't have it all figured out, Madigan. I didn't then, and I still don't now. Not even a little bit."

Staring up at her, he only raised a brow. Like, *go on. I know you're not done.*

Pushing off his desk, she started pacing again. "Part of me feels like I *should* go back. Like that would be the right choice. Take the second chance while I can. Finish what I started. Do what's expected of me. But another part of me is like, no. No way. That's not what I want. And if I do decide to commit all my time and energy to school again, shouldn't it be for something I actually want? Something I'm passionate about?"

"Those all sound like reasonable concerns," he said calmly.

Scoffing out a harsh *pah*, she said, "They don't feel reasonable. They feel awful."

"I'm sure they do. Concerns are still concerns, even if we understand why we have them." Pulling the necklace her mom had given him last Christmas out from under his shirt, he slid the pendant from side to side and said, "I guess the question is, do you know what you want? Is there something you're passionate about?"

This was the right question at the right time. This was Madigan cutting to the chase with surgical precision. This was why she'd come to talk to him instead of anyone else. This was her chance. Now she just had to take it.

Sitting down again, sliding her chair in close, she remembered the look on Brayden's face when he'd said, "You know, you're kind of good at this." How Ace and Stanley had cheered, high-fiving each other when they'd gotten most of the questions right on the practice quiz at the end of their first class. She thought about how her excitement to set up the new computer lab was eclipsed only by the knowledge that she might not be here long enough to help the men get the most use out of it. She thought about Kev, because she always thought about Kev. Because it seemed impossible to make any kind of decision without considering him too. And that was a problem. Because when she did consider him, there was only one decision her heart wanted to make.

Gathering all her random thoughts and internet searches and program comparisons, she took a deep breath, blew it out, and laid it all out on the table. "I think I might know what I want," she said. "But I need your help first."

CHAPTER TWENTY-TWO

KEV

They stood together in the empty Bluebird parking lot, the mountain rising to the sky behind them, the birds singing in the trees above them, her tan skin and golden hair glowing in the early morning sunlight.

"Here's my plan." She raised her phone, showing him the route she'd marked off on her biking app. While he studied the bright red line that followed along the highway in some sections, breaking off into the trees in others, merging with trails that wove snakelike through the mountains, she said, "It's forty miles."

Even though he could see her phone screen well enough, he leaned in closer, breathing in her sweet, herbal shampoo scent. "How long will it take you?"

"I'm hoping I can do it in a little over three hours. But realistically?" She hummed. "Probably closer to four."

Realizing he was maybe a little too close, so close he could see down the front of her tank top, he straightened, stepped back. They had been very good lately about maintaining their only-friends barriers. Even though he white-knuckled his sheets every night, dreaming about all the ways he'd reduce those barriers to fucking rubble with his bare hands if she'd let him. "How many pitstops do you want?"

"Maybe two," she said. "I can do the first fifteen miles or so without a break. But then, how about you meet me here?" She pointed at the intersection of two mountain roads. "This spot has a pretty little meadow and lots of trees. Great for shade. And then I'll do another fifteen, and you can meet me here. This is the last rest before the big climb up the road back to Bluebird. I'll need, like, a big-ass Gatorade or something at this one."

"Got it," he said, drawing a little map of his own on a pad of paper since he didn't have a cell phone, marking their meeting spots off with two little X's. After muttering "Big-ass Gatorade" to himself as he wrote the letters B.A.G. next to the second spot, he looked up from his pad and asked, "Do you want any specific kinds of snacks?"

"Just granola bars or an apple. Whatever you can find in the kitchen."

"Granola bars, apple, what-ever," he said, writing her request down word for word. But it was all for show. Because he'd made his own plans for her rest breaks the second she'd asked for his help. "Done."

Sliding her phone into the holder on her bike, she strapped her helmet on, slung a leg over the frame and said, "See you in a little over an hour or so at the first stop?"

He slid his hands into his pockets. "I'll be there."

When she smiled at him, his heart gave a kick so solid he thought it might leave a bruise. "Thank you, Kev. Seriously. I've been doing all these rides alone, but it's nice to know you'll be waiting for me. Especially since this ride is so long."

Not acknowledging a single one of the countless inappropriate comments about *long rides* banging around his head—barely even acknowledging her tight little bike shorts, her even tighter tank top, the way both hugged every curve on her body—he smiled and said, "No worries. I'm happy to help."

She settled over her bike seat—an inanimate object he was abruptly jealous of—and smiled back at him. "I'll do my best."

After he watched her ride off toward one of the trails they'd walked down together just the other night, he hopped into the truck he'd already stocked with a cooler full of water and sports drinks, turned the key, and backed out of his spot so fast his tires skidded across the gravel. Because if he wanted to do this right, there was no time to waste.

THE BELL above the door chimed, "The Lovecats" by the Cure tinkling through the speakers, the beat keeping uncanny time with Kev's pounding heart.

Mira stood behind the counter, her long black hair up in a ponytail, her black bangs swept off her forehead as she wiped her hands on her apron. In jeans and a gray Siouxsie and the Banshees T-shirt, Cole sat on one of the stools across from her, about to take a sip from a tiny cup of coffee, when they both turned toward the door.

Cole's eyes went wide, his mouth hinging open when he set his tiny cup down on its tiny saucer with a soft *clink*. While Cole remained silent, Mira said, "Hi, Kev," looking equally shocked to see him but at least able to speak. "How are you?"

Feeling more awkward than he ever had in his entire life, realizing he probably should have called first, Kev said, "I'm good. How are you?"

"We're good...too," Mira stammered. And then they all three stared at each other, not saying a word. Until Mira waved at the empty stool beside Cole and asked, "Do you want to sit?"

"No, thank you," Kev replied a little too quickly, his blood pressure spiking. "I, um, just need to get some cupcakes."

Without warning, Cole grunted like he'd been punched in the gut. After Mira gave him an apologetic wince, they both turned, staring at Kev again.

"And, uh, a couple scones," he said, knowing he was just stalling, delaying. "And maybe one of those meat and cheese trays over there."

Mira nodded.

Cole blinked.

Robert Smith hissed.

And Kev finally said, "And I also need to apologize." The words rasped out of him like sandpaper, gritty and coarse. Painful, but necessary to smooth things over. "To both of you. But especially to you, Cole."

With a dismissive half smile, Cole raised his hand, poised to wave Kev off. Which wasn't surprising either. Cole was one of the nicest dudes Kev had ever met. And he knew what Cole was about to say. He was about to say that it was fine. That he didn't need to apologize. That it was all good.

But it wasn't all good. It was far from all good.

So Kev didn't give him a chance, asking, "Is this an okay time for you to hear an apology?" before Cole could tell him it wasn't necessary.

When Cole dropped his hand back to the counter, Mira reached out, taking it in hers. Then they both nodded.

Trying to take a deep breath through the fist-like grip around his chest, Kev readied the words he'd practiced last night, this morning, and again on the drive into town.

"Cole," he said, "I took advantage of you when you were supervising Little Timber. I knew you wouldn't be watching me as closely as Madigan always did. I was going through something, and I didn't know how to talk about it. Because of that, I made a bad decision. I was thoughtless, dishonest, selfish, and I put you in a terrible position." Taking another moment to drag air into his lungs, he said, "I know that my actions worried you, scared you, and might have even made you feel responsible for something that wasn't your fault. And I am sorry. I'm really, really sorry."

Mira raised her other hand to her chest, her palm pressing flat over her heart. But Cole only stared at him, motionless, still silent. Like someone had pushed his *pause* button.

Fighting to keep his voice steady, Kev looked down at his shoes and said, "I'm happy to talk more about everything that happened if it would help you feel better about what I did. But the last thing I ever wanted to do was hurt you. Either of you. And if there's anything I can do—"

"Stop."

Kev looked up.

Running a knuckle under his eye, Cole said it again. "Stop. You didn't need to apologize. Because we'd already forgiven you, Kev." Rising to his feet, he crossed the bakery, grabbed Kev's hand, and used it to pull him into a tight hug. "We're just so glad you're okay."

"So glad," Mira repeated, dabbing at her eyes with her apron.

When Cole pulled away, he gripped Kev's arms gently and said, "But thank you for saying all of that. Thank you for coming here. I can't imagine it was easy."

Finally letting the shaky exhale that had been bound up inside his chest loose, Kev said, "Gets a little bit easier each time. But it's true. I really am sorry."

After yanking Kev into another hug, Cole returned to his stool while Mira asked again, "Do you want to sit? I can make you a coffee."

"Thank you for the offer," Kev said. "But I can't. I'm actually on a bit of a time crunch."

"Okay. Then what flavor *cupcakes*," she whispered, bracketing her hand around her mouth, shielding her lips from Cole's view, "would you like? I've got peach pie surprise on special today."

A sudden, visceral revulsion ripped through him, his fingers tingling, stomach roiling. "No. No peach." Somehow, he caught himself mid-spiral, remembering his manners. "I mean, no thank you." Shoving away visions of empty cupboards, the syrupy sweet smell of canned peaches, the knotted-up pain of a belly so empty it had stopped wanting food, he asked, "What about chocolate?"

Nodding, even though he could tell his reaction had worried her, worried both of them if Cole's furrowed brow was any indication, Mira said, "Coming right up."

On his way back to the truck a few minutes later, armed with two bags of food and his own little espresso, Kev unlocked the passenger side door and placed the bags carefully on the seat, then froze when he heard "Kev?"

The voice was thin, jangly, familiar.

Turning around slowly, bracing himself in all the ways he knew how to brace himself, tight jaw, rigid shoulders, wide stance, Kev came face to face with his past. It was Thom, his old friend who probably wasn't really a friend at all. His drug buddy and previous Little Timber roommate. The escape hatch he thought he'd finally boarded up tight.

Yet here it was, creaking open before him in broad daylight, right in the middle of town, clashing with the everyday soundtrack of shoppers walking by and children laughing in the park across the street.

"Didn't know you were out," Thom said while Kev made himself breathe. "When?"

Thom was still too skinny, but he had a clean shave and his hair was brushed, and there was color in his cheeks. Kev wondered if he'd kicked. "About a month ago. How's things?"

"Oh, you know," Thom said with his wired, nervy chuckle, flashing his toothy grin. "Same shit different day. How about you? You good?"

It was one of those questions most people didn't really think about when they asked it and definitely didn't think about when they answered it. But right then, Kev did. Kev thought. Because *good* meant something different to him now. Figuring out how to feel good, how to *be* good without drugs, without living each day in fear that it might all get ripped away from him, meant something.

"I'm getting there," he eventually said, thinking of all the good things in his life right now. *Madigan, Jen, River, Davis.* Davis, who he was going to be late to meet up with if he stayed there much longer. Even so, he needed to ask, "How's Trish?"

Running a hand through his shaggy brown hair that, when Kev looked closer, definitely looked unwashed, Thom said, "Haven't heard from her." He rolled his eyes. "She's not really speaking to me right now, or whatever. But she's still in rehab." Before Kev could dig deeper, Thom took a step toward him, and with a sideways grin, he pulled all the boards off the hatch and yanked it open. "I'm holding," he said. "If you want to come over and take a break from being 'good.'" He drew air quotes around the word, like it was obviously a cover. Like obviously Kev was just playing along until he could use again. "It's amazing shit too."

Even though Kev had felt it coming, the offer to hook him up, the chance to sink back again, fall again, it still shook him, made his breath catch and his skin pull tight. Scanning himself from his fingers to his toes, his head to his heart, he felt for the pull, the tug, recognizing this moment for the test that it was.

He didn't live in a temptation-free world. Escape hatches would continue to exist all around him. There was no closing them, no boarding them up. There was only seeing them, recognizing them, and stepping to the side. So he readied himself for the fight. He readied himself for the voice in his head that would nudge him, telling him, *Only once. Once won't hurt anyone. One time and then you can be done, go back to your nice little life, go back to Davis and Madigan and the men and nobody would ever know.*

But as hard as he listened for it, the voice never came. At least not this time. This time, he saw the open hatch and stepped to the side.

"Nah, I'm good," he said. Then he put a hand on Thom's shoulder. "You could be good too, you know. Madigan will help get you into treatment whenever you're ready. It really is better here on the other side." Words he never thought he'd say. Words he believed with his whole entire heart.

"First Trish, now you too?" Thom backed away, shaking his head.

"Look, I'm happy for you, Kev. But that life isn't for me. I tried it once, remember? Hated every fucking second of it."

"I'm sorry to hear that," Kev said, wanting to help but also recognizing that he wasn't the man for the job. He couldn't let himself get wrapped up in that world again. Even with the best of intentions, it would be too easy to lose focus, lose track. He might have succeeded this time in not being tempted, but he thought he'd been on the right track last time too. And temptation found him anyway. So he only said, "It's good to see you, Thom. Take care of yourself, okay?"

Pushing his hands into his pockets, Thom nodded with his head down and said, "You too, man." And then he walked away.

Kev didn't feel proud, necessarily. He didn't feel triumphant that he'd had some clarity this time. But he did feel hopeful that maybe the next time his old life snuck up behind him, he'd have even more. That he'd keep stepping to the side before he fell. And now he had to haul ass to get the meadow set up in time.

WAS IT OVERKILL? Possibly. Did he care? Fuck no.

He'd passed Davis twenty minutes ago. She'd been standing out of her saddle, charging up the road toward the little meadow. When he'd rolled down his window to shout, "Hey! Nice ass!" at her, he'd grinned so wide his eyes watered when she shouted back, laughing, "Friends don't say that to each other!"

But now he was panicking. Now he was sitting on the picnic blanket he'd spread out in a patch of soft grass, arranging the meats and cheeses and scones and apple slices on the charcuterie board Mira had let him borrow when he'd told them what his plan was today.

This is fine, he told himself. Friends did this sort of thing. Friends brought each other treats. Fancy, delicious, spent-every-penny-they-own-on-them treats. There was no need to be nervous. No need to freak out as badly as he was freaking out. No need to be one racing heartbeat away from jumping up and pacing out his nerves.

And then he saw her in the distance.

She must have ditched her tank top because she was only wearing her sports bra and her biking shorts. Her head was down, her perfect ass out of her seat while she pedaled up the hill to the meadow. When she reached him, she stopped, hopped off to straddle her bike, ripped off her helmet, and yanked her water bottle out of its holder.

As she angled her face toward the sky, the spray from the water bottle flowing into her mouth, running over her chin, sluicing down her throat, disappearing between her breasts, Kev groaned internally at the highly detailed fantasy playing out in real time before him. There was nothing particularly extraordinary about a woman drinking water after exerting herself. But the way Davis looked doing it, the way the sunlight glistened off her dewy skin, the way her chest heaved with every breath... It was the single most erotic thing he'd ever witnessed. There wasn't a scene in any of his romance books that held a candle to it.

His mouth suddenly felt too dry, his chest too hot, his shorts too tight.

Squirting another stream of water directly down the back of her neck, then over her chest, making him come to terms with his actual mortality, she finally noticed him. "Whoa." A smile crept across her face. "Kev? What's all this?"

Well, Davis, he thought, *this is called a grand gesture.*

"It's just a picnic," he said, waving his hand over the spread. "I stopped by Glazed. Thought you might like something a little nicer than a granola bar."

Lowering her bike to the grass, her expression sobering, she asked, "Did you see Cole?" Because she knew he hadn't seen Cole since he'd gotten back. She knew that encounter would have had a weight to it.

He nodded slowly. "I did."

"How did that go?"

"Honestly," he admitted with a huffed laugh when she sat down beside him, "it kind of sucked. Super awkward. But I needed to apologize. To both of them. I'd probably already waited too long. I think we're good now. But"—he shrugged, because whether one apology was enough wasn't really up to him, and he'd make more if he needed to—"I guess we'll see."

She looked up at him, smiling like she was proud of him. Which might have closed his throat right up if she hadn't immediately changed the subject.

"This is amazing," she said, and with only a moment's hesitation, her eyes locking on his and her lips curling at the corners, she leaned over and kissed his cheek. Because friends did that too. Friends gave each other proud smiles. Friends kissed each other's cheeks. Friends felt those kisses sear their skin like a brand, leaving an indelible mark behind they'd feel forever.

While he fought the temptation to cover his cheek, holding her friendly kiss in place for as long as he could, she dug in, making a little sandwich out of two slices of salami and a hunk of Gruyère. After her first bite, she moaned in a way that threatened his grip on consciousness.

"Seriously. Amazing," she repeated while he fished one of the ice-cold bottles of water out of the cooler. Taking the bottle, she spun off the top and downed half the contents in three gulps. Then she wiped her mouth with the back of her hand, smiled at him again, and said, "*You* are amazing."

So are you, he thought, trying not to stare at her flushed cheeks, the tendrils of damp hair sticking to her neck. Failing spectacularly. "How's the ride so far?"

"Good," she said before taking a bite of a second salami sandwich. "Really good. Some days I feel like my legs are made of lead and every road and trail goes uphill. But today I feel strong."

He felt strong today too, sitting next to her, supporting her. He felt like he had a direct line to the sun.

"Can I do anything for you?" And because, at the moment, he was willing to sell his soul to the devil himself to touch her, he suggested, "Are you sore? Want a neck rub? Back rub?"

"Oh my god," she groaned, reaching up to squeeze her neck. "If you'd rub my shoulders, I'd love you forever."

If she noticed what she'd said, the electrical current her words had generated through his bloodstream, she didn't let on. Either way, she'd just signed up for the single best shoulder rub of her entire fucking life.

Sliding in behind her on the blanket, he balled his hands into fists for a brief, bracing moment. Then he spread his fingers out, rubbed his palms together to warm them up, and slid his hands gently over the tops of her shoulders. When she hummed in pleasure, he made himself pause, breathe, feel. Her skin was so warm, so soft and smooth under his hands. So perfect. But her muscles were tight as hell. When he gave the tops of her shoulders a testing squeeze, she hummed again, low and throaty.

Christ. That hum. He wanted to chase the sound, draw it out, see what it took to transform it into a moan.

"That feels so good," she said, dropping her chin to her chest, giving him better access. "I've been so tight."

Fuuuck. He screwed his eyes shut, bit his cheek, anything to keep the words *Davis* and *tight* from commingling in his mind.

His voice straining just as much as the rest of him, he said, "Tell me if I do something you don't like."

Either she truly had no idea how much this massage was taking him apart piece by piece, or she was purposefully trying to torment him. But when she said, "I doubt there's anything you could do that I wouldn't like," he knew he was going to die. Right there in that beautiful meadow on that perfectly warm day with his hands on her perfectly smooth skin, he was about to meet his end.

"Kev?" she said when he stopped moving, stopped breathing. "Are you okay?"

Giving his head a shake, he said, "I'm good. Sorry." Then he pressed his thumbs into the muscles traveling along her spine, which earned him another hum, almost a moan. A matter of semantics, really. *And* now he was getting hard.

Despite the precarious situation in his shorts, he spent the next ten minutes kneading and pressing and squeezing until her head hung limply and the tension in her muscles melted away. And with every press of his thumbs, with every moan and sigh he pulled from her, his fingers itched to slide beneath the straps of her sports bra, to pull them down over her shoulders, to brush his lips over the skin he exposed...

"I should probably get back on the road," she said, hauling him out of his fantasy. "But thank you. That was amazing."

He almost scoffed. Because *that* was nothing. If she wanted amazing, he'd show her amazing. He'd knead and squeeze and work every single muscle in her body if she let him. He'd kiss every inch of her skin, worship every sensitive spot she possessed with his fingers and his lips and his tongue until there was no part of her left sore or stiff or wanting.

"Anytime," he said, getting a hold of himself, wishing things were different. Wishing they weren't just friends. Wishing she wasn't leaving.

Standing from the picnic blanket, she turned to him, and he didn't miss her flushed cheeks, the dazed look in her heavy-lidded eyes.

"Thanks for the food, and for the"—she waved a hand in the air, swaying a little on her feet—"other stuff."

While a smile tugged at his lips, she scampered off, tripping over the corner of the blanket as she grabbed some ice and another water from the cooler to refill her squirt bottle, not looking at him once.

"Meet you at the next stop?" he asked, a little relieved that he still knew how to fluster a woman.

"Mm-hmm," she chirped, passing him the empty water bottle from a good four feet away, leaning forward at the waist rather than taking another step closer.

"Davis?" He hid his smile as best he could while he got to his feet. "Is everything okay?"

She made a *pfft* sound. "Totally. I'm great. Ready to go." She snorted. "I mean, ready to ride." Her eyes flared. "I mean my bike. I'm ready to ride my bike. Of course."

Running a hand through his hair, letting his dimple pop because, *fuck*, she was cute when she was worked up, he said, "See you soon?"

"You bet." Backing away a step, she stumbled over her feet.

"Careful out there."

Waving him off with an airy laugh, she said, "There...was a rock. I tripped."

Glancing at the grass around her feet, not a rock to be found, he nodded. "Gotcha."

While color surged up her throat, a flush flooding her cheeks, she snorted again, turned around, and practically ran the rest of the way to her bike.

CHAPTER TWENTY-THREE

DAVIS

His hands. *Good god, his hands.* He'd scrambled her brain with those hands. He'd made her moan, like *moan*, with those hands. He'd taught her something with those hands. Because a woman, she now knew, could tell a lot about a man by the way he massaged her shoulders. A lot about their patience, their responsiveness, their attentiveness. A lot about the way their big, warm hands and skilled, nimble fingers might feel on other parts of her—

"Shit!" she yipped, yanking her handlebars to the right when her front tire veered off the trail. Narrowly avoiding skidding into the trees, she mentally slapped herself. She needed to focus. She needed to focus, specifically, on the trail—which was fairly technical on this portion of her ride—and not on Kev's preternatural ability to work a muscle until it tensed, twitched, clenched, and then released.

But focus was hard to come by, fleeting and slippery. Because aside from blessing her with his stellar masseur techniques, he'd also made her a picnic. He'd gone to see Cole and Mira. He'd faced them, apologized to them, tried to make things right with them. And then he'd bought more food than she could have possibly eaten.

Kev didn't have a lot of money, and she knew what that stop had cost him. But he did it for her, without fanfare, without wanting any acknowledgment at all. But just because. Just because that's the kind of man he was.

The kind of man who made her insides light up like a Christmas tree whenever he was close. The kind of man who threw pinecones at the stars with her. The kind of man who was so thrilled that the pony at Jen's barn got along with River, and that River wouldn't be alone in her pasture anymore, that his eyes had gone all glassy when he'd told her about it. The kind of man who had done everything in his power to get his life back on track, to heal their relationship as much as possible, to make amends. *Truly* make amends in the way he'd defined it in his letters. Not just by saying sorry and trying to move on. But by living with his choices, owning them, working through them, letting them transform him into someone new.

He probably didn't know this, because the realization only fully dawned on her right then as she broke through the trees, leaving the shade of the forest behind to bask in the sunlight, but he'd transformed her into someone new too. Someone who was willing to give second chances. Someone who'd learned that being brave sometimes meant being vulnerable. Someone who no longer believed that things could be broken beyond any hope of repair.

Someone who admired him, cared about him, thought about him from the moment she woke up to the second she fell asleep again. Someone who was wrong. Because she didn't want to be only friends with him. She wanted more. She wanted everything.

And she wanted it now.

Despite pedaling so hard her quads caught fire and each breath she took scorched her lungs, it still took her another forty minutes to reach the next stop. Forty minutes of fantasizing about the rasp of his soft stubble under her fingertips, his even softer lips brushing against hers, curling into a smile as he whispered things she was suddenly desperate to hear into her ear. Forty minutes of wanting and needing with a sharp clarity that rang through her bones and heated her blood. Forty minutes that proved beyond a shadow of a doubt that time was not fixed but relative, stretching out depending on the thirst of the observer.

And just when she thought she couldn't take another torturously slow tick of the clock, there he was.

At the bottom of the hill, he sat in a folding chair, one ankle hooked over the other knee, sunglasses covering his eyes, reading one of his romance books. Because of course he was.

He'd set up a little bistro table beside him with several cupcakes and a champagne glass full of yellow sports drink on top of it. And she didn't care what she looked like. She didn't care that she was sweaty and red-faced and gasping for air. When she hopped off her bike, pulling off her helmet and chucking it to the side, she didn't care that she was being rash and wild. And when he set down his book, slid his sunglasses up into his hair, and said, "Davis?" with a mildly concerned expression, she didn't even care that it was the middle of the day. That they were in broad daylight and anyone driving by might see them.

Marching up to him while he rose to his feet, she took his shirt in both hands and said, "I want to kiss you."

Even though she'd entered his space with the force of a tidal wave, he stood his ground, his hands rising to cup her face. "Whoa, slow down," he said, brushing her damp hair back off her forehead.

"I don't want to slow down," she said, because time had decided to speed up now, reminding her of how much of it she'd wasted already. "I know I'm gross and sweaty, and I probably look terrible. But I want to kiss you. I *need* to kiss you. Please, Kev." She knew how desperate she sounded. She didn't care about that either.

His gaze shifted restlessly between her eyes and her lips and back again. "That's not it, baby. Believe me."

Baby. Oh fuck, he'd called her baby. The word was a key springing the lock on some box of hope and longing and need she'd buried so deeply inside herself she'd almost forgotten it existed. But now she knew. Now she felt it all. Now she wouldn't survive another minute without his lips on hers.

"You could roll around in literal garbage and you'd still be the sexiest woman I've ever laid eyes on. But friends don't kiss."

Grabbing his shirt even more tightly, she practically growled, "I don't want to be friends."

"But—"

"I know what I said. But I was confused then. Everything was so intense, and I was scared. But Kev, you made me a picnic. You wrote me letters. You make me laugh." She glanced down at the little table, her voice wobbling when she said, "You got me cupcakes and fancy Gatorade." She met his stare again, insecurity trickling over her skin. "I know I'm kind of a mess. I know I'm indecisive and flailing and trying to figure it all out. And if that's too much for you right now, I'll understand. I'll leave you alone. I'll get back on my bike and ride away. I'll—"

His lips crashed into hers before she had a chance to finish her sentence, his hand gripping her neck while hers slid over his chest. Touching him. Feeling him. Kissing him. *Finally*.

Wild, primal noises tore from their throats as he kissed her like she'd never been kissed before. Like she'd wanted him to kiss her for so long it almost hurt. With tongue and teeth and unrestrained craving. With hands roaming along her back, down her thighs as he hoisted her into his arms, as she wrapped her legs around his waist, clinging to him while he sat on the edge of the little chair some still-functioning corner of her mind really hoped was sturdy enough to hold their weight.

On second thought, who cared. If it broke, she'd ride him down to the ground.

"*Fuck*, baby," he whispered between her lips.

"I know," she whispered back. She'd forgotten how good he was at this. How perfectly his lips molded to hers. The softness of his tongue even when it demanded entry into her mouth, seeking a deeper connection, seeking more. She'd forgotten how phenomenal it felt to press herself against him, her breasts against his chest. Her heart against his heart. The rightness of it, like this was where she belonged. This. Right there. In his arms. In his lap, with his hands sliding from her hips to her ass, squeezing.

"Davis?" he asked between kisses. "What...is that?"

"Hmm?" she replied, her eyes rolling back while he broke away from her lips to trail kisses down her neck.

Squeezing her ass again, he asked, "Are you wearing a diaper or something?"

Laughter burst out of her as she met his hungry gaze, his pink, smiling lips. "It's padding. Bike shorts have padding. Four hours in the saddle is brutal on my ass."

"Can't have that," he said, kneading her sore muscles through the padding, rocking her against him, letting her feel exactly what the kiss had done to him. "I fucking love your ass."

Because she'd wanted to for so long—because she could now—she slid her hands along his jaw, the rasp of soft stubble against her palms feeling just as perfect as she'd remembered. She realized how much she'd missed looking at him at this distance. The triangle of freckles dotting his right cheek, the dark gold forest of his eyelashes, the strands of silver fanning out from his pupils, floating like tinsel in a sea of dark blue waves. He was so gorgeous. So beautiful. So perfect.

He was staring at her too, his gaze traveling from her eyes to the bridge of her nose, sinking to her lips, her chin, her throat.

"I'm sorry," she said, grasping for her bearings while his fingers closed around her hips. "I'm sorry I jumped you. I guess surprise fancy snacks are my weakness."

With a low chuckle and a smile that displayed his dimple like another little gift, making her heart go *whump*, he said, "In that case, expect them every day." He licked his lips, rolled them together. "And never be sorry for kissing me. Ever. Definitely don't be sorry if you do it again."

Staring at his mouth, wanting more of him already, she said, "But anyone could drive by—"

"I don't fucking care," he said, leaning forward to close his teeth over the spot where her neck met her shoulder. Enough to feel, not enough to hurt. Then he kissed her there, gentle and sweet. And she melted like ice cream left a second too long in the sun.

"I don't care if you're a mess," he said. "I don't care that you're still trying to figure it all out. I'll take whatever you'll give me. Anywhere you're willing to give it to me. For as long as I can."

She wanted to give him everything. She wanted to give him her entire heart, now and forever. But they'd moved too quickly last time, racing headlong into something they'd never even had the chance to define. Something they'd barely even talked about. Something they'd just leaped into because it had felt so perfect.

Only it hadn't been perfect.

Something had let him slip away from her. Maybe if they took things more slowly this time, more carefully, she could find out what that thing was. Maybe she could keep it from happening again. Maybe, if they didn't rush, if they were careful, she could keep...him.

"Hey, it's all right," he said softly, sensing her hesitation, grazing his lips along the length of her neck as shivers skittered down her arms. "You don't need to say anything." His breath ghosted over her jaw. "Just kiss me. That's all I need, Davis. Just kiss me."

This time when her lips met his, the kiss was exactly the way she needed it to be. It was deep and slow and patient. The breeze caressed her cheeks while his hands slid up her back. Trees rustled in a soft whisper above them while his fingers curled around the nape of her neck. His tongue brushed over hers, and a cloud drifted in front of the sun, cooling the air between them.

When they pulled apart, they did it wordlessly, pressing their foreheads together, sharing the same breath. Until she said, "I've missed that."

He turned his head, just enough to roll his forehead tenderly over hers. "Me too."

"Can we do it again? Like, later?"

Pulling her in close, he nestled his face into the hollow of her neck and said, "Absolutely."

CHAPTER TWENTY-FOUR

KEV

Peeking into the brand-new computer lab Davis had surprised the men with a few days ago—the one she'd single-handedly set up after cleaning out the storage room without telling them, not even telling him—Kev leaned against the doorframe, crossed his ankles, and watched her.

Ever since their kiss, ever since he'd had her in his arms again, tasted her, felt the softness of her skin against his lips, the need to do it again had drummed inside him like a second heartbeat. He'd been so distracted by it on the trails yesterday he'd almost weed-whacked his big toe off. Making Madigan add a twelfth Little Timber house rule to the list: No Flip-flops On The Trails.

But watching her now as she talked to the guys after their class, listening intently while answering their questions, looking competent as hell, he had to bite his lip against the desire stirring in his post-shower sweats. He couldn't help it. She was always DEFCON levels of sexy, but hair-up, all-business, stern-but-helpful teacher Davis needed a whole new scale. This Davis made his mouth water. This Davis made him harder than the ruler he imagined her smacking against the chalkboard when someone misbehaved...

"'Sup, Kev?" Brayden said, his hair messy like he'd been running his hands through it for the last hour, his mechanical pencil sticking halfway out of his mouth until he pulled it out and said, "You already missed the class today, if you were thinking about joining us."

Stepping inside the room, Kev stifled a groan when Davis turned around, when she noticed him, when her cheeks went a little pink and the corners of her lips curled into a smile that looked shy but definitely wasn't.

"Thanks, Brayden." Kev's voice dropped an octave all by itself. "But I'm not here for class."

Ace rolled his eyes while quiet and reserved Noah, of all people, muttered, "Ugh, time to go."

"Come on, everyone," Stanley said, standing from his chair, stretching his back with a mighty bear-like groan. "Let's get out of Davis's hair."

But it was Brayden who caught his attention. Because he was staring at Kev with a strange sparkle in his eye, an even stranger smirk on his face as he leaned toward Davis to mutter something that sounded a lot like "Remember, maybe it's just true or false."

After Davis huffed a laugh, nudged Brayden's shoulder with hers, and then gave Ace some parting remarks about variables and quadratic equations—a thing that turned Kev on so thoroughly he wondered if he had a secret teacher kink—she leaned back against one of the desks, taking her turn to watch him. While the men walked past him through the door, Kev got an encouraging thumbs-up from Brayden, a firm pat on the shoulder from Stanley, a tight nod from Noah. And then Ace pretended to smack him in the dick, making him leap back out of the way.

But eventually, *finally*, they were alone.

"Hi," he said in the sudden silence surrounding them.

"Hi," she said back, still leaning against that desk, her fingers curled over the sides.

The sight of her did something to him—her coy smile, her snug yellow shirt, her tanned, muscled thighs filling out her cutoff jean shorts. The way she sucked her lower lip into her mouth, then let it slide back out. The way she stared at him under her lashes, running a fingertip along her collarbone. And when she tilted her head, he recognized the moment for what it was. This sudden aloneness. This charged silence. This tension strung so tightly between them it hummed. *This* was a scene from a romance novel.

So he asked himself, what would Smithson Kane do right now? Alone with Daphne at last? How would they fill the next few pages? Kev could see it. Smithson would reach behind him, pull the door closed, and turn the lock without ever breaking eye contact.

Which, slowly, Kev did.

Tightening her grip on the desk, Davis asked, "Why did you lock the door?"

He prowled toward her, one slow step at a time. "Did I?" he asked instead of answering. "Must be habit." He raised a brow. "Can't ever be too careful."

"Did you"—her throat bobbed through a swallow—"need help with something?"

Funnily enough, he actually did. He wanted to do some research about wild horse roundups, get some better insight into what River might have gone through. But for some reason that had a lot to do with her heaving chest, her pupils expanding as she continued to grip the desk, looking like she wanted to back away but having nowhere to go, he could only tell her, "I think I do."

"Kev," she whispered as he entered her space, as he noticed the little vessel in her throat bounding with every beat of her heart. "What are you doing?"

"Hmm," he murmured, leaning on the desk across from her, letting his gaze travel down her throat, over her breasts, her thighs, knees, all the way down to her perfect toes in her sandals. "Nothing."

"Nothing?" she repeated, and when she swallowed again, he pushed himself off the desk.

Stepping toward her, he leaned forward to place his hands next to hers. When she didn't tell him to back away or place a hand on his chest or do anything other than stare into his eyes, he angled his head, dipping to run the tip of his nose along the length of her neck. Entirely aware that he was being rash and wild and all the things he wasn't supposed to be, not caring one fucking lick, he muttered, "That's right," against her skin. "Nothing at all."

She raised her chin toward the ceiling, giving him full access to her throat. And as she slid her hands up his arms, widening her legs to let him nestle between them, she said, "It doesn't feel like nothing."

"It doesn't?" he asked, grasping her hips, lifting her onto the desk while she clutched at his shoulders. "What does it feel like?"

Sliding her hands up his neck to thread her fingers through his hair, she gently scratched his scalp in that way that made him purr. "It feels like everything," she said, hooking her heels behind him, grasping his face between her hands, drawing his lips to hers.

She was right. It was everything.

Kissing her again was timeless, thoughtless, formless everything. Timeless because he wanted it to last forever, eons, an eternity between her lips. Thoughtless because thought didn't belong here. Comprehension had no place in the vanishing sliver of space between their bodies. Formless because he was no longer confined to the boundaries of his body. He was everywhere at once, surrounding her, pulling her, pushing her, driving against her.

He slid his hand up her side, his erection pressing through his boxer briefs and flimsy sweats into the firm denim seam at the apex of her thighs. "Have I told you how incredible you are?" he asked between kisses. "How amazing this room is?" He gave her a gentle thrust. "How indescribably sexy you look today?" He did it again, letting his hand drift across her ribs until it covered the soft swell of her breast.

"No, you—*Oh*," she gasped when he grazed his thumb over her stiff nipple. When he realized from some distant shore of his mind that this situation might be getting a little out of hand.

"Well, you are," he said. "It is." He pinched her nipple through her shirt, nearly losing himself in his pants when she bucked against him. "And you really fucking do."

"Kev." This time she moaned it into his mouth, her hips rocking against him, meeting him thrust for thrust. "This, *oh god*. This is... I'm too—*Fuck*."

"Too much?" he asked, pulling back, removing his hand from her breast to brush her hair off her cheeks while she continued to move against him, chasing a release he could tell wasn't very far away. "Should I stop?"

"I don't know. Maybe." She closed her eyes when he thrust against her again. "No. Never mind. Don't stop."

Ghosting his lips over her ear, he said, "I'm so hard, Davis. From the moment I saw you in the doorway. With your hair up and your shorts clinging to your ass. With your confidence. Your fucking swagger. I'm so hard you're making me leak."

She shuddered in his arms, let loose a keening little whimper.

"What about you, baby?" he asked, kissing her jaw, grasping her hips again, rolling her over his rigid length. "Are you feeling it? Are you wet?"

"Come on, Kev," she whispered, dropping her forehead onto his neck. "You know I am."

"Oh, but I don't," he insisted, moving his hands from her hips to her thighs, her knees, spreading her legs wider. "Tell me, Miss Thompson. Teach me. Show me how I can find out."

Yep, definitely a teacher kink.

Curling her fingers around his neck, she pulled him into another kiss and grabbed his hand. She'd just started to guide him to the button of her cutoffs when someone knocked on the door.

"Honey?" The handle rattled, the sound like a slap to his face, a bucket of ice water dumped over his head. "Are you still in there?"

Davis froze, her eyes doubling in size when she hissed, "It's my fucking mother."

Hauling himself away from her, Kev shook his head, shaking off the effects of her hands, her lips, her body. As potent as any drug he'd ever used.

"I'm here," Davis called out, snapping her fingers, pointing at Kev to sit in the chair behind the computer. "Come on in."

Adjusting himself in his sweats, which didn't do much to hide his raging hard-on—something he gave Davis an almost bashful smile about when she mouthed an appreciative "wow" at him—he tucked himself behind the computer, grabbed the mouse, and started clicking at random shit.

"I can't," Ashley called through the door. "It's locked."

"Oh?" Davis said, innocent as spring rain while she collected her hair into a cleaner ponytail since he'd made a mess out of it. "That's... weird."

Kev snorted. They were so busted.

Getting herself in order, smoothing her soft yellow shirt back into place, Davis walked to the door, turned the lock, and pulled it open.

It took Ashley less than one second—a second in which she looked at Davis, and then at Kev, then back to Davis—for her to know *exactly* what had just happened.

"Hi, Ashley," he said, sinking down into his chair when she arched a brow at him.

Smiling tightly, knowingly, she said, "Kev. You're here late."

Davis cleared her throat. "I just wrapped up with the other guys. And then Kev came by, needing help with..."

"Horse research," he added helpfully when she stalled out.

"I see," Ashley said, propping a hand on her hip. "Learning anything interesting?"

"Um..." He ruffled his hair, his knee bouncing so hard it probably registered on the Richter scale. "Yes?"

Davis palmed her forehead. "Did you need something, Mom?"

"I just wanted to let you know that your grandma is getting started on dinner, if you were planning on helping out."

"I'll be there in a few." Taking Ashley by the shoulders, Davis physically turned her toward the door. "Thanks for the heads-up."

"Don't push me," Ashley said, half laughing. "I'm leaving. Bye, Kev!"

After making sure her mom was gone, Davis turned around. Then she walked back to him, leaving the door open behind her this time.

Sitting back in his chair, blowing out a heavy breath, he said, "That was close."

She made her way around the desk, sliding her fingertips along its surface, stopping just shy of where he sat, and said, "In more ways than one."

While her gaze raked over him, he rolled his lips together, his poor cock twitching back to life. "I know you need to go." He reached for her, hooking his fingers through her belt loops and tugging, not feeling even the slightest bit bad about it this time. "But just give me five minutes, Davis. No, three. I can finish you off in three."

With a pained laugh, she dropped her head until he rose to his feet, snaked a finger under her chin and brought it back up. Sliding his hand over her cheek, cupping her jaw, he said, "We probably shouldn't have done that, huh?"

She nodded, then sighed, then said, "We need to be more careful."

It was a statement with so many meanings. *We might get caught. We might be rushing things. We might be losing control. We might end up hurting each other again.*

"Yeah." He met her stare, making sure she knew that he felt the weight of her words, that each hidden meaning sank into him like rocks in a river. "You're right."

He wanted to talk to her about them, about what they were doing and what it meant. But everything felt so good, so right. He didn't want to risk saying the wrong thing, messing up, losing her again before she even left. Even though he wasn't sure he actually had her. Even though he was too scared to find out.

Reaching up to toy with one of his curls, she asked, "Did you really need to research horse stuff?"

"I did, believe it or not." Snatching her hand, he kissed her palm, then asked, "Can I hang out in here for a few minutes?"

"Sure. Just"—she laughed, because the irony was funny—"lock the door when you're done."

He sat back down, then gazed up at her, studying her freckled nose and bow-shaped lips, her electric blue eyes, already trying to remember, already preparing himself for when he wouldn't see her every day, maybe not for weeks at a time. "See you at dinner?"

She stepped closer, crowding between his open legs, and he felt the payback for his behavior coming when she leaned in, dropped her lips to his ear, and whispered, "Yes." The word sent shivers across his neck. Shivers that shot straight south when she added, "But I have to change first. I think you might have ruined my underwear. They're absolutely soaked."

And before he could even begin to release the groan building up in his chest, she backed away, turned on her heel, and left him alone with that mental image invading his thoughts, her kisses still sweet on his tongue and an almost painful erection tenting his sweats.

CHAPTER TWENTY-FIVE

KEV

Tex sat on Kev's couch, his jaw practically resting on his knees when he asked, "You kissed her? In the lodge?" He adjusted his hat. "And Ashley almost caught you?"

Kev nodded. He wouldn't tell the guys much more than that, but ever since their...encounter today, all through dinner, even after, while he helped with the dishes, while Davis worked right alongside him, her hands and wrists all wet and sudsy, Kev was out of sorts, giddy, high. It felt too much like the euphoria of using, the bliss of oblivion, and he figured he needed to check himself, talk it out, get some advice before he stopped using his head entirely. Because in his life, that was generally when bad things happened.

"What's the big deal, Tex?" Brayden asked, finally invited to the let's-help-Kev-through-yet-another-crisis party. Without looking up from the Swiss army knife he was using to clean under his painted-blue nails, he said, "You kissed Shannon."

"Wait, what?" Kev blurted out. "When did you kiss Shannon?"

"And then Clay kissed Maude Alice," Brayden went on, like all of this was normal.

"What?" Kev practically shouted.

CHAPTER TWENTY-FIVE

"It's worse than damn summer camp around here," Stanley said, giving his head a shake.

"Oh, please," Brayden said with a dramatic eye roll. "You're no innocent. I've seen the way you've been checking out the UPS guy who comes to the lodge."

"That's different," Stanley said, his face turning redder than a fire hydrant. "That's just appreciation. I appreciate great calves."

While everyone muttered their agreement—because the UPS guy definitely had some killer calves—Kev stared at Tex and repeated, "When did you kiss Shannon? Is it serious?"

Ignoring his questions, Tex said, "The big deal, Brayden, is that Kev and Davis haven't talked their shit through enough yet to be kissing."

This knocked the wind out of Kev's sails. He knew without question what his heart wanted, but that didn't mean his head wasn't spinning. The thing was, he didn't want to make the same mistakes he'd made last time. And he figured a real important part of that process was figuring out what those mistakes actually were—which was something he still hadn't been able to do.

"We've talked through some stuff," Kev said, unconvincing even to himself.

"Sure," Brayden said, the word dripping in sarcasm.

"You can lie to yourself," Stanley chimed in. "But you can't lie to us."

When Ace suggested, "I think you need to talk to Boss about it," Kev choked on nothing.

"I agree," Tex said.

"Hard no," Kev insisted, still coughing. "I'm not talking to Madigan about kissing his stepdaughter."

"Oh, man. That's right," Ace said, like he'd just realized the complexity of their entire relationship. "What a tangle, huh?"

Tex clicked his tongue. "Kev, I hate to break this to you. But if you really want something serious with Davis, something real, as long as you're living here"—he pointed to the floor beneath his shoes—

"Madigan is going to need to know about it. The rules are the rules. Believe me," he said, heaving out an *I kissed the head of maintenance —who is also kind of my boss* sigh, "I should know."

River could have kicked him in the chest, and it would have been less of a blow.

"Kev?" Stanley asked. "You okay?"

Ace grimaced. "Are you gonna pass out or something? You're real pale right now."

"I'm fine," Kev said, rubbing his sternum, not actually fine in any sense of the word. It wasn't that he wasn't aware of his reality. It wasn't like he didn't know that Madigan would eventually need to be involved in his relationship with Davis. It was just that coasting along in complete denial was so much easier.

"Come on." Stanley pushed up from the couch. "We'd better get out there."

Letting Ace help him up, Kev followed them out to the firepit for group. While they waited for the other men and Madigan to arrive, he picked up a stick and started drawing shapes into the dirt: clouds, a horse's head, a heart pierced by an arrow...

"You good?" Ace asked him. "You still kind of look like you're going to faint."

"Who's going to faint?" Madigan asked, finally arriving to take a seat on his log.

Nobody answered, and Kev felt the weight of ten sets of eyes staring at him, until Tex said, "Uh, I am," with a nervy laugh. "But... not really."

"Okay," Madigan said slowly. "What does 'not really' mean?"

Pulling his hat off and holding it in his lap, Tex said, "I've just been thinking about something lately. It's stressing me out."

"This is what group is for." Madigan's legs spread wide as he leaned forward to rest his elbows on his knees. "Let's talk about it."

Tex cleared his throat. "Well," he said, "I've got this friend," and Kev almost barked a laugh. Was Tex seriously about to *fake scenario* their love lives in group? "And he's feeling a certain way about this woman."

Yep. This was happening. If the ground had picked that precise moment to crack open and swallow Kev whole, he wouldn't have minded.

After a long moment of tortured silence, Madigan said, "Go on."

Tex squeezed his hat between his hands. "My friend, he thinks she feels the same way about him. But...it's complicated."

"How so?" Madigan asked, obviously doubtful of the existence of this *friend,* but willing to play along.

"They live together, sort of," Tex explained. "And they work together. They have other roommates too." He flicked his gaze in the direction of the lodge. "And some very nosy neighbors. But they're not ready to have the entire world know that they're catching feelings for each other. So they have to hide it. They can't be out in the open. Like I said. It's stressful."

As Kev listened to Tex, watching him twist his hat within an inch of its life, he felt, at the very least, a little less alone. Even though it probably should have, it had never occurred to him that he might not be the only person feeling the pressures of their situation, of the rules they had to live by, the limitations on their freedoms at Little Timber. But, of course, he wasn't.

Every single man around the firepit had a story. Every single man had hardships. A lot of them had suffered abuse. All of them had made bad choices. They had more in common than they didn't, and Kev needed to stop insisting that he was so unique, so special in all the wrong ways. He needed to realize that he wasn't alone.

"That seems like a difficult way to start a relationship," Madigan said. "How is your *friend*"—he put special emphasis on the word because this wasn't his first rodeo—"feeling about it?"

Reaching up, Tex scratched his head. "He's willing to do whatever he needs to do to make her comfortable," he said. "But he also feels wrong about it, in a way. It's one thing to want privacy in a relationship. It's another thing to feel like he *has* to keep the relationship a secret. It feels too much like lying. And since it was his idea to move into this...particular house, he's feeling guilty about all the special accommodations she's having to make for him."

Madigan covered one hand with the other, pushing on his FEAR-tattooed knuckles until they popped. "That does sound stressful."

"It's also frustrating," Tex said.

"How so?" Madigan asked as all ten men leaned in a little closer.

Tex pursed his lips. "It's frustrating that it can't just be them, taking their time, figuring things out like normal people. Like any normal new relationship. They're both frustrated that so many other people need to be involved in what should be only between them. It feels unfair. It feels like a burden. And he feels like if he had more money or better luck or had made better choices, they wouldn't be in this position. But now they're stuck." His lips pulled to the side. "And he's worried he'll lose her because it's all too hard. Too complicated."

When Madigan asked, "What do you think would happen if they just told their roommates? What would happen if they told the people around them about their feelings, even if they were new and they were still figuring them out?" Kev was so focused, listening so intently, that a spark from the flames could have set his pants on fire and he wouldn't have noticed.

"Well, Boss. It's not just their roommates." Tex glanced down, finding something suddenly fascinating on his boots. "They also have this super strict landlord who gets real mad whenever anyone who lives in their apartment complex hooks up."

It took every ounce of self-control Kev possessed not to palm his forehead.

Madigan rolled his lips together, biting back a smile. "Nothing worse than a super strict landlord," he said, then he cleared his throat. "Okay. So they're frustrated that they don't have enough privacy. But they're also worried about the repercussions of being together. Which might include getting in trouble with their landlord. Do I have that right?"

CHAPTER TWENTY-FIVE

"Not only getting in trouble." Tex looked up. "But maybe even getting evicted."

Wood crackled, embers floated into the sky, and Kev's blood went cold. Because that was the fear. That was the risk. That was the fire he was playing with.

If he broke that particular rule, rule number five, the no overnight guests—which really meant no sex—without permission rule, especially here on his second chance and knowing he wouldn't get a third, it wouldn't be a bathroom duty situation. If he broke that rule, Madigan would kick him out. He'd have no other choice. Kev needed to be here. He wasn't ready to be on his own. At the same time, he knew he'd risk even more than getting kicked out to be with Davis. He'd risk everything. And he almost had.

His brows slid together, his attention shifting from this night to that one. The night everything had fallen apart. The night in her car. The night he'd wanted her so badly he would have packed his bags himself just to be with her.

Only, he hadn't.

He'd stopped himself. He'd said no. He'd blamed the rules, but that had just been an excuse. There was something else. Something that had kept him from taking that step with her. Something that had made him move away instead of closer. Some curtain that had fallen down between them. Something that had triggered him to use again. But what? What was it? Why couldn't he remember?

"Sometimes," Madigan said, then he corrected himself. "A *lot* of the time, our decisions, our choices, affect other people in ways we can't anticipate. They can affect people from our past, from our present. But they can also affect people who will show up in our future. People we haven't even met yet." His eyes slid toward Kev, who was still in full spiral. "Maybe people we're meeting all over again. Because our decisions, especially as addicts, have consequences. And the people we care about often have to share in those consequences with us. I know I've talked to all of you before about how difficult relationships can be for people recovering from substance abuse. Especially if you happen to live in a communal setting that makes intimacy challenging."

Kev's chin sank to his chest, his hope dimming, flickering, snuffing itself out. *Difficult. Challenging.* The words rattled through his head, churned in his stomach, because Davis didn't deserve difficult. She shouldn't have to deal with challenging.

With his magical ability to see into people's souls, Madigan looked directly at Kev and said without hesitation, with nothing but a solid, resolute understanding, "Difficult. Challenging. But not impossible." He scratched his beard, glancing around the firepit, at all the men one at a time. "And I hope you all know that the rules concerning intimacy at Little Timber are not meant to be punitive or to make your lives harder. They're not meant to stifle you or keep you alone. They're only meant to protect you. All of you. I believe Little Timber needs to be a safe, calm, and stable place for you to focus on your recovery. Privacy is so important here. Especially in a small town. I don't want any of you to have to worry about who your cabinmates might bring home. And I will not risk having someone from the outside bring drugs or alcohol here. That's why we have specific visiting days and curfews for guests. That's why overnight passes or intimacy visits need to be scheduled and approved. Does that make sense?"

"It makes sense," Tex said, sliding his hat back onto his head. "Doesn't mean it's not embarrassing as hell."

"Is it embarrassing?" Madigan asked, leaning so close to the flames they flickered in his eyes, turning crystal blue to deep orange. "Or is it something else? Is it shame?"

Something inside Kev's chest began to buzz.

"Because if you're still feeling ashamed of who you are," Madigan said. "If you're still ashamed of your substance abuse, of being here, of how you got here, of needing rules and structure and everything a sober living home provides, then you might have more work to do before you're ready for intimacy. Shame makes healthy relationships nearly impossible. It will become a wall between you and everyone else around you."

With a dull, resounding *clunk* Kev felt like a shove, a punch, a slap to the face, a puzzle piece clicked itself into place. Fears. Beliefs. Insecurities. Events leading to other events leading to choices he wished he'd never made. Clarity finally surfacing through endless miles of murky haze. And he knew. As suddenly as dreams ended, he knew why he'd pulled away from her. He knew why he'd said no to her. Why he'd left. Why he'd been so sure she'd be better off without him. Why he'd turned back to drugs. Finally, *finally*, he knew.

"Oh my god," he said, shooting to his feet.

"Kev?" Madigan stood from his log. "You okay?"

Meeting Madigan's stare across the fire, Kev shook his head, turned around, and started walking toward the trees. He had no idea where he was going, didn't even really know why he left the fire. He only knew he had to move, to get away, to try to breathe. But he couldn't. He couldn't breathe.

Hinging at his waist, he braced his hands on his knees when he heard footsteps at his back.

"Kev?" It was Madigan. His voice soft but deep. His warm hand settling on Kev's shoulder. "Are you okay? What's happening? Are you sick?"

Are you sick? The question was fair, since he was hunched over and gasping for air. But it was also ridiculous. Because he wasn't sick. Far from it. He finally had a shot at truly healing.

In a rush of air, his shoulders shook, his eyes burning, tears seeping from their corners.

"It's okay," he heard Madigan say, his hand dropping from Kev's shoulder to slide up and down his back. "Just let it all out. I've got you."

"I'm...not," Kev said between giddy, unstoppable, body-racking spasms, "crying." When he straightened, then turned around, laughter burst out of him, his watering eyes blurring Madigan's confused expression.

"You're...laughing?" Madigan's head cocked. "Is this some sort of a breakdown situation?"

Grabbing Madigan's shoulders and squeezing, Kev said, "No, Boss. It's some sort of a break*through* situation." He sniffled, his relieved smile stretching wide across his face. "Because I know. I know why I used. I know why I left."

With a tightly furrowed brow, Madigan said, "You do?"

Kev nodded. "I've had this feeling, like this weight hanging on me, dragging me down. I thought maybe it was fear. Or even guilt. But it wasn't. It isn't. It's"—even though he knew, it was still so hard to say it out loud, to admit it—"shame. It's all just stupid, selfish shame. I need to tell her." He turned, looking back toward the lodge. "I need to tell her everything."

As much as he trusted Davis, he'd never told her about his past. It wasn't that he didn't want her to know. He just wanted to believe that it didn't matter. That what had happened to him then didn't affect him now. He'd even tried to convince himself it had all happened to someone else. Some other kid. Some other life.

He thought he'd moved on, stopped hiding. But he hadn't. He just hid differently now. He hid behind easy laughter and setting-people-at-ease smiles. Behind silence and denial. But he wouldn't hide from Davis anymore. He wouldn't hide from himself.

"I need to go see her."

"Kev."

"No," he said, balking at the note of warning in Madigan's voice. "This isn't a joke. This is my life. I have to go see her."

Reaching out to grasp his shoulders, making him focus, making him meet his stern stare, Madigan said, "No, Kev. Not yet. You're right; this is a breakthrough. It's not a joke. It's huge. But you're worked up, and it's late. Come back to the fire. Come finish group. Come back, and let's make a plan. Let's do this right. Let's be steady." He tucked his chin, a small pause emphasizing his point. "Because she deserves your steadiness."

Letting Madigan's calm wash over him, letting his words sink in, letting the truth of them settle him down, Kev took a breath, nodded, and said, "Okay."

T*AP, tap, tap.*

This wasn't necessarily part of the plan he'd worked out with Madigan after group, but while he watched her through her bedroom window, biting his lip as she rolled over and kicked a leg out from under her covers before falling back to sleep, he tried not to be too hard on himself about the improvisation.

He tapped on her window again.

She raised her head and groaned. "Murphy? That you?" Sitting up in bed, her head turning from her door to the window when he tapped a third time, she finally noticed him through the glass. A slow, sleepy smile spread across her face. And if anything more beautiful existed in the world, he'd certainly never seen it.

"Hey," he said when she slid the window open. "Sorry to wake you."

She glanced at the alarm clock on her desk. "You're out past curfew. Is everything okay?"

"I know," he said. "I won't stay long. I just"—he blew out a slow breath, taking in her barely there white tank top, her pink underwear, her bare legs. "I've missed you."

"I've missed you too," she said, leaning her elbows on the window frame, reaching out to brush his hair back off his forehead.

"Can I kiss you?" He hadn't meant to ask her that. Hadn't meant to let this visit get physical. Despite this little late-night ad-lib, he did have a plan for making things right with her, for truly apologizing because he finally knew what he was apologizing for. A very solid plan that didn't involve kissing her through her window. But her eyes, the way they sparkled in the moonlight...

When she nodded, when their lips met, the kiss was slow and

sweet. And maybe even the best-laid plans were really just guidelines. Suggestions, at best.

After a length of time that was nowhere near long enough, they pulled apart, and he asked, "What are you doing tomorrow?"

"I'm riding in the morning, then helping mom with rental inventory after lunch."

Tucking that unruly curl of hers, his favorite one, behind her ear, he asked, "Do you want to come to the barn with me when you're done?"

Her eyes popped wide as her mouth fell open. "Really? Will I finally get to meet your other girlfriend?"

His heart skipped right over its next beat. "My *other* girlfriend?" he asked as warmth spread out beneath his ribs.

She blushed like a rose, color flaring through her cheeks. Then the motion sensor light from the deck flicked on.

"You should go," she whispered, staring at his lips, her tongue sneaking out to wet hers. "Don't want to get caught."

He wanted to kiss her again, kiss her all night long, kiss her lips and her neck and her belly, the soft, supple skin of her inner thighs... But the weight of everything he planned to tell her tomorrow kept him rooted. Would it be too much? Would he scare her off? Would he only make her leave him faster?

Feeling himself start to spin out, he heard Madigan say *she deserves your steadiness* in his mind.

Taking a breath, centering himself again, he took her hand, brought it to his lips, and said, "Some things are worth the risk."

CHAPTER TWENTY-SIX

KEV

It was one of those days that made him wish he'd been born more poetic. The sky was so blue it glowed like neon. So clear he could see every rocky ledge climbing up the mountains on either side of the road to the barn, every needle on every pine tree, every pointed aspen leaf quaking in the breeze. Every round freckle dotting Davis's nose.

"Beautiful day," he said, breaking the silence they'd been sharing.

She smiled at him, but it was a strange one—too small, almost sad. "It's gorgeous."

He wanted to say something romantic. Something about how she was more gorgeous than any sky could ever be, any cloud or mountain or leaf, but his nerves were already near their breaking point. So he only took her hand in his and squeezed.

Looking up at him, she gave him another smile—this one with a heart-stopping host of emotions behind it. He didn't know what to make of her smiles. Knew even less what to make of the deliberate way she watched him, like she was already trying to make this moment a memory. He couldn't shake the way it all felt like goodbye. And with how little time they had left, with how long he'd waited to have this conversation with her, he knew it could easily be just that. He might not have done enough, said enough, *been* enough. It might be too late.

It would make sense, considering the one constant in his short life was his almost cosmically bad timing. But even if he was too late, it didn't change anything. Even if he'd missed his chance with her. Even if the steps they'd taken back to one another weren't big enough to survive only seeing each other on weekends and holidays. Even if she left him next week and they slowly drifted apart. Today was still important. It was still necessary. Because she deserved it. She deserved the whole story. She deserved to know every part of him. She deserved the truth.

"Here we are," Kev said, pulling up to the barn and killing the engine.

Opening her door, Davis hopped out of the truck and looked around. "It's so pretty here." Kev's chest grew tight, because the smile she gave him now was the one he recognized. The one he wanted. The full-on Davis smile that had knocked him on his ass from the first day he'd met her. "I can see why you love it."

Through the loft in the main barn, Jen tossed a hay bale down to the ground and shouted, "Hey, Davis! Welcome to Strawberry Farms!"

"Hey, Jen!" Davis shouted back up. "Need help?"

Of course she would ask. Of course the first thing Davis would think about was helping someone else. Because that was just who she was. She worked the trails with the guys when she didn't have to. She helped her mom and grandma with Bluebird seven days a week, always saying yes when they asked her to do anything. She helped the guys in the computer lab because nobody else had the time. And now she was going back to school to help cure cancer or something. She would literally save lives. The same way she'd already saved his.

He wondered if she had any idea how much he respected her, how in awe of her he was. He also wondered if she knew how bonkers hot she looked today in her emerald leggings that stopped mid-calf and a black tank top that barely covered her ass. Her hair up in a loose bun except for the few curls that refused to be tamed, trailing down to caress the graceful curve of her neck.

"Nah, I'm good," Jen said, waving them off. "I think River's been waiting to see her boyfriend, anyway. She's been pacing the fence all day."

"See?" Davis said, so low only he could hear her. "I told you I was the other woman."

Shrugging, trying to play it cool, trying to ignore the way his heart rate accelerated, trying to keep himself together at least long enough to get through this, he said, "What can I say? Antisocial horses love me." While Davis gave him an easy laugh, he called up, "See you later, Jen."

"There's mints in the office," Jen shouted back as another hay bale fell to the ground.

After a string of sweltering days, it was a pleasantly cool afternoon as they walked down the road toward River's pasture. Clouds filled the sky, the breeze lifted his curls from his forehead, and Davis slid her hand into his.

Even though they'd kissed, touched, pushed every clothes-on boundary within a country mile, they hadn't really held hands since he'd come back. It felt important in a way, this bit of normalcy in a relationship that hadn't felt normal in a very long time. Because of what he'd done. Because of his choices. Because of what he was about to tell her.

"I'm nervous." Davis tucked one of those wild curls behind her ear. "What if she doesn't like me?"

"Ah, she'll love you," he said, then amended it with "I mean, despite what Jen says, I think she really only tolerates me. So maybe *love* is a little strong."

He felt her gaze settle on him, sensed the weight of her stare, but he kept his eyes on the road ahead. Considering the little he had of it was still mostly faked, his confidence wouldn't survive much shaking today. He had to keep his shit together. He had to get through this.

As if in solidarity, River whinnied from her pasture.

"Is that her?" Davis asked, shielding her eyes from the sun's bright glare.

"That's her," Kev said.

When River whinnied again, practically a holler, Davis laughed. "Does she always freak out like this when you show up?"

"It's not me." Digging into his pocket, he pulled out one of the mints he'd grabbed from Jen's office. "It's these. Here."

Davis took the mint, then she pointed her chin toward the mare galloping toward them, dust flying up from her hooves. "I don't know much about horses," she said, breaking into laughter when River whinnied again. "But I think it's more than just the mints."

"Hey, girl," Kev cooed when River slid to a stop at the fence. She leaned her head over the gate, sniffing his shirt, his pants, nudging him with her nose. "This is Davis. Davis," he said, tilting his head to urge her closer to the fence, "this is River."

"She's stunning," Davis said. Lowering her voice, making it sweet and soothing, she told River, "You are stunning."

While Kev's heart melted into a puddle, River's nostrils flared, her attention homing in on Davis when she realized which one of them held the mint.

Out of the side of her mouth, Davis asked, "How do I give this to her without getting my hand bitten off?"

"Here. I'll show you." Kev took Davis's hand and spread her fingers flat. Then he unwrapped the mint and placed it in the middle of her palm. "Just hold out your hand like this. She'll do the rest."

With her eyes locked on his, she asked, "She really won't bite me?"

He shook his head, a half smile tugging at his lips. "No. She won't bite you." River snorted, pawing at the ground. "But she might break through the fence if you don't give it to her soon."

Holding her breath, Davis closed her eyes, let out a tiny squeak, and extended her hand. Then she laughed when River snatched the mint in less than a second. While the mare crunched away, contented for the moment, Davis reached out carefully to run her fingers down the soft hair between River's eyes. "This was the horse who wouldn't let anyone near her before she met you? The same horse? You're not messing with me?"

"It's not like it was me specifically who turned her around," Kev said, his cheeks heating under the spotlight she'd put on him. The spotlight he always tried to stay out of, even though it meant diminishing everything good he'd ever done in his life. "Nobody else was able to give her the time she needed."

"You think so?" Davis asked while River dropped her head into Kev's arms, pushing her nose against his belly while he scratched the spot under her chin that always made her lower lip droop.

Leaning into the warmth of the mare, letting her support him for the brief moment she allowed it, he asked, "Do you remember when I told you how she ended up here?" Because it was time. It was time to stand in the spotlight. Now or never.

"She was wild, right?" Davis said. "In Wyoming or something?"

Kev handed Davis another mint, and while River left his arms to nudge Davis's shoulder until she got the mint unwrapped and fed it to her, he said, "Yeah. She lived in a herd. She probably had a big family. She might have even had children of her own. And then one day, humans came along and snatched her up, separated her from her family, took her from her home. Most likely ran her within an inch of her life."

"That's awful," Davis said, running her palm carefully down River's nose. "Is that what you were researching the other day? The 'horse stuff'?"

Kev nodded, his fingers curling inward when he remembered some of the stories he'd read.

Davis said to River, "Poor thing. You must have been so scared."

The sky was changing, the vibrant blue dome above them fading at the edges as the sun moved west toward the trees, lining the clouds in thin silver rings. "When I first saw her, I think I saw myself. She was like a mirror," he said softly. Then he cleared his throat, letting himself take up space, letting himself be heard, be seen.

If what he told Davis made her not want him anymore, it would hurt like hell. But it would be okay. He would survive it. Because he had survived a lot in his life. He was stronger than he gave himself credit for.

"I looked at her that first day," he continued, "hiding out in her pasture, trying to keep herself safe from a danger that didn't really exist anymore. And I thought *I do that too*. I mean, I do it differently, I guess. I'm not holing up in my cabin or anything. But I don't really let people in. I smile and I laugh and I crack jokes, but I don't really trust anyone. I don't trust people to see me for who I really am."

Davis took a step toward him. Just a small step, but he felt it. He felt her listening. He felt her attention on him, warming him, like sitting closer to the firepit on a cold night. Knowing this might be his last chance to stand in her warmth didn't make the sensation any less comforting.

"I think we do it, keep our guards up, protect ourselves, because we're scared," he said. "She's scared of losing everything again. She's scared of getting comfortable here and then having someone come out of nowhere and run her out of her home, shove her into a pen, into a trailer, take her somewhere she doesn't want to go."

Turning to look at him while River, realizing the mints had stopped appearing, walked off to drop her nose into a patch of green grass a few feet away, Davis said, "You said *we*. *We're scared*. What are you scared of, Kev?"

His teeth sank hard into his cheek. It wasn't something he'd done on purpose, just a reflex. Just his brain attempting to distract the rest of him from the words slicing like broken glass in his chest. As sharply as the words cut him up inside, he knew it would hurt even worse when he pushed them out. But then they'd be gone. Then he could heal.

"I know I've told you some things about my past," he said while River grazed calmly in the shade of a puffy white cloud. "But there's more. A lot more. And it's not that I haven't trusted you with knowing about my life," he told her, in case she'd been wondering. In case she'd been worried. "It's just, sometimes it feels like *I* don't even want to hear it. Like I don't want to admit that it actually happened to me. Like I really thought I could just process all of it myself, and then I could move on. Be done with it. Never have to talk about it again."

"That makes so much sense," she said softly. "You don't have to tell me anything you don't want to. You know that, right?"

"I know." His chin tried to drop to his chest, but he held it up. "The thing is, I want to tell you this. I need to. Because it did happen." He let his gaze travel over her face, over the earnest concern in her eyes, the tight set of her jaw. "And as much as I hate to admit it. As much as I wish I could just put it all behind me and leave it there, it's affecting me now. It shaped who I am. It's the weight on my shoulders. It's the voice in my head. But because I didn't realize it, because I've been refusing to accept it, because I've been in denial, I've allowed it to affect you too. I've let it hurt you too. And I will not let that happen again," he said with a sudden severity. "Never again."

"Okay," she said, stepping even closer, not scared away by his intensity but leaning into it. "Okay. I'm here. I'm listening."

She's here. She's listening. You can trust her.

"My mom was an addict too," he said, that memory shard cutting so deeply he had to look away, dig his palm into his chest to soothe the pain. Because he never talked about his mom. Barely even let himself think about her. Almost never looked at the one picture he had left of her, standing in their backyard garden when they'd had one, wearing faded denim overalls, a floppy hat, the kind smile he'd grown up wishing he could see again but knowing he never would. "But from what I remember, she was a good mom. She loved me. The drugs took her when I was five, leaving me alone with my dad."

River's long white tail swished gently from side to side in the breeze, the motion lulling him like a metronome. "He started drinking after she died. Couldn't cope without her. Left alone with this kid. And he was a mean drunk too. Hit me a lot. I learned pretty quickly to be quiet. I learned that being invisible meant I didn't get hurt. I didn't really talk in my house, barely came out of my room, never left the few toys I had lying around in case he accidentally stepped on one of my matchbox cars. Which happened once. I'll spare you the details."

Out of the corner of his eye, he saw Davis's hand curl around the fence rail and squeeze.

"Turned out, I was really good at being invisible." He laughed, even though what he was about to say was miles away from funny. "Because, eventually, he forgot I was even there. He started leaving. He'd leave for days at a time, sometimes up to a week. And then, when I was twelve, he was just...gone.

"At first, I tried to pretend like everything was normal. Like even though he'd been gone for almost a month and hadn't called once, that he'd still be coming back. So I kept going to school, walking four miles there and back every day. I ate whatever food we had in the house until all that was left was canned peaches. I lied to all my teachers, my friends. I told anyone who asked about him that my dad wasn't feeling good and that's why nobody had seen him around town. I thought it was working too, until one day, on my way to school, a couple of my friends stopped me outside the football field. They told me that Child Protective Services was inside looking for me."

River raised her head, meeting his gaze with something almost encouraging in her sweet brown eyes. It was about to get harder, but he had to keep going. He couldn't stop. Couldn't even slow down.

"I guess I'd worn the same clothes too many days in a row or something," he said, embarrassment trickling down his spine. "That's what had finally tipped my teachers off. So I turned around. Went home. I stopped going to school. I hid from CPS for as long as I could.

I never answered my door, never left the house. I hid, stayed quiet, kept the lights off, pretended nobody was home. Because I knew what happened to kids who didn't have parents. I knew they went into the foster system. And I wasn't one of those kids. I had a dad. I had a dad, and of course he was going to come back for me. I mean, who just abandons their kid? Who just leaves a twelve-year-old to fend for themselves? My dad was an asshole, but even he wasn't that cold. He just got lost or his car broke down. Maybe he hit his head and was in a coma in a hospital somewhere, fighting to wake up. I made up all sorts of stories. But I knew he was coming back for me. I knew he'd show up before the canned peaches ran out."

"Kev," Davis said, her voice thick and wobbly. He didn't have to look to know that she was crying. And that was okay. This was a sad story.

"Only, he didn't," Kev said, letting some of his anger loose so it could ride over his pain. "He never came back. The food ran out. And, *Christ*." His stomach roiled. "I still fucking hate peaches."

While River sliced her tail through the air, Davis pressed her forehead into his arm.

"I think it was the third day without food when the cops showed up with CPS. I was hungry and tired and really scared by that point, so I caved. I let them in, but I refused to say a single word to them. Except for maybe 'fuck you.' Until two older people walked in behind them. They were both crying, both looking around the house I'd been hiding out in by myself with these horrified expressions. I had no idea who they were. But then my grandmother knelt in front of me and introduced herself. That's when I saw the resemblance. She had my mom's eyes. My mom's kind smile. That's when I finally lost it."

Davis pressed her lips into his biceps. A small kiss. Just to tell him *I'm here. I'm not going anywhere.* When she turned her cheek, he felt the dampness of her tears through his shirtsleeve.

"My grandparents had known about me, but my mom—probably

because my dad had made her—had gone no-contact with them before I was born. They told me they wanted me to come and live with them on their ranch. I refused at first, still convinced my dad would come home. But they told me he was in jail in Florida. They told me they'd gotten custody. I had no choice. It was done. And, *god*, I hated them for it. I tried to run away at least five times." He laughed at himself. "It's amazing how much anger a kid can hold on to. And I was burning with it. I didn't trust anyone, especially not these two happy people who were always nice to me and never yelled at me and got me clean clothes and made me good food I barely ate any of. It took me six months before I even unpacked my bag."

Davis slid her hand up his arm, curling her fingers to press it close to her body.

"It was the horses who finally turned me around. My grandpa took me out every day after school and every weekend, teaching me how to feed them, how to check their pastures for holes, mend their broken fences, build new ones. My grandmother taught me how to groom them and tack them up. She taught me how to ride, how to move cattle, how to tend to a herd. The more time I spent with the horses, the more time I spent helping my grandparents, the more I felt like I was a part of something. Like I was important instead of an inconvenience. Like I was wanted. Like I was in a family."

She gave him a tight squeeze, interlacing the fingers of her other hand through his, wrapping his entire right arm in her warmth.

"My father never came to get me, even though he was released from prison about a year later. By that point, I never wanted to see him again anyway. I was safe. I felt loved for the first time since my mom died. I felt like I had a home. And I was getting really good at riding. I'd imagined this whole cowboy life for myself. Out in the open. Free and happy." His throat spasmed, forcing him to take a dry, painful swallow. "But my grandparents were getting older. And when I was fifteen, my grandmother cut herself on one of the fences. It got infected. She went septic, and then she was gone. It all happened so quickly it felt like a dream. Like it couldn't possibly have been real. I guess it was too much for my grandpa. Three months after she died, he had a heart attack out in the back pasture."

Davis's strangled sob was a perfect echo of the sob he'd let loose that day. The one he held trapped inside his chest now.

"I was put in foster care after that. I never rode a horse again." He could smile at this part, at least. "Not until I came here, anyway. My foster parents weren't bad, all things considered. But I think I'd just lost too much by that point. I got in trouble a lot, spent some time in juvie, fell in with the wrong crowd, moved in with Thom and Trish. I started using. And, well, you know the rest."

She pulled her forehead away from his shoulder, but only so she could look up at him.

"All that stuff, my past, it's part of me. It lives inside me." Pointing his chin at River, he said, "Just like her past lives inside her. We both have these scars nobody else can see. I try not to think about mine. But they're here." He tapped on his chest. "Right here, all the time. These wounds that make me feel like I'm never good enough. Like I'm still that kid hiding alone in my house waiting for someone to come back, even when I know they never will. Like I'm still so terrified of getting close to someone, so terrified they'll just leave me, that I find a way to make sure I leave them first."

He wanted to look down at her. He wanted to see her face, to dry her tears, to pull her into his arms and hold her while he told her this next part. But he couldn't move. He could barely breathe. There was too much at stake.

"Do you remember that night?" he asked, not giving his resolve a chance to waver. "In your car? The night we almost—"

"I remember." She said it quietly, but fast enough to cut him off. And there was something in her voice he couldn't decipher. Something cold and stiff.

Hoping the something in her voice wasn't regret, he said, "All through rehab, through all my group sessions, all my appointments with Rick, even when it was happening, I had no idea why I'd relapsed. As hard as I tried, I couldn't figure it out. I couldn't remember. Everything was so good with you, with this place. My life was amazing, and then...it wasn't. It scared the shit out of me, Davis. Because I kept thinking that if I never figured out why I'd failed, how could I keep it from happening again? So I've kept trying. I've kept searching, going over those weeks before I left in my mind. Trying to find a reason. Trying to find a single clue to explain how everything had gone so wrong so quickly. And then Madigan started talking about shame last night, and it hit me. Seriously," he said, pounding his fist into his chest. "Like a brick. It was that night in your car. That was when it all started."

She didn't let go of his arm, but he felt her grip loosen, felt the tremble in her fingers.

"That night, I'd wanted to be with you more than I'd ever wanted anything in my life. I didn't care about anything else. I didn't care about taking my next breath. Or at least I thought I didn't. But when things got heated, when you reached for me, when you reached for my jeans, the voice in my head reminded me they were the only pair I owned. When you slid your hands under the shirt I'd been wearing, the voice reminded me that it wasn't even mine, that it was a Little Timber shirt. That a bunch of men had worn it before me and a bunch more would probably wear it after. And I felt it then. Shame. So much fucking shame. I was drowning in it. I had this beautiful, perfect woman in my arms, and I didn't deserve her. I was a man without money. Without a real job. Without a high school education. A man with a record. A man with a past that would haunt him forever. A man whose dad didn't even care enough about him to stick around. A man with no family, no home, nothing. A man who would only bring her down. And that was it. That was the moment. Something inside me just broke. That was when all my scars opened back up."

The breeze died down. Even River stopped chewing, adding to the sudden, profound silence of the moment.

"I knew you loved me," he said softly, because anything louder would have felt like shouting. "I knew you'd told me you didn't care that I was poor or uneducated or had nothing to offer you. But I didn't believe you. I couldn't. Because I didn't believe it myself. The only thing I knew for sure was that you'd find someone much better than me if I wasn't around anymore. So I said we had to stop. I blamed it on the rules. And I was going to end it. The next day, I promised myself I'd let you go. But I even fucked that up because I couldn't. I was too weak. I loved you too much. So I stayed with you, but only halfway. Like a ghost. I knew I was hurting you. I knew it. I could *feel* it," he said, more glass scraping out of him. "And I still couldn't walk away."

He paused, waiting for the sharp pain to pass. Then he said, "I made a lot of mistakes, Davis. But the biggest mistake I ever made was when I started struggling, instead of telling you about it, or even telling Madigan or the guys about it, I just did what I did best. I hid. I hid behind the same shame and fear I'd hid behind since my mom died and my dad left. I locked myself up in that house again, refusing to answer the door, refusing to accept help. I didn't realize it then, but I was as good as gone the second I made that choice."

He filled his lungs with as much air as they'd take in, and then he let it all out. "I wish I'd seen it sooner. I wish I'd recognized what was happening inside me. It still scares me that I didn't, and I hate that I hurt you. But Madigan told me that each one of his relapses taught him something about his addiction. That each slip made him understand himself better. So I'm trying really hard to learn from this one. I'm trying to understand. I'm trying not to be ashamed."

Through some miracle, he'd kept himself together through all of this. But he was crumbling now, breaking apart, every one of the flood gates he'd built around his heart failing at once. "Because how can I be ashamed of my past?" he asked, fighting to keep his voice steady, blinking through the mist clouding his vision. "How can I be ashamed of my parents? My one pair of jeans and my borrowed shirts? My drug use? Even my relapse? When those are all things that brought you into my life. If someone came along right now and gave me the chance to start over, to have all the things I grew up without, to have a happy, normal childhood, I wouldn't take it. I wouldn't fucking take it. I'd go through my same life again, over and over a thousand times. As long as it meant I got to meet you at the end."

Her hands were on his shoulders, his face, turning him, making him look at her.

"I used to think that only the bad things in our lives left scars," he said while she tried to dry his tears, while hers flowed in rivers down her cheeks. "But I don't believe that anymore. I think good things can leave scars too." Taking her hand in his, he kissed her palm, then placed it flat over his heart. "I have permanent marks here. Some are from terrible things. But not all of them. Because some of them are from you. Marks you've given me. Little Davis lines traveling over all my old scars, reminding me that I have felt love. That I have *been* loved. That even the worst kinds of pain can lead to something beautiful."

He covered her hand with his and pressed down. "I won't stop trying to figure myself out. I won't hide anymore. And I know you're leaving soon. I know it's the thing we don't talk about. I hope you don't think that I haven't brought it up because I don't care. Because I do. I care so much. I only want you to be happy. But I've been too much of a coward to tell you how I feel. I've been too scared to ask if you'll let me wait for you while you're gone. If you want us to be together even though you aren't here. But I need you to know that I want to. I'm ready to. I need you to know that I'll wait for you for as long as you need. Even if I'm waiting forever. Because you're it for me. You're everything. Because I love you, Davis. I love you so fucking much."

Silently weeping, she stepped into him, wrapped her arms around his waist, and pressed her tear-soaked cheek against his chest. "I love you too, Kev," she said through her tears, cracking him open, splitting him right down the middle. "I love your one pair of jeans and your borrowed shirts. I love the man your life has shaped you into. I love your mistakes. I love how hard you're working not to make the same ones again. I love your scars. I love the marks I've made on your heart. I love the marks you've left on mine."

Just when he thought he couldn't take another word without falling to his knees before her, she made the world stop turning, made everything inside him grind to a ground-trembling halt when she said, "And I love that you'd be willing to wait for me. But you don't have to. Because I'm not leaving."

CHAPTER TWENTY-SEVEN

DAVIS

"What?" His body went rigid in her arms. "What did you just say?"

When he tried to pull away, she squeezed him more tightly, holding him still. "Wait," she said, closing her eyes, slowing her breathing, doing everything she could to stop crying. "Please. I need to get a few things out too."

Softening, sliding one hand along her low back, the other around her neck to cup her head, holding her closer, so close she felt his heart beating inside his chest, he said, "Okay."

Pulling herself together was next to impossible. His story, his life, the last twenty minutes of his unrelenting honesty, had cored her out so deeply that she knew some part of her would remain hollow and aching if she didn't do this right. So even though it was impossible, she had to try. She had to stop crying, stop hurting for him. For them. At least long enough to say what she needed to say.

"Thank you for trusting me with your story," she said, wishing more than anything that she could go back in time and find him in his house, surround him with her arms like she was now, make him feel safe again, let him know he was loved. "I know it probably won't help, but I am so sorry all of that happened to you. None of it was your fault. You were just a kid. You were just doing what you had to do to survive."

His cheek dropped to rest gently on her head.

"Thank you for telling me about that night too. The night in my car." Shame tried to dig its sharp claws into her, but she pushed it back. That was the point, wasn't it? To no longer be embarrassed? No longer be ashamed? If he could do it, she could do it too. "I think I knew that was the night everything fell apart too. I felt it. Only, I thought it was me. This whole time, I thought it was all my fault."

"Why?" he asked, incredulous. "Why would it have been your fault?"

"Because of what I said to you. Because of how selfish I'd been."

"You weren't selfish. You didn't say anything wrong." He pressed his lips into her hair, the sweetness of it giving her the courage to pull away, to raise her chin, to look at him.

"I did, though," she said, while he cupped her face, drying her tears with soft swipes of his thumbs. "I wanted to be with you too. I wanted you so badly I could barely see straight. And when you said no to me, when you pushed me off your lap, it felt like rejection. Like you didn't want me. I was so embarrassed. I was hurt and confused and so frustrated about the entire situation that I lashed out. When I got out of the car and slammed the door on you, when I shouted at you to fuck the rules, I was ashamed too, Kev. I was so ashamed of myself. I'm still ashamed. Because I didn't support you. I put my own selfish needs over your recovery. I got pissed at you because you were trying to do the right thing. Who does that?"

"Davis." A hint of a smile curled his lips. "When did you ever tell me to fuck the rules?"

Pulling up short, she said, "What do you mean? I said it that night. I shouted it."

His huffed laughter brushed across her cheeks. "You must have only thought it. Because I think I would have remembered if you'd told me that. All I remember is I said no. You said okay. You walked back to the lodge while I walked back to my cabin. And that was that."

"No." She shook her head. "That's not how it happened." Shock was, quite frankly, not a strong enough word for her current emotional state. "You said we had to stop. I got pissed. I flew out of the car, slammed the door, told you to fuck your rules. And then I ran away like a spoiled child. Nothing was the same between us after that."

Snaking an arm around her waist, urging her close again, he said, "Total coincidence." He was trying to calm her, absolve her. After all he'd just told her, he was still more worried about her than himself. "If you did tell me to fuck the rules, either I was too messed up to hear it, or you said it while the car door was closing. Either way, I can guarantee you, one hundred percent, that my relapse had nothing to do with you or your actions that night. It was all me. Now can we please get back to the part where you said you're not leaving? Because I am freaking the fuck out."

Just then, River nickered. Davis had never heard a horse laugh before, but that's definitely what it was.

While it was true that he'd just shifted her entire worldview on its axis, tipped it on its head, punted it off a cliff, she didn't want him to freak the fuck out. So she rose up onto her toes, her lips a breath away from his, and repeated, "I'm not leaving."

"Davis." It was a plea. A prayer against her lips. So she answered it, kissing him as sweetly as she could.

Pulling away, she explained, "No matter how hard I tried over the last month, I couldn't make a single decision about school, about my future. I've had this feeling, these thoughts pulling me in a different direction for a while. And then I started getting more involved with the men, helping them with their education, with *their* futures, and it felt so good. Being helpful felt good to me. And then you and I made up. We started talking. We started...more than talking. And even though I was already leaning away from going back to the U, and even when I started leaning toward you, I knew I had to find something for me. A reason to stay beyond just us, beyond my mom and grandma, beyond Bluebird. I had to find my own path."

While he watched her, still listening, still waiting, she asked, "Do you remember when you got back from rehab, and I told you that you couldn't fix us?" He nodded, and she said, "I told you that because I believed it. I believed we were so broken that we couldn't possibly find our way back to each other. But I've been here, watching you piece your life back together, watching the men support you, watching Madigan and Jen support you. And I realized that I was wrong. I realized that maybe, with enough time and support and love, nothing is ever so broken it can't be fixed. Because you've pieced my life back together too. You've pieced *us* back together. And maybe I can do the same thing for others. Maybe I can help other people piece their lives back together after they've been broken."

"You'd be really good at that." Brushing his knuckles over her cheek, he said, "You put me back together every time I see you."

Her eyes stung, fresh tears rising to cloud her vision, fresh Kev lines meandering across her heart. "I met with Madigan the other day," she said. "And I asked him to talk me through some things, help point me in the right direction. And then yesterday, after we"—she cleared her throat, the sense memory of his lips on her skin and his fingers closing around her hips threatening to derail her train of thought—"after...*talking* to you in the computer lab, I knew the path I was on was the right one. The path where I got to help people, but I also got to be with you. Because I'd spent so many nights while you were gone wishing you were here, and I don't want to do that again. I don't want either of us to spend one more second wishing we were together. So as soon as I got back to my room, I emailed my professor. I told him that I appreciated his offer, but that I was interested in something else now. I told him I'd applied to several online programs to get my master's in social work—which I spent all night doing before you knocked on my window. I told him I was staying where I belonged. Because I am. Right here is where I belong." She placed her hand over his heart, feeling it beat a steady, solid rhythm under her fingers, a rhythm that would count out their days, their years, their lifetime together. "With you is where I belong."

He looked down at her with tears shining in his eyes. With pure love shining in them too. "You're really staying?"

Smiling up at him, she said, "It wasn't a mistake when I said that River was your other girlfriend."

He made a sound that was half sob, half laugh, and when she reached up to cup his cheek, she asked, "How could I leave you, Kev? Your face is all I want to see when I wake up. Your voice is all I want to hear before I go to bed. You're it for me too. The only man I'll ever love. Because I love you. I love you. I am so in love with you. And I'm yours, completely. If you still want me, I'm yours."

He didn't answer her with words, only by pulling her close, lowering his lips to hers, and kissing her so deeply their tears mingled on her tongue. So passionately her body turned liquid in his arms. And for so long even the horse looked away.

It was dark by the time they got back to Bluebird, even darker with the steam building up on the truck's windows. She was in his lap, his seat reclined, his hands on her ass while he kissed her and she kissed him back. Through her thin leggings, she felt everything. Every hard inch of him sliding against her, every firm press of his fingers. They'd parked at the far end of the lot, under the trees, far from the lights. Far from the world.

"You're so fucking beautiful," he said against her neck, rocking her over his erection, driving her to the edge so fast her breath stuttered and her toes tingled. "So perfect."

"So are you," she whispered in his ear before sucking his lobe into her mouth, making him groan.

Slowly, his hand moved lower, his fingers sliding between her cheeks, under her. Until he found the need throbbing between her legs.

"*Fuck*, baby," he said, practically grunting it while sparks exploded behind her eyes. He pressed on her clit, circled once, making her bite her lip, bite back a moan. But it was when he paused and asked, "Is this okay?" that shit got real.

Was this okay? Was this how she wanted things to go? Some stolen, sweaty moments in the parking lot like high school? Like last time? But this wasn't high school. This wasn't last time. This was now. This was real life with real-life consequences. This was a rule break. If they got caught, he could get kicked out of Little Timber. If they got caught, he could lose his home. And he'd already lost enough.

While she'd been thinking, he'd been circling. Slow. So mind-meltingly slow. Her thoughts blanked, sensation pulling her down, dragging her under. But she fought back, kicking hard to the surface.

"Stop," she gasped when he pressed down on her again. "We gotta stop."

"We do?" His breath was hot against her skin, his tongue even hotter as he licked a searing trail up her neck.

"Yes," she said. "The rules."

"Fuck the rules."

She barked a laugh.

Pulling his fingers away from her—but not before giving her one final, torturously slow swirl that made her eyes roll back in her head—he said, "But I don't want to leave you like this. That would be twice I've left you so close."

Still rocking against him, still chasing the climax she was intent on denying herself, she said, "I know. But we have to. I love you, Kev. I want to be with you. For real. Out loud. And I don't care who knows it."

Meeting her gaze, the hunger in his nearly making her change her mind, he said, "You know what that means, right?"

"Yes," she said as resolutely as she could. "Tomorrow morning, I'll tell Madigan that we need to talk to him. We'll set it up. We'll follow the rules. We'll do this right."

"Are you sure?" That telltale crease sank between his brows. And now that she knew the life that had worn that groove into his skin, all she wanted to do was smooth it away. "I don't want you to be uncomfortable just so we can be together," he said. "I can wait until I'm ready to leave Little Timber. Until we can be intimate without having to get permission."

Leaning forward to kiss his forehead, right over his crease, feeling it melt under her lips, she said, "Maybe *you* can." Then, to prove her point, she took his hand and placed it over her breast, over the hard tip of her nipple that could probably cut glass. "But I can't. Besides, literally nothing could make me more uncomfortable than I am right now. Telling Madigan I want to be with you will be a walk in the park compared to—*oh my god*," she gasped when he pinched her nipple through her tank top, rolling it between his thumb and finger.

"Good point," he said darkly. "There is no way in hell I'll be getting any sleep tonight."

"Same. But, *fuck*, if you keep touching me like that, we'll never leave this truck." She pushed his hand away before sliding hers over his shoulders. "We can wait, right? We can be good?"

His gaze was still pinned on her breast, his tongue darting out to wet his lips. And if he leaned forward, if he pressed his open mouth over her and sucked her nipple through her shirt, it would be game over. Luckily, while hers was frayed beyond recognition, his restraint was still intact.

"I can wait," he said unconvincingly. "Just...not for very long."

CHAPTER TWENTY-EIGHT

KEV

STANDING NEXT to Davis outside Ashley and Madigan's office, ready to knock, ready to be seen for their appointment—their *we would like to have sex* appointment—Kev could have crawled right out of his skin. If anyone had ever told him he'd be creeping up on thirty and about to ask permission from a grown-ass man to get it on with his girlfriend, he'd have laughed himself hoarse. And yet...

"This'll be fine, right?" Davis stared uneasily at the door, squeezing his hand so tightly it hurt. "He won't, like, say no, right?" She did one of those *puh* laughs. Then she peered up at him. "Wait. Will he say no?"

Putting on his most unruffled expression, even though he was more than mildly worried about the same thing, that this simple request might turn into a teachable moment about restraint and patience and some mortifying mention of birds and bees, he said, "It'll be fine. The other guys do this all the time. It's just part of the deal."

"I guess that makes sense." Davis blew a breath out loudly through her lips. "Okay. Let's do this."

"No shame," he said.

Smiling up at him, she echoed back, "No shame." And then she raised her fist and knocked.

"Yo," Madigan called out.

Davis snorted, muttered, "Seriously. Who says *yo* anymore?" And then she opened the door.

As soon as they stepped inside the office, Kev snorted too.

Madigan sat at his desk, his back stick straight, his hands folded, a bright red blush flashing above his beard. His buttoned-up expression was almost the opposite of Ashley's as she stared at them from her desk, her eyes round with emotion, her smile intensely proud.

"Oh," she said after the moment of awkward silence it took for her to realize she was who they were waiting for. Because as much as Kev would have appreciated a full family sex discussion about as much as a punch to the throat, Ashley hadn't been invited to this meeting. "Right, I'll just be..." She stood from her desk, stopping on her way out the door to give Davis a tight, lengthy—long enough for Davis to give him a mildly concerned look—hug. And then she was gone.

"What can I do for you two today?" Madigan asked, sitting even straighter, his expression even sterner. Seriously, he looked like he was about to tell a group of kindergartners that Christmas was canceled this year.

Feeling less certain than he had before they'd entered his office, and he hadn't been overflowing with certainty then, Kev said, "Um. Well." *Oof.* Not a stellar start. But the potential energy sparking inside him was outrageous. He wanted to make the time-out sign just so he could do fifty jumping jacks to get rid of it. Then Davis squeezed his hand, and when he looked down at her, she mouthed, "No shame."

He closed his eyes for a long blink. *No shame.*

"Madigan," he said, even somewhat steadily. "I am here today to request a night off site. To, um, spend with this woman." He waved his other hand in Davis's direction, up and down like she was a brand-new car in a showroom. "With Davis, I mean." He laughed.

"Because you know her name. She's your stepdaughter. I want to spend the night with your—with Davis. Please and thank you."

"Wow," Davis said under her breath. "Nailed it."

With his jaw clenched and his armpits starting to sweat, Kev awaited the verdict.

"Okay," Madigan said calmly, like Kev had just asked for a dental appointment rather than a date to bang his stepdaughter. "When? And where will you be going?"

Was that it? Kev thought. Would it really be that easy?

"Tonight," Davis said. "If that's okay."

Sitting back, Madigan ran his knuckles through his beard the way he did when he was deep in thought—or when he was about to say something nobody wanted to hear. "Typically, I need a bit more notice before giving out an overnight pass." And when he added, "Even for family," Kev wanted to turn into dust, leaving nothing but a pile of clothes and shoes where he used to be.

But Davis was undeterred. "Okay, what about tomorrow night?"

Straightening some already straightened papers on his desk, Madigan said, "I think that would be fine. But," he said when Davis wheeled on Kev with triumph in her eyes, "you have to let me know where you're going and check in if any of your plans change. And you have to be back on the premises by noon. Those"—he clasped his hands on the table again—"are the rules. Please don't break them."

"We won't," Kev said, not only his knee but his entire body wanting to bounce. "We'll be back on time. Early, even. Promise."

"And Kev, Davis," Madigan said before she tried to pull him from his office. "Have fun." He raised both brows. "But please, please, *please*, for the love of god, be safe."

Knowing he wasn't talking about wearing their seat belts, Kev nodded, telegraphing *there's a fresh box of condoms in my nightstand* as best as he could with the gesture. And then Davis yanked on his hand.

But he couldn't go with her. Not yet.

"Can I have a minute with Madigan?" he asked. "I'll come find you after."

Her head tilted, her smile fading as she sensed the shift in Kev's mood. When he squeezed her hand to let her know he was okay, she squeezed him back and said, "Of course."

Waiting until she left the room, Kev turned toward Madigan, took a deep breath, and said, "Um, there's something I need to say to you."

"Kev." Madigan's deep voice was a sword slicing through the tension in the air. "You do not need to make amends with me. If that's what you're trying to do."

"I don't?" Kev slid his hands into his pockets. "Why not?"

"Because I am already too emotional right now," he said, blinking hard, touching a finger to the corner of his eye. "And also, because you already have. You've made your amends to me with every minute of work you've done since you got back. No words you could ever say could be more important to me than that. But I appreciate that you're here." His crystal blue eyes stared straight into him, straight through him. "I appreciate that you wanted to try."

Taking a moment to let it all sink in, or at least trying to because it would probably take more than a moment, Kev said, "Okay," to the man who was more supportive of him, more accepting of him, and more of a father to him than anyone he'd ever known.

Even though he had a whole speech prepared, there was only one thing he wanted to say now. It wasn't an easy thing, but he knew that it should have been. And since it should have been, he decided to pretend that it was.

"Madigan," he said. "You're the best man I know. I wouldn't be where I am without you in my life. And I love you."

"Aw, hell, Kev," Madigan said gruffly, squeezing his eyes closed, pinching the bridge of his nose. With a quivering chin and a tear tracking into his beard, he said, "Thank you for saying that. I'm going to need a minute alone now. And I love you too."

CHAPTER TWENTY-EIGHT

WONDERING how a single day could last as long as the one he'd just barely managed to get through had—even if he had spent every second of it dreaming about what would happen tonight, fantasizing, *preparing*—Kev stepped out of the shower when someone knocked on his door.

"Who is it?" he shouted, towel drying his hair.

"Your fairy godmother," Tex answered. "Open up."

Wrapping his towel around his waist, he walked to the door and pulled it open.

Without so much as a hello, Tex, Ace, Stanley, Brayden, and Noah all barged through the door, filing in one right after the other like man-sized ants.

"Hey guys," Kev said, watching his cabin fill up. "Can I help you?"

"The correct question is," Brayden said, "how can we help you?"

Kev frowned. "Huh?"

"A little birdy told us you had a date tonight," Ace said, sitting on the bed for exactly zero point five seconds before snatching the wolf shifter romance book Kev had torn through last night off his nightstand and flipping through the pages.

"Wow." Kev ran a hand through his still damp hair. "News travels fast." He knew it was too much to hope that he and Davis wouldn't provide more grist for the Little Timber gossip mill. The mountain had eyes, after all. He'd just kind of hoped the chatter would have waited until tomorrow.

"Has anyone ever told you that you are absurdly good-looking?" Brayden asked, his eyes narrowed as he stared at Kev's abs. "You could be a movie star. It's ridiculous."

"Facts," Noah said, crossing his arms as he leaned against Kev's closed door.

"Thanks?" Kev's voice pitched upward because he never really knew what to say when people complimented him on his looks. It wasn't like he had anything to do with them. "Uh, you too, guys."

"Really?" Brayden asked. "You mean that?"

Kev nodded. "Hundred percent."

And for the first time since Kev had met him, Brayden actually blushed. Noah just snorted and shook his head.

While Ace raised a hand to cover his open mouth, deeply concerned by whatever he was reading in Kev's book, Tex said, "You're probably wondering why we're here."

"I'd be lying if I said I wasn't," Kev replied, feeling suddenly underdressed in his towel and nothing else. "Can I put some clothes on first?"

"What are you planning on wearing?"

Kev looked at Tex, baffled by the question. "You want to know what I'm wearing?"

Taking off his hat while he sat on Kev's couch, making himself comfortable, Tex said, "Yup."

"Uh, okay." It wasn't a difficult question to answer. It wasn't like he had a lot of options. "My jeans," he said. "And a T-shirt. Maybe my flannel." His lips twitched. "Davis likes that one."

"Nah," Stanley said while Brayden made a massive fart noise and a thumbs-down gesture.

Kev laughed. "What's wrong with that?"

"Listen, Kev," Tex said. "This is a big night for you. And I know Davis wouldn't care if you showed up wearing your stinky trail clothes. But we would. You deserve to look good."

"That's right." Like it was some sort of magic trick, Stanley pulled out the plastic bag he'd been hiding behind his back. "Sorry we didn't wrap it or anything. We were in a hurry."

"What's this?" Kev asked, taking the bag.

"It's a million dollars," Brayden teased. "That's how much we love you."

Ignoring Brayden's snark, Tex said, "It's a gift. From us to you."

Kev opened the bag, and when he peered inside, the towel

around his waist slipped. Barely grasping it before it fell to the floor, he said, "Oh my god." He looked up again. "Where did you find these?"

"Took a quick trip to the Goodwill this morning," Tex said. "But we washed everything this afternoon. And shined the shoes."

Kev blinked, stunned. "You shined my shoes?"

"Sure did," Ace said, his nose still buried deep in the pages.

Reaching into the bag, Kev pulled out a nice pair of navy chinos, a white button-up that looked brand new, and a pair of brown dress shoes so well shined they practically glowed.

"They're all my size." He shook his head. "How did you know?"

"The pants and shirt were a guess," Stanley said. "But Brayden's apparently got a weird thing of comparing shoe sizes with everyone he meets."

"I knew it would come in handy eventually," Brayden said on his way into Kev's kitchen to raid the cupboards. "Hey, can I have a Pop-Tart?"

"Knock yourself out," Kev said, holding the pants up to his waist. "This is amazing." He looked at the men hanging out in his cabin, realizing that each and every one of them was his friend. Realizing how lucky he was to have them all in his life. "Thank you."

"Go try them on. We want a fashion show," Ace said distantly, and then he gasped. "What did I just read? Did he just get *stuck inside her?*"

Laughing at Ace's horrified expression, Kev explained, "Knotting. It's pretty wild."

"I'm sorry." Ace stared blankly up at him while Noah crossed the room, taking a seat next to Ace to get a closer look. "Did you just say 'knotting'?"

"Wait." Racing back from the kitchen with a Pop-Tart in his hand, Brayden sat on Ace's other side. "I need to see this."

While they all read *My Secret Alpha* in shocked, wide-eyed silence, Kev gathered his new clothes into his arms and said, "Okay. I'll be right back."

Emerging from the bathroom a few minutes later, his shirt tucked in, his shoes tied, his curls scrunched, he barely felt like himself. He felt new, put together. He felt like the man he'd always wanted to be.

"How do I look?" he asked, spreading his arms out wide.

"Oh honey." Brayden clasped his hand over his heart. "Our little baby is all grown up."

After hurling a pillow at Brayden's face, barely missing Ace too, Tex said, "You look good, Kev."

"Real good," Stanley added. "You're gonna knock Davis off her feet."

"He's still stuck." Ace pointed at the book. "It's two pages later. That can't be healthy."

"Oop," Noah said after flipping the page. "Just popped free."

"Come on, guys." Tex put his hat back on. "Let's let Kev finish getting ready in peace."

After accepting knucks from Ace, a whispered "can I borrow that book when you're done with it?" from Brayden, a firm handshake from Stanley, and another tight nod from Noah, Kev watched them leave.

"You got condoms?" Tex asked, staying behind.

Kev nodded.

"Need help paying for the hotel room?"

"No, we're good." His cheeks heated. "We were gonna stay at the Motel 6, but Maude Alice got us a room at the Sapphire Lodge. Apparently she gets a discount there or something." Kev shrugged a shoulder. "I guess she goes there a lot."

"That's a really nice place," Tex said with an approving nod. "Only stayed there once, but it's classy."

Kev smiled, running a hand down his outfit. "I guess it's a good thing I'm not going in jeans."

Then they stood there for a moment, until Tex leaned in, placing a hand on Kev's shoulder, and doubled the gravity in the cabin when he said, "You're a good man, Kev. I know what it's like for guys like us. I know how we can feel like we have nothing to offer the world.

Like we'll never be good enough. Like the people we care about deserve better. But it's a lie. Because we have a lot to offer. *You* have a lot to offer. And Davis is lucky to have a man like you. Uh-oh," he said when Kev wiped his eyes. "Are your fingers getting wet again?"

Kev exhaled a laugh, and when Tex tried to let him go, he grabbed his arm and said, "Hey, Shannon is lucky to have a man like you too."

"Oh, I know." Tex winked, then tugged on the brim of his hat. "We're going on our first date next week."

"Nice," Kev said, slapping Tex's hand twice before they slid their fingers back, making them snap against each other. "Poor Madigan. He's gonna have his hands full with us."

"Well, this was the life he chose," Tex said with a shit-eating grin. "Can't feel too bad for him."

When Tex left his cabin, shutting the door behind him, Kev realized the man had a point.

CHAPTER TWENTY-NINE

DAVIS

"Whoa," she said on an exhale when the automatic doors slid open, and they stepped inside. The Sapphire Lodge was perched on a cliffside high in the mountains overlooking Red Falls, and although she knew it existed the same way she knew the moon existed, something that was always there, glowing steadfast in the distance, she'd never set foot inside it. But it was beautiful, with rustic stone walls, dark wood beams crossing a lofty arched ceiling, and massive chandeliers sparkling above a pebble-lined creek that ran through the center of the atrium.

She still didn't want to know why her grandmother had a frequent stay discount here—although she suspected it had something to do with a certain big-hearted man who lived in Billings. But she couldn't deny that the woman had great taste. She also wondered how much her grandmother had spent to fund their sex sleepover, because this place had to be expensive as hell no matter how often a seventy-year-old woman used it for her clandestine hookups.

Then she looked up at Kev, dressed in the fine clothes his friends had gotten him, with his fresh shave and his perfect hair, not a single curl out of place, and sighed, realizing those were concerns for another time. There was only one thing she wanted to concern herself with tonight, and he was standing right beside her, so gorgeous it hurt to look at him—a little pang in her chest.

Smiling down at her, his dimple on full display, he said, "I think this is the nicest place I've ever seen."

"Are you hungry?" she asked, noticing the hotel restaurant across the lobby. They hadn't had dinner yet, and it was about that time.

His gaze roved down her throat, across her collarbone, tracing the neckline of the little red dress she wore. The one she loved for the way it hugged her curves and made her tits look phenomenal. When he licked his lips, his eyes dipping briefly to her cleavage, they could have been standing in the middle of a deserted frozen wasteland and flames still would have flickered up her neck when he replied, "Starving."

"Do you"—her breath caught, her stomach swooping when he stepped closer, slid his hand into hers, and pulled her to his side—"want to get dinner before we go to the room?"

Leaning in, brushing his lips along the side of her neck, he whispered, "The only dinner I want is you."

After the ten indescribably long minutes it took to check in, they barreled through their door, his overnight bag landing on a chair while she tossed hers...somewhere. She didn't know. Didn't care. Too frantic and wild and a single breath shy of ripping his nice new clothes off his body just to get at him. She couldn't kiss him enough. Couldn't touch him enough. Couldn't wait another second.

"I love you," she said, or tried to, the words half lost between his lips. "I need you."

She reached for his pants, for the top button. But he grabbed her wrists, stilling her, and said, "Wait."

The word was a slab of ice, and she froze inside it. *No. Not again. Please.*

"Did you say wait?" Fear flashed through her, her heart stalling out, a lump of lead taking its place in her chest. Her eyes stung. *Shit,* she was going to cry. "Kev, y-you don't want—"

"Oh, fuck. Baby, no." He grasped her face, his devastated expression making it clear he'd just realized what he'd said. Then he took her hands and placed them on his chest, holding them there over his pounding heart. "We are absolutely doing this tonight. Multiple times if I have anything to say about it. Nothing short of this lodge catching fire will stop me from getting inside you—and even then, I'll keep fucking you until the walls burn down around us."

In an almost violently relieved rush of air, her lungs started working again. "Okay," she said, her heart finding a steadier rhythm even as his words, the intensity behind them that felt like a promise, yanked some string inside her, leaving her unraveled. "Okay, good."

"It's just, this night means so much to me. I mean, look at me." He held up a trembling hand. "I'm shaking. I've never felt like this before. I've never been so nervous. I don't want to rush this. I want to take my time with you. I want to remember every single second." His eyes turned half a shade darker, a storm out at sea with its sights set on land. "I want *you* to remember every single second."

Gazing up at him, wondering how it was possible to need someone so thoroughly it barely fit inside her, swelling and expanding until it was all she could see or hear or feel, she said, "I want that too."

"Will you"—when he swallowed, she wanted to lick the bobbing point of his Adam's apple—"undress for me? I want to watch you. I want to see you. Is that okay?"

Yes, it was okay. But right then, she knew she'd do just about anything he asked. Whatever he needed. Whatever he wanted. She'd do it.

With a slow nod, she placed her hands on his chest, urging him to take a step back. "Sit down," she said. "On the bed."

He obeyed, his erection straining against his pants in a way that looked painful. And she wanted to touch him, to undo his zipper, reach inside, and finally know how soft and warm his skin would feel under her fingertips, how hard he would feel with her hand wrapped around him. But if he needed them to take their time, she could do that for him. She could slow down. She could behave.

Their room was beautiful too: dark wood furniture, ornate curtains, an enormous bed with a crisp white comforter and a padded headboard. But it was too bright. So she walked to the door and dimmed the lights. On her way back to him, she removed her earrings one at a time, set them on the dresser, and stood directly across from where he sat on the bed. Close but just out of reach.

His eyes seared a path to her, his gaze so blistering it felt, for a moment, like the walls really were burning down around them. While he watched, she reached back, tugged at her zipper, released it slowly. His pupils were blown, lips parted, and she realized that as much as she wanted him, she wanted this too. His attention wholly on her, his hunger for her so clear in the tight, flickering muscles of his jaw. In his hands fisting the bedding at his sides.

Turning her back to him, she slid one dress strap over her shoulder, and then the other, letting the bodice pool around her waist. Then, slowly, she bent forward, working the dress inch by inch over her hips, down her legs before kicking it off to the side.

"Davis." He exhaled sharply behind her. "You really do have the best ass in the entire fucking world."

Straightening up, she looked back at him over her shoulder. "The best?" she asked, running her palm over the round curve of one cheek, feeling sexier than she ever had with another partner. Feeling sexier than she ever had, period. It was impossible not to when Kev looked at her like that. Like he was two seconds and one pair of panties away from losing his mind, tearing off his clothes, and taking her right there on the dresser.

When he nodded, she gave him a soft smile, an even softer "thank you." Then she hooked her finger under the slender strap of her lacy black G string, pulled, and released it with a muted *snap*.

He reached down, repositioning himself in his pants. And then he let his hand linger on his erection. Like he couldn't leave himself alone while he watched her. Like he knew the deep ache it generated between her thighs when he stroked himself absently, his attention glued on her G-string strap. The strap she hooked her finger beneath again, running it up and down the silky material, pulling it free of her cheeks before tugging it snuggly between them again.

"*Fuck.*" It was a low, pained groan, and it spurred her on, heating her blood, making that ache swell into a hot, incessant throb.

She unclasped her bra, slid it down her arms, and dropped it onto the dresser. Then she gathered her hair off her neck, holding it up while she peered over her shoulder again, twisting just enough to give him a view of the outer curve of her breast.

"Was that slow enough?" she asked, tracing her fingertips down her neck, skimming the side of her breast.

"Turn around." His voice was dark, commanding. And when she did, his gaze feasted on her, devouring her from her lips to her neck. From the base of her throat to the tips of her breasts. "Come here."

One slow step at a time, she moved toward him, not stopping until she was so close his breath ghosted across her bare skin.

Grasping her hips, he pressed a kiss onto her belly and said, "Thank you."

"For what?" she asked, threading her fingers through his hair.

He glanced up at her from beneath his lashes, sliding his fingers along the waistband of her panties. "For leaving these." His voice was so low it rumbled through her bones, through the floorboards beneath her feet, when he said, "For me."

If she thought she'd taken her time undressing for him, it was nothing compared to his patient, brain-scrambling pace as he worked one side of her panties down, and then the other, kissing every new inch of skin he uncovered.

She was breathing hard, fighting for air, lightheaded and swaying as his teeth closed gently around the point of her hip, as his tongue skated across the skin below her belly button. He'd barely touched her, and she was already near loss-of-consciousness levels of turned on. And he knew it too, staring up at her with a mischievous grin while he slid her panties down, but only halfway, breaking all the laws of physics to keep them suspended on her ass. Even though the triangle of black fabric in the front still covered her, it was a technicality. It gaped away from her body, loose enough to pull to the side, to slip a finger inside, maybe a tongue. But he didn't. He didn't do any of those things.

Instead, while she considered begging him to free her from the suddenly unbearable restriction of flimsy lace, he spun her back around.

Her heart hammered against her ribs, her vision going white around the edges. Being almost naked already made her feel vulnerable, but not being able to see him behind her, not knowing what he was about to do. She could barely stand it.

At the first graze of his tongue along the crease where her ass met her thigh, she gasped. When he did it on the other side, she moaned. When he bit the string of her panties, pulling them down the rest of the way with his teeth, a tremble tore through her. But it wasn't until he brought her panties up to his nose, closing his eyes and inhaling deeply, that blind need nearly doubled her over.

"Kev," she whispered as he rose to his feet behind her, his lips brushing over her shoulder, his fingers sliding across her stomach. His erection a firm and insistent presence against her back.

Naked except for her heels, she ground her ass into him, doing it again when he groaned into her ear. His hands found her breasts, cupping them, his thumbs circling the sensitive skin around her nipples.

"Do you ever read romance novels?" he asked, slipping a hand down her body, his fingertips brushing a featherlight trail of flames across her belly, his other hand still cupping her breast, his thumb still teasing her nipple.

With his hard body at her back, his soft lips at her neck, his skilled hands roaming all over her, she felt like there were ten of him, twenty, everywhere at once, surrounding her like wind, like water, overwhelming her senses while soothing them at the same time.

"No," she answered him, her chest heaving, breaths coming hard. "I like mysteries. Thrillers."

"So you've probably never read a wolf shifter romance."

Squirming when his fingers dipped in a low pass from her right hip to her left, skimming so close to where she ached for him before leisurely skating away, she asked, "That's a thing?"

His laughter fanned out over her skin, firing goosebumps along her neck, across her shoulders. "Oh, it's a thing," he replied with another shallow pass of his fingers, his thumb gliding back and forth over her nipple in a slow, almost lazy pattern. Like he didn't know what it did to her. Like he wasn't aware of the way it pulled her insides tight, winding, coiling, making her shudder and writhe in his unbothered arms.

"In these books," he said while she shuddered, while she writhed, "the couples are always mates, fated to find each other and love each other forever. And when the male, who's been searching for his mate his entire life, finally gets that first taste of her." His fingers slid down another inch, almost there, so close. "When he first licks her."

"W-what happens?" she asked, delirious, pushing herself up to her tiptoes to get him where she needed him.

He closed his teeth over her shoulder, a slow glide of pressure and warmth that centered her spiraling nerve endings, then whispered harshly against her skin, "He loses his goddamned mind."

And just when her eyes closed and her knees threatened to buckle, his hand dove between her legs, holding her up, cupping her.

"Fuck, Davis," he ground out. "You're so smooth. So bare."

Reaching back to grasp his neck, clinging to him while he pressed the heel of his palm over her clit, she stammered, "I wanted to...for you. Did it yesterday. Had to...beg my girl to—*ah*," she gasped when he pinched her nipple, "fit me in."

"You did that for me?" he asked, a little awed, while he stroked her, petting her silky, ultra-sensitive skin.

She nodded.

"Did it hurt?"

"Only for a second," she said, remembering the bright sting, the sudden burn fading to an almost comforting glow.

"How does it feel now?"

How did it feel? Was there even a word to describe his touch? The gentle reverence of his hands? There wasn't, but she settled on "Amazing."

His forehead dropped to her shoulder as he slid his fingers between her folds, parting her. When he found out what she already knew—that she was so wet, so slippery, it wouldn't take more than a single firm thrust to be inside her—he let out a tortured moan.

"Those books are fucking wrong." He burrowed his face into her neck, his voice strained and muffled. "I haven't even tasted you yet, and I'm already losing my mind."

She arched back, her hips rocking helplessly into his hand, her mind careening past lost and hurtling toward utter oblivion.

Dipping two fingers shallowly through her core, he painted her slickness up one side of her labia, leaving her even more sensitive to the cool air in the room. "So soft," he said, dipping inside her again, dragging his fingers up her other side. "So sweet." The next time he slid through her center, he found her opening and sank one long finger in deep.

She'd never had a religious experience before, but when a second finger joined the first, she thought this must be close. The euphoria, the clarity, the overwhelming rightness of it as he squeezed her, his palm putting some golden ratio amount of pressure on her clit, his fingers pumping, curling, stroking. But the sensation was short-lived, and when he pulled out of her, she whimpered at the loss.

"I've been dreaming about tasting you since the day I met you," he said, bringing his glistening fingers to his lips. "Fantasizing. Obsessing over it."

Twisting toward him, she watched as he closed his eyes, parted his lips, and sucked his fingers into his mouth. While she staggered, struggling to stay on her feet, not entirely sure she was conscious anymore, nothing but sensation and desire and need, he hummed. "Do you know what you taste like?"

She shook her head, the motion making him swim in her vision.

Sucking on his fingers again, groaning in pure, unguarded satisfaction, he pulled them free, brought his lips to her ear, and whispered, "Mine."

Then he spun her around again, pulled her close, controlling her body like she was a puppet and he held her strings. He sat back down on the bed, looked up at her with eyes that were almost entirely pupils, nearly black, and said, "I want to watch you the first time I make you come."

Incapable of doing much else, she nodded, grasping his shoulders as he kissed the hollow between her breasts. "I can feel your heart pounding," he said, pressing kisses over the swell of her left breast. "Like a drum against my lips."

She could feel it too, battering her ribs. Each beat making only one sound over and over again: *yours, yours, yours.*

He swirled his tongue around her nipple, catching her around her waist when her legs tried to give out. When he sucked her nipple into his mouth, flicking his tongue over the peaked tip, some primal sound escaped from her throat. The kind of sound that, if she were a lioness, would have every lion from every neighboring pride prowling the plains to find her.

"You're already so close," he said, not a question, as he took her other nipple gently between his teeth, kissing, licking, sucking. "Do you want it now? Do you want it fast? Or can you wait? Can I be slow?"

"I...don't know," she admitted, barely able to hold her head up, barely able to keep her eyes open. "Just, don't stop."

"I won't," he promised, taking her ass in his hands. "But I think it would be better like this." Rising from the bed, he hoisted her into his arms and spun her around, swapping their places. And then he sank to his knees. "Yes," he said, almost a hiss as he spread her legs wide and settled between them. "This is *so* much better."

It all felt almost indecent. Being naked aside from her heels while he was fully dressed. Sitting on the bed while he was on his knees in front of her. But when he spread her legs even wider, when he spread her apart with his thumbs, baring her to him, it also felt like the most perfect thing she'd ever known.

"Lie back if you need to," he said, brushing the pad of his thumb over her clit, his barely there touch making her legs shake.

It was less that she needed to and more like she had no other choice. Collapsing back onto the bed when he brushed his thumb over her again, his touch so soft she almost wept, she raised her arms above her head. Her entire body thrummed with anticipation, so keyed up for so long she had to grasp at a pillow, needing something to hold on to, almost terrified of the pleasure he was drawing out of her.

"I don't think I got enough last time." He ran his finger through her slick center again. "I think I need more."

She expected the firm sensation of that finger penetrating her again. Waited for it. So when warm breath and soft lips found her instead, his tongue slipping deep inside her, she released a rasping moan.

"Shh," he soothed, kissing her right inner thigh, then her left. "Save your voice, baby. I want to hear it all night long."

Oh god. She wasn't going to survive this. She'd known he'd be good in bed. It was obvious by the way he touched her, kissed her, handled her. But this was something else. This was a man who'd done his homework, read up, took fucking notes. Like the way his tongue slid inside her again. The way it licked a slippery path up to swirl around her clit, making her dig her heels into his back, pull her pillow over her face in case he made her scream into it.

"No," he said, reaching up and tugging the pillow free. "Don't hide from me."

Then he disappeared between her legs again, his hand cupping her breast, his fingers pinching her nipple, his tongue feathering over her clit so fast she had to bite her knuckle not to cry out.

None of this was normal. None of it made sense. He was too good, so incredible she wondered for a brief, delirious moment if she was dreaming. If she'd wake up before she even finished, covered in sweat and panting with need.

But then he slid his hands under her ass, tugging her hips forward, lifting her up to his mouth, holding her there while he kissed her, made love to her with his tongue, dragging slow, firm licks over her clit, and she knew this wasn't a dream. This was real. And the sharp edge of pleasure he kept her balanced on was excruciating.

Dropping her head back, her chest heaving while he pulled away from her and lowered her down to the bed again, she felt the hot sting of frustrated tears prickling her eyes.

"Do you need to come?" he asked, his voice quiet, tone soothing even as he brushed his thumb over her swollen clit once, twice, three times.

"Please," she begged, her prickling tears welling, filling her eyes while he held her down with one hand on her belly and pushed two fingers inside her.

And as he slid them in and out so slowly her mind blanked, her inner walls fluttering around him, he said, "I shouldn't have left you like this for so long." His fingers curled, his fingertips dragging over that spot deep inside her that made her entire body turn liquid, thick as honey. "It was rude of me."

She floated above the bed, lost track of herself, the boundaries of her body starting to blur.

"Davis, look at me." The command grounded her, and she tried to follow it, she really did. But her head was so heavy, her limbs so far away from her control, her muscles so rubbery and useless. "Look at me," he said again, and with a straining, punishing effort, she finally did.

In less than a single breath, the hunger in his gaze transformed into a heartbreaking, soul-deep sincerity. "Anything for you, baby," he said, sliding his fingers out, back in again, picking up speed. "Everything I have. Everything I am. It's all for you."

With her last remaining shred of strength, she raised herself up onto her elbows. And when their eyes locked over her belly as he sank between her thighs again, electricity sparked. It flashed along her spine when he gave her clit a long, deep suck. It ignited in her core when he flicked his tongue over her again and again. It flared white hot through her entire body when she reached down and grasped his hair, holding him in place while she bucked and cried and came apart against his mouth. While pleasure gripped her, unrelenting, holding on to her for so long, wringing her out so thoroughly, she only realized it had wrung out her tears too when her harsh moans faded and his soft whispers rose to fill the void they'd left behind. When he crawled up onto the bed beside her. When he brushed her hair back from her tear-soaked cheeks and said, "Davis? Shit, are you okay?"

She couldn't answer. Because she didn't know. It was all so good. So perfect. So much better than she'd ever dared to hope for herself. And this was only their first night together. What would it be like when they really knew each other's bodies? What would it be like with practice?

"Baby?" There was a note of panic in his voice. "Did I hurt you?"

"No," she said through jagged, body-racking sobs. "You didn't hurt me."

Gently, he ran his hand down her body, slipping it between her legs, cupping her. It wasn't sexual this time, not entirely. It was only pressure, comfort. "Then why are you crying? Was it bad?"

"Bad?" So abruptly it shocked her a little, her tears transformed into gasping, breathless laughter. "Kev, it was the best thing that has ever happened to me. I left my body. I transcended this astral plane. I'm pretty sure I know the meaning of life now."

Smiling down at her, he lowered his head and kissed her so tenderly she almost started crying again. But she held herself together. She had to, because they weren't done.

While she came back to herself by degrees, gradually regaining control over her emotions and her limbs, she placed a hand on his chest and pushed him back. Urging him to stand at the end of the bed, she sat up, reached out to unbutton his shirt, and slid it from his shoulders. Then she unbuttoned his pants, relief and thrill and so much love tumbling through her when she realized he wasn't going to make her stop. Not this time. Hopefully never again.

Still needing to prove it to herself, she pulled his zipper down and reached inside. His boxer briefs were wet, the round head of his penis slick and dripping, the rest of him hard and ready and *everything*.

"I'm not sure how long I'll last," he gritted out, his abs flexing when she spread his slickness over his slit, swirling her thumb around his head. "I almost lost it already just from watching you."

Reluctantly pulling her hand free, she slid his pants down over his hips, then his boxer briefs. While he toed off his shoes, she finally did the same. And then they were both naked. Completely.

"Stay there for a second. Right there," she said when he tried to move toward the bed. "I've been wanting to look at you like this for so long, Kev. Every time I saw you without your shirt on," she admitted, not even slightly embarrassed, "this is what I imagined. What I fantasized about. Your naked body close enough for me to touch, to feel."

While he stood for her, perfectly still except from his heaving chest, she took him in. His broad shoulders were the perfect shape for her fingers to curl around. His pecs were made for her palms to press against. The firm ridges of his abs called out for her tongue, wanting to be licked and traced. The proud, swollen jut of his erection begged for her mouth.

"You're so beautiful," she told him. "You're beautiful here." She reached up, cupped his cheek, brushed her thumb over his lower lip. "And here." She trailed her fingers along his collarbone, down the line between his pecs, through the valley between his abs. "Here too." When her fingertips danced along the underside of his shaft, his skin there just as warm and soft as she imagined, he sucked air in through his teeth. When she closed her fingers around him, sliding her grip up and down his rigid length, he threw his head back, grunting a low and long "*fuck*" at the ceiling.

Giving his head a single slow lick that made him shudder, she released him, sliding her hand back up to his chest, resting her palm over his heart. She waited for him to look at her again before she said, "You're beautiful here too, Kev. All the things that happened to you could have turned you cold, closed you off. But you have the warmest heart. You have the most beautiful heart."

When he covered her hand with his, his expression fell, the fire in his eyes banking, flickering out. "Are you sure?" he asked, the sexy, confident man he'd been a minute ago looking suddenly so defenseless, so scared. "What if you're wrong, Davis? What if I—"

"No." She shook her head. "I'm not wrong. Not about this. I trust you with my whole entire heart. Now you just have to trust me too." Sliding her hand free, she moved back in the bed and said, "Come. Be with me."

Silently, he followed her, crawling over her, settling his hips between her open thighs, lowering himself onto her chest. The soothing heat of his skin seeped into hers. The solid weight of his body pushed her into the bed, calming something inside her that had been unsettled over the last few months. Because she'd needed to feel him like this too. She'd needed to feel his warmth, his weight. She'd needed him healthy and vital and safe in her arms.

While the moment seared itself into her memory, carving out a space in her heart where it would live forever, she took his face between her hands and said, "I love you." She kissed one corner of his mouth. "I trust you." She kissed the other corner. "Make love to me."

CHAPTER THIRTY

KEV

It was so quiet, only their breaths, only her words echoing between his ears. Words he'd never thought he'd be lucky enough to hear.

I love you. I trust you. Make love to me.

He wanted to, needed to. But he was bare. Hard and leaking and so close already that all it would take was a single thrust inside her and he'd be gone.

He needed to get a condom. He needed to get his head on straight and think clearly. But right then, sliding his erection through her soft, wet core, her head dropping back with each thrust over her clit, her lips open and begging to be kissed, clarity was no longer on the menu.

"You feel so good," he told her, kissing her neck, her throat, her jaw. "So perfect. You're everything I've ever wanted." He slid a hand down her side, over the soft swell of her breast, the dip of her waist, the rise of her hip. "I love you," he said, hooking his fingers behind her knee, hoisting her leg over his hip, opening her up to him. "I trust you." She was so slippery, so ready. It would be the easiest thing ever to slide inside her, to sink into her heat, to be surrounded by her.

"I need you," she said while she tilted her hips, lining his head up with her entrance. "I need you now. Please."

He groaned while she rocked beneath him, making him slippery too. "Baby," he said, lucidity deteriorating, ecstasy beckoning. "I have to get a condom."

"We don't need one."

Wrangling his reason back online, he met her stare.

"I don't have any STIs," she said, her cheeks flushed, tits flushed, everything flushed. "And I've got an implant."

He'd heard people felt cold when they went into shock. So when incandescent heat flared through him, he knew it wasn't that. But it was something. Something dangerous, cataclysmic, maybe even fatal. Could he fuck her bare? Would he survive it? Or would he thrust inside her, see that white light, step through the pearly gates, and never turn back?

"I don't have any STIs either," he heard himself say, even with the full knowledge that he may be using his last few breaths to say it. "I haven't been with anyone in years. And they tested me at rehab."

"Good." Grinning, triumphant, she reached down for him.

"Wait." His heart galloped beneath his ribs, especially when her fingers wrapped around his length. "Um, birth control isn't one hundred percent, though, right?"

Stroking him, her soft grip gliding up and down his shaft, she said, "It's pretty damn close."

And he realized in that moment, about to make love to the woman of his dreams, that he was scared. Check that; he was terrified. "Remember when I told you I wanted kids?"

She nodded, stilling her hand until he shook his head and said, "You don't have to stop." With a breathy laugh, she stroked him again. "I remember. You said you wanted four."

"Right. And I do. I mean, I would. With you. If you wanted that too. Someday." He was stammering, fritzing out completely when she reached down and cupped him. "But what if—oh my god. *Fuck*, baby," he groaned, barely able to speak, barely able to keep his eyes open as she massaged him. "What if you accidentally get pregnant," he ground out, "and I'm not ready to be a father? Like, what if I'm really bad at it?" *What if I turn out like my dad?* he thought but didn't say. "I have too much work to do still. I'm not ready."

He saw it in her eyes, the change, the concern clearing out the haze. Pulling her hand away from him so she could slide her fingers around his neck, she said, "It's okay," as a furrow dove between her brows. "I understand. Let's just get a condom. Let's be safe."

But at that moment, through some mystical twist of sex physics, the head of his cock slid into her, just barely. And it was the single most exquisite sensation he'd ever experienced in his brief exquisite-sensation-seeking life.

Hanging his head, he wheezed, "Christ, that feels good."

"So good," she said, her eyes fluttering closed.

"What if... What if I pull out?" This was a bad idea. Really bad. Or maybe it was the best idea he'd ever had. Impossible to say. "I can pull out. Right before." He wanted to come inside her more than anything. Except for this. For the chance to feel her orgasm grip him, squeeze him. Because he wasn't going to stop until she came again. He denied himself a lot of tempting things these days. He wouldn't deny himself this.

"Only if you're comfortable." She tilted her hips. Enough that all he had to do was push and he'd be home. "I trust you. But hurry. *Please*, Kev."

And that was all it took. That *please* stretched out on a needy moan. "Okay," he said, his cock aching to bury itself inside her. "Okay."

She gave him a smile. A smile that faded like a sunset, her lips parting, her expression darkening into something so sensual, damn near erotic, when he took himself in hand and pushed into her, a single slow inch before sliding back out.

While he savored every new sensation of his body joining with hers, delaying his pleasure with every slide in and back out, in and back out, she moaned, begged, pleaded for him to stop teasing her.

"I'm not trying to tease you," he said, kissing her closed eyes, her pink lips. "I'm just not willing to rush this. I've waited too long, baby." Another slow slide in and out. "I've spent too many nights dreaming of this."

"I love it when you call me baby," she said, kneading his lower back like a cat, pulling on him. Her hips rocking, tilting, trying to reach more of him.

He slid in another inch, and another, so close to bottoming out. But not quite. Then he backed out again, almost to the tip.

"Kev," she whimpered, her fingernails digging into his skin.

Taking mercy on them both, because he'd gone nearly cross-eyed from holding himself back, he slid into her fully in one hard thrust. And when she cried out, "Yes!" When her walls closed around him, her inner muscles squeezing, pulsing, pulling him toward a promise of blackout bliss, *there* was that white light. There were those pearly gates. There was heaven. He'd found it at last, surrendered to it, content to spend eternity inside Davis Thompson's perfect pussy.

And because he was in heaven, it took every bit of willpower he possessed to hold off his orgasm, to stem the pleasure trying to barrel down his spine. But willpower was a skill. And he'd been practicing for months.

She slid her other leg up the bed, hooking her ankles behind his hips, urging him even more deeply into her. When she grasped his neck and drew his lips to hers, he kissed her fiercely, their tongues tangling, her fingers diving into his hair while he fought to find a steady rhythm. With each thrust inside her, each needy moan he pulled from her throat, each roll of her hips, his control slipped, sensation wrenching it from his grasp.

He wasn't going to make it. He needed to slow things down. He needed to breathe.

Grasping her hips, he rolled them over, refusing to break their connection. He'd thought it might be better having her on top, easier to keep a leash on his need. But with her breasts pressed against his chest, her nipples brushing over his. With her hips moving and her ass in his hands, he realized he was wrong. So, so wrong.

"Slow down, baby," he gasped on a ragged breath. "I won't last."

Sitting up, she braced herself with her hands on his chest, finding a sweet, syrupy pace that made his eyelids sink. "Is this better?"

He nodded, even though it wasn't. Not even close. But he wasn't about to give up this view. He wasn't about to keep himself from sitting up with her, from kissing her breasts, from swirling his tongue around her nipples, sucking on them while she held him close, while the slow grind of her hips pulled him one step closer to the edge.

"You're so good," she said, shuddering when he took one of her nipples between his teeth. "You fit me so perfectly. Like you were made for me."

Reclining again, he bent his knees, giving her a place to rest, and said, "Lean back."

In this position, it was harder for her to move, but easier for him to keep himself together. It also opened her up to him, and because she was so bare, he could see everything. Her clit was right there, so pink and swollen, so ready to be touched, caressed, teased.

While she struggled to slide up and down his shaft, he said, "It's okay. This is all for you." Then he drew his hands up her sides to cup her breasts, rolling her nipples between his thumbs and fingers. Leaving her alone only long enough to suck his fingers into his mouth, bringing them back wet and warm. While he circled his slick fingers over her hard, sensitive tips, pinching and flicking, she threw her head back, all her weight resting on his bent legs. Then he slid one hand down her belly, between her thighs, and hovered his thumb over her clit.

"Kev," she moaned, rocking up to meet his touch.

"Look at you," he said, finally pressing down on her, drawing slow circles with his thumb while his other hand continued to tease her nipple. "So fucking sexy. So gorgeous. So perfect."

Lifting her head, watching him through half-closed eyes, she grasped his thighs, using the leverage to roll her hips.

"Fuck," he grunted, circling his thumb faster, watching her abs contract, her chest heave, feeling her inner walls pressing in all around him. She was close. Unfortunately, so was he.

"You're almost there," he said. "I can feel it. I can feel you squeezing me, gripping me."

Her thighs started to tremble, her hips jerking while he worked on her, building her orgasm. And even though it was one of the most satisfying moments of his life, pushing her like this, driving her headlong toward the inevitable cliff. It meant that he raced in that direction too. So he pulled his thumb away, denying her, telling her, "But not yet."

He wasn't ready. It couldn't be over yet. He needed more.

With a frustrated whine, she said, "Don't stop."

Giving her a firm thrust, and then another, making her tits bounce, he brought his thumb up to her lips and said, "Make it wet for me."

She opened her mouth, closed her lips around his thumb, and sucked, rolling her tongue over his skin, rolling her hips in time with his thrusts.

He grunted, bit down, falling prey to some deep, preternatural connection between his thumb and his cock. "That's it." Pulling free of her mouth with a soft *pop* before she sucked his soul straight out of his body, he lowered his hand again, his thumb sliding so easily over her clit now, spinning her up while he worked her closer and closer to the edge. And after enclosing himself in a steel trap of self-control, after a few rapid taps to her clit followed by firm, swirling swipes, he pushed her over.

She cried out his name—a sound he'd never forget—and leaned forward to ride him hard through her climax. And *god damn* it was nearly impossible not to follow her, not to let the pulsing clench of her walls drag his orgasm out of him. But he bit down, held his breath, narrowed his focus to one single directive while she shuddered and jerked and collapsed back onto his bent legs: Do Not Come.

Breathing through several thundering heartbeats, he relaxed a fraction while she went limp, pliant and panting, with her arms hanging at her sides. But before she came all the way down, before her sated expression and languid limbs destroyed him completely, he flipped her over, settled between her legs, and drove into her.

Fuck, this'll be quick, he thought while ecstasy blurred his vision, buzzed along his spine, gathered in his tightening balls. While his hips snapped, her eyes slid open, her hands slipping down his back to cup his ass, squeezing, pulling him into her harder, faster, deeper. And he was done. He lost the fight, waved his white flag, surrendered everything. After three more thrusts, and a split second before it was too late, he yanked himself out of her.

While she watched him, her eyes wide, her mouth caught on a gasp, he fisted his cock, stroked, grunted as his orgasm barreled through him. As the first rush of his release splashed across her stomach, some earth-shattering mix of gratitude and love and hunger poured out of him with it. As she bit her lower lip, running her fingers gently up and down his thighs while he pumped his fist, while he painted his release over her sun-bronzed skin, he knew he'd never feel anything as phenomenal as this. No drug. No drink. No high would ever compare.

She stared at him silently until he was finished, completely drained, barely able to keep himself upright. Then she said, "I love you so fucking much. Kiss me."

Carefully, he held himself above her and leaned down. He only meant for it to be a quick kiss, a brush of his lips against hers before he crawled off the bed. But when he tried to pull away, she hauled him back.

"You're...messy," he said between kisses. "Need to...clean you up."

"I don't care," she whispered into his mouth, and his resistance flagged, fading out of existence when her tongue slid over his top lip, when she took his bottom lip between her teeth, when she reminded him "You're messy now too."

CHAPTER THIRTY

It was true. He could clean them both up later. It was worth it. *She* was worth it.

Eventually, the kiss shifted from deep and needy to sweet and soft. And then it was only their gazes meeting, her hands cupping his face, his forehead pressed against hers, their breaths slowing.

"Let me get a washcloth," he said, kissing her one last time before she said, "okay," and let him go.

When he crawled off the bed, he did it slowly, staring at her, memorizing her flushed skin, her contented expression, her knees still spread wide. Then he smiled at the evidence of their shared pleasure glistening on her skin in the dim hotel room lighting.

He left the bathroom door open, and while he turned on the faucet, waiting for the water to warm up, he caught his reflection in the mirror. The man staring back at him was one he barely recognized—healthy and happy and lucky as fuck.

Leaning back to peek through the door, making sure she wasn't watching him, he gave his reflection a high five. "This is why," he whispered to himself. "This is why you never gave up. This is why you'll never give up again."

With bliss surging through his veins, he wet a washcloth and wiped himself clean, then he wet another. Stepping out of the bathroom, his smile slipped, replaced by a stunned, slack-jawed gape. He staggered back a step. Nearly fell to his knees. Nearly met his end again at the sight of Davis swirling a finger around her belly button, making a path through his release.

Meeting his stare, she brought her finger up to her lips, slid it into her mouth, and sucked it clean.

"Davis," he said on a rushed exhale, his cock giving a firm twitch.

"You taste good," she told him, gazing at her stomach again, a little stunned, a lot well-fucked. Then her head fell back. "I'm dizzy."

Make that *extremely* well-fucked. He'd high five his reflection about that later.

Joining her on the bed, he said, "You need water. I'll get you some in a second."

She nodded easily, and with that same distant, sated expression, she watched him clean her stomach, her sides. Each swipe of the warm washcloth over her skin, each flex of her muscles, each breathy moan while he made sure every one of her dips and valleys was spotless, shot blood straight to his dick.

When he returned from the bathroom again with two glasses of water in his hands, she patted the bed beside her. "Come here."

Because beside her was the only place he ever wanted to be—and because denying her anything was impossible—he set the glasses on the nightstand and slid back into bed.

On their sides, their bodies close but not touching, they breathed, stared, smiled at each other. Then she asked, "Do you remember the first day we met?"

"Of course," he answered. "I think about it all the time. I was talking with Madigan at the Moonlight lift like it was any normal day, and then I spotted Ashley walking up to us, bringing the most beautiful woman I had ever seen with her. I think I forgot how to speak for a second."

"But you didn't." Her smile reached her eyes, making them shimmer. "You said *hi* to me right away. My mom hadn't even introduced me yet, but you extended your hand and said, 'Hi, I'm Kev. I'm one of the Little Timber goofballs.' It made me laugh."

"I think I fell in love with you right then." He slid his hand over her hip. "Right when I heard your laughter."

"I saw you before that, though." She cupped his neck, coming willingly when he reached around her waist and tugged her close. "From my mom's window in the lodge." Brushing her fingers along the angle of his jaw, she said, "I thought you were so fucking hot."

He snorted. "Sure you did."

"It's true. And kind of embarrassing." She pressed her smile between her lips. "Like, I'm not proud of it. But the first thing I thought when I saw you standing in the snow with the sun shining down on you was *someday I am going to have white-hot sex with that man*. And my mom and grandma were standing right next to me."

"Oof." He winced, laughing. "Horny in front of the fam."

"For real."

Pulling her even closer, so close he could hitch her top leg over his hip, which he did, he said, "Then either you're a psychic or a mastermind, Davis. Because you definitely just had white-hot sex with this man."

It had been a long, long time since he'd been with a woman. But he couldn't even remember the last time he'd laughed with a woman in bed. Maybe never. It was a singular sensation, feeling her laughter everywhere their bodies touched, in all the places where his skin met hers. And in each of those places heat swelled, friction intensified, until he was hard against her. Until they weren't laughing anymore.

Meeting his stare, she said, "Can I ask you a question?"

"Always," he replied, dragging his fingertips up her side until he cupped her breast.

"Why do you like romance books so much?"

It was such an unexpected question, he almost asked her to repeat it. "You really want to know?"

She nodded, wiggling closer until his erection pressed into her belly.

"Well, first of all." He ducked to guide her breast toward his lips, giving her nipple a slow, wet kiss. "I get horny too."

Sinking her fingers into his hair, scratching her nails along his scalp, making his toes curl, she said, "And second?"

He raised his head again, resting his cheek on his pillow. "You're serious about this, aren't you?"

"I am," she said. "It's something about you that I don't know. And I want to know everything."

"Okay, just...don't make fun of me." When she shook her head, like she would never, he said, "I wasn't good at reading when I was young. Because of my homelife stuff, I had a late start. And in school, reading seemed to come so easily for everyone else, while it was impossible for me. All the kids were reading chapter books, and I could barely make it through a single sentence. Which really pissed me off. So I just stopped trying. Kind of gave up on it. But when I moved in with my grandparents, my grandmother wasn't having it. She told me I would always be at the mercy of other people if I couldn't read. Vulnerable. So she got me some graphic novels, *Holes,* all the Narnia books. I still wasn't interested. It was still ridiculously hard. But instead of making me struggle through the books on my own like my teachers did at school, she read them with me. Every night. And eventually, it worked. I really got into it. Then, one day, I finished the book I'd been reading and went into her room to grab another one. I was probably thirteen, maybe fourteen, and it was the first time I noticed that the entire bottom of her bookshelf was full of romance books."

"Uh-oh," Davis said with a glimmer in her eyes. "Young Kev was about to get an education."

He laughed, remembering lying sprawled out on his belly, his eyes burning because he kept forgetting to blink. "I probably spent two hours on her floor, flipping through pages to find all the steamy scenes. And you're right." He waggled a brow, earning an even bigger smile. "I learned a lot that day. But eventually my grandmother got back to the house, so I snuck one of the books to my room. I read it cover to cover that night, didn't sleep at all. The next day, I returned it and snuck another one. At first, let's be real, I was just in it for the sex. But the more I read, the more I realized there was something about the stories that gave me hope. Lots of bad shit can happen to the characters in romance novels. People get sick. People die. People are abandoned. But I felt safe reading about that bad stuff because the ending was always happy. Like, the characters went through even worse shit than I'd been through, but everything always worked out. Everyone always got their happily ever after. I think I needed that." He laughed at himself. "Maybe I still do. And, of course." Grasping her ass, he yanked her into him. "They're hot as fuck. I'll admit, though, it is a little weird that your mom is my main supplier right now."

Her eyes popped wide. "She's what?"

He tried not to crack up. "You didn't know?"

"No, I didn't know. I figured you ordered them. Or got them at the used bookstore or something." She blinked, several times. "My mom?"

Tucking his favorite loose curl behind her ear, gliding his fingers along the curve of her neck, he asked, "Is this, like, a dealbreaker?"

"I don't know." She rocked against him. "Maybe I need to see more of the things you've learned before I decide."

He licked his lips. "Is that a challenge?"

"Maybe. Wait." Her bravado faltered when he slipped out of her arms and off the bed. "Where are you going?"

Finding his overnight bag on the chair, he pulled out the box of condoms. Turning back to face her, her hungry gaze dropping to his straining erection, he removed a strip of condoms from the box and tossed them onto the bed.

"This time," he said, prowling back to her, "nothing is going to stop me from coming inside you."

CHAPTER THIRTY-ONE

DAVIS

WHAT TIME WAS IT? She had no idea. What day? No clue. All she knew when she woke in the darkness from a deep, dreamless sleep was that Kev's head was resting on her chest, his arm heavy and draped across her stomach. All she knew was she was not the same woman she'd been the day before. All she knew was she was so madly in love with the man in her arms it hurt, a physical pain she felt in her chest, a bruise beneath her ribs, an ache she hoped would never heal.

In his efforts to show her everything his romance books had taught him, he'd given her more orgasms than she could count, stretched her into positions she didn't think were possible, and told her the sweetest, most beautiful, and then the filthiest things she'd ever heard.

Look down. Watch me fuck you. Get on your knees. Grab the headboard. Grab your ankles. Come for me. Come on my tongue. Come on my cock. Let me feel it. Breathe for me, baby. You're doing so good. Give me one more. Give me everything.

She had a new kink now: Kevin Lowes dirty talk. She was half tempted to roll him over, slide down his body, and wake him up with her mouth just to hear it again. But she was already sore, her muscles melted under her skin, her eyelids so heavy she could barely hold them open. Her heart so full she thought it might burst.

So she enclosed him in her arms, kissed his curls and whispered, "I don't know how we made it here, but I'm so proud of us for never giving up." And then she let sleep claim her again. Only to wake up later with the sun peeking through the curtains and his head between her thighs.

THEY'D FED each other room service breakfast, making such creative use of the syrup from Kev's pancakes they had to shower together after. And then he made love to her while they stood in front of the bathroom mirror, her towel barely clinging to her breasts, his hand sneaking inside the open slit, slipping between her legs. They watched each other in their reflection, his wet bangs swinging in front of his eyes, his teeth sinking gently into her shoulder as he took her from behind, her mouth open on a silent gasp. Until she couldn't watch anymore, she could only feel, only cry out, only quake in his arms as he brought her right to the edge, held her there, and then jumped alongside her.

She wanted to stay in that room with him forever, talking, laughing, making love until they could barely move. But their time was up. And well before she was anywhere close to ready, they were back on the road, their overnight bags resting against each other in the back seat of her car, like even they didn't want the night to be over.

Kev was driving, and in the bright sunlight of midmorning, out of his nice clothes and back into the T-shirt and jeans that she loved, he glowed.

"That was the best night of my life," she told him, reaching across the center console to take his hand.

Bringing her knuckles to his lips, he said, "Mine too."

It was all so sweet, just the two of them, alone in the quiet stillness of mountain roads, stealing these last few minutes to hide out from the rest of the world. So, of course, her phone would choose that precise moment to buzz.

Ignoring it would have been her preference, but they didn't live in this quiet stillness. They lived in the real world. And in their real world with real consequences, it could have been a text from Madigan or her mom. It could have been important. So she reached back, pulled her phone out of her bag, and frowned at the screen.

> Chuckle Puppet: Hey honey. I know I'm supposed to be giving you space. And I'm trying, I really am. But I just saw these three, and they reminded me of you. I know how much you love them. I'm still here to talk if you ever change your mind. I love you, Dad.

"He still signs his texts," she said with a deep sigh, waiting for the three dots to turn into whatever her dad wanted her to see.

"Is that Chuck?" Kev asked.

"Yeah." When the picture came through, she recognized Conquest Mountain's fancy lodge, the expansive deck where she used to sit with her dad, watching the sunrise. Where they used to drink hot chocolate—and later, coffee—when she'd spent every other weekend with him after the divorce. Where now an enormous cow moose stood with her twin calves, their little ears pointing straight up, their shaggy red fur glinting in the sunlight.

"They're so cute," Kev said, sneaking a glimpse of her screen. "Did he take that?"

She nodded.

"Because they're your favorite," he said to the road.

She nodded again, pressure building behind her eyes, unwanted emotion burning her nose.

"Have you talked to him?"

"No." She looked up from her phone, her heart heavy, tired of holding on to so much anger. "Do you think I should?"

He blew air through his lips. "Baby, that's up to you. But I'll support you no matter what you decide."

It was all he needed to say. It was all she needed to hear. She wasn't ready to forgive her dad, not yet. But maybe she could at least do this.

Clicking on his caller ID, she changed his contact name back to *Dad*, pressed her thumb over the moose picture, and clicked the heart emoji. It wasn't much, but it was a start.

After Kev parked in the Bluebird lot, Davis slipped out of the passenger seat while he got their bags out of the back. It was quiet on the mountain too, only a few notes of distant birdsong while they walked to the front of the car and stared at each other.

Moving close, he asked, "So what do we do now? What's next?"

He sounded nervous, uncertain. So she stepped closer too and said, "I think we do what we always do. Take it one day at a time."

Amusement flashed in the tilt of his lips, the crinkling corners of his eyes. "I think this is the first time in my life I've actually loved the sound of those words."

Taking his face between her hands, a sudden intensity swelling inside her, she said, "Just don't shut me out again, Kev. If you're struggling. If you're feeling insecure or sad or scared or anything, even if it's my fault. Even if we're fighting and we say mean things to each other, because it's bound to happen. Even if you're worried that what you're thinking or feeling might hurt me or scare me. Please don't shut me out. Talk to me. Tell me everything. And I promise I'll do the same for you."

Lowering his forehead to rest gently against hers, he said, "I promise. I won't shut you out again." And then he kissed her.

Before she registered where they were, whether it was a good idea or not, she let him lift her into his arms while she wrapped her legs around his waist and kissed him back like there was a giant meteor headed right for them and this was the last chance they'd ever get.

And then Murphy barked.

And then Madigan cleared his throat.

"*Shit*," Kev whispered, setting her gently back onto the ground. "We're not late, are we?"

"No, you're not late," Madigan answered from the lodge steps. The man had bat hearing. "But you *are* making out in broad daylight, so…"

"Oops," Davis said, flicking her hair off her shoulder before waving at her stepdad. "My bad."

"Not to be presumptuous," Madigan said while Kev looped the strap of her bag over her shoulder. "But I'm guessing you both should probably get some sleep."

"Not me," she said through a jaw-cracking yawn. "I've gotta ride."

"Seriously?" Kev asked, stepping up behind her while Madigan made his way back up the lodge steps. "Haven't you already *ridden* enough?"

Spinning around again, she bit back a grin. "Not even close."

"Seriously, though," he said. "You must be exhausted. We barely slept."

"I'll sleep after. But my race is in three weeks. Gotta get my ass in the saddle."

While his lips quirked, he said, "What if I want your ass back in my saddle?" Then his expression fell. Slowly at first, then sinking like a stone.

"Kev?" she asked as her smile faded too. "What's wrong?"

"It'll still be awkward, Davis. As long as I'm living here, being intimate, being in a relationship, will be awkward. It'll be hard."

"I know," she told him, reaching out to squeeze his fingers, unbothered by the potential awkwardness, by the infinitesimal hardness of being with him compared to the crushing impossibility of *not* being with him. "I don't mind. You won't live at Little Timber forever. I can handle a little awkwardness while you do. Besides, this," she said, kissing him one last time, "is worth it." While his eyes fluttered open again, she took a backward step toward the lodge and grinned. "Besides, it's kind of fun watching Madigan squirm."

"Hey," he called out to her when she started to turn around.

"Want to walk tonight? I can watch you throw pinecones at the stars."

Tilting her head, she asked, "You don't want to throw some too?"

His smile was back, brighter than the sun, because he'd set a trap, and she'd fallen right into it. "Don't need to. All my wishes have already come true."

CHAPTER THIRTY-TWO

KEV

"What do you think?" He touched the folded wool saddle pad to River's neck, brushed it over her withers. "Is today the day?"

By way of answer, she threw her head into the air, pawing viciously at the dirt in the round pen.

"I'm not sure that was a yes," he conceded, unfolding the pad. "But we've got to try it, sweetheart."

Waiting until she stopped digging a hole to disappear into, he slid the saddle pad over her neck. He'd already saddled her twice in the last few days, but she still wasn't used to it. And when the heavy pad touched her shoulders, she startled, jumped her legs out wide, her muscles straining, primed to run. But she didn't run. And after a tense moment, he eased the pad down carefully until it settled into place over her back.

In a heartbeat, her withers started twitching violently, her ears pinned while she tried to shake off what likely felt like a gigantic fly that had just landed on her.

"Shh," Kev soothed, running a hand down her neck, trying to calm her nerves, trying not to let her see the way his shot off like a bottle rocket.

"She's doing great," Jen said quietly, watching him from the other side of the rail.

"This is so neat," Stanley chimed in, standing with Madigan, Davis, and the other guys a few feet back from the pen.

"She is one good-looking mare," Tex said, tipping his hat.

Eyeing River warily, Brayden said, "I think you're all nuts. She looks like she's about to bite his balls off."

"Brayden," Madigan warned.

"Sorry, Boss," Brayden said. "She looks like she's about to bite his *junk* off. That better?"

Pinching the bridge of his nose, Madigan sighed deeply.

Kev hadn't necessarily intended to try to ride River for the first time with this big of an audience. But based on how well Kev had responded to Jen's equine therapy, Madigan had wanted to give the other guys a chance to try it out too before winter hit.

"You want me to hold her reins while you saddle her?" Jen asked, her focus rock solid despite the distractions all around them. Just like his needed to be.

Turning his attention back to River, to her upright neck, her wide eyes, tight mouth, Kev said, "She still doesn't like the saddle. I think she'll panic more if we hold her. If she feels trapped."

Taking a step back, releasing the pressure, Jen nodded. "I think you're right. You know her well, Kev. Let's see how she does."

Guiding River over to the rail, he let her sniff the saddle, snort at it, nudge it with her nose. While he waited for her to lose interest, Davis made her way over to them.

"Hi, River." She held out her palm, letting the mare snatch a mint from her hand. "Good girl." Glancing up at Kev, she asked, "Are you scared?"

"A little," he said, underplaying the fear pulsing through him by a mile. He grabbed the saddle's horn to rock it back and forth on the rail, letting River snort at it again. "I think if I can get her to take the saddle without bucking like a bronc this time, we'll be good."

"I've got more mints in my pocket," Davis whispered. "If you want me to distract her."

Giving her a crooked grin, he said, "My savior. Yes, please."

In the week since their night together, the night that had redefined love and joy and perfection and pleasure for him forever, Davis had somehow become even more beautiful. Sometimes, like now, he had a hard time looking at her. Because when he did, all he wanted to do was kiss her, hold her, make love to her. A thing they hadn't been able to do since the hotel. A thing he dreamed about doing again every waking moment.

"I have good news," she said, unwrapping another mint.

"Oh yeah?" Kev slid the saddle off the rail, lifting it into his arms while River balked, then sniffed at it again, then decided Davis's mint was more exciting. "What's that?"

"I got accepted into the social work program. I start next week."

"Really?" His smile practically cracked his face in half, but his eyes misted too. It took him a second to realize why—that at least some small part of him was still convinced it wasn't real, that she wasn't really staying. That something would happen to make her leave. He supposed the effects of a lifetime spent worrying that everyone he loved would leave him wouldn't vanish overnight. He could give himself that much grace at least. But he'd be lying if he said that her news didn't set his soul at ease. This was real. She was staying. She loved him, and she was staying. "Baby, that's amazing."

"Did he just call her baby?" he heard Ace ask, followed by Madigan gruffly clearing his throat. Boss shorthand for *zip it*.

"Sorry." Davis winced. "We can talk about it later. In private. Right now, you've got a horse to ride."

Mouthing, *love you*, earning the sweetest *love you more* mouthed back, Kev held the saddle under River's nose and said, "All right, sweetheart. It's time."

"You've got this, Kev," Jen said, brimming with a confidence in him that he definitely didn't share. Even though it had been years since he'd hopped onto a green horse, he could still feel the bruises, the sore neck from bucking-induced whiplash, the overwhelming weight of lungs that refused to expand after a fall knocked the wind out of him. But the last thing he wanted was for River to sense his nerves. At least one of them needed to act like they knew what they were doing. At least one of them needed to stay cool.

Taking a deep breath, he let River sniff the saddle one more time, then he hoisted it over her back without fanfare. Like they'd done it a hundred times before. Because sometimes that was just how the hard things needed to be done, eyes closed, heart in throat, but hands steady. Knowing things might not work out, but believing without fail that they would. And this time, they did.

River took the saddle surprisingly well, only objecting once with a half-hearted rear before Davis distracted her with another mint. Eternally grateful for food-motivated horses, Kev did up the cinch—which took another three mints—and then he led River around the round pen.

While they walked, while he got her used to the saddle, the cinch, these things she didn't know, didn't understand, probably didn't like yet had allowed him to put on her, he thought about trust. He'd lived so much of his life believing that he shouldn't trust anyone or anything. People left. They died. They said one thing and did another. They hurt him, lied to him, abandoned him. It took seeing that same belief reflected in River's big brown eyes for him to start questioning whether what they both feared the most was actually true or just really bad fucking luck.

Because he trusted Davis. He trusted Madigan. He was even starting to trust himself. And if he could just convince River to trust him too, that he wasn't going to hurt her or abandon her, maybe they could help each other move on in their lives. Maybe they could heal from their pasts together.

Leading her to the mounting block, asking Davis to bring more mints—because even something as daunting as trust was easier to earn with treats—Kev climbed the steps. He waited, put his foot in the stirrup, pushed down a few times. But the second he pulled on the horn, River flinched.

When she swung her haunches away from the block, he let her, hopping down to walk her around the pen again. Eventually, he brought her back to the mounting block, lined her up, stepped into the stirrup, pulled on the horn, and let her walk off again. After two more rounds of this, he lined her up, tugged on the horn, and steeled his nerve when she finally stayed put. "Okay," he whispered to her, or maybe to himself. "Moment of truth."

Holding his breath, he stepped into the stirrup and eased his leg over her back. Immediately, a primal, fist-of-god type fear closed in all around him. There was so much potential energy coiling beneath the saddle it felt like he was riding a bolt of lightning instead of a horse.

"Easy girl," he soothed, trying to keep his body relaxed while hers practically vibrated. "Easy."

At his voice, his gentle tone, she calmed a fraction, enough to let him center his weight over her back without feeling like she'd explode. And then her ribs expanded against his legs. Which was good. At least she was breathing. At least she wouldn't straight up keel over with him on top of her.

"Wanna walk?" he asked, his tone light, heart pounding.

She didn't budge at first, but after a moment, she took one step, and then another. And then they were moving. Sitting quietly, he let her lead the way as she ambled around the pen. After a few uneventful laps, she stopped, dropped her head, and blew into the dirt. When she started pawing at the ground, Jen said, "Don't panic, Kev. But I think she wants to roll."

Not wanting any part of that action, he gave her sides a gentle squeeze. When that didn't work, he clicked his tongue. When she kept pawing, when he felt the swooping drop of her hind legs bending, he did, in fact, panic.

Yanking her reins up while Jen said something to him he couldn't hear over his hammering heart, he dug his heels into her sides, kicking—

CHAPTER THIRTY-TWO

The sky was truly beautiful, a deep, vibrant blue. Delicate white clouds drifted by, totally oblivious to Kev's throbbing head and aching ass.

"Kev!" Davis cried, leaning over the rail, looking down at where he'd been deposited unceremoniously into the dirt. "Are you okay?"

"And *this* is why we wear helmets," Jen said under her breath. Then, louder, "Need help?"

"Nah. I'm good," Kev grunted, pushing himself up onto his elbows. He spotted River standing on the other side of the round pen, staring at him with a thoroughly unimpressed expression that said, *You kick me, I dump you. I'm glad we understand each other.*

While Eleanor jumped up onto the railing—adding to River's silent scolding with an unimpressed glance down at Kev before licking one of her paws—Jen said, "Well, then." She ducked her chin. "You know what they say."

"When you fall off," Stanley began, also staring down at Kev over the fence.

"You get right back on," the rest of the men finished.

"You've got this, Kev," Brayden said, seeming sincere for once. "Even though I still think you're nuts."

Tex came to the rail, his hat shading his eyes. "She won't have as much fight in her this time. Sit back, hold on, and ride her out."

Kev repeated the words in his head while he walked back to River's side. *Sit back, hold on, and ride it out.* He could do that.

When he eased his leg over the saddle a second time, the lightning didn't even wait to strike. His butt touched leather, and River bolted. But he sat back, he held on, and he let her run and buck and kick and fight as much as she needed to. And even though his life flashed before his eyes more than once and his neck would definitely be aching in the morning, *damn*, it was fun.

"Atta girl," he said, finding a rhythm with her while she slowed from a wild, sideways gallop into a less-wild lope and then to a fairly calm trot. Not squeezing his legs or trying to guide her with the reins. Resigning himself to passenger status, giving her the power to decide where they went, how quickly or slowly they got there, when they stopped. Staying with her every step of the way.

"Wow," Jen said, exhilaration lighting her up when River finally decided to stop. "Excellent job, Kev."

Pride rushed through him, intense as a flood. "Thanks, Jen," he said, pulling the words straight from his heart. "Like, for everything."

"Careful getting down," she told him. Her eyes were wide and clear, but there was weight behind the words. "Sometimes the dismount is the hardest part."

He sensed the deeper meaning. *Don't lose your focus. Don't assume you can stop working because you feel like you've crossed some finish line. Don't rush the dismount in your own life.* Like all the others Jen had given him since he'd started working with her, he appreciated the lesson.

As luck would have it, River was more than happy to have him off her back, standing still as a statue while he slid down her side.

"Good girl," he praised, loosening the girth, running his hand down her neck, knowing they'd try again tomorrow, and the next day, and the next. Every day that Jen would let him keep coming here, keep working with her. Realizing how much he never wanted his time at Strawberry Farms to end.

After untacking River, accepting an ecstatic high five from Davis and a tight hug from Jen, Kev made his way to Madigan and the men. They were watching him silently, their expressions stern, their arms crossed.

Squinting at them, because something was up, he said, "Guys?"

While Madigan looked to the sky, fighting back a swell of emotion Kev had a hard time imagining was due to a horse, Tex stepped forward. Pulling a box out from behind his back, he said, "We all chipped in. Clay too."

When Kev took the box, his hands trembled. Why? He wasn't sure. Probably the adrenaline comedown after getting dumped in the dirt. Couldn't have been anything else. "What is it?" he asked.

"It's a boat," Brayden answered dryly, but his voice was too thick for the sarcasm to hit. "Just open it."

Cracking the lid, Kev peered inside. Then he jerked his head back up, his friend's faces swimming through his suddenly misty vision.

"You're a cowboy," Tex explained, the only one of them maintaining his composure, as Stanley ran a knuckle under his eye. "And cowboys need hats."

Fighting the wobble in his voice, Kev said, "But there aren't even any cows here."

Tex chuckled. "It's a state of mind, Kev. Just go with it."

Lifting the hat from the box—a replica of Tex's, but far less ratty—Kev held it like it was made of solid gold. While Davis and Jen came to his side, he said, "I can't believe you did this for me." He slid the hat onto his head, tipping the brim up and down until it felt right. "It's too much."

"You've been through a lot, Kev." Madigan's deep voice cut through the din, commanding everyone's attention without even trying. Even River's ears perked up. "But instead of letting the setback hold you down, you've worked hard, opened yourself up, learned from it, grown from it. And you've shown all of us that a relapse isn't the end. That sometimes, it's just a new beginning."

While the guys nodded, while Davis interlaced her fingers with his, Kev pulled himself together as best he could and said, "Thank you. All of you. I can't tell you how much this means to me."

True to form—even though his eyes were shining—Brayden broke the tension, making everyone groan when he said, "Take it down a notch, people. It's just a hat."

As they watched River head back out into her pasture, watched Maggie race up to meet her, squealing at the top of her pissed-off lungs for being left alone all day, Jen said, "She did so great today."

When Kev nodded, Jen added, "You did great too. I honestly never thought I'd see the day when she'd accept a rider, let alone a friend."

After showing the guys around the barn while Jen explained the purpose of her therapy, then seeing them off, thanking them again one at a time before they headed back up the mountain. After hugging Davis for a solid minute before she headed home too, Kev was already so emotionally drained he wasn't sure how much more he could take.

Adjusting his new hat on his head so it shielded his eyes from the slant of afternoon sunlight, he said the only thing he could think of. "Horses are amazing."

"They really are," Jen agreed. Then she turned to face him, her red braid burnished gold. "Do you have a second before you head back? I want to show you something."

Walking in step with her down a road behind the main barn he'd never walked down before, he kicked at a few rocks, enjoying the silence between them, the crunch of gravel under his boots, the soft sounds of horses grazing in their pastures, the world finally winding down after one hell of a day.

"So." Jen kicked her own rock. "Here's the thing. I'm a busy woman."

"Understatement," he said. He'd wondered more than once if she ever slept.

"My rehab facility has offered me three days a week instead of two, and as much as I want to be here, I really can't turn down the money. Not right now, anyway."

Not sure where this conversation was headed, and mildly concerned she was about to tell him she was going to sell the barn or something, he said, "That makes sense."

When they rounded a corner, the road smoothing out into a driveway, Kev finally recognized where they were. He'd seen the white shed they were walking toward in the far corner of River's pasture.

"I haven't had any help with Strawberry Farms since Scott left,"

Jen said. "It's taking a toll on me. My back is a mess, my neck is even worse. And I'm not getting any younger."

Dread swirled inside Kev's stomach. "I'm sure it's not easy," he said, crossing his fingers and toes in his mind because he didn't want to lose this place. He'd only just found it.

"With such limited time," she said, "I want to be able to focus on the therapy with the horses when I'm here and less on the work of running a barn."

"I could help out more," he said without even thinking, just letting the words cartwheel feverishly out of him. "Volunteer or something. I could come early in the mornings before my shifts at Bluebird and come back after dinner. Help feed and clean stalls. You've done so much for me. I feel like it's the least I could do."

"Well, Kev. That's just it," she said while a row of juniper bushes sprang up on either side of them, a willow tree swaying gently in the breeze off to their right, providing an umbrella of shade over the property that was clearly not a shed, but a house, old but well maintained, with big windows and a small porch. "I need more than a volunteer. I need someone to be here when I'm not, to love these horses just as much as I love them. I need someone who can help me run the therapy program. Someone who understands addiction and cares about people with substance abuse issues. I need a barn manager."

Stopping in front of the house, just off the weathered stone path wandering through its big green yard up to the porch, Jen said, "I can't pay you much more than minimum wage. But if you're interested, I can—"

"Wait," he said, shock shoving him a full step back. "What do you mean *pay* me? What... Jen, what are you saying?"

"It's a paid position, Kev. Full time."

He blinked at her. "You want *me* to be your barn manager?"

With a gentle smile, she said, "I can't think of a single person better for the job."

His jaw simply fell open. How was this possible? How was any of this real? How had he gone from one of the lowest moments of his existence to this? To this glowing, warm, wonderful life? He kept expecting to wake up, to open his eyes and find himself all alone in his bed in rehab, in the upstairs room of Thom and Trish's house, in his childhood home.

It's not a dream, he told himself, closing his eyes so he could convince himself of it, so that when he opened them again, this life, this future, would still stretch out in front of him. *You've earned this. You've fought for this. You deserve this.*

"There's no rush," Jen went on, her voice a shade softer. "This is only for when you're finished living at Little Timber. Only for when you're ready. And, like I was saying, I can't pay you much. But you can live here." Turning away, taking the steps up to the front door, she said, "Rent free." Realizing he wasn't behind her. That he was, in fact, frozen in place, she said, "Are you coming?"

Forcing himself to thaw out, forcing his legs to move, he nodded. As he climbed the steps, each footfall echoed the words *live here* and *rent free* and *full time*. When she turned the key in the lock, it sounded like hope. When she turned the knob, it felt like purpose. When she pushed the door open, when he peeked inside, independence peeked back at him.

Jen flicked on the lights, illuminating the charming front room, and said, "I know this is a lot. You don't need to give me an answer today. Look around. Take some time to think about it."

The house was perfect. From the narrow plank hardwood spanning the floors to the bright living room, the two small bedrooms, the adjoining bathroom with creamy floral wallpaper and a clawfoot tub, the sweet little kitchen with a farmhouse sink and a big window overlooking River's pasture. *Perfect.*

"I don't need any time," Kev said, his throat closing up tight. "I just..." He ground the heel of his palm into his chest, even though there was no hope of soothing the ache inside it. "I can't believe it."

"Believe it, Kev. And I saved the best part for last." Sliding the kitchen window open, Jen placed her pinkies into the corners of her mouth and blew a sharp whistle.

Out in their pasture, River and Maggie whipped up their heads, dropped their haunches, and bolted toward them. While they ran, dust flying up from their hooves, something inside Kev broke wide open, some final wall around his heart crumbling until only rubble remained.

The pasture fence was so close to the kitchen window that River could lean over and stick her nose inside. Not Maggie. She was too short. But while River sniffed the windowsill, the sink's faucet, Kev's imagination spun out. He saw himself waking up early in the morning and making coffee for himself and Davis. Saw himself standing in front of this window while he fed River apple slices, making sure Maggie got some too. He pictured the plants he'd hang from the ceiling, set on the windowsills, the garden he'd grow in the backyard. He saw himself taking care of a house. Making it a home. Making it *their* home.

Maybe Jen noticed the emotion hunching his shoulders, the way his fingers gripped the edge of the sink until his knuckles turned white, the wobble in his chin, because she said, "I'm going to go check on the fence back here. Take all the time you need." She rubbed his back, from one shoulder to the other and back again, then she turned around. He barely made it until the door snicked shut behind her before he fell the fuck apart.

While tears streamed down his cheeks, while a life he'd never dared to hope for himself fell at his feet, River snorted at him.

"I know," he told her through a broken sob. "I'm just a lot more emotional than you are, okay?"

She snorted again, but this time there was no indignation in it. And then she placed her warm, velvety nose into his trembling outstretched hand.

ON HIS WAY back to the barn, still in his head, still wading through dreams of a future he couldn't believe might be his, he slowed when he noticed Bud's side-by-side parked next to his truck. And Jen standing with her husband at the other end of the lot.

"Hey, Kev," Bud said from the driver's seat.

"Hey, Bud." Pointing his chin in Jen's direction, Kev asked, "Everything okay over there?"

Bud shrugged. "He's not drunk right now. That's all I know."

The last thing Kev wanted to do was intrude, but considering how much of a shit show it was the last time Scott showed up, he needed to check in. "Thanks, Bud," he said, then he started their way.

"Hey, there," Scott said when Kev walked up. His brown eyes were sharp, his stubble darker and thicker since Kev had seen him last, the start of a beard covering his chiseled jaw. And somehow, his shoulders seemed even broader today, his chest even more expansive. "You're Kev, right?"

Stepping up beside Jen, trying to present some sort of a united front, Kev said, "That's me."

Scott smiled at him, and Kev saw the magnetism in it, the confidence. The undeniable swagger. "Jen tells me I met you the last time I was here," he said, more apologetic than embarrassed. Almost charming in an intimidating kind of way. Or maybe it was just that he was so huge. "It's all a little blurry."

"I'm sure it is," Kev replied, coming off as much more judgmental than he had any right to be. But his protectiveness of Jen won out over his concerns about Scott's feelings. "You look better today, though." This was true. Today Scott was clear-eyed, well-dressed in Wranglers and a button-down. And Jen was so motionless beside him Kev was tempted to snap his fingers in front of her face to make sure Scott hadn't hypnotized her.

Running a hand through his silvery-black hair, Scott said, "Jen also told me you'll be helping out around the farm. And that River let you ride her. I'm impressed."

"Um, I hope so," Kev said, trying not to let the praise make blood rush to his cheeks. "And thanks." Then he turned to Jen, giving her a look that asked, *are you okay?*

CHAPTER THIRTY-TWO

When she nodded tightly, smiled even tighter, Kev said, "Good to see you again, Scott." Giving Jen a parting look he hoped conveyed that he'd be right inside if she needed him, he walked back into the barn to load hay onto the little forklift for the morning.

Twenty minutes later, Kev heard the rumble of Bud's side-by-side heading back up the road, and Jen walked numbly in through the barn door.

"Jen?" He took a step toward her.

Lifting her gaze, she said, "He's...checking himself in to rehab."

"Oh," Kev said. "That's good, right?" By the unnerving blankness of her expression, he wasn't so sure.

"I..." She released a breath, not quite a laugh. "I mean, it's great. It's something I've been asking him to do for years. I just didn't think he'd ever go." She looked down at the ground again, at her boots, at nothing.

The light in the barn dimmed as the sun finally sank behind the western mountains, fingers of deep amber stretching across the dirt floor. "Are you okay?"

Raising her head, and with an almost unrecognizable uncertainty surfacing in her eyes, she said, "I don't know. But I think so."

CHAPTER THIRTY-THREE

DAVIS

Olivia: Good luck tomorrow!

Callie: Break a leg. Or don't. I don't know what to say with a bike ride.

Lying in her bed, Davis smiled at her phone and responded.

Davis: I'm so nervous.

Olivia: About the ride? Or about finally telling Kev your sneaky little secret?

Davis: Both. Hard both.

Callie: I never knew you were such a romantic, but I am loving this side of you.

Olivia: I want to be you when I grow up.

Davis: Girls' night next weekend?

CHAPTER THIRTY-THREE

Olivia: Yes please.

Callie: Yes, but bring Kev. We can go out for pizza or something.

Davis: Then it wouldn't be a girls' night.

Olivia: We don't care!

Callie: Text us tomorrow when you cross the finish line, you absolute badass!

Olivia: Be safe too, okay?

Davis: I will 🩶

ROLLING OVER, she plugged in her phone, set her alarm for four thirty a.m., and thought about how she was going to tell him. It was silly, how long she'd kept the real reason she was riding tomorrow a secret. There were so many times she could have easily told him. But she was invested now. And even though she wasn't a romantic at heart, not like Kev was, she wanted to try. She wanted to be more romantic for him. She just hoped she'd pull it off.

SHOVING her bike shoes into her bag, she zipped it up, hauled it over her shoulder, and trudged up the stairs.

"There she is," Madigan said, his coffee mug paused halfway to his mouth. He was sitting with her mom on one side of the dining hall counter, her grandma on the other side. All of them looking bright-eyed and bushy-tailed even though the sun hadn't even considered rising yet.

"You're all up early," she said through a yawn, rubbing her eyes and joining them at the counter.

"We had to see you off," her grandma said. "Besides." She gave a deep, long-suffering sigh. "I'm always up this early."

Leaning in to kiss her temple, her mom asked, "Are you excited?"

"I'm more nervous than anything," she admitted. "I just hope I finish the ride."

"How much did you end up raising?" her grandma asked. She set a plate of blueberry muffins on the counter. "These are just out of the oven."

"Thanks, Grandma," Davis said, her stomach already tied up in knots. "But I'm not hungry."

"Oh well," her grandma said in a huff, one hand on her hip. "You have to eat. You can't just raw dog your bike ride, Davis."

Madigan—*not exaggerating*—spit out his coffee.

"Raw dog?" Davis repeated while her mom snorted out the laugh she'd been trying to hold back.

"What?" her grandma asked, baffled by their responses.

"Where did you learn that term?" Davis asked back.

She straightened. "Clay said it when he was here. He said it like," she paused, cleared her throat, and stated as clearly as if she were in a court of law, "like it was being unprepared."

Madigan was gone, wheezing, actually getting up from the counter and taking a lap around the dining hall to pull himself together.

"I guess that's kind of right," her mom said, barely getting the words out through her laughter.

"Oh, ha, ha." Her grandma flicked a hand through the air, swatting at all of them. "If you were there, you would have gotten it."

"Sounds like *someone* definitely got it," Davis muttered, barking, "ow!" when her mom elbowed her in the arm.

Immediately apologizing, still trying not to laugh while she rubbed Davis's arm, her mom attempted to shift the conversation back on track. "Anyway, sweetie. How much did you raise?"

"Around two grand, I think," Davis said. "Thanks mostly to all of you. But Cole and Mira donated too. And Jen. And Bud. And Clay. Jimmy. All the Little Timber men chipped in what they could."

"What you're doing for Kev," Madigan said, returning to the counter, still red-eyed but at least able to breathe, "and for people like him, it's pretty amazing."

Her mom gave her a squeeze. "We're so proud of you."

"Couldn't be prouder," her grandma said, completely composed again as she reached across the counter to pat her hand.

Sitting there, surrounded by some of the most important people in her life, a light switched on inside her, flickering, growing brighter. Her mom, her grandma, Madigan, each one of them, in their own way, had been helping her, supporting her, rooting for her—and for Kev. This whole time, they'd been there for her, never trying to tell her what to do or judge her choices, never trying to intervene, at least not in any way she was aware of. It had probably been hard for them, watching from a distance while she and Kev found their way back to each other. Watching them struggle, seeing them hurting. Waiting for them to figure it all out, one way or another. Because that was the thing about growing up; nobody could do it for you.

She wondered if they knew how grateful she was for them. She wondered if they knew how much they meant to her.

"Guys," she said, meeting their stares one at a time. "Thank you. Thank you for being there for me, for us. I love you all so much."

After Madigan and her mom hugged her tightly, and then each other, her grandma stiffened her spine and said, "We love you too, dear," reining in the emotions in the room before they spiraled out of control. Placing two warm muffins into a paper bag and handing it to her, her grandma said, "Now go ride your bike for far longer than anyone ever should, you ridiculous child."

Taking the baggie, Davis shook it gently and said, "No raw dogging for me."

While Madigan coughed on his coffee again, she gave her grandma a loud, smacking kiss on her cheek. Then she stopped at the stairs to give Murphy—who seemed to be waiting for her—scratches behind both ears before she went to find Kev.

"What do you want to listen to?" he asked, scrolling through her music while she drove them out of the parking lot.

"I don't know." She tightened her grip, clinging to the steering wheel like it was a fraying rope suspending her over the Grand Canyon. "How about something fast and hard?"

"Hmm," he hummed. "A little challenging while you're driving, but if it's what you need, then I am up to the task."

She laughed, but it came out too loud.

"You're nervous, huh?" he said, still scrolling. "I would be too, after all the training you've done. But you're gonna do amazing."

If only he knew *why* she was so nervous. She'd wanted to tell him about the fundraiser so many times. Almost had after he'd ridden River for the first time. But when he came back home after Jen had offered him a job and a house that Davis couldn't wait to see, he'd taken one look at her, fallen into her arms, and wept. After he'd told her why he was crying, they were both too wrecked to add any more emotions into the mix.

"Here." He clicked play. "I think this will do the trick."

While techno started thumping through the speakers, she turned up the volume, slid her sunglasses over her eyes, and stepped on the gas.

Two hours and several rambling conversations later, she checked the GPS. Three miles until their exit. She was running out of time. Stalling. If she didn't tell him now, he'd figure it out on his own before she could.

Turning the music down, she said, "Kev, I have something to tell you."

His head swiveled toward her. "Is it something bad?"

"No. It's not bad. It's just... I haven't been completely honest with you."

"Uh, baby. I don't mean to disagree with you, but this is usually how bad conversations start."

Reaching over the center console, she took his hand and squeezed. "I promise, it's not bad. It's not even that big of a deal. I mean, I should have told you this a while ago. Like, you probably won't even care." She knew that wasn't true. Because Kev cared about everything. It was one of her favorite things about him, how much he cared. "At first I didn't tell you because we weren't talking. And then I didn't tell you because I was embarrassed. And now, I don't know." She laughed at herself. "The closer we got to the ride, the more I wanted to surprise you with it."

Squeezing her hand back a little too tightly, he said, "Okay, so this might be a good time to tell you that I hate surprises."

"It's a good surprise," she said. "Really good. But it might take a second to get to the good part. Because a few months ago, something happened." A little fire kindled to life inside her chest. "Someone I loved needed help. And as hard as I tried, I couldn't figure out how to help him."

His fingers threaded through hers.

"And because I couldn't help him, I thought I might have lost him forever. I thought it was too late. But I was wrong." She flicked on her signal, taking the off ramp at their exit. "It wasn't too late. It was just that he needed to go away for a while. He needed to be with people who were like him, people who understood him."

"Wait," he said, looking around at the intersection at the top of the ramp, probably recognizing the gas station on the right, the mountains rising to their left. "I know where we are."

"But even though he was where he needed to be," she continued, turning left at the light, "I missed him. I missed him so much. And I felt helpless because I couldn't talk to him or see him. I wasn't a part of this thing he was going through."

She felt him watching her again as the road took them toward the mountains, pavement giving way to dirt beneath their tires.

"And even though we weren't talking anymore, even though I thought I might never see this person again, even though my heart was so broken I wondered if it would ever heal, I still wanted to help him. I *needed* to help him. Even if it was only in a small, insignificant way."

"Davis," he said, his voice thick. "This is where my rehab is. Willow Creek. It's right down that road."

She nodded, swallowed the lump rising up her throat, then explained, "So I found the place he'd been sent to. I found their website. I saw how he might be spending his days. I read about all the programs available to him. I learned about all the support he was getting. And I felt better. Because even though *I* couldn't help him, I knew they could."

She turned onto another mountain road, heading up a switchback, the trailhead where the race would begin looming on her GPS. "And then I saw that they had a yearly fundraiser. They called it the Ride For Recovery. It was no joke either. Fifty miles—"

"—of pure hell," he finished for her. And when she looked at him, his eyes were wide. "You're doing this fundraiser for my rehab? You're doing this ride for me? You're grand gesturing"—he placed his other hand over his heart, his round eyes going glassy—"for me?"

Her eyes went glassy too, and with a watery laugh, she said, "Yep."

"But you've been training for this ride all summer, right? I mean, when? When did you sign up?"

For some reason, admitting this, saying it out loud, felt like reaching into her chest and yanking her heart right out into the open. *Oh well.* It belonged to him anyway. "I signed up the day after Madigan checked you in. He had a brochure for Willow Creek. I stole it. I found the website."

"But you hated me then. Why—"

Jerking the wheel, she pulled off onto the shoulder, slamming the brakes so hard rocks shot up from their tires. If she was late, she was late. But he couldn't go one more second believing that was true.

Throwing the car into park, she twisted in her seat, took his face between her hands and said, "Kevin Lowes, I have *never* hated you. Not a single day of my life. I have only ever loved you. That love may have hurt more than anything else for a while. I may have tried to push it down. I may have tried to hide from it. But it has always been there."

Dropping his chin to his chest, he said, "Thank you, Davis. I'm so..." He squeezed his eyes shut for a long blink. "I can't find the words. Just, thank you."

"You can thank me more thoroughly in about six hours. But for now..." She cupped his jaw, raised his head, leaned in, and kissed him. Then she said, "You're welcome."

HAD she ever ridden a bike before? Had she even trained at all? Was it all some cruel and meaningless fever dream? Or had she died here, and this was her purgatory, pedaling up this fucking mountain for all of eternity?

These were the questions rolling around her head while she pushed herself up the final climb of this evil, seventh circle of hell ride. She only had five miles left, but the previous forty-five had redefined pain, knocked her down all the pegs, humbled her to the point of tears not once, but three times.

They'd made it to the trailhead where the race started, and might someday finish, in the nick of time. And after she'd stood by Kev's side during an emotional reunion with his lovely rehab therapist Rick —which included one of those intense man hugs complete with two hearty back slaps—she'd waited with the other riders at the starting line so long ago now it felt like a different geological era. Like she'd need a time machine to find her way back.

And now she was pedaling alone, almost at the back of the pack, with what she was pretty sure were no longer feet but just socks full of blisters. With each pedal stroke, she pictured Kev and Rick sitting comfortably in their camping chairs, chatting, soaking up the early fall sunshine while she wiped beads of sweat off her forehead before they dripped into her eyes, unable to do anything at all about the sweat dripping down her ass.

But she kept going, kept pedaling. Because even if she was dying, even if this was the way she'd meet her end, she wasn't going to stop. She wasn't going to give up. She'd come too far now.

Finally reaching the top of the last climb, the finish line coming into blessed view below her, she paused to catch her breath and drink some water. Then she took in her surroundings. The larches were already turning, yellow and orange branches dappling the mountainsides. The sky was the deep, almost nautical blue of early fall. And the love of her life was waiting for her at the bottom of a run that, despite her complete exhaustion, actually looked pretty fun.

Pointing her tires down the trail, she rose out of the saddle, pedaled hard to clear a wicked rock drop, and bombed it down to the finish line. Where she found Kev, up on his feet with a champagne glass of Gatorade in one hand, a chocolate cupcake from Glazed and Confused in the other, and a million-dollar smile on his face.

Smiling back, she thought, *this is my life*. It hadn't always been easy. It hadn't always gone the way she'd wanted it to. It would certainly get harder in ways she couldn't anticipate. But right now, it was good. It was really, really good.

EPILOGUE

FOUR YEARS LATER

Kev pulled down the blinds, shielding her sweet, brand-new eyes—eyes he just knew would turn a vibrant blue like her mom's—from the morning sunlight streaming in through the bathroom window.

Placing his daughter's warm and impossibly small body down on the changing table—a gorgeous antique Jen found for them in her attic that just barely fit in their bathroom—he flinched when the smell hit him.

"Oof, baby girl," he said, leaning back. "What did you eat?"

He knew the answer. He'd watched Davis breastfeed their daughter Max as often as he could since they'd brought her home from the hospital over a week ago. It was the most amazing thing he'd ever seen. But, *damn*, this tiny miracle in human form could stink up a room.

"I told you it was a bad one," Davis called out from their bedroom, sounding exhausted. "Do I need to come help?"

"Nah." Wiggling Max's tiny toes between his thumb and first finger, he said, "I think I got it," in a goofy voice he might have been embarrassed about if he'd given two shits about that sort of thing anymore.

Peeling back the adhesive tab on one side of Max's diaper, and then the other, he braced himself for the fallout. "Dear lord," he cooed while she grunted and squirmed. "Did you do all that? How? How did all of that come out of your teeny, little..." He trailed off, his eyes going wide. "Babe!" he shouted. "Oh my god, Davis!"

"What?" A dull *thump* came from their bedroom, probably her feet hitting the hardwood. "What's wrong?"

When she stumbled into the bathroom, her golden hair a tangled mess, dark circles camped out under her eyes that matched his but only worse, and still more beautiful than any woman had a right to be, he pointed at the diaper and said, "It finally happened."

"What finally happened?" She rubbed her eyes. "She pooped? She does that, like, a hundred times a day. Aside from eating and sleeping and crying, it's all she does."

"Yeah, but not like this." He could sense how manic his smile was, how manic *he* was. Sleep deprivation did that to a person. But this was important. "That's it, isn't it?" he asked, pointing at the diaper again. "That's baby-shit green."

With a breathy, worn-out laugh, Davis collapsed against his side while he wrapped his arm around her shoulders.

"Yep," she said, staring down at their perfect, precious daughter. "That is baby-shit green."

Squeezing her close, he said, "Well, now I finally know for sure. That is definitely not my favorite shade."

Davis laughed again, then yawned for a full five seconds before asking, "You got her?"

Pressing a kiss onto her head, he said, "I got her. Go back to bed, baby."

She turned her face up to his. "Do you have any idea how much I love you?"

"Yes," he said, leaning down to brush his lips over hers. "About half as much as I love you." He squeezed her ass, then swatted it. "Now go get some sleep."

After planting a soft kiss on their daughter's forehead, Davis gave Kev a quick hug, then staggered back into the bedroom.

Kev cleaned Max up—a task that required six whole wipies—snapped her into a fresh onesie, and carried her into the kitchen. Cradling her in his arms, he slid open the window above the sink, where River and Maggie were already waiting for their morning apple slices. While Max watched the horses chew their apples, utterly transfixed, Kev smiled at his daughter like she was the sun and the moon and every single one of the stars—including the ones he'd thrown pinecones at back when he hadn't even known how to wish for a life this wonderful.

Once the apple slices had all been fed, he closed the window again, and as quietly as he could, crept past their bedroom, glancing at their bed, at his wife, who'd already fallen back to sleep. Grabbing a blanket from the couch, he let his attention linger on the one remaining picture of his mom that hung on their living room wall. The one Davis had surprised him by having framed for his birthday three years ago. Then he stepped out onto their porch.

The September morning was chilled but not cold, with a clear, deep blue sky that seemed to stretch on forever. A few leaves on the willow in front of their house had begun to change color. A crescent moon still hovered over the mountains. And everything around him, including the fresh horses bucking and squealing in their pastures, felt like fall. Like change. Like the end of one thing and the beginning of something else. It was the sort of sensation that used to scare him. But not anymore. Now it just filled him with hope.

What he'd said to Madigan in his truck that day four years ago had been true. He'd never touched another drug, never again felt the pull of that life. At least not in any way that made him consider giving up everything he had now. All the good things he'd been blind to before that surrounded him every day, like sunlight. The barn that felt like home, River, the love of his life sleeping in their bed, the angel in his arms.

Wrapping the blanket around his shoulders, tucking it snuggly around their daughter, he sat in one of the two wooden chairs on the porch—the chairs he'd found in Jen's storage, the chairs that Davis had taken one look at, then said to him with tears standing in her eyes, "They both rock."

A part of him had cowered in fear when they'd found out Davis was pregnant. The part of him that wondered what kind of father he'd be, if he'd be a source of comfort and solace in their daughter's life, or if he'd somehow trip and fall into a genetic sinkhole and leave her feeling unloved, alone, never good enough. Looking at Max now—and after talking his fears through with Davis, and later with Grandpa Madigan—he almost laughed. Because from the second Davis pushed Max into the world, from the second she took her first breath, then released her first wailing cry, he knew. He knew it like an arrow aimed true, shot straight through his heart. He would never leave her. He'd do everything in his power to protect her, to love her and support her and be there for her always. Always and forever.

Filling his lungs with a deep, grateful breath, he started rocking. And while Max settled into a contented milk coma, her mouth falling open into a blissed-out little O, her body warm and heavy and substantial in his arms, Kev felt the sun on his face, listened to the birds singing in the trees, and wondered—the same way he'd wondered every single day since Davis came into his life—how he'd ever gotten so lucky.

For a Kev and Davis bonus scene, visit jesskhardy.com

ACKNOWLEDGMENTS

I had this running internal dialogue while I wrote Kev and Davis's story: I would never put my older characters through this type of shit. It's funny if you think about it, but my older characters don't have time for this level of emotional devastation. They've got kids, parents, jobs, and lifetimes of heartbreak they've already learned a few things from. Their stories are just different.

That being said, I absolutely loved every second of writing this book. Even the parts that made me cry (all 100 of the times I reread them). So if you had a difficult time watching Kev and Davis go through hell to find their way back to each other, believe me, so did I. But growing up is hard. We tend to be much more giving of our hearts when we're younger. I won't say that we're careless with them, but we're less guarded, more trusting, and if we're lucky, nothing happens that makes us put those barriers up. But most of us aren't lucky. And although luck is a major theme in this book: what it means, how it can change, how it's a concept that is based so much on environmental and socioeconomic factors we may have little to no control over, Kev, and Davis especially, had to go through some things that made them put their barriers up. Then they had to learn how to take those barriers back down together.

It was also important for me to address the way that a lot of people with substance abuse issues get blindsided by their relapse(s) in this story. Kev had buried his past so deeply, hiding from his trauma as much as an adult as he did as a kid, that he couldn't connect the dots to figure out how he lost his way. And with his incessant need to please everyone around him as a form of self-protection, he was unable to check in with himself or identify his triggers, held down under the thumb of shame so firmly he couldn't ask for help when he finally did realize things were going sideways. We don't get Madigan's POV in this book, of course, but I think he knew all along that Kev had a lot of shame to work through. And that's why he waited until just the right moment, when he knew Kev was ready to face his past, to bring it up. Speaking of Madigan. They say two words can't make you cry. The words: Grandpa Madigan.

Wish You Were Here is about the journey of finding ourselves, the work of making amends, the courage required to forgive, and, ultimately, the ways that loving someone and being loved in return can be a great source of healing in our lives. And, of course, the importance of community.

It takes love and community to successful publish a book as well. And I need to thank my community for this one. I want to thank Nicole at Emerald Edits and Beth at VB Edits for taking such amazing care of this story and helping me make it the best it could be. Thank you to my sensitivity readers: Sam and William. A very special thanks to Livy Hart, Sarah T. Dubb, J Calamy, Kate Clayborn, Kate Canterbary, Sarah MacLean, Nikki Payne, Anita Kelly, Maggie North, Erin Hahn, Lauren Morrill, Regina Black, Mia Hopkins, Cathy Yardley, Cass Scotka, and Denise Williams. And a massive enormous gigantic thank you to every ARC reader who spent time with this story and talked about it on SM. It means so much to me!

Thank you to my agent, Katie Shea Boutillier.

Thank you to Aljane Compendio for continuing to rock my character art.

Thank you to my hysterical and wonderful husband, my amazingly thoughtful and talented son, my beautiful sisters, my parents, my friends, my dogs, and MotoGP for getting me through. It'll be your year again soon FQ20.

And, as always, thank you from the bottom of my heart to

everyone who has taken the time to read this story. It means the world to me.

Final note. This series continues in my mind with a mix of older and younger people's stories. It's just how the characters are speaking to me. And that's how I write. I write the stories that want to be written. I have no other choice. But I can't tell you how excited I am to get back to older folks with book four: Jen and Scott's marriage in trouble. Hoo boy!! Hang on to your saddles, y'all.

ABOUT THE AUTHOR

Jess K. Hardy is an award-winning, bestselling author of contemporary and sci-fi romance. Jess writes about characters at any age, but especially over 40, finding second chances, proving that life, and love, only get better with time. She has ben featured in Publisher's Weekly and People.

ALSO BY JESS K HARDY

SPACE CRUISE ROMANCE SERIES
SUNASTARA & THE VENUSIAN
ELANIE & THE EMPATH

BLUEBIRD BASIN ROMANCE SERIES
COME AS YOU ARE
LIPS LIKE SUGAR
WISH YOU WERE HERE

THE CURSE OF NONA MAY TAYLOR

www.ingramcontent.com/pod-product-compliance
Lightning Source LLC
LaVergne TN
LVHW010307070526
838199LV00065B/5475